Brigid has a diverse professional background, having worked as a teacher, solicitor, and criminal barrister. Immersed in a world of crime and having authored numerous legal articles, she was inevitably drawn to the realm of crime fiction. Surprisingly, this literary world wasn't so dissimilar from the reality of the crimes she encountered in her everyday work.

Born in Glasgow to a Scottish father and Irish mother, she moved to the North of England as a teenager. She has a son and now lives in Greater Manchester.

For Ian Alexander Macdonald QC

Till a' the seas gang dry

Brigid Baillie

JOINT ENTERPRISE

AUSTIN MACAULEY PUBLISHERS™

LONDON * CAMBRIDGE * NEW YORK * SHARJAH

A CIP catalogue record for this title is available from the British Library.

ISBN 9781035820351 (Paperback)
ISBN 9781035820368 (Hardback)
ISBN 9781035820382 (ePub e-book)
ISBN 9781035820375 (Audiobook)

www.austinmacauley.com

First Published 2023
Austin Macauley Publishers Ltd®
1 Canada Square
Canary Wharf
London
E14 5AA

A huge thanks to my first readers—Mary Baillie, Liz Taylor, Alison Straw and Monica Garvey, without whose helpful comments and feedback this book would never have been finished.

The journey to writing this book was difficult and emotional, and my love and thanks go to friends and family for their unstinting love and support. It's difficult to single out people here. You know who you are but particular thanks go to Cameron Baillie and Mary Baillie.

Part One

Chapter 1

It reminded him of raspberry ripple ice cream, rivulets of red flowing through white. He'd seen blood against all sorts of backgrounds—spattered up walls, soaked into clothing, dripped on pavements, dried brown splodges on carpets, but dribbling through a pool of milk was a new one.

DI Ian Pearce arrived in the Fisher estate alley after the uniforms had cordoned it off. He should have been here earlier but his sixteen-year-old son, Jack, came first. After an argument about too much X-box, Jack had dissolved into tears saying he missed his mum. Ian couldn't just walk out and leave him till he was sure he was okay. Or at least as okay as he could be.

Ian felt he was in two places at the same time. His mind was with Jack but his body was at a crime scene. It was like being in limbo. Just stuck, not knowing which way to go. *I have to be here*, he thought, *otherwise there was no point in doing the job.*

He stood taking in the surroundings in the cold February night. An alleyway, or ginnel as the locals called them, a cut through surrounded by terraces and inter war council houses. You could tell the ones which had been bought, new doors and windows with pristine gardens and fencing.

His body was held tight as if holding his muscles in would protect him from the cold. It wouldn't. It was freezing. He zipped up his jacket as far as it would go, wishing he'd worn a scarf.

The press were already here as he'd spotted Tricia Gibson from the Yorkshire Daily Post. She was shouting over at him for an update.

'Hi, Tricia. You know I can't give you anything just now. Contact the press office.'

'Come on, Ian, just tell me if it's another county lines case.'

He used to think county lines was a southern phenomenon but with more drug dealing and local gangs it had arrived in Carfield.

'Too early to say, Tricia. You know that as well as me. As I said, contact the press office.'

'Thanks, Ian, you're a fount of all knowledge.'

Ian liked her perseverance and forthrightness even if she was a journalist. *Right*, he thought, *change the head space and focus.*

Sergeant Mel Garvey was already in the alley wearing a paper suit, long blond hair tucked into the hood, directing operations. How come some people could look good in the shapeless paper suit? She was efficient, knew instinctively what to do, could be relied on and he liked her. But. There was always a "but".

She'd been with the team for six months now having come from the Met. It seemed an odd move but maybe she'd just had it with London and a move north gave her something new as well as breathable air. Plenty of people were moving out of London for a change of life but he wasn't sure why she'd moved north. It wasn't as if she was from Yorkshire.

She was guarded with him and he couldn't work out why. He'd tried to be welcoming and friendly but she kept her distance. She was clever, efficient and would no doubt go far providing she lost that southern aloofness.

He donned a paper suit, gloves and overshoes before lifting the tape to walk the few yards towards Mel and the raspberry ripple ice cream. He couldn't get that image out of his head now. It was the visual equivalent of an ear worm. He could see the alleyway was one of those cut throughs used for drug dealing, illicit sex and any other scummy activity you could think of.

He could smell the dog shit, the piss and see a used condom and syringe against the wall. It was a stereotype of a downtrodden place but a stereotype immersed in reality. It was dirty with takeaway wrappers, discarded paper and empty cans and bottles. The temperature must have been hovering around zero. *What a place to end up in*, he thought.

'Okay,' he said, 'fill me in.'

He could see the wisps of his warm breath coiling upwards as he spoke. God, it was cold.

'Seventeen-year-old boy with stab wounds to the abdomen. He's still alive but only just,' said Mel.

He could tell by her disapproving look she was thinking that he should have been here earlier. Maybe he was just being overly sensitive because that was what he was thinking.

'Paramedics have taken him to Carfield A & E. He had a provisional driving licence on him, name of Josh Smithies, address in Moss Green, so not from round here. Sergeant Dykes has gone to the hospital to speak to the parents.'

Ian knew John Dykes was sensitive and good in difficult, emotional situations. He came across as a big gruff Yorkshire man but underneath that taciturn exterior he really cared and empathised with those who were in the depths of despair whether they were victims of crime or the perpetrators who'd taken a wrong turn in life.

'Who called it in?'

'A woman, Chelsea Brittan, had just been to the local shop which is at the bottom left of the alley. She said she'd popped out to get some milk and fags, heard shouts, looked up the alley and saw figures running off. She saw the lad on the ground, ran up to him and in her shock she dropped the milk, hence the Jackson Pollock on the ground.'

Jackson Pollock? He still thought it was more of a raspberry ripple.

'Where is she now?'

'She's been taken home by PC Aitken. I've asked him to take a first account but she's pretty shaken up.'

'House to house?'

'We've started that and CSI are on their way although they might not get very far tonight even with lamps.'

'Well done,' Ian said, 'you've covered all the initial bases.'

'Thanks.'

Shit, he hoped that didn't sound patronising.

'Let's see what John comes up with,' said Ian. 'He's good in these situations, sensitive, good with families, lots of sympathy. What is a lad from Moss Green doing round here?'

'Sergeant Dykes might be able to fill us in on that once he's spoken to the parents.'

'Right,' said Ian Pearce. 'Let uniforms carry on with house to house. Mel, can you get everyone else in the briefing room in an hour.'

'Of course.'

He caught Mel looking at him in an odd way. Maybe she was being judgmental. Maybe it was just his paranoia but he felt he could read her thoughts. He knew he looked rough, even rougher than usual. Bags that were more like suitcases under the red eyes, being late at the scene of a crime when you're the senior investigating officer and generally being knackered.

But that's what happened when you were on your own with a teenage boy. Still, he was aware he wasn't the only one in this situation, just the only man he knew it had happened to.

Right. Time to get his shit together.

Chapter 2

Carfield police station was not one of the newly built high-tech glass and steel police stations that are all a carbon copy of each other on the edge of towns. It was a Victorian building in the middle of the town. It was built to be visible, to be a warning to those who passed by. It might have been in the past but not now.

The briefing room was a grand name for a large room reminiscent of a Victorian classroom. High windows and ceilings, old pipes and a wooden floor. There had been attempts to modernise over the years but that meant 1980's laminate desks, uncomfortable chairs and fluorescent strip lighting. Sometimes a mix of styles looked chic. This didn't. It looked old and tatty.

'It's freezing in here,' said John Dykes. 'Can't think when you're this cold.'

'You should be okay, John,' said Prita Patel.

'What do you mean?'

'All that extra padding.' She prodded John in the side to make the point.

'Ha bloody ha. My wife appreciates a few extra pounds to keep her warm in bed. Not a stick insect like some.'

'Just jealous that I'm in good shape,' mocked Prita.

'Get a coffee. It'll warm you up until the heating comes on. If it comes on,' said Mel.

'Right,' said DI Pearce. Ian stood in front of the white board and cork board where pictures, problems, leads and connections could be displayed. Just now it was empty.

Mel thought he looked tired. The bright blue eyes were shot through with red; he was unshaven and the grey marled jumper had seen better days.

'I want updates so we can work out a plan of action. You can go home after that, not before; so the quicker we get through this the more sleep you get.'

'John, what have you got on the victim?'

John Dykes turned to his daybook. He screwed up his face and his eyes disappeared into the flesh. An occasional wearer of reading glasses who didn't want to admit he needed them. 'Josh Smithies, seventeen, from what seems like a good home, parents divorced, mother is a teacher and dad is a builder. He lives with mum and nineteen-year-old sister who is at university.

'Parents are still on pretty good terms. No-one has any criminal convictions. He's at college doing his A levels but his work started slipping about six months ago and mum doesn't really know why. He's got a girlfriend, Naomi Edwards, also at college doing A levels and lives round the corner from him. Mum and dad are at the hospital now.

'Mum is in a complete state, can't understand what he was doing in the Fisher area. Didn't think he knew anyone there but he's been a bit secretive recently. She couldn't fill us in any more at this stage and I left her to be with him. Dad's a bit less involved as he's got a new partner who has two children of her own. Doesn't appear to be any conflict though.'

'Any more on the injuries?'

'One stab wound to the left side of the abdomen, pretty deep, lost a lot of blood. Doctor said it pierced the mesenteric artery and spleen. He's in the operating theatre now.'

'Let's hope he pulls through,' said Ian. 'He's just a year older than my Jack.'

Mel wondered how long it would take him to get to his personal circumstances. She realised it must have been hard. Abandoned by the wife who was fed up with the husband's long hours, got a better offer and now he's saddled with the sixteen-year-old who is going through a "difficult phase". If a woman talked about it as much as he did, it wouldn't go down well but it's somehow different for a single dad.

Still, she thought, maybe she should be more sympathetic. It can't be easy being a DI in major crime with a troubled sixteen-year-old.

'Mel, update on the scene?'

Focus on the task, Mel, she thought to herself.

'CSIs are there now. No weapon has been found yet. Ground is pretty frozen so footprints unlikely. House to house continuing but no-one wants to get involved. Lots of drug dealing amongst teenage gangs according to one householder who refused to give a statement for fear of reprisals. Some houses appear to have CCTV which we need to check out. The shop at the bottom left of the alley also has CCTV which might be helpful.'

'Thanks. Prita, what have you got?'

'There's a bus route at the end of the alley so there might be some helpful footage from a bus camera but that's a bit of a long shot. We've got Josh's phone which was on him and might show what he was doing in Fisher once we get it analysed, but nothing else as yet.'

Sergeant Prita Patel, newly promoted, felt she had a lot to prove but her outrageous and gallows sense of humour meant she was popular. Unlike Mel, thought Ian, she was human as well as efficient and didn't have that robotic side to her that Mel displayed. If only Mel would relax a bit, she'd be great. Mel was beautiful and clever but to say she was buttoned up was an understatement. He hoped that working together on this case might improve things between them.

'Right,' said Ian Pearce. 'I know the rest of you haven't been to the scene yet but this is an attempted murder; yet another stabbing of a teenage boy, possibly gang related, maybe also drug related. Fisher was a thriving community till the 1980's when the pit closed. Now it's an area without jobs and without hope, where generations have been unemployed and the main industry is drugs.'

Oh no, thought Mel, *I hope he's not going to go all bleeding heart liberal on this one. Let's face it, its little shits who come from shitty families where no-one gives a toss and they're making easy money with drugs.* As soon as she thought it, she knew that was harsh and unfair. Maybe she was carrying her bitterness from the Met with her.

'Prita, I want you to co-ordinate CCTV searches and house to house. Some of the houses will have cameras so we want to see who is in the area at the relevant time. Let's also look into bus cameras as they might have caught someone running off or even jumping on a bus to get away.

'John, I want a search of Josh's house and see if you can get any more from the parents. If this is gang related, there should be something on his phone or laptop.

'Mel, I want you to co-ordinate CSIs and search of the area for any weapon. Speak to his school teachers, school friends and the girlfriend as well. The rest of you will be in the teams headed by Mel, Prita and John.

'Meet back here at 1.00 tomorrow so we can see what we've got. If you're in the middle of stuff, then ring in at 1.00 with an update. Thanks everyone. Go and get some sleep before you have an early start.'

The door banged open as PC Merrick burst in. He didn't need to say anything as the expression on his face said it all. He looked at Ian and almost whispered, 'Call from the hospital, guv. I'm afraid Josh didn't make it through surgery.'

Chapter 3

Ian drove home to the other side of Carfield. It was six miles from Fisher yet a million miles away. A four bedroomed detached house built around 2000 with a garage, lovely big kitchen with bifolding doors leading out to an enclosed garden and in the catchment area for good schools. Sounded like an estate agent's dream. So many people would give their eye and teeth for this but it wasn't the warm, family home it had once been.

He needed to stay positive as he had so much going for him. The good job, the comfortable home and Jack. It was a lot more than Josh's parents had now. He went up to Jack's room. Jack was in bed but not asleep and, more importantly, not on Xbox.

'You feeling a bit better?' Ian asked.

'Yeah, I suppose.'

'It's good to have a cry and get it all out. I always feel like my head has been hovered out and it's all clean again when I have a cry. It sort of builds up and you need to let it out every so often.'

'I haven't seen you cry since mum left.'

'That's the thing about adults. We do it in private so as to kid everyone that we're fine but we're not fooling anyone. I still get upset but not as much as I did a year ago so it gets easier. It will for you too and you'll go to London to see your mum during the half term holidays.'

'I know but I don't like staying with him as well. I just wish it could be like it was.'

'If it was good she wouldn't have left. She was unhappy and we've got to get on without her. Count your blessings as my old Irish granny would say. Now, get to sleep, school tomorrow. I love you.'

'Night, dad, love you.'

Ian went downstairs and the emotions were almost bursting through. At one time, he'd have had a glass of wine and wept but he needed to sit with his feelings and a cup of tea before bed, not necessarily in that order. No crying tonight but it was close to the surface. All he'd have to do was put on some music and he'd be off. What must Josh's parents be going through?

'Get in touch with your emotions,' his counsellor had said. If only he'd done that a couple of years ago, Jenny might not have left. Sometimes life is easier if feelings are held deep inside, if they can't be reached, if you're surrounded with armour plating. It's when they come out that things become difficult. Getting in touch with your feelings is certainly not an easy option.

He would feel wrung out after a session with his counsellor. He knew he would never make the same mistakes again if he ever had another relationship and that was a big if. He couldn't see it happening but he missed that companionship and it could feel so lonely with just him and Jack. It wasn't just the sex he missed. It was having no-one to cuddle, to feel their warmth, or read the Sunday papers and do a crossword in bed.

He couldn't stop thinking about Josh's parents. He'd been on enough murder investigations but it was so much worse when it was a child who'd been killed. He couldn't imagine their pain. Didn't want to imagine their pain, just knew it would be unbearable.

He knew that if anything happened to Jack, it would send him over the edge. When it is just you with a child, the thought of losing them was unimaginable. He could survive the loss of his wife but never the loss of a child.

Right, bed time, he thought. He had a job to do and a team to lead if they were going to catch Josh's killer. He went up to the bathroom and looked at his reflection. Bags under the eyes, unshaven but not in a sexy way and needed a haircut. He had kidded himself on that it was a tousled look but it was an out of shape mess. Looking on the bright side, he had a full head of hair and his own teeth. He needed to stop the self-pity now and focus on the job.

Chapter 4

Naomi

She lay in bed unsure whether or not to get up.

She'd left Josh there and ran. *Was he badly hurt? He'd fallen over but that didn't mean anything.*

Did he get the bus home?

He didn't respond to her texts. What did that mean?

She'd get up and call round for him. That way she would know how he was.

She pushed the duvet back and swung one leg out of bed followed slowly by the other. No energy.

Shower. That would wake her up.

In the shower, soaping herself, last night flashed back. She didn't want to see it.

What had happened?

It was a blur. She couldn't remember. She ran, got a bus home and went straight to bed.

She had panicked.

She had to get away from them.

They might have done anything to her. She had to run. She couldn't help Josh.

Should she have stayed?

No.

Quick towel dry.

Jeans and a jumper would do. No makeup. No point.

She grabbed her books and folders and ran downstairs.

Piece of toast and run round to Josh's house.

She's not thinking straight. She recognises this and knows there is an underlying panic. What to do?

'Hi, Mum. I'll have some toast and call for Josh.'

But part of her knows there is no point, although she doesn't want to recognise this.

She butters the toast and is about to take a bite but thinks she will be sick.

The news is on and she hears it.

'A seventeen-year-old boy has died after being stabbed on the Fisher estate in Carfield.'

He can't be dead, she thinks. *It can't be Josh.*

The alleyway is shown with blue and white police tape, people in white paper overalls and a television reporter.

This can't be happening.

'Mum. It's Josh.'

She screams and vomits.

It was never supposed to end like this.

Chapter 5

Anna

He is her baby boy and he's gone.

She sits, not moving, and stares at him. His beautiful long lashes on eyes that will never open again. His clear skin that escaped the teenage spots. His nose, like her own, slightly too big on her but it suited his face. His lips that will never again kiss.

She bends to kiss his cheeks, his forehead. She strokes his hair, remembering that only yesterday he said he needed to get it cut. He didn't. It is copper and beautiful. He was perfect. He is perfect.

She doesn't believe it. She looks at him and sees him sleeping. She holds his hand, which is still warm, examines his fingers with dirt in the nails. She sees the bruise on his arm, a blemish on his perfect body. A body that will grow no more, a boy who will never have children, never get married. A boy whose dreams of going to university will never come true.

She strokes his smooth, hairless chest. He is so perfect is all she can think. She keeps stroking as if her love will bring him back. But it won't.

She feels him kicking inside her as if it was yesterday. It's not a memory, it's a feeling. She would grab hold of his foot, always at night, always on the right side of her body and she loved it. The thought of meeting her boy, for she knew he was a boy, the excitement of the new life. She couldn't wait.

And now he is no more.

She doesn't cry. She just strokes and touches and kisses. She wants to sit with him till he wakes up. She examines every visible inch of him. She doesn't pull the sheet back as she doesn't want to see the imperfection that has taken him away.

There is something about the arms and hands that she can't leave. The hairs so fair and fine. She feels she knows every one of those hairs. The nails broken, the graze on one of his knuckles, the fingers slightly curled like a baby's gripping her hand. She strokes and strokes.

She sees him as a toddler. He was just the best. Hardly any tantrums so she'd escaped the terrible twos. They weren't terrible for her, they were magical. His beautiful strawberry blond curls that she never wanted to cut. When she picked him up from nursery, he would run to her and throw his arms around her legs asking if tomorrow was a mummy day.

No more mummy days.

The start of primary school when he asked for a boy's haircut because everyone thought he was a girl. It was the end of a beautiful phase but the start of a new one.

Now there will be no new starts.

He loved stories and when she'd get to the end he would smile and say, "the end", because he knew that was what she said.

No more stories. No more family holidays, where they would splash in the pool, and no more swimming races. He is faster than her now. Was faster.

No more holidays. No more anything. She can't go on. She can't bare him not to be here. She can't live without him. There is no future.

And that's when the wailing starts. From the very depths of her, like a devil escaping, the noise is unearthly. It comes from the soul, a soul that has died like her son.

'Josh, Josh, I love you, don't leave me. Please don't leave me. Please. Please. I love you. I love you.' She can't bear it.

Greg runs in to the room and she pushes him away. She doesn't want him. She just wants her baby boy back again.

Chapter 6

Everyone reacts to a death differently. Greg is angry. Why couldn't the doctors have done more? They all look about twelve. Why weren't there more staff, more experienced doctors on duty? If only they'd got him here sooner. If only. That was what everyone thought after a death, after a sudden and pointless death.

And what are the police doing? Fuck all. They're not even here, only the plod sitting outside the room.

He's shouting at Doctor Hartford. 'Why didn't you do more? Why couldn't you fix the artery? Why didn't you give him another blood transfusion? Why did you just give up?'

Why, why, why? The pointlessness of it all.

And that's when he hears Anna.

The screaming pierces his noise, his rants, and he runs in. He holds her but she pushes him off. He has his pain and doesn't want to see hers. It is too much. They are each locked inside their own pain.

He can't stop thinking what the fuck was Josh doing in Fisher?

He sees the copper, Sergeant John Dykes he said his name was, in the doorway and then he just walks off. *Go and fucking catch who did this*, thinks Greg, *instead of just standing there*.

John walks along the corridor and sees the doctor just standing there.

'Hello,' he says. 'I'm Sergeant John Dykes from Carfield CID. Have you got five minutes?'

'Of course, we did everything we could you know, but the piercing of the artery meant he was beyond help.' She must only have been mid-thirties but the tiredness around her eyes aged her. She looked absolutely exhausted. He didn't suppose he looked much better.

'What's the cause of death? I know you can't be definitive at this stage.'

'That's for the pathologist but what I can say is the stab wound caught the mesenteric artery which led to massive blood loss and is the likely cause of death. I don't know if there is anything else but toxicology might show that. To me, it looks like a stab wound that was unlucky.'

'Was it just the one stab wound?'

'Yes, but it was deep.'

'Thanks. You look as if it's taken it out of you,' he said. 'Hope you don't mind me saying that.'

'It's tragic to lose a young boy in such a pointless way. It just doesn't make sense.'

'I know. I'll go and see if the parents are up to a quick word, although I will understand if they tell me where to go.'

'Dad is angry and mum is in a state of shock so good luck.'

She walked off slowly, slightly hunched over. He thought, not for the first time, just how many people are affected by such a killing. It's like ripples spreading to places you'd never think of. Doctors, nurses, police, teachers, apart from the family and friends. He's even known the odd hard faced lawyer fight back the tears.

He went back to the room and spoke to the PC waiting outside.

'Anything you can tell me?' John asked.

PC Holroyd wasn't long out of police training college and John knew this was hard for him as well.

'Mum and dad have taken it very differently. Mum was really quiet and then started screaming and wailing. Dad is angry at the world.'

'Can't say I blame him. Stay here until I can get someone to relieve you then you can go home. I'll have a quick word with them if they're up to it.'

John Dykes knocked on the door. No answer. It wasn't fully closed so he pushed it open slightly.

'Hello again. Sergeant John Dykes. I'm very sorry for your loss.'

'Why aren't you out there trying to catch the bastard that did this,' said Greg.

'There are a number of lines of inquiry and we will get a liaison officer to keep you updated. I don't want to intrude now but would like to come and talk to you in the morning if that's ok?'

'Yes,' said Anna, 'come to my house. Greg will be there.' She was motionless, obviously in shock, and John could barely hear her she was so quiet, as if it took all her strength to utter those few words.

'Thank you. I won't intrude any further just now. I'm really sorry about your son.'

He turned and left, just grateful that it wasn't him in their position. He could go home to his wife and three children knowing they were safe and sound asleep.

Chapter 7

Prita arrived in the briefing room at 8.00 and Mel was already there. 'Morning, I'm going to make a coffee, fancy one?'

'Great,' said Mel. 'I think we'll be living on coffee for the duration.'

Mel really liked Prita, her sparkiness, her friendliness. She seemed so energetic and full of life. Maybe they could go for a drink some time. She needed a friend round here. She'd been here six months and, apart from meeting up with an old university friend in Leeds, hadn't really been out or got to know anyone. She was lonely but didn't want to admit it.

Who likes to admit to themselves, let alone others, that they are lonely and they need people. Six months wasn't long though and starting a new life takes time. One step at a time.

'Anything so far?' Prita asked.

'CSI are there now and I'm going to ring the school as soon as they open. You?'

'Give us a chance, I've just walked in. Hopefully, there will be some CCTV. Have you seen John or Ian?'

Just then, DI Ian Pearce walked in. Mel thought he looked so much better after a sleep and a shave. He'd also brought coffees and croissants for whoever was in. Thoughtful.

'I didn't know who would be in yet but there's coffee and pastries for anyone who wants them.' Ian placed them on the table that was becoming a bit of a dumping ground for cups, plates, biscuits and any other bits of food or sweets going.

'Thanks, that's great,' said Mel. She'd never considered him to be thoughtful but it was a kind gesture. Not one her old boss in the Met would have done. He'd have expected someone else, one of the women probably, to get the coffee and cakes.

'We've got coffee, pastries and the heating has kicked in. This is as good as it gets for the time being. I've just spoken to John. He's on his way round to the parents. Understandably they're not in a good way. You all know what you're doing so I'll leave you to it and we'll gather here in a few hours to see what we've got.'

*

Prita began searching the bus companies on the route that went by the top of the alley. There was only one which made life easier. On some of the routes there were three or four bus companies all vying for trade. She got through to the guy in charge, Fred Brocklehurst.

'Hello, Sergeant Patel from Carfield CID. We're investigating an incident that took place in Fisher last night and we're trying to track down any CCTV footage that might help. We're looking at between 8.00 and 9.00 pm. Any buses that travel along the Western Road?'

Fred had a look at the timetable. 'There are buses every twenty minutes in each direction, all have cameras but they only capture the inside of the bus and people getting on.'

'It's worth having a look so I'll send an officer down if that's ok with you. We need to see the footage from all buses that passed along that road between 8.00 and 9.00 pm.'

'Okay, it's all on the central system so won't be a problem.'

'Thanks for your help,' said Prita and put the phone down.

She decided to go and have a look at the local shop and have a scout around. Rummaging around in her pockets, she checked she had the necessaries. Got mints, got keys and phone, good to go.

But first she'd better get someone down to the bus depot. She rang DC David Metcalfe. 'Morning, David, Prita here. I've just spoken to Fred Brocklehurst at County buses. Can you get down to the bus depot and have a look at any CCTV on buses passing along the Western Road between 8.00 and 9.00 last night? It's a long shot but the camera points to the bus doors and might show kids running off or getting on. Fred's expecting you.'

'Okay, I'm on it.'

He's been watching too many American cop shows, thought Prita.

'I'm off to the local shop in Fisher and will have a general scout around for CCTV. See you later.'

When she got outside, the light struck her and she screwed up her eyes. There was something intense about winter light. It was one of those beautiful, cold days. Clear blue skies, sun shining, even the smells were somehow clean, the sort of day that makes you glad to be alive and grateful to be outside. She never took anything for granted. Every type of weather held its own beauty and today was no exception.

She drove the few miles out to Fisher. The drive out of town was uphill and the frosted hills against the blue sky were just stunning. It was a day when you wanted to walk in the hills, feel your face frozen with the cold but fresh and alive at the same time. A day which should end with a hot chocolate after trekking through the countryside. However, that was for another time.

It wasn't far but it became more depressing the further she drove despite the beauty of the hills in the background. The odd house was boarded up, shops all had metal shutters and social facilities were non-existent. The occasional pub and bookies seemed to provide the entertainment for the area.

She knew it was one of those post-war council estates that had been built on the edge of a town with space and gardens and, most importantly, jobs, where once upon a time people had dignity and hope. Generations later, most of that was gone. Horizons were limited in a dictatorship of minds. It looked as if it had been forgotten. Despite what the government said, there was no levelling up here.

She pulled up outside the Fisher local shop, just at the bottom of the alley where Josh was stabbed. She could see a couple of reporters, or vultures as she thought of them, trying to get information out of CSI.

The alley was taped off and CSIs were painstakingly searching. Mel was already there. She liked Mel even though she had that southern reserve about her. Mel had hinted that she'd had a hard time in the Met and wanted out but she wasn't sure what that was about. Maybe they needed a girlie night out together. Let's face it, women in CID needed to stick together.

She greeted the uniform standing by the tape and went to chat with Mel who was at the other end of the alley. She could see why the alley was a handy cut through between the main Western Road, the bus route, and Green Street where there was a concentration of terraces and council semis.

Mel was well wrapped up in scarf and beanie hat but still managed to look frozen, which somehow suited her. A hint of red cheeks on her pale skin, her blond hair below the hat was blowing across her face and her pale blue eyes standing out more brightly now the sun was shining.

'Hi, Mel. Anything yet?'

'No weapon. We've looked in bins, gardens, adjoining waste ground and nothing. We're going to widen the search. It was dry and cold last night so doesn't look like there are any shoe impressions. I'm just going to the school now. How about you?'

'David Metcalfe is looking at CCTV from buses and I'm going into the shop to see if there's any footage they might have. The bus is a bit of a long shot though. We go up so many blind alleys in an investigation. No pun intended.'

They both laughed, each recognising the gallows humour.

'Good luck,' said Mel. 'I'll see you later.'

Mel set off for Moss Green Academy, a sixth form college with a reputation that had parents clamouring to move into the catchment area.

First the headteacher.

The school receptionist took her along a brightly lit corridor with art on the walls and student names underneath, pictures of students and glass display cabinets with trophies and shields. It gave the impression of talented, aspiring, high achieving students. No wonder parents were clamouring to get their kids in here.

At the end of the corridor, she knocked on a door with a highly polished brass plate displaying the name, "Sian Jones, Headteacher".

Mel could remember going to the head's office when she was at school and a slight nervousness came back to her. She knew it was ridiculous but having to see the head was always a big deal.

The voice from inside shouted "yes" and in they walked into the warm, bright office with more student paintings on the walls. The receptionist introduced Mel and Sian Jones to each other formally as Sergeant Garvey and Ms Jones. Mel noted the 'Ms' rather than 'Mrs' despite the wedding ring she was wearing.

'Thanks Janice. Would you get drinks and biscuits for Ms Garvey please?'

She turned to Mel and asked with a slight Welsh lilt to her voice, 'Tea or coffee?'

'Coffee would be great, thank you.'

Sian Jones came from behind the huge mahogany desk and gestured for Mel to sit on a comfy chair by a coffee table where she joined her.

Mel took her in. Petite, navy fitted suit and a short blonde bob. She exuded efficiency with an air of being in control. She'd read the psychological studies saying employers made up their minds about candidates in the first fifteen seconds of an interview. Mel wasn't sure that was strictly true but she could already tell she was a no nonsense sort of woman.

Sian Jones began immediately, a woman who was used to talking and being listened to.

'No-one can quite believe it. We're all in a state of shock, staff and students alike. I imagine you will want to talk to some of Josh's friends and his girlfriend, Naomi Edwards. Naomi isn't in college today, understandably. I imagine you will find her at home.'

'Yes. We need to build up a picture of Josh, get to know the kind of person he was and work out why he was in Fisher.'

Just then, the receptionist brought in a tray with a pot of coffee, two cups with saucers and a bowl of sugar cubes and a plate of chocolate digestives. She'd never had that when she was at school but didn't imagine this was the treatment the students would get.

'It might also be useful to speak with the head of year and Josh's form tutor. I can arrange that after we've spoken. You will of course need the permission of the parents to speak to the students and they will no doubt want to be present or have an adult present. I'll get on to that as I imagine you want to do that as soon as possible.'

'It would be good to start that this afternoon if we can as there is no time to lose in an investigation such as this.'

Mel didn't want to use the term "murder investigation" as some people recoiled at the use of the word as if it was too macabre.

'Of course. I'll get my secretary, Kate, to take you up to Mr Ricketts, head of year, and Miss Sansom, Josh's form tutor, and then I can speak to the parents. You can give Kate your number and we'll contact you about speaking to the students.'

With that she stood up, went to her desk, pressed a button on her phone and told the person on the other end, who Mel assumed was Kate, to escort Mel to Mr Ricketts and Ms Sansom and to get her number.

Mel knew when she was being dismissed but if Sian Jones got things done, that was absolutely fine with her. Pity she'd only managed a few sips of coffee and one biscuit though.

Sian Jones came across as a very caring, efficient woman, maybe a bit scary at times, and one who clearly wanted the best for her students. She was also, understandably, very protective of them.

After conversations with the head of year and form tutor, she was building up a picture of Josh. A bright lad, university material but not grafting the way he should have been with the A levels coming up. He had plenty of friends but they needed to speak to his girlfriend, Naomi Edwards, urgently. Hopefully, they could fill in some blanks about what he was doing in Fisher.

Mel's phone rang with a number she didn't recognise.

'Hello Sergeant Mel Garvey.'

'Hello, Sergeant Garvey, it's Kate Atkins, Ms Jones' secretary. She has asked me to let you know that some student interviews have been lined up for this afternoon and can start at 2.00 pm if that's convenient.'

'Yes, that's great. I'll get some officers down here in plenty of time. Thanks so much for your help.'

'My pleasure. If they just come to reception, I will take them to the common room and arrange the interview slots.'

Well, thought Mel, *that was certainly efficient*. Let's hope they can throw some light on what Josh was doing on a sink estate in the arse end of town.

*

John Dykes arrived at Anna's house with Immie Lord, family liaison officer. He wasn't looking forward to this. It was always difficult to see the pain in the face of a loved one and it was just shitty when the loss was a child.

Anna opened the door. You could tell she hadn't slept. Her eyes were swollen and red, lids drooping but there were no tears now. Perhaps you can only cry for so long. Her brown hair was roughly tied back from her face with strands of hair fighting free of the scrunchie that held most of it back.

'Come in, Greg's here.'

They walked into the bright hallway and Anna showed them into the living room where Greg was sitting, staring into space. If anything, he looked even worse than Anna. Maybe it's just lack of a shave that gives some men that look of squaller and exhaustion.

'I'm really sorry to be imposing just now but we need to build up a picture as quickly as we can. This is Immie, she will be your family liaison officer, help you with everything you're going through and keep you updated on progress.'

'Hi. I'm very sorry for your loss and I will be here to help, answer any questions and update you as John said.'

'The only update I want is to know when you've arrested someone.' Greg was still angry and John couldn't blame him. Sometimes anger was easier to deal with than seeing the raw agony of loss.

'We're building up a picture now. We have officers at the scene, making house to house enquiries and looking for CCTV. It would be really helpful if I could take a look in Josh's room and perhaps Immie could put the kettle on?'

'You won't find his killer in his bedroom,' said Greg.

'No, but it helps in getting to know Josh and might give us some clues as to what he was doing in Fisher last night. We've got his phone and I'd like to take his laptop if he has one. Any passwords would also speed up the process if you know them.'

'He told me he was going round to Naomi's to work on a geography project,' said Anna. 'I had no reason to think that wasn't true but I haven't heard anything from Naomi. She might know why he was there.'

Greg was silent now. He was limp and bent over as if the anger had sucked his very being, draining every bit of him.

'I'll show you up,' said Anna.

Anna showed him in to Josh's room, then turned away and left him to it. John could tell it was too immediate for her. The socks and T shirt on the floor, Leeds United insignia on the walls and various posters of bands that John had never heard of. It was just a teenage boy's room.

He looked in drawers, above the wardrobe, under the bed and bedding. He found a small amount of weed in a drawer consistent with personal use. Josh was a teenage boy after all.

Before leaving the house, he took the laptop and hoped the techies at the station might find something helpful.

*

Prita showed her ID and asked to speak to the owner of the shop. 'That's me.' Sunni Singh was dressed in grey joggers and sweatshirt. He looked at her warily. Prita knew people round here didn't talk to the police and if they did, they didn't want anyone else knowing it.

'I'm part of the team investigating the incident in the alley last night and I'd like to have a look at your CCTV. I believe you've spoken to an officer.'

'Yes, but I didn't see anything. I live above the shop, heard some shouting about 8.30 but didn't take any notice of it. Shouting is not unusual round here.'

Prita paused and looked at him instinctively, knowing he just wanted to fit in and not make waves. He was too quick to say he hadn't seen anything which was always a flag to suggest he had. 'Were you working in the shop at that time?'

'No. There's a part time assistant, Julie, who was on last night. You can speak to her. There's teenagers in and out of the shop all the time so nothing unusual.'

'When you heard shouting, did you look to see what was happening?'

'No. Like I told you, I didn't see anything and didn't hear anything out of the ordinary.'

He took her to the back of the shop where she could view the CCTV. She looked around the small space where boxes of drinks and crisps were kept, a kettle and some mugs and behind all that was a staff toilet and sink. Talk about not being able to swing a cat.

On a shelf above the drinks and crisps were the CCTV controls. He described the angles of the four cameras covering the interior of the shop, one covering the door outside and one covering the side of the shop and bottom of the alley.

'Let's start with the having a look at the one covering in the alley,' said Prita.

Watching CCTV was terminally boring but took all your concentration so you didn't miss anything. It was all too easy to switch off.

At 8.34 on the clock, she could make out five figures at the end of the alley. It was too dark and the quality too poor to see their faces or what they were doing. When a bus goes past at 8.39, it momentarily illuminates the alley and the figures are easier to see. Definitely five figures but you couldn't tell whether they were male or female. From some of the quick movements they seemed young. That footage needed enhancing.

'Can we have a look at the camera covering those coming into the shop?'

At 8.16, she saw a teenage boy and girl in the shop buying some coke. Josh and Naomi.

'Have you seen either of these teenagers before?' Prita asked.

'I don't recognise them but I'm not usually in the shop in the evenings.'

The way he avoided looking at her told Prita he was lying.

'I'm going to send a colleague up to get a full download of all the footage.'

'That's fine. I'll help with the CCTV but that's it.'

'Why?'

'I just don't want to get involved. I live here, have a business here, and don't want any comeback. Anyway, I didn't see anything.'

'Okay,' said Prita, 'but you do know a seventeen-year-old boy was murdered and we need all the help we can get. If we catch them, then everyone around here will be safer. Here's my card and if you think of anything, give me a call.'

She left him to it. She understood why he didn't want to get involved. Indian shopkeeper on a predominantly white council estate. He wasn't going to help and she wouldn't hold her breath that he would call. She couldn't blame him but unless they caught whoever killed Josh he would always live in fear.

Outside, the weather was still gloriously bright and freezing cold. She rang DC Metcalfe.

'How are you getting on, David?'

'Nothing here. There is a bus stop at the top end of the alley on Western Road but none of the buses stopped during the relevant time.'

The frustrating thing about an investigation is the time you spend going down blind alleys. Sometimes you can spend weeks on something that looks promising but, in the end, takes you nowhere. At least investigating the bus cameras hadn't taken long.

'Okay. Can you come back to Fisher and look at the local shop CCTV. The proprietor is Sunni Singh and there is some CCTV footage of Josh and a girl in the shop between 8.16 and 8.19 last night and footage of what looks like a scuffle in the alley. Take a download of everything and get the techies to enhance any relevant clips. I know it will take some time to go through and for the techies to enhance it but get PC Butler to give you a hand.'

'Oh no,' groaned David, 'that'll take ages.'

'I know but it's got to be done and I know how much you love watching CCTV footage.'

'Okay, I'm on it.'

'You're watching too many American cop shows, David.'

'I don't know what you mean,' laughed David.

Prita decided to have a wander round the area and check out any CCTV there might be in surrounding houses. After a wander round, she found four cameras which might show something.

She decided that was another one for David.

If people are too frightened to talk, their only hope was getting evidence on film. Even better.

*

Mel rushed into the briefing room, cheeks flushed. Most people were there and Ian was just getting started, marker pen in hand.

'Okay, everyone, let's see what we've got. Updates please. John?'

'Seems like an ordinary seventeen-year-old, nothing of any help in his bedroom. Found a small amount of weed consistent with personal use. We've got his laptop, phone and passwords which I've given to the tech department. Seems he was with the girlfriend, Naomi Edwards, for at least some of last night so she needs to be spoken to urgently.'

'Thanks for that, John. Prita?'

'No helpful CCTV from the bus depot but there is from the shop. It shows Josh and a girl in the shop buying a bottle of Coke between 8.16 and 8.19. There is a camera in the alley which shows five people at the top of the alley at 8.34. It looks like this might have been when Josh was stabbed. It's very unclear but David Metcalfe is getting a download, going through it and getting the techies to enhance any relevant parts.

'There are also four houses in the vicinity with CCTV which might show something. David is going to have a look at that. I get the feeling people won't talk to us so CCTV might give us the answers.'

'Great stuff. Is the girl Naomi Edwards?'

'We don't know but it seems likely given what John said.'

'Thanks Prita. Mel?'

'Nothing from CSI. No footprints anywhere. It wasn't helped by the freezing temperatures last night. No weapon. We've widened the search area. The school is accommodating us in speaking to the students to see if we can get more background from his friends. All of that will all start this afternoon. Naomi Edwards wasn't in school today but I agree she's a priority.'

'Good. It would help if we could find the weapon. Post mortem is taking place now. Preliminary findings suggest the blade must have been at least six inches but we'll know more when they've finished. I've spoken with DI Martha

Holroyd about local gangs. There's the Z99 gang operating in Carfield which seems to have control of Fisher. Drug dealing, threats and violence.

'People are too frightened to talk but everyone knows who they are according to Martha. She's given me a list of the main players so let's see if they crop up anywhere else. Mel, see if you can speak to Naomi Edwards as a priority.

'Let's hope the CCTV and techies can throw up something. I want it rushed through as a priority. Meet back here at 6.00 for updates. Thanks everyone. Mel, can I have a quick word before you go?'

Ian thought she was his most efficient sergeant and, with her Met experience, his number two although he felt she could do with a warmer, more sympathetic approach. She did what was asked of her and did it well but there was something missing. She kept herself to herself as if she was reluctant to get closer to anyone. Part of policing was relating to people, including colleagues.

Maybe it's just how she is but he wanted to get on a better footing with her. There was an awkwardness between them that was not helpful and he was sure there was a human being underneath that cool exterior.

'Good work on co-ordinating all of that. I know there's a lot to cover there. Coming from the Met, you've more experience than most with these sort of investigations.'

'Thanks. Let's just hope we get something. I'll take Sally Black with me and go along to Naomi's now. As she's not in school, she should hopefully be at home. If Prita is right that she was there last night, she could be our main witness.'

'Or only witness by the looks of it, so let's see what she has to say.'

Chapter 8

Naomi's house was in a quiet cul de sac of semis five minutes' walk from Josh's. Mel rang the bell and a tall, mixed race woman with striking green eyes answered the door. She looked like she was dressed for work in the black trousers and white fitted shirt and not for a day at home.

'Hello, I'm Sergeant Mel Garvey and this is DC Sally Black. We're from Carfield CID and would like a word with Naomi about Josh Smithies if she's up to it.'

'It's terrible. We can't believe it. Naomi's in a complete state. Who would want to do such a thing? He was such a lovely lad. And what must his parents be going through? It doesn't seem real.'

She took a breath as if suddenly realising they were still standing on the doorstep.

'I'm sorry, I've not even asked you in. I'm not thinking straight. Come in please,' as she ushered them into the hall and through to an almost anally tidy living room.

'I'm Naomi's mum, Pam. I've tried talking to Naomi but she's in a state of shock, very tearful and hasn't really been able to speak a word about Josh. We found out about what happened from the television this morning as Naomi was getting ready for college and Harry, my youngest, had just left for school. Naomi just screamed and was sick. She sometimes vomits when she's anxious.

'Been like this since she was a baby. You should have seen her during her GCSEs. Josh and her were very close and even hoped to go to the same university. I know they were young but they seemed so suited and we all thought they'd end up being together permanently. We're all devastated by this and can't really believe it. I'll go and get her so you can speak to her but you've got to be very gentle and very brief. I'm not having her vomiting again and if she's not up to speaking to you yet, you'll just have to be patient and wait.'

Mel recognised it was the anxiety that was making her talk non-stop.

'Of course, and you can sit with her if that helps,' said Mel. 'It's just an initial chat while things are still fresh in her memory.'

'From my point of view, I just hope her memory will fade. She's in her bedroom. I'll go and talk to her and see if she's up to it.'

When Pam left the room, Mel could see her walking up the deeply carpeted stairs. She looked around and took in the room they were in. A comfortable, bright, sitting room with an archway through to a dining area and large windows at the back. The sunlight streamed in from the front and back of the house lighting up the space and, from the framed photographs of Pam, a man, presumably her husband, and two children, you could tell it was a real family home despite its obsessive tidiness.

Looking at the photos was like seeing scenes fast forward showing the children from babies, through the toddler stages and into various school uniforms.

You could often tell a lot from sitting in someone's home. The family photographs, a bookcase with books on wildlife, travel and natural science all gave a warmth to the surroundings. You get a feel of a house and Mel felt it was a happy place.

Naomi came downstairs and stood in the doorway. She was tall like her mum and had the same beautiful green eyes which stood out all the more against the red rims surrounding them. Long wavy brown hair framed her face and underneath the grief stricken face, Mel could see how beautiful she was. The baggy pink hoodie and joggers she was wearing was almost a uniform for teenage girls.

Poor kid, thought Mel. *She was too young to be coping with this.*

'Hello, Naomi, I'm Mel and this is Sally. We're from Carfield CID and we'd like to speak to you about last night.'

Naomi shuffled over to an oversized armchair, sat down and said nothing as she looked at the floor and twiddled with the ties on the hoodie. Mel could see the bitten nails and bleeding skin around a couple of them. Surely that can't just be from this morning, thought Mel.

'Would you like a cup of tea or coffee?' Pam asked.

'That would be lovely. Two teas, milk, no sugars.'

Having a drink, whether you wanted it or not, relaxed everyone and it gave Pam something to do.

'We know this is going to be hard for you and this is just an initial chat to see if you can help us find Josh's killers.'

Naomi sat there like a statue until her mum came back with the tea and biscuits.

'We understand Josh came round here to do some work on a geography assignment last night. Is that right?'

'Yes,' she whispered, still not looking at them.

Mel could tell this was going to be a slow one and it was probably one for a video interview in the vulnerable witness suite at the station. She was grateful she'd had that experience as she knew things like this couldn't be rushed.

'Can you tell us what happened when he came round?'

'We did a bit of work and Josh wanted to go to Fisher.'

'Did you go too?'

Naomi started crying and nodded while Pam sat next to her and held her hand.

'Why did he want to go to Fisher?'

She shook her head, unable to speak. 'I was frightened and ran away before it all kicked off. I didn't really hear what they were saying. I ran off. I'll never forgive myself. I left him to die.'

The sobs became uncontrollable as her mum knelt and cuddled her, crying with her.

They sat, waiting, hoping more would come but not wanting to push too far.

As Naomi calmed a bit, Mel thought she would just try a couple more questions.

'Do you know why he wanted to go to Fisher?'

She looked at her mum, clearly reluctant to say.

'If we know what he was doing there, it will help us catch his killer.'

'He owed money for drugs. That's all I know.'

Pam looked shocked, clearly not expecting this. She looked like she wanted to interrupt but kept silent no doubt wondering if Naomi was involved.

'Did you see who did this?'

She nodded.

'Do you know their names?'

A shake of the head.

'Would you recognise them again?'

Another shake of the head.

'Could you tell us anything about them such as how many, colour, age, what they were wearing?'

'There were three of them, all white, a bit older than me. That's all I can remember. I ran away.'

Naomi started crying again. Throughout this brief interview, she hadn't made eye contact once.

'I think that's enough,' said Pam. 'She's in a state. We all want you to catch Josh's killers but she's too distraught to keep answering questions. She got home about 9.30 and went straight up to her bedroom. I didn't think anything of it.

'Did you ring the police, Naomi?'

Pam answered again. 'She told us a little bit about it this morning and said she didn't want to ring the police. She didn't think he'd been badly hurt and just wanted to leave it. We only learnt what had happened from the news this morning when we were getting ready for college and work.'

Mel knew there no point carrying on now that Pam had stepped in and was answering for Naomi.

'It might be helpful if we can show some images to Naomi when we have some suspects. Not now but it might just jog her memory. We will also need to do an interview but that's something I will chat to you about later.'

Naomi nodded but still didn't look up. Mel felt this was as far as they would get today. Let's hope they get some suspects that Naomi can identify.

Back in the car, Sally asked, 'What did you make of her?'

'She's traumatised. Did you notice there was no eye contact at all?'

'Yes. Might be she's hiding something.'

'I think it's more likely that she's in shock. I've seen that sort of response in survivors of sexual abuse. They can't bring themselves to talk about it because it's reliving it all and just too painful. The trauma she's been through in seeing Josh attacked is likely to have the same sort of effect on her as the trauma of being the victim of a sexual offence. We'll need to organise a video interview.'

'Getting some suspects and organising a VIPER might jog her memory. I reckon she's seen more than she's saying as she knows why he was there, so it's more than likely she knows who they are and that's why she ran.'

The video identification parade electronic recording was a mouthful so it was VIPER for short. It meant that identifications were much easier to organise now that witnesses viewed a video of nine similar looking persons, one of whom was the suspect.

'We'll see if the CCTV footage from the alley can help with identifying anyone. Unless someone talks, it's definitely going to be our best bet.'

'It might be our only bet,' added Sally.

Chapter 9

Back at the station, they sat there, each with a piece of the jigsaw but missing the crucial connecting pieces held by others.

Ian explained they had updates on CCTV, cause of death, Naomi's first account and the Z99 gang. It was a lot in such a short space of time.

'Right, everyone, thank you for feeding back the information you've gathered. We've got some important developments which I'm going to briefly summarise.

'First of all post mortem initial findings. We're still waiting for the report but its confirmed cause of death is blood loss caused by a single stab wound to the left of the abdomen piercing the mesenteric artery and the spleen. Blade was probably at least six inches to penetrate that deep. There is also cannabis in his blood stream, maybe some amphetamine, but not a huge amount and not a contributor to his death. We're waiting for a full tox screen.

Next, CCTV. We've got some of the attack in the alley and we've managed to fast track the enhancement. It's still fairly unclear and the techies are working on it further, but it looks like Josh and Naomi Edwards. The other three have been identified by a community police officer as Ben Sutton, Harley Brown and Luke Price. I will come back to them.

All five are together when there's a scuffle, Josh seems to fall and the others run off. We then see Chelsea Brittan walk up, drop her bottle of milk and get on her phone. We've also got some footage from a house to the top left of the alley which shows Naomi running off. I'm assuming the others ran in the opposite direction but there are no cameras in that direction so we've no footage of the others after they leave the alley.

DI Martha Holroyd has confirmed that Sutton, Brown and Price are suspected members of Z99, all have previous for drugs and violence and all three have convictions for carrying knives.

'Martha has had one case of cuckooing where the gangs use the home of a vulnerable target, who is too frightened to refuse, as a place for storing and dealing drugs. County lines, previously something that was a big city problem, is also a reality in Carfield. Young, vulnerable kids are used to carry drugs from one area to another. We don't know if Josh was involved in this but we can't discount it yet.

'Apparently one of the local journalists, Tricia Gibson, has been doing some work on it for a piece she is researching. Although, I wouldn't normally suggest it, Martha thinks it might be worth speaking to Tricia as people will speak to a journalist rather than the police. I'm happy to do that.

We're in the process of speaking to some of Josh's friends at school. He was clearly a popular lad according to staff but had distanced himself from friends recently. We've got names of his closest friends and interviews at school are underway.

'Naomi has given a first account. She confirmed being with Josh, going to Fisher, gave a vague description of three white male suspects a bit older than her. That was the extent of the description. She said she ran off and probably wouldn't recognise them again. We will need to arrange a VIPER for that if we can't identify them from CCTV.

'Looking at the CCTV footage, it is clear she did run off but she was in the alley at the time Josh appears to fall, so looks to be in the thick of it and she must have heard what was said.'

Mel interrupted at that point. 'She said she was frightened and if this is a case of gangs and drugs, it's understandable that she ran off and might be reluctant to identify them.'

'Maybe, but she was there. I know it was dark but she's right next to them and she's there when it looks as if Josh falls over, presumably stabbed. The impression she's given is that she ran before and was too distant to identify them.'

'To be fair to her, she didn't really say when she ran off and, given what has happened to Josh, she's probably frightened it could happen to her.'

Ian was in front of the white board now with marker pen in hand. He wrote Josh's name, circled it and above it wrote "victim".

To the right, he wrote "potential suspects" and underneath put the names of Ben Sutton, Harley Brown and Luke Price. Next to that, he wrote "motive" and underneath wrote "drugs?" To the left, he wrote "witnesses" and put Naomi's name underneath.

'I'm sure Naomi is frightened but she's our crucial witness. Mel, I know you've done a lot of work with vulnerable witnesses so I'd like you to organise a video interview with her. We're waiting for a lot more such as analysis of Josh's phone and laptop but that will take a while and we need further enhancement of the CCTV. We can see them all there but can't tell what anyone is doing. We've also got enough to arrest Sutton, Brown and Price. John, I want you to take some officers and go to Sutton's house for his arrest. Prita, you're on Brown and, Mel, you're on Price. You will each lead the interviews with another officer of your choosing. Let's see what they've got to say for themselves.'

Chapter 10

DC Mick Buckley was at the school with a team of uniformed officers interviewing Josh's friends and year group. It would take a while. Some of the parents refused to give permission for their sons and daughters to be interviewed, some of the children had parents with them and others had the school counsellor or a teacher.

Mick had been told who were the friends of Naomi and Josh so he decided he would do those interviews.

Callum Matthews had been Josh's best friend but they'd grown apart recently according to Sian Jones. Mick decided he'd start with him.

The year 13 common room was out of bounds to students just now and was being used for interviews. It was big enough for them all to be well apart if there were a couple of interviews going on at the same time. Things had changed since his days in the sixth form. The chairs grouped round low tables, were comfier and less tatty.

He remembered his old common room, such as it was, with vinyl chairs and foam stuffing poking through the tears. No snack machines or drinks machines in his day.

'Thanks for agreeing to talk to me, Callum, and thanks to you too, Mr Matthews, for taking time to come down. It won't take long.'

'It's okay,' said Trevor Matthews. 'We want to help. Josh was a lovely lad.'

'We're just trying to build up a picture of Josh which might explain why he was in Fisher.'

Callum fidgeted uncomfortably and looked at the floor.

'I'd not seen him much recently. We'd a lot of work on and were doing different A levels. I don't know why he was there.'

Callum was not making eye contact and Mick could tell there was something he wasn't saying.

'Whatever you tell us might help in piecing together a picture of Josh. There had to be a reason why he was there and anything you can tell us, no matter how small, could help catch his killer.'

There was another awkward pause. Mick wasn't going to fill the silence and just waited for Callum to speak.

'He got into drugs so that was probably why he was in Fisher.'

'Okay. Thanks for that. I know you feel like you're being disloyal but that could be the key to why he was killed. Do you know what sort?'

'Definitely weed but I think he was also using cocaine and maybe pills but not sure. He was also selling or at least trying to, but I don't think he had many takers.'

'Do you know anyone who was buying?'

'Try Phil Murray. He might have or might know someone. I hadn't bought any, neither had my mates. Josh changed. We used to be really good mates but he didn't want to do anything or get together. He was on the football team but just stopped coming to training and said he had too much on to play. I don't know why Naomi stayed with him. I don't want anyone to know I've told you this.'

'What you tell me is confidential but I will need you to make a statement as it could be relevant. If it is relevant, I'm afraid it might not remain confidential. Don't worry, we don't go around telling people what you've said.'

'I don't know any more than that. I missed him when he stopped doing stuff. We'd been in the same primary and secondary schools and were always best mates.'

At that he couldn't hold the tears back and his dad put his arms around him.

'I'm so sorry I'm having to ask you questions. I know the headteacher is suggesting anyone affected should talk to the college counsellor and she's organising some more counselling to be available for those who want it. It's not a bad idea to take it up.'

'I know and I'll probably do that. I hope you catch them.'

'Thank you, Callum, and thank you too, Mr Matthews. I know it's not easy for anyone.'

Mick watched them both leave. He needed a coffee before he continued. The intensity in these interviews was exhausting. He went over to the snack machines and got a coffee and bar of chocolate. He needed to take five before he saw the next one. Phil Murray wasn't on his list so he checked the other lists.

Karen White was seeing students in one of the classrooms and was due to see Phil Murray in about half an hour. He decided to give Karen a call.

'Hi Karen, Mick here. You've got Phil Murray on your list and something's come up so I'd like to see him. Can you redirect him to me when he arrives?'

'Will do. One less for me is a result.'

'I would say any time but that's too much like a commitment.'

They both just laughed as Mick ended the call.

The next one, Yvonne Carter, was waiting for him by the drinks machine. Right. Onwards and upwards.

'Hi. You must be Yvonne.' The woman next to her was too young to be Yvonne's mum. He looked at her and she introduced herself as Stacy Mulligan, art teacher. Yvonne was one of her students and asked Stacy to sit in. Now that she said she was an art teacher, he could see it. He could play a game of guessing the subject taught when the teachers came in.

Stacy was dressed in green dungarees, white T shirt and her long black hair was tied loosely back in a blue silk scarf. Lots of black kohl around big blue eyes. He couldn't help but notice she wasn't wearing a wedding ring and he automatically smoothed his hair down. *Right, focus on Yvonne, not Stacy or she'll think you're a real sleaze,* thought Mick.

'Thanks for coming, Yvonne. You too, Stacy. I just want to ask you some questions about Josh so we can get a better picture of him.'

Yvonne was another reticent one. His information said she was a good friend of Naomi's but she couldn't tell them much. Hadn't heard anything about drugs. Hadn't seen Naomi much. Too busy getting her portfolio together for the university applications due soon.

'Naomi spent most of her time with Josh so I haven't seen her much.'

She was adamant Naomi wouldn't do drugs though.

Right, no help there.

'Thanks for coming. You too, Stacy.' He reserved the big smile for Stacy.

Get a grip, Buckley, he told himself as he watched Stacy leave.

He assumed that it was Phil Murray sat a few tables away. He was with a man who was probably in his sixties. Mick thought he was probably too old to be Phil's dad so more than likely he was a teacher. Beige trousers, a bit baggy but not in a fashionable way, brown jumper over a white shirt. Science, guessed Mick.

They both came over and Mick held out his hand. 'Hi, thanks for coming, I'm DC Mick Buckley and you must be Phil Murray.'

The young man nodded.

'Hello. I'm Jon Bryant, head of physics and one of Phil's teachers.'

Mick smiled to himself. *Bingo*, he thought. *This game could be light relief.*

Phil turned out to be more forthcoming than anticipated.

'Josh was selling drugs. I bought some weed from him but that was it. He was trying to sell cocaine and amphetamine but I wasn't interested. He said it would help me concentrate on assignments and keep me awake when I had a lot of work on. That wasn't me. I didn't mind the occasional bit of weed but that was it.'

'Any idea where he was getting it from?'

'All I knew was that he had a supplier in Fisher. He was trying to sell around college but no-one was interested that I knew of. Ask Naomi.'

Mick carried on but didn't get much more than the link to Fisher.

After thanking them, he looked at his list and the next student waiting patiently. He was with a man who had to be a teacher, too young to be a parent. Very smart, expensive looking navy pinstripe suit, pink shirt with co-ordinating blue and pink tie, shiny shoes and sharp haircut. If he was older, Mick would have guessed deputy head but unlikely as he looked about thirty.

Possibly business studies, maybe economics or law. Something safe and conservative.

They came over and the boy confirmed he was Pierce McGuire. The teacher introduced himself as David White, sociology teacher.

Oh well, thought Mick, *can't win them all.*

Chapter 11

Naomi

Naomi wished she could get it all out of her head.

She couldn't sleep, couldn't eat, and the images were with her all the time.

Not just last night but from all the other times she'd been to Fisher.

All the times she'd gone with Josh because he asked her to.

Had begged her so he didn't have to go on his own.

If she did manage to get to sleep, she'd wake up in the night and see it all. It was like reliving it over and over again and having no control.

Groundhog Day.

The times they hit and kicked Josh.

The way they all bullied, humiliated and threatened. It was how they were, their way of being.

She saw him fall, saw the look in his eyes, the fear, the questions, not understanding.

It was that haunted look she couldn't get out of her head.

But that was only then.

And all the other times when they were there. She could hear their laughter in her head.

But not just the laughter. That was the least of it.

Why had he started down this road in the first place?

He was clever and had it all but he'd thrown it away. He could be so stupid. And bossy.

She wished she hadn't gone with him. Why didn't she just say she wanted to work on her project?

Maybe she did say. She couldn't even remember now.

He wasn't bossy with them.

He did what they told him.

But so did she.

Everyone was frightened of them. They were young but so cocky. They acted like they owned the estate and no-one could stop them. They were kings.

Or at least Sutton was. The other two just did what he said.

They dealt their drugs in the shop when it was cold so they could keep warm. They would even help themselves to a can of Stella if they felt like it and the shopkeeper turned a blind eye.

He was scared too.

Sometimes in the night, her head would take her back to all the other times she'd gone there with Josh but she couldn't bear that.

The countless images of horror and fear and humiliation.

She'd shake her head just to try and get rid of the sights as if the action would rid her mind of the countless pictures.

It wouldn't.

Time is a great healer her mother had told her.

She just hoped that time would get rid of the never ending wheel of pictures she was stuck with.

Chapter 12

Four officers went round to Ben Sutton's house. He knew it was police by the way they hammered on the door. Only the bizzies would hammer on the door like that.

Anyway, he knew they'd be here sooner or later so better get it over with. They wouldn't find anything anyway and, although he was just nineteen, he knew the score. He'd been at the cop shop often enough.

The bit of weed he had in his bedroom was probably enough for a caution but that was it. They couldn't be arsed most of the time. Too much paperwork.

His mum, Liz, answered the door in leggings and baggy T shirt, complaining about the banging as her youngest was asleep.

'We need to speak to Ben,' said John.

'Why, he hasn't done anything? You're just harassing him. You've got it in for him.'

Ben sauntered slowly to the door. 'It's fine, Mum, I've not done nothing.'

'Ben Sutton, I'm arresting you on suspicion of murder. You do not have to say anything but it may harm your defence if you do not mention when questioned something that you later rely on in court. Anything you do say may be given in evidence. Turn round and put your hands behind your back.'

He did it as slowly as he could and John cuffed him.

It was obvious it was not a surprise to him that he'd been arrested.

The guilty ones often complied and the innocent ones kicked off. If this was anything to go by, then he was guilty as sin.

John could hear a child crying from inside the house, no doubt woken by the commotion.

'No,' screamed his mum. She went forward to grab Ben but John held her back. He could see that she loved him despite him being a little shit with a record as long as your arm.

Ben was booked in at the station, gave the name of his solicitors, saw the duty doctor who said he was fit to be interviewed, and was put in a cell while they waited for the solicitor to arrive.

Waiting in a cold cell, sitting on a plastic mattress on top of a concrete platform used for a bed and with nothing to do made the wait seem forever. All they'd given him was machine coffee in a plastic cup which was undrinkable.

His solicitor, Charles Haig, arrived and they went into a private room for a consultation. At least it broke the monotony of sitting in the cell.

The white cuffs of Charles' shirt showed just below the sleeves of his fitted navy blue suit. The understated blue cufflinks, neatly combed fair hair and brown briefcase completed the look. Every inch the solicitor.

'Right,' said Charles as he sat down and took the Mont Blanc pen, pad and, most importantly, legal aid forms from the briefcase.

'They're doing this by the book. You've seen the doctor and they're getting an appropriate adult from Social Services to sit in even though you are twenty-one and don't technically need one. They say they've got CCTV footage of a scuffle in an alley during which a lad called Josh Smithies was stabbed and killed. I've not seen any CCTV so I don't know how clear it is or what it shows so my advice to you is to go "no comment".

As they're not showing us the footage, my guess is it's not very clear. If you don't answer questions, it can go against you in a trial but I think, at this stage, as they've not disclosed any evidence, that's the best course of action. The decision has got to be yours though.'

'Yeah, I'll do that.'

'You sure? Once you do it, there's no going back.'

'I'm not answering any of their fucking questions. I didn't do anything so they can go and fuck themselves.'

'Fine. Sign here to agree I've advised you about your options and it's your decision not to answer questions. And drop the attitude when we're in the interview. It won't do you any good.'

'Okay, okay, I hear you.'

'Right, let's tell them we're ready for interview.'

*

53

Prita arrived at Harley Brown's house in two police cars with four officers and knocked loudly on the front door. No answer but she saw the curtain twitch and seconds later, heard shouting coming from the back of the house. *He must think we're clueless*, she thought. *Didn't he realise we'd have officers covering the back? Trying to escape out the back door was not exactly original.*

Prita and the other two officers ran down the side of the inter war semi just in time to catch a glimpse of Harley Brown leaping over the fence into the neighbouring garden with Bob and Sharon in a slow pursuit. Oh, to have the mobility of teenagers!

'Bob, Sharon, cover the backs of the houses. Hayley, Phil, go round the front. He can't have got far. I'll stay here in case he tries to sneak back in.'

No-one else came out of the house so either the others didn't want to get involved or there was no-one in.

After a few minutes, Hayley radioed in. 'Nothing, Sarge. He's disappeared. Maybe he's gone into a mate's house.'

'Okay. Stay where you are and I'll see if Bob and Sharon have spotted him.'

She radioed Bob, 'Anything?'

'No sign of him.'

'Okay, I'll get the dog team but stay there in case he sneaks out.'

She radioed for the dog team and just waited.

She couldn't go in the house, not that she would on her own anyway, but at this stage they didn't have a right to enter. They would soon though. She got the impression there was no-one inside so it was tempting but she couldn't break the rules and possibly bugger up the investigation.

It was too cold to be waiting around but the dog handler eventually arrived with a mean looking German Shepherd you wouldn't want to mess with.

'About time. What kept you?'

'Sorry. Traffic. Which direction did he run in?'

She pointed in the direction. 'That way. He must be hiding out somewhere as he just disappeared.'

'Right, leave it with us.'

She watched the dog straining at the leash, spittle dripping from its jaws pulling the dog handler behind it. She'd never been keen on dogs. They always made her a bit nervous. More of a cat person.

After a couple of minutes, she heard the whistle and ran in that direction. Hayley and Phil arrived seconds later with Bob and Sharon just behind. The dog was barking furiously attempting to get at Harley Brown who was half way out of a wheelie bin, a very smelly wheelie bin at that. She'd seen a lot of suspects with dog bites so she warned him.

'Out of the bin slowly unless you want to risk the dog ripping your arm off. Stand up and put your hands behind your back.'

The look of fear on his face told her he'd decided to co-operate rather than face the dog.

She cuffed him saying, 'Harley Brown, I'm arresting you on suspicion of murder. You do not have to say anything but it might harm your defence if you do not mention when questioned something you later rely on in court. Anything you do say may be given in evidence.'

'What? You're taking the piss.'

'In your dreams, soft lad.'

Bob escorted him to the car placing one hand on Brown's head as he guided him into the back seat. Can't have any knocks or bruises at this stage.

Prita got in the front and Bob drove to the station.

God, he stunk. They don't warn you about the smelly suspects at police training college.

At the station, she booked him in telling the custody sergeant the reason and circumstances of the arrest. She could see her trying to take a step back to avoid the stench and, after getting his solicitor's details in double quick time, had him taken down to a cell.

'When his solicitor arrives, we can put them in the small consultation room at the end. The smell in that space should be particularly ripe.'

'Perks of the job,' laughed Prita.

'There aren't many so get them where you can.'

Once Brown's solicitor arrived, he was given the disclosure and then went into consultation with him. He didn't take long.

'Ready for interview?' Prita asked when he emerged.

'Yes. I gather you found him in a bin?'

'I'm surprised you could tell.'

'Very funny, Sergeant.'

Prita walked him to the interview room smiling to herself.

Winding up solicitors could definitely be a perk of the job.

She showed him into the room and one of the custody staff brought in Brown and the appropriate adult.

After introductions were made, it was straight into the questions.

And the answers.

"No comment" to every question.

Shit. But to be expected in a murder case when the evidence was in its very early stages.

*

Mel had no problems with Luke Price. He opened the door, was in his house alone, said nothing when she arrested and cautioned him and came quietly. With his lanky frame, shaved head, bum fluff on the chin and grubby hoodie and joggers, he cut a pathetic figure. He must be over six feet but was just skin and bone. He didn't utter a word in the car, when he was booked in or when he saw the doctor.

She was concerned that he might have learning difficulties but the doctor didn't think so. Definitely needed an appropriate adult though. He was just so silent. Maybe it was a tactic but she didn't get the impression that he had enough upstairs to work out tactics. His solicitor arrived from Hitchcock and Co. and Mel showed him into a consultation room before getting Price out of his cell. Mel didn't really know any of the local solicitors yet but she had heard this firm's name a few times.

After half an hour, the solicitor emerged.

About time, thought Mel. At least he can't say he's not had long enough with his client. Maybe he needed a long time to try and get through to him. Definitely not the brightest.

'We're ready for interview, Sergeant Garvey.'

'I'll show you both through to the interview room.'

Once they were seated, Mel asked Luke if he needed drink before they started and when he declined, she went through the caution again explaining it very slowly to Luke.

'Do you understand, Luke?'

'Yeah.'

Well at least she's crossing the I's and dotting the T's with this one so no defence barrister further down the line can say that it was an oppressive interview.

She wasn't hopeful the interview would be productive. It wouldn't have been in the Met but who knows up here. She wasn't wrong. A "no comment" interview.

*

Back in the briefing room, feelings were mixed. They'd made early arrests but the interviews were all "no comment". They had all used the same firm of solicitors.

'Isn't that a conflict of interest?' Prita asked.

'Not at this stage. If they start cutting each other's throats, it will be but they're saying nothing,' explained Ian. 'I've been on to Ged at the CPS. Not enough to charge with that footage but let's keep them for twenty-four hours and see if anything else turns up. We might have to apply for an extension but we'll see what else we get from the section 18 house searches which are underway.

'If we find anything, we can interview again in the morning. Mel, have you spoken to Naomi about bringing her in for a video interview?'

'Yes, we're booked in for two days' time.'

'Nothing tomorrow?'

'We're lucky to get a slot in two days with the number of vulnerable witness interviews they do.'

'Fair enough, I'll leave it with you. I'm going to meet up with Tricia Gibson from the Yorkshire Daily Post and see if she can fill us in a bit on the local gangs and county lines. We might have to give her something but I will run it past the press office first. That goes for all of you. I don't want any leaks that could jeopardise the investigation. Go home, get some rest and I'll see you all tomorrow.'

Ian knew they'd made good progress in a short space of time but it wasn't enough for charges. Yet.

*

Tricia was already in the Brown Cow when Ian arrived. She looked cosy in a sheepskin jacket and cream polo neck shirt, her auburn hair cascading over her shoulders.

57

'Thanks for agreeing to meet up, Tricia. DI Holroyd said you might be able to fill me in on the county lines research you've been doing.'

'And I thought you were after my body, Ian.'

Tricia always flirted outrageously around everyone, male and female. Ian knew she didn't mean anything by it but he quite liked it all the same. It was a long time since anyone flirted with him and it was a skill he'd never really mastered.

'What would you like to drink?' was all he could say in response. He knew it was a bit wooden.

'Dry white wine. If you throw in some salt and vinegar crisps, I'll reveal all.'

Ian could feel himself blushing as he turned his back and walked to the bar. He really was out of practice.

Half a pint of shandy later, Tricia had told him what she knew about Z99, the main players, how they targeted kids from schools out of the area, then got them hooked on clothes, money or drugs. Sometimes it was violence or threats of violence that was enough. The kids from other villages or towns often lived in reasonably affluent areas and were terrified to tell their parents.

They were often more frightened of their parents' reaction than they were of what the gang would do to them. The main hub for the gang was Leeds with satellite gangs spreading to other towns and villages. Each town had a main player who was usually too clever to do any dealing and just organised the street dealers.

Everyone knew what was going on but getting solid evidence to prosecute was another story. A few street dealers had been prosecuted but no-one further up the ranks.

Ian was grateful for that information but wasn't sure if it cast a new light on Josh Smithies' murder.

'Your turn now,' said Tricia. 'Is your case a county lines case?'

'The honest answer is that I don't know so I don't want you printing anything that suggests it is. It's too early to say and we are pursuing a few lines of inquiry.'

'Don't give me that, Ian. That's what you would say to any journalist.'

'It's true though. What I will say is that as soon as we have something solid that doesn't jeopardise the inquiry, you will be the first to know.'

'It's a date then,' said Tricia grinning at him.

He felt as if she was undressing him the way she looked at him with those big brown eyes. *As if,* he thought.

'I'll look forward to it,' returning her look and smiling inanely. That was the closest Ian came to flirting. He could get to enjoy it. He liked Tricia. She had a bit about her but he had enough on his plate to think of anything else just now.

Chapter 13

Ian was in the briefing room bright and early going over the list of items seized in the house searches. Clothes, a phone and, most importantly, a knife, from Sutton. Clothes, a knife, a phone and £200 in cash from Brown. Clothes, a phone and a knife from Price. All the knives were found in their bedrooms so they'd struggle to get anyone to believe they were household knives used by everyone.

No burner phones by the look of it and no drugs. Sutton was the brains according to DI Martha Holroyd, if any of them could be described as being the brains. *We might have the murder weapon*, thought Ian. Everything had been sent to forensics with a request that it be fast tracked but there wouldn't be any results for a while.

Definitely enough to re-interview the three of them though. John and Prita could do Sutton and Brown and Mel would do Price. Same teams as before.

Mel decided to ring Pam before they started the interviews to explain there was going to be a video interview the following day, what that would mean and the reason for it.

'Why do you need to speak to her again so soon?' Pam asked.

'We've made some arrests and have got some CCTV footage so we'd just like to clarify some points with Naomi. It's a video interview, she's a vital witness and might be able to remember more as we go along.'

'She's in a state of shock so I'm not happy about this. She's grieving and in a bad way. Can't it wait?'

'It's better to get it done while it's still fresh in her mind,' explained Mel.

'That's what you said before but I don't think a few days will make it fade very much.'

'We want to get Josh's killers behind bars as quickly as possible and Naomi is the one who can help us. I understand you're looking out for her but it's really important and I wouldn't ask unless it was so urgent.'

'Okay. I'll go and talk to her but it's her call and if she doesn't want to do it yet you'll just have to wait.'

She could hear Naomi speaking in the background but couldn't hear what was said.

Naomi came on the phone.

'I'm sorry this is sooner than we anticipated but we've made some arrests and need to clarify some points with you. It won't take long and I will bring you both home after the interview.'

'Okay. It was too dark to see what happened though so I'm not sure how much help I will be.'

'I'm sure you will be more helpful than you think.'

When Mel got off the phone, she couldn't help but worry about Naomi's reluctance. She understood she was frightened, after all, the likelihood was that one of these three had killed her boyfriend, but it just felt as if there was something else.

Just then, Prita came in and saw the worried look on Mel's face.

'Oh dear, that's some face you're pulling. Any particular reason?'

'Just told Naomi and her mum about the video interview. Neither of them are happy about it and I think Naomi is really frightened. I'm just not sure if there's more to it than that.'

'You're overthinking. She probably just can't face it. What you need is a night off. How about a drink in the Brass Cat tonight. About 8.00?'

'Great. Probably just what I need.'

*

Sutton, Brown and Price had all been re-interviewed and the results of the house searches put to them. All gave "no comment" interviews again as Ian expected.

He called Ged at the CPS and gave him an update.

'We can put them at the scene,' said Ged, 'but we need a bit more to charge them. If we can get initial findings on phones and forensics, we can go ahead and charge. Just now they should be bailed with a return in about seven days, conditions of residence at their home addresses and no contact with each other. That should be long enough to get some results through.'

'You're hopeful. Have you not heard of cutbacks?' Ian said.

'Cutbacks are everywhere. We just need to do the best we can with what we've got.'

'You sound like a politician.'

'Would certainly pay better than being a CPS solicitor,' laughed Ged. 'Get back to me if you get anything else.'

'Will do.'

Without more evidence the grainy CCTV footage showing presence wasn't enough and Ian knew it.

Chapter 14

Mel

Like most teenagers, Mel had no idea what she wanted to do when she grew up. If she grew up. She enjoyed school, had friends and boyfriends and then went off to study psychology at Bristol university where she had a great time. There was no teenage angst, no depression, and no problematic boyfriends. So far life had been good.

All she wanted to do was make a difference, do something that was socially useful. But what?

When she decided on the police, all her friends and family were shocked. Some tried to talk her out of it which just made her more determined.

She was the star of her intake at Hendon Police Training College and everyone, including her, thought she'd go far.

After a stint as a PC, she got an attachment to the sexual offences unit.

For most police officers, the very worst were the indecent images of children. These had to be categorised depending on what was being done to the children and how old they were. She just couldn't get her head around how people could do these things to children and get pleasure from it. She felt sick at some of the things she saw.

No-one stayed in that particular job for long as the things you saw crawled through your head like an insect that couldn't be dislodged.

Interviewing both men and women, but mostly women, who had been subjected to sexual assaults and helping them tell their story in a way that was clear and compelling gave her satisfaction and earned her a promotion to sergeant. She knew this work was useful but hearing what men could do for sexual gratification and power ground her down. She started to really understand a term she'd learnt about at university, vicarious trauma.

The agony of the victim was, in some way, becoming her agony too. She knew she wouldn't last long there.

When a post became available at the major crime unit, she went for it. In some ways murders were easier. There was no victim to describe what had happened to them. It just had to be pieced together like a puzzle so she could be objective about it. The forgotten victims in a murder were the family and friends.

The major crime unit in the Met was very sociable and they'd often end up in the pub after a suspect was charged or after they got a conviction. It was a much needed release from the intensity they had all felt.

Her boss, DI Miles Greatorex, was very helpful, friendly and seemed to appreciate her work. Until he got too friendly and too appreciative. Until she told him loudly one evening to take his hand off her knee. The pub went quiet and he laughed it off saying he accidentally brushed her leg and he was sorry.

A woman knows when it's an accident and when it's intentional. That was no accidental brushing.

It was after that incident that he became picky with her work, gave her the menial tasks and belittled her suggestions in briefings.

She'd had enough. She reported him to his superior and involved her police federation representative. After an investigation, such as it was, he was cleared. It was the old boys' network even though there were some women in managerial positions. The message was loud and clear. The Met would not be tarnished. She couldn't stay.

A fresh start was what she needed. Away from people who knew her and Yorkshire fitted the bill.

She'd had a walking holiday in the Yorkshire Dales once and loved the light, the countryside and the people who were friendly, often behind a gruff exterior. It was far enough away and she could make new friends and a new life.

That was easier said than done when all you did was work. She had good intentions. Joined a walking group but working shifts meant she'd only been a few times. Joined a book group but never had time to read the books. Joined an evening class to improve her French but had only been twice.

There was a reason why police officers socialised together and married other police officers. They didn't have time to meet anyone else.

The last relationship she'd had in London was with a pathologist she'd met on a case. She felt he enjoyed his work too much as that was all he talked about so he had to go.

She wasn't doing much better in Yorkshire but it was early days.

Chapter 15

Mel arrived at the Brass Cat five minutes late and out of breath. Prita was already nursing a glass of white wine and some crisps. Prita's long, dark hair had copper highlights which emphasised her amber eyes and, sitting down in the low seats, she looked even smaller than usual. She was so petite that Mel felt like a giant next to her.

'Sorry, I'm a bit late. I decided to walk and it took longer than I thought.'

'Don't worry. I think a few minutes late is within the margin of error. You look fantastic.'

'Thanks. It's amazing what a shower and some makeup can do. You look good too. Do you think it's just getting out of the station and leaving the frowns behind?'

Prita laughed. 'Could be. The facial muscles become rearranged and we look human again. We need to get out more. I've a group of girlfriends, no police, and we try to get out at least every couple of weeks. You should come with us next time we meet.'

'Thanks, I'd like that. It's been hard trying to meet new people when you relocate to a different part of the country.'

'Well, it's an open invitation. I'll let you know when we next meet up. They're a lovely, diverse and really interesting group of women. I think you'd like them. Now, I'm very nosy so tell me what brought you up to Yorkshire away from the Met. It can't have been a career move.'

'It's a long story. Let me get the glass of wine first and we can have a good old chin wag.'

'Brilliant. You're really learning the Yorkshire patter.'

Mel went over to the bar, ordered a bottle of wine, more crisps and thought about what she would tell Prita. She wasn't sure she wanted to bare her soul but it would be good to have a chat with another woman who knew what it was like to be female in CID. She wasn't the sharing type but didn't want to come across as a blocked southerner. Still, Prita was friendly and it would be nice to open up a bit.

'Not sure where to start. I loved it and was doing well till it all imploded.'

Mel told Prita about her old boss, the sexual harassment and what happened when she complained. Offloading it all to someone in the job, knowing they weren't judging, felt liberating. Maybe she should have done it sooner.

'I couldn't stay there. He was one of the lads, popular and I was the woman dragging his name through the mud. Some people stopped talking to me and those that were supportive felt they couldn't be open about their support. I found out I wasn't the first he'd harassed but no-one else would make a complaint. I could see why. Anyway, enough of my sob story. I want to make a go of it up here. Tell me about you.'

'Not much to tell. Parents came over from India as children in the 1960's. I grew up in Leeds, went to university in Leeds, never wanted to leave Yorkshire. God's own country. I love it here; the dales, the people, everything about it really. Always wanted to be a police officer and have loved it so far.

'Some of my friends at university tried to put me off saying an Asian woman will have a hard time but I've not experienced much overt racism. I'm sure there's been plenty of comments behind my back but not to my face, and I seem to get on well with most people. I can take the piss as well as anyone. The major crimes unit is a good place to work, although I've only been there a year.'

'You've worked with Ian Pearce longer than I have so what's he like?'

Mel had wondered about Ian and was gradually thawing towards him but it was good to get someone else's take on him.

'I really like him. His wife left him and their son about a year ago which seemed to really cut him up. She went off with a younger man. I think he's found it hard coping but he's good, he's fair and he's intuitive. It's what you need from a boss in major crime.'

'He seems to get a lot of sympathy as he's a single dad. It happens to women all the time but if they play the single parent card, it doesn't get the same sympathy.'

'I know and that's wrong. It doesn't mean it isn't hard for Ian and that he shouldn't get sympathy.'

'Point taken. It's just that I'm not sure we always see eye to eye on things.'

'The good thing about Ian is that you can disagree with him and he doesn't hold it against you. He's a good sounding board and, let's face it, quite dishy too.

I like his slightly unshaven look and those soulful blue eyes. He used to run marathons so I'll bet there's a great body underneath that suit.

'Bit too much baggage for me but he's got a few admirers. Anyway, enough shop talk. There's a good Italian round the corner. I need something to eat before I drink any more, otherwise you'll be carrying me home.'

'Good idea, I'm starving.'

Chapter 16

'I'm going round to see Anna and Greg this morning. You should come.'

'I'm not sure I can face them.'

'Why? It's not as if it's your fault. I wish you'd told me about the stuff Josh was into. You didn't need to deal with that on your own.'

'I felt I couldn't betray him and didn't know what to do.'

Naomi started crying again. It felt as if that was all she did.

'Come with me. I don't know if it will help but it might, and you can't stay away for ever. Your dad will get back from Berlin tonight and he wants to go round then. It's understandable that Harry doesn't want to go round as he's young but you can't be the only one avoiding them.'

'Okay, it's just hard and I don't know what to say.'

'There won't be much to say and they won't expect much but you might be a comfort to each other.'

'All right. Give me five minutes.'

Pam watched Naomi heave her body out of the chair as if she was an old woman and slowly leave the room to go upstairs. She wished to god she'd never set eyes on Josh. What was he thinking dragging Naomi into all of that? Her heart went out to Anna, Greg and Kit. What they must be going through.

When Naomi came back into the living room, she'd brushed and tied her hair back but didn't look any better.

'Come on, love, get your coat and we'll go round. It won't be easy but it might help.'

Or will it make it worse? Wondered Pam.

They made the short walk to Josh's house; a walk they'd both done so many times. Each set of parents would take it in turns to pick them up from school trips or other events. Just popping in, no need for an excuse. There was now.

Pam's stomach was churning. She wanted to see Anna but, at the same time, didn't want to see her. She wanted to blame her. How could she not see Josh was on drugs? She knew it wasn't her fault though. Maybe it was since Greg left but that was six years ago and they all got on fine.

She wanted to blame everyone for getting her daughter into this. She even wanted to blame Naomi for not saying anything. She couldn't exactly get angry with her though, not after everything she'd been through. Was still going through.

Neither of them spoke on the way round to Anna's. They were each locked inside their own thoughts. What was there to say?

They walked up the path and rang the bell. A woman they didn't recognise looked out of the window and came to the door.

'Hi, I'm Immie Lord, family liaison officer. You must be Pam and Naomi. Anna said you'd rung and would be popping round. Come in. Anna and Greg are in the living room and Kit is upstairs.'

They walked in with leaden steps and saw Anna and Greg looking like they'd never seen them look before. Pain was etched in Anna's face and she'd aged about ten years.

Anna stood up and Naomi went over to her, hugged her and they both broke down sobbing. It was hard to watch.

'I'll make some tea for you all and leave you to it,' said Immie, and off she went.

Anna and Naomi sat down on the sofa holding hands.

Pam sat opposite and cried with them.

'I'm just so sorry. There's nothing else to say.'

'We just need to catch the bastards who did this,' said Greg. His anger was palpable in the same way that Anna's pain was.

Different ways of showing emotion, thought Pam.

'I had no idea what Josh had got himself into,' said Anna. 'Why didn't you say anything?'

Naomi looked like a cornered animal. She didn't know what to say. What could she say that would make it better? That would make Anna not blame her? Nothing.

'I was frightened. The whole thing was a mess. I hoped Josh would see sense but he just seemed to get deeper into it, owing money and trying to sell stuff for them.'

'Immie told us they'd arrested some lads but not charged them yet. It's not going to bring him back anyway. I know you must have done your best, Naomi. I just wish you'd talked to us. I wish Josh had too.'

'I know. I wish I had but Josh told me not to say anything and I was frightened of the lads on Fisher.'

Anna sat staring into space. No one knew what to say. What did you say in these situations?

Anna took a deep breath in and looked at Naomi. It was almost as if she was willing herself to come to life.

'We know you're going through hell too. You have your whole life ahead of you. Make Josh proud and do wonderful things.'

'I don't feel like doing anything. I've not been back to college yet. Can't face it. I've tried getting my books out but I can't concentrate. It seems so pointless.'

Immie brought the tray with tea and biscuits and left it on the table before going back into the kitchen.

'I'm sick of tea. When people don't know what to do or say they make you a cup of tea.'

'I suppose no-one knows what to say,' said Pam.

'I know. And no-one can do right for doing wrong. I don't know what I want. I want it to go away. I want to wake up and it's been a bad dream. I dream about him all the time and in my dreams he's here. It's all been a mistake. He's not really dead and he's home.'

At that, Pam started crying again. Silently this time, the tears running down her cheeks.

Anna and Naomi sat there holding hands while Pam poured them yet more tea.

They were bound together in their grief and no-one could unlock that for them.

Chapter 17

Ben sat on a swing in Fisher's only park. A slightly tubby nineteen-year-old with a ginger number one cut wearing a stone island jacket and Nike trainers. Drug dealing meant designer clothes and respect. You couldn't beat it.

It was 9.30 pm; too late for the kids to be playing and too cold for most people to be out.

He was waiting for Luke and Harley. He couldn't ring them but it was easy to slip a couple of quid to a kid to get them to tell Luke and Harley to meet him here. He couldn't risk the burner phones and there was no cameras in the park so it was safe.

Luke would be late as he could barely tell the time but he'd do as he was told and turn up. He could see Harley walking towards him. They were on the same wavelength and he knew he could trust him. He'd be too frightened not to do as he was told.

Harley looked rough. Ben knew he was using but, from the look of him, he was using a hell of a lot more now. *As long as he wasn't using the profits*, thought Ben. Harley walked towards him as if he was some sort of cowboy trying to look hard. At five feet five, he didn't.

'All right, mate?'

'Sound, Ben. We need to watch our backs as there are loads of bizzies around. Me mam says she's seen them on the estate.'

'She's probably shagging half of them,' laughed Ben.

Harley was easy to take the piss out of. Everyone knew his mum was on the game.

'Anyway, we use runners, no phones and keep our heads down. Here's Luke. We need to make sure he's on side and keeps his mouth shut.'

'All right, Luke?'

'All right, lads.'

Luke was wearing the same joggers and hoodie that he did most days. *For fucks sake*, thought Ben, *he was earning enough to get some decent clobber. Not a good look for a Z99 man.*

Ben launched straight in. 'We need to get our stories straight. Did you give a "no comment", lads?'

'Course,' said Luke. 'I was told to by my brief. I'm not going to do anything else, am I?'

'Me too,' said Harley. 'We need to keep our mouths shut.'

'So which one of you sliced him?'

'Not me.'

'Not me.'

'Well, I know it wasn't me so it's got to be one of you,' said Ben. 'Were you both carrying?'

'Yes.'

'Aye but I didn't use it.'

'Neither did I. I thought it was you, Ben.'

'Don't be daft. I'm not going to slice him and risk a collar so it's got to be one of you. Own up.'

Luke stared at his feet and said nothing so Ben poked him in the chest. 'It was you, wasn't it,' said Ben.

'No, I swear on my mam's grave, it wasn't.'

'The amount your useless mam drinks, she won't be long before she pops her clogs anyway.'

Luke kept his eyes focussed on the ground. He didn't like what Ben said about his mam but everyone knew she was an alkie.

'Harley?'

'Don't look at me. I just wanted to rough him up a bit and scare him. What's the point of slicing him? He had a load of our weed and coke to sell. He owed us. We're out of pocket now and we've got to make it up or we've had it.'

'Maybe you didn't mean to go so far, just cut him a bit, but now you're running scared,' said Ben.

'What about that slag Naomi?' Harley said.

'Don't be daft. She's terrified and she followed him around like a bloody puppy. Why should she stab him?'

'Because of, you know, what happened.'

'No, I don't know,' said Ben. 'Nothing happened, got it?'

73

'Yeah.'

'Okay.'

'She'd stab one of us if she was going to stab anyone. Can you imagine that scared little bitch carrying?' He laughed.

'It's got to be one of us and I know it wasn't me, so which one of you is lying?'

Harley could feel the tension and fear in the air.

Ben could see they were both shitting themselves.

'Where did he keep the stash?'

'Fuck knows. Maybe he got that slag Naomi to hide it for him.'

Ben was worried about the loss of the stash that they now owed on. They'd have to make good on that. Too risky to do any dealing now as the bizzies were on to them.

'Ok. Let's all keep shut then. No-one says anything to the bizzies but if it comes to a trial, one of you is going to cop for it cos' I'm not risking going down,' said Ben.

'They can't charge us. I haven't done ought,' wailed Luke.

He was such a fucking baby, thought Ben.

'Get real. That doesn't stop the bizzies from fitting us up. We were there so that's enough.'

'I heard they were interviewing Naomi so she might blab and finger one of us,' said Luke.

'She wouldn't dare if she knows what's good for her. Where did you hear that anyway?'

'My cousin goes to the same college as her so that's the word.'

'Didn't think you had any cousins at college. What is he, the cleaner? Anyway, sounds bollocks but if they do pull her in, I'll make sure she keeps quiet.'

'How?'

'The less you know the better. We don't get in touch unless I send a runner telling you to meet. No phones or anything else. Got it?'

'Yes.'

'Okay.'

'Right, piss off now and remember what I said.'

Ben watched them walk off in different directions. One of them had sliced Josh but he didn't know which one and no-one was going to admit it. If they all kept quiet, no-one could dob anyone in. Safest.

It might be worth paying Naomi a visit though.

Ben rang his brother. 'Hi, mate, I need a lift, you around?'

Ben knew Mark was always happy to help him, after all he was his dealer, and agreed a meet up in ten minutes.

Next, the text to Naomi. 'Bottom of your road in half an hour. Tell anyone and u r dead. Delete this.'

They waited in Mark's car near the end of Naomi's cul de sac.

'Not a good idea to be here, mate,' said Mark who was always the careful one. 'You don't know how many cameras we've passed on the way.'

'I've been crouched down all the fucking way so no camera is going to pick me up. Anyway, it's got to be done. Won't take long.'

Naomi was in her bedroom when the text came through. She just knew it was Ben Sutton, even though he wasn't in her contacts list, and could feel the anxiety rise. She felt sick but knew she had to go or he'd do what he said.

'Mum, I've got a bit of a headache. I think it's because I've not been out the house and need some air so I'm just going to walk round the block for ten minutes.'

'You can't go out now, love. It's freezing and it's late.'

'I know. I should have gone out earlier but I'm starting to feel like a caged animal and need to get out.'

'I'll come with you.'

'No, I want to be on my own and just clear my head.'

'Okay, take your phone and be back in fifteen minutes or ring me. I can't help but worry after what's happened.'

'I get it. I won't be long.'

She grabbed her coat, opened the door and went out before her mum could say anything else.

She could see a figure at the end of the cul de sac. As she got closer, she recognised Ben Sutton.

Naomi hated him but feared him too. Hands in pockets, she started to shake as she got closer. Tears sprang to her eyes.

'Hey up, Naomi, how you doing? Shame about Josh but thought we needed a little chat.'

Naomi was openly crying now.

'No need to be like that, Naomi, I'm not going to hurt you, providing you do what I say.'

Naomi just nodded.

'Where's Josh's stash?'

'I don't know. Honest. He never told me where he hid it.'

Ben just looked at her. She wasn't lying. She was too shit scared to lie.

'You need to keep your mouth shut. If the police interview you, you saw Luke with a knife and I were shouting "no" to Luke. Got it.'

'Yes.'

'Good. We wouldn't want anything to happen to that lovely face of yours, would we?'

Naomi shook her head. She shivered but it wasn't with the cold.

'I've got to go or my mum will be worried. I won't say anything about you.'

'Good girl. See you around. Maybe get together some night.' He laughed.

She felt physically sick and turned to go.

'Bye, Naomi. Be good.'

Pam heard the key in the door and got up. 'You okay, love?'

Naomi just nodded. 'I don't feel great, Mum, to be honest. I think I might be getting a cold or something.'

'It'll be stress. You don't look great. Let me make you a hot drink.'

'I just want to go straight to bed. I think I'm worried about the video interview tomorrow. I just want to get it over with and try and get back to normal.'

'Okay love. See you in the morning.'

Naomi went up to her bedroom but couldn't stop shaking. She had to do this even though it terrified her. She got her phone out and played the recording.

Got the bastard, she thought.

Chapter 18

Naomi

The flashbacks came again.

The noise, the light, the pain and the smells. The smells were the worst of it. Of all her senses, she couldn't get rid of the smells deep in her nostrils.

The smell of clothing that hadn't been washed, stale sweat, deep fat frying, the dirty house.

And them.

She could hear the laughter, the dog barking, the sound of kids playing in the street, an argument from the house next door.

She thought flashbacks were about pictures but not this one because she had her eyes closed, the one sense she had some control over.

Josh falling was a picture though. A picture she couldn't unsee. The look of fear in his eyes, not understanding, pleading.

And all the "if onlys".

If only Josh had never started using.

If only he had been stronger.

If only she had never gone to Fisher with him.

If only she'd stayed in to do her geography project.

If only she could turn the clock back.

If only they'd never got together.

If only, if only, if only.

She knew she had to be strong but knowing and feeling were two different things, and she felt broken, an emotional wreck.

She knew she had to get over this but she wanted to curl up under the covers and hide.

She knew she had to study and get to university, get away, start over but all she could do was sit there and stare into space.

The reality of the emotions was stronger than the knowledge she could have a future.

Counselling, that was what was needed, her mum said. But where would she begin. She couldn't open up. It all had to stay buried deep inside underneath the armour plating she'd erected; that was the only way she could cope.

Once you opened Pandora's Box, there was no going back.

Chapter 19

Despite her best intentions, Mel was slightly hung-over but she had needed the night out with Prita who looked fresh as a daisy in the briefing room.

Mel looked at Ian with fresh eyes since Prita's description. She had been hard on him and maybe he was okay. He did have nice eyes and his body looked slim but strong beneath the shirt and trousers. Mel couldn't believe she was thinking like that. Must be the hangover.

Prita gave Mel a knowing smile as she caught Mel staring at Ian. *Right, concentrate*, thought Mel as Ian began the briefing.

'I want to summarise what we've got and what's outstanding so you're all up to speed. Naomi is going to be video interviewed today so we'll see if she can give us a clearer picture of what happened and why they were in Fisher.

'We're waiting for the lab results on items seized from the homes of Sutton, Brown and Price but, until we get that, they've been bailed with conditions of residence at their home addresses and no contact with each other. The chance of them sticking to those conditions is pretty slim but the CPS say we haven't got enough to charge them yet.

'We've got some additional enhancement of CCTV which the CPS hasn't seen yet. I'd like us all to have a look at it and see what we think. Prita, your call on the CCTV so take us through it.'

Prita loved giving a good performance and she'd been through this footage enough to talk about it with confidence.

'Right, everyone. The techies have colour coded everyone and added daylight enhancement so each individual is easier to identify and we can see more of what is happening. Josh Smithies has a blue arrow, Sutton is green, Brown is red, Price is yellow and Naomi Edwards is orange.

'I'll start it now and talk you through it. We can see Sutton, Brown and Price near the top of the alley which is the end furthest away from the shop. Unfortunately, it's also the end furthest away from the camera. They're looking towards the bottom of the alley and we can see Josh and Naomi coming into view and walking towards them. They come together and it looks like they're arguing, although we don't have sound. Sutton is gesticulating with both hands, Josh is backing off, then Sutton pushes him.

'Josh is surrounded by Sutton, Brown and Price. Naomi is stood next to Josh. Sutton throws a punch at him. Brown and Price join in. Naomi is stood on Josh's left side and her arm moves out towards Josh. He then falls to the ground and Sutton, Brown and Price run off.

'Naomi waits for a second and she too runs off in the same direction. From house CCTV footage just beyond the top of the alley, we can see that Naomi runs off to the left. There is no CCTV to the right of the alley and we must assume the other three run off in that direction.

'We can clearly see that Sutton, Brown and Price assault Josh. As there is no doubt about their identities, we don't need a VIPER. We can't see who has a knife but we know that one of that group of four did have a knife that stabbed Josh. We can also see that Naomi's right arm reaches out towards Josh's left side, the side he was stabbed. We can't see what she was doing.

'On the basis that we can see an assault by the three males, I think there is enough to charge all of them on a joint enterprise basis. They are in it together even though only one of them stabbed him.'

Ian asked, 'Could Naomi have stabbed him? She's on Josh's left side.'

'We can't rule it out, although I would say it's pretty unlikely as she's our star witness. In any event, why would she? It's more likely that she'd be grabbing out at him to pull him away. It's simply not clear enough to say. I don't think the techies will get the footage much better than that but they're still working on it.'

'I agree with you, Prita. We can see an assault by those three and I think it's enough to charge them on a joint enterprise murder. I'll run it past the CPS now but I want to wait and see if we get anything more from Naomi's video interview before charging. That's assuming the CPS agree. We'll meet back here at 2.00 after Naomi's interview.'

The meeting broke up. Everyone looked more positive and upbeat. They could see a charge in sight.

'I've arranged to pick up Naomi for interview and Sally Black is again going to be with me to operate the video equipment.'

'Fine by me,' said Ian. 'Let's see what she has to say.'

Ian spoke to Ged at the CPS, explained where they were up to and that Naomi was being video interviewed this morning.

'It would be better if we had some forensics,' said Ged.

'At least a few days but the CCTV clearly shows an assault and Josh falling even if we can't see a stabbing.'

'I agree it's enough for a charge but let's wait till this afternoon and see what Naomi has to say.'

'I knew you'd say that and it's fine by me. Speak later.'

Naomi must have seen what happened. It was dark but she was right next to him. Let's hope she's a bit more helpful in her interview, thought Ian.

Mel showed Pam and Naomi into the witness waiting room and explained the video interview. Pam looked round and could see teddy bears, a slinky, cuddly toys and games.

'Why have you got teddy bears?' Pam asked.

'Sometimes we have very young witnesses and we want to make the process of an interview as comfortable as we can. Children might bring in a cuddly toy if they like or there are some here they can hold while they are interviewed.'

Pam shuddered and didn't want to think what young children might have gone through to end up being interviewed here and needing toys to cuddle. She didn't know if it was better or worse that Naomi was older. Maybe the younger ones could forget more easily.

'Are you ready to start, Naomi? Your mum will be here waiting for you when you've finished but can't come in with you. I see you have your phone in your hand but you'll need to leave that with your mum.'

'I need to bring my phone in as there's something I need to show you.'

Mel and Pam looked at each other but said nothing.

'I just want to get it over with.'

Mel took Naomi into the video recording room, made sure Sally Black in the other room got the recording started and then did time, date and introductions.

She needed her to relax as much as possible and the protocol for these interviews was to begin by asking her about herself, her favourite subjects and what she hoped to do at university before moving on to Josh and what they were doing in Fisher.

Naomi described how she got to know Josh, how they got together, and his involvement with the Fisher estate.

'Josh started using drugs, weed initially but then moved on to cocaine and amphetamines. He was getting really stressed about his work, felt he couldn't concentrate and that the drugs helped him. He got them from some lads in Fisher. He got into debt so they threatened him. He had to start selling drugs as a way of paying his debts.

'He said it would also give him money so that when we started uni we wouldn't be skint. I didn't care about that. I just wanted to be with Josh. We'd get loans, jobs, we'd be fine. We didn't need money from drugs.

'He didn't sell much. He thought people at college would want to buy but apart from selling some weed he was not doing well and they were on his back for the money he owed them.'

'Where did he keep the drugs he had to sell,' asked Mel.

'I don't know.'

'Okay, so what brought you to Fisher that night?'

'Josh owed money and was told to meet Ben Sutton by the local shop in Fisher. He wanted me to go. He said he'd be safer with me there but I didn't want to go. We waited outside the shop and a kid came down saying Ben was waiting for us in the ginnel so we went up.

'Ben asked Josh about the money and the drugs. Josh said he was trying to sell but didn't have many takers and he'd get the money to him. Ben said he was fed up waiting and that he'd had enough time. They all started jostling Josh, they punched him and he fell over.

'They ran off and I ran too. I was frightened and didn't know what to do. I should have stayed but I panicked.'

'Josh was stabbed. Did you see who had a knife?'

'No. It was too dark and it happened too fast.'

Naomi was fighting back the tears remembering that night. She described how she felt when she ran, the guilt of not staying, not calling for help.

This would stay with her for a long time, thought Mel.

'I want to show you what's on my phone.'

Naomi took out her phone and played the recording. She then showed Mel the text.

Mel was surprised but this was great stuff. It was almost an admission, an attempt to pervert the course of justice and witness intimidation. She knew there would be arguments about admissibility of this evidence but it nailed them as far as she was concerned.

'Can you confirm who this is that's speaking?'

'It's Ben Sutton.'

'Did you recognise his number when he sent you that text?'

'No but I just knew it was him and then when he turned up, it just confirmed it.'

'Thank you, Naomi. I will need to seize your phone for evidence. Is there anything you want to add before I ask Sally to switch off the recording?'

'No.'

'Okay. We'll end the recording now.'

Back in the witness waiting room, Mel explained that she couldn't say anything more but suggested Naomi tell Pam what had happened.

Mel drove them both home and said she would ring them later but would also arrange for an alarm to be fitted to the house and for Naomi to carry a personal alarm with her. She couldn't help but admire Naomi for her bravery and the foresight to take her phone and record Sutton. That really took guts.

Back at the station, Ian was getting everyone together in the briefing room for the latest update when Mel arrived.

'I've spoken with Ged at the CPS and said I'd update him once we hear what Naomi has said in her video interview. Over to you, Mel.'

'Thanks Ian. Naomi has confirmed she was present at the scene. Josh was punched and jostled by the others but she didn't see a knife and didn't see the stabbing because it was dark and it happened so fast. She's also confirmed Josh's drug taking and drug dealing, although she didn't know where he kept the drugs. They've not turned up in any house search yet. He had a drug debt which was why he started dealing. Nothing new in that.

'But this is the interesting thing. Naomi brought her phone in. There is a text on it which says, "Bottom of your road in half an hour. Tell anyone and u r dead. Delete this". She didn't recognise the number but assumed it was Ben Sutton.

'She went to the end of her cul de sac where Ben Sutton was waiting. She had the foresight and bravery to record the conversation on her phone. It's a bit muffled as the phone was in her pocket but Sutton is telling her to do what he says and that if she is interviewed, to blame the murder on Luke Price with him and Brown saying "no" to Price. It ends with a veiled threat to Naomi if she doesn't do what he says.'

'Bingo. That's brilliant,' said Ian. 'We need to interview all three again and see what they've got to say for themselves. Mel, will you give the phone to the techies, get them to download the recording so we can play it in interview and put the text to them. Let's see if it's still a "no comment" then.

'We need to make sure Naomi is protected. They're not due to answer their bail yet but let's get them in this afternoon. Same interview teams as before.'

Ian knew they'd be looking at charging them before the day was out.

Chapter 20

Naomi

She'd done it.

She'd been terrified but she'd done it.

She faced Sutton and did something he'd never have guessed she'd do in a million years. She'd trapped him.

He made her flesh crawl and seeing him again took her back to that day, that house, to what they'd done.

That grin on his stupid, ugly face. The way he'd looked at her remembering what he'd done. She could see him wallowing in the memory with that smug look on his face.

And the not so subtle threat to hurt her if she said anything.

Well, she had said something and she was glad she had.

She didn't think she'd have the strength to do it but she did it. She'd show him that he'd underestimated her. She wasn't just a victim.

She remembered her life skills teacher had talked about women having agency.

Well, she had agency now.

And, okay, it was terrifying. But she had done it. She may have been shaking from fear. She may have been crying at the thought of what he had done to her. What he could still do to her. But she had still managed it.

He and the others were going to pay for what they'd done to her and what they'd done to Josh. If it wasn't for them, Josh would never have got involved in dealing, she would never have been in Fisher and she would be a normal seventeen-year-old doing A levels and looking forward to going to university.

If it wasn't for them, her world wouldn't have been turned upside down.

Chapter 21

You could feel the excitement in the air at the station when they went for Sutton, Brown and Price.

Sutton had kicked off saying he wasn't due till next week and he'd stuck to his bail so why the fuck were they arresting him again. He'd soon find out. Getting three solicitors down from the same firm could take some time so it was a waiting game now.

Ian was anxious. They couldn't mess this up. Treat all three with kid gloves, get them drinks, food, let them have as long as they need with their solicitors and see what they say.

'John, it's your call but I'd like to sit in on the Sutton interview with you if you have no objection.'

'Fine by me, Boss.'

Mel was amazed Ian had actually asked for John's permission. How different from the Met. She was warming to him even more. Maybe Prita was right and she'd been a bit too hard on him. Emotional baggage has a lot to answer for.

Luke Price was in for a bit of a shock this time. *Wait till he hears that recording*, thought Mel.

When Sally knocked on his door, there was no answer but they could hear the television so knew someone was in. They kept hammering on the door then Mel looked through the window where she could see him wearing headphones and playing some game on television. They tried the door and it opened so in they went.

'Police,' Mel shouted again and this time he looked up with a puzzled expression on his face.

Mel took in the untidy room, clothes everywhere, chipped paintwork and the smell of dirt permeating the air.

He just sat there so she went over, grabbed his arms, put them behind his back and cuffed him before removing his headphones.

'What are you doing? I'm in the middle of a game.'

'Not any more you're not.'

No-one else was in the house. Or at least no-one emerged. Mel had looked into his background and knew that Social Services had been involved with the family. There was no dad on the scene and the six younger children had been taken into care leaving Luke with his mum. Hopefully, the younger kids were faring a bit better than Luke.

He was wearing the same hoodie and joggers as before and gave off a stale smell of grubbiness.

No comments on the way down to the station, no kicking off saying he wasn't due till next week. Just silence.

His solicitor arrived and Mel gave him the typed sheet of disclosure.

It was the same for all three solicitors who arrived pretty quickly. A typed page setting out that Sutton met with a potential witness after sending a text, the conversation had been recorded and Sutton was telling the witness to blame Price. It also outlined what the enhanced footage showed.

He read through it quickly before looking up at Mel.

'I'd like to see the footage and hear the recording before the interview please?'

'We will play the recording in the interview. The footage is being further enhanced and we will not be showing it today.'

He'd had enough information to advise his client so he wasn't getting any more, thought Mel.

She showed him through to a consultation room and went to get Price from his cell. He was just sitting there staring into space.

She took him down the corridor and into the consultation room to see his solicitor.

After that, she just waited for the fireworks.

Unsurprisingly, he was the first one ready.

Mel could see he was fizzing. He wasn't quiet now. *Bet he'll be answering questions this time*, she thought.

After introductions, he didn't even wait for questions before launching in.

'That's a load of bollocks. I didn't stab no-one. I was there, hit him because he owed us money but I didn't stab him. I'm not having it.'

'Do you recognise that number?'

Price hesitated. 'No.'

Mel didn't believe him for a minute but suspected he was still trying to avoid a charge of supplying and it was likely this was a burner phone.

'Do you recognise the voice?'

'It's Ben Sutton. He's blaming me and it wasn't me.'

'So who was it?'

'I don't know. That's the honest truth. It was dark, we hit him and someone must have slashed him but I don't know who. I just know it wasn't me.'

He carried on ranting and Mel believed him but he might just be a good liar. She'd met plenty.

'What was your intention when you met him?'

'Just rough him up a bit. Make him get us the money.'

'Did you have a knife on you?'

He hesitated. 'No, I didn't.'

'You've got form for carrying knives. We've found a knife at your house. Are you sure you didn't use it.'

'I did have one but I swear I didn't use it.'

'So who did?'

'I don't know. I don't know. He owed us money so why would we slash him. We wanted the money.'

It was a fair point, thought Mel. Why kill him when you're owed? Unless they didn't intend to kill him.

'Why did he owe you money? You might as well admit it was a drugs debt because we know already.'

Price sat there. He looked at his solicitor for help but the solicitor couldn't answer the questions for him.

'Okay. He owed us for drugs and he also had a stash he was selling so why slash him when he's got our drugs and money?'

'Maybe you went too far. Didn't mean to kill him but it got out of hand. Maybe Sutton is blaming you because it was you.

'No, it wasn't me. I swear on my mam's life. It wasn't me.'

He started to cry. At that point, he looked just like any vulnerable kid. He was out of his depth but he was also part of the group that had caused the death of Josh Smithies.

'My client needs a break.'

'Okay, stopping the interview now.'

'Do you intend to charge my client?' the solicitor asked.

'Not my decision. We'll need to run it past the CPS and in the meantime, I'll take you back to your cell while we await a decision.'

Prita had gone with three other officers to Harley Brown's house. She didn't want to risk him running off again. She knocked loudly and he answered the door. No running away this time.

'What do you lot want? I've stuck to my bail.'

'Tough. We've got more for you down at the station so hands behind your back.'

He complied but couldn't resist the insult, 'Paki bitch.'

'Careful. You don't want a charge of a racially aggravated public order offence as well. Wrong country anyway.'

'Eh?'

Subtlety was wasted, thought Prita.

When Luke was back in his cell, Mel went into the briefing room to get a coffee. Ian was there with another man she didn't recognise.

'Mel, this is Ged Harris from the CPS.'

'Hi, Mel. Ian has been singing your praises.'

'Good to hear but it has been a real team effort and Prita has been brilliant on CCTV.' She couldn't help feeling pleased and a slight blush crept up her neck.

Prita came in at that point. 'Hi, Ged, wondered when you'd make it out of the ivory tower to us mere mortals.'

'Complimentary as always, Prita. You know I've just come to see you.'

'I could tell that, Ged, but there's a long queue so you'll have to get to the back.'

'You break my heart, Prita.'

Mel took it all in. It was just banter. There was no power trip and no innuendo which was so unlike the Met. Maybe she could relax more and get rid of the shield she kept so tightly wrapped round herself.

'Charles Haig, Sutton's solicitor, is in with him now and as soon as he's finished, we'll go for interview,' said Ian.

'Looks like that's him ready,' as a head poked round the door. 'See you soon.'

Once John had introduced everyone and cautioned Sutton, he started with the questions and played the recording. No comment to everything. Both Ian and John were expecting some sort of reaction. As they were coming to the end of the questions, Charles Haig asked for a break to consult with his client. Tapes were turned off, Charles and Ben Sutton were shown back into a consultation room and Ian and John went back into the briefing room.

'That was quick,' said Prita.

'We're just having a break for consultation. It's been "no comment" so far. Not what I thought he'd do but let's see what he does after the consultation.'

'Coffee anyone?' John asked. It was something to do as they waited and the tension was mounting.

'How are you getting on, Prita?' John asked.

'He's in with his brief now but shouldn't be much longer.'

'Here we go. That was quick. See you shortly,' said Ian and off they went.

John switched on the recording, introductions were made and it was confirmed that no questions had been asked by officers during the consultation.

Charles Haig launched in.

'After consultation, my client would like to make a statement which I will read out:

"I, Ben Sutton, deny that I sent a text to anyone asking them to meet me. The police have confiscated my phone and I do not have another phone. I do not recognise that number. I did not meet up with anyone, did not make threats and did not tell anyone what to say. It is not my voice on that recording.

'I believe Luke Price did stab Josh Smithies. I did not carry a knife, did not stab him and was not part of any plan to do so. Luke was closest to Josh and I saw a knife in his hand. I accept I punched Josh Smithies but did no more than that".

'That is signed and dated by my client. You may take a copy. My client will not be answering any more questions.'

'Thank you for that,' said John. 'I will be asking you further questions. You don't have to answer them but let me remind you of the meaning of the caution. If you come up with an explanation in court, that you don't give now when you have the opportunity to do so, the court may draw inferences, hold it against you, in other words, wonder why you didn't say it at the time.'

'My client understands the meaning of the caution and will not be answering any questions you put to him.'

John persisted.

'Is that a burner phone you use?'

'Do you recognise that number?'

'Do you know who this phone belongs to?'

'Where were you between 9.00 and 10.00 yesterday evening?'

'Do you know Naomi Edwards?'

'Did you ask her to meet you yesterday evening by sending a text to her?'

'Did you threaten to harm her?'

'Do you ever carry a knife?'

'Have you got a conviction for carrying a knife?'

'Why did you punch Josh Smithies?'

'Did he owe you money?'

'Did you supply him with drugs?'

'Is that why you stabbed him?'

And on it went. 'No comment, no comment, no comment.'

At the end of the interview, Charles Haig asked, 'Do you intend to charge my client?'

Ian answered. 'We will consult with the CPS and give you a ring as soon as we know. In the meantime, you will be returned to your cell, Ben. Do you require a further consultation?'

'No.'

Charles wanted out of there and was pretty certain there would be a charge. All good work for the firm.

Back in the briefing room, Prita was the last to come and give an update.

'He was pretty vague but blamed it on Price and he knew nothing about any knife or any plan to rough up Josh. He answered some questions but when it got uncomfortable he just went "no comment". Won't look good in court.'

Ian summarised what they'd got and then they started to pick it apart.

'We've got Naomi as a witness and we have the text,' said Ian.

'But we have no attribution for that phone. It's obviously a burner and ideally we need to find it. That text could have come from anyone,' pointed out Ged.

'We have the recording.'

'Poor quality. Unlikely we'll get any sort of voice identification.'

'We have Naomi's interview.'

'Granted. We have an eye witness account. We might get the voice ID in evidence but unlikely, although the text might go in but not if we can't identify the phone. We've also got them cutting each other's throats now. Sutton and Brown are blaming Price and Price will no doubt turn on them. What bothers me is motive. As they have already said, why kill Josh when he owed them money and had a stash belonging to them. That doesn't make sense.'

Ian was desperate for a charge. He knew Ged had to point out the pitfalls.

'The chances are they just wanted to frighten him and it went too far. That happens.'

'I agree. With the CCTV and Naomi's interview, we've enough to charge all three.'

A cheer went up. 'Bloody brilliant,' said John.

'But, before you get carried away, this is when the hard work starts,' interrupted Ged over the cheers.

'We need CCTV going back twenty eight days. I want to see if there's a pattern of Josh and Naomi going to Fisher, if we can see any other assaults or drug deals. We need to get the phones analysed and attributed. We need further house searches. We haven't identified a murder weapon yet so we need to get on to forensics and see what they've come up with. They could still wriggle out of it so we need to make it watertight. Has Naomi's house been searched?'

'No,' answered Mel. 'I didn't see the need.'

She was now thinking she'd missed something but at the same time, why search Naomi's house. The poor kid had been through the mill.

'There wasn't a need initially but we don't know where Josh hid his stash so it could have been at her house. She might not even be aware of it or she might have felt she had to go along with it.'

'Okay, I'll coordinate that,' said Mel.

'So, it's forensics, phones and more CCTV and searches. In the meantime, I'll get a prosecution team together and we'll have a meeting as soon as possible. Good work, everyone.'

'You mean great work,' said Ian. 'I know there's a lot to do but I think we can have an evening off to pat ourselves on the back. Who's up for a curry at Akbar's tonight?'

Hands shot up amid whoops of delight. Mel held back a bit.

'Come on, Mel, you've been brilliant and you won't have tasted a curry like Akbar's.'

Mel gave him a look of disdain. 'We do have curry houses in London you know.'

'And they charge twice as much. Life is better in the north for all sorts of reasons and the curries are just one of them.'

'Okay, I'll give you that one.' She smiled at Ian and he smiled back holding her gaze. She could feel herself blushing again.

'Right, everyone. 8.00 Akbar's for ten of us. See you later.'

The atmosphere was electric. They just had to make sure nothing went wrong.

Chapter 22

Mel was the first to arrive and was shown to a table which had been booked in Ian's name. As she looked around, she took in the red walls accented with gold, the dark wood carved screens and chairs and the white tablecloths. It could have been an Indian restaurant anywhere.

She ordered a Cobra. You had to have an Indian beer with a curry. Prita and John arrived together and sat down with her before ordering beers.

'We might as well have some poppadoms while we're waiting,' suggested John.

'And here's me thinking you were watching the waistline,' laughed Prita.

'Bugger the waistline. I'm starving.'

The others arrived and were just waiting for Ian. John heard a text ping and looked at his phone.

'It's Ian, he's been held up and says to start without him.'

Mel couldn't help feeling a little disappointed. *Come on, Mel*, she was giving herself a good talking to. She guessed it was because she felt lonely, didn't really know anyone outside of work and it was easy to just latch on to someone. She hoped she wasn't giving off that desperate vibe that was so off putting.

It was just more friends she needed rather than a relationship, and a relationship with someone at her work who had a difficult sixteen-year-old was a no-go area. God, she couldn't believe she was thinking about a relationship. Not a good sign.

'Come on, Mel, you're miles away. The lamb saag is really good or saag paneer if you fancy veggie,' suggested Prita.

'Okay, I'll go with what you suggest and have the lamb saag. I can pretend I'm being healthy by having spinach.'

The starters arrived just as Ian did.

'Add a lamb rogan josh and pint of Cobra for me,' he shouted as he walked through the door greeting Ismail, the proprietor. It was obvious Ian was a regular.

'Sorry I'm late, I had to help with the maths homework. Not my strong point.'

More beers arrived. 'Cheers, everyone, you've all done a brilliant job and deserve a pat on the back. I know Ged said this was where the hard work started but we've got a charge, they're in court tomorrow and will be banged up till the trial at least. I think that's some cause for celebration.'

They were buzzing, food was great and conversation was flowing. John, who Mel thought was the taciturn Yorkshireman, turned out to be very funny as he told story after story about hopeless cases.

'Did I tell you about one of my first ones out of uniform, the hopeless drug dealer in Adfield?'

He didn't wait for a reply and just carried on.

'Charlie Bramwell used to sell fake drugs. Talk about having a death wish in Adfield. He even tried selling privet hedge to undercover officers trying to pass it off as weed. The best one was when he was picked up with snap bags containing white powder and was carrying two machetes, obviously for protection. Turned out the white powder was soap powder and the machetes were about eighteen inches long, I kid you not.

'He said that one was his vegetable knife, the other was his fruit knife and he must have put them in his pocket, forgotten about them and left his house unaware he still had them on him. Eighteen inch bloody machetes, they couldn't even fit in his coat pockets.'

There was a roar of laughter, although many of them had heard the story before.

'You must have some stories from the Met, Mel.'

'I can't remember the light hearted ones as they were all pretty heavy in sexual offences. I do remember one that was both funny and sad. A woman who'd been abused by a variety of men, she'd had a really sad life, pimped out by one of them, was illiterate and an alcoholic, came in to report an assault by the latest man in her life. She was a big woman, had a black eye and described this man jumping on her.

'I asked if she had any other injuries. She stood up, pulled her skirt up, knickers down and showed the most gigantic bruise covering most of her gigantic bottom. It was incredibly sad but I just wanted to laugh at the sight of this bottom only inches away from me in the interview room.'

'What did you say?'

'I couldn't think of anything to say so I went and got the camera and took a picture of her bottom. I didn't feel I could do anything else. I wanted to laugh but I think it was nerves at the unusual sight of this very large, bruised bottom before me. It was sad though because she got back with him and refused to support a prosecution.'

'That's not a light relief story,' said Prita.

'The sight of the bottom was though,' added Mel.

The stories and beer continued until it was closing time.

Taxis were called, a couple of them decided to walk home and, as Prita, Ian and Mel were going in the same direction, they shared a taxi.

'You've both been brilliant,' said Ian.

'We know,' laughed Prita, 'don't we, Mel.'

'Definitely. We're bloody fantastic.' They'd all relaxed a bit after a couple of pints but it was the relief and the excitement at getting a charge that had relaxed them.

'Well, don't get too big for your boots.'

They were still buzzing and laughing when the taxi pulled up outside Prita's block of flats. 'Great night, guys. Thanks for suggesting it, Ian. We need to do this more often.'

'We will have to make time to do it once a month. That's the theory anyway. You obviously need to work harder so we can fit it in,' said Ian.

'Don't be cheeky,' replied Prita, almost falling out of the taxi. 'See you tomorrow.'

'Night.'

'Bye, Prita.'

'This is the best night I've had since I moved up here,' said Mel.

'I suppose it takes time to settle in to a new place but you've really been accepted by the rest of the team and they obviously value the experience you've brought with you.'

'Thanks, I'm starting to enjoy it. And if you need a hand with the maths homework, just give me a shout as I was always pretty good at maths.'

She couldn't believe she'd just said that. What was she thinking of.

'Just pull up here on the right please.'

'I might just take you up on your offer,' said Ian, turning round in the passenger seat and smiling.

Mel got out of the taxi and ran into the large Victorian house that had been converted into period flats. Without looking back, she ran straight up the stairs to the top floor, her place of sanctuary, with windows overlooking Carfield and out to the hills beyond.

What have I said, thought Mel. *Does he think I was coming on to him? It's such a bloody cliché, not liking the boss, then fancying the boss, then coming on to the boss. Shit. Still, I can't unsay it now and hopefully he just thought it was a kind offer.*

She was buzzing and tired at the same time as the adrenalin wore off. It's the emotional intensity and exhaustion rather than the long hours. Better take the makeup off before crashing into the king-size bed. It would be nice to share this bed with someone she thought before drifting off.

*

Ian's house was about two miles further on. The houses got bigger and newer as they drove along and the roads quieter. Was that just an offer of help, wondered Ian. He was sure it was as Mel was out of his league. Anyway, he'd made it a rule never to have any sort of a relationship with a colleague. If it goes wrong, which it usually does, the fallout is horrendous. He couldn't believe he was thinking like that.

As he was thinking about Mel, his phone pinged with a text message.

Tricia Gibson. "Heard there's been charges. Call me x".

Shit, he'd forgotten about Tricia and it was too late to call now. A text would have to do. "Knackered and need to sleep. Drink tomorrow at 8.00 in the Brown Cow with update?"

He still couldn't get in the habit of the perfunctory x at the end of a text.

"Great. See you then x".

As the taxi pulled up outside his house, he found himself looking forward to seeing Tricia which was a good feeling; a feeling he hadn't had in a long time.

Chapter 23

Anna had to do it at some point. She knew she couldn't put it off forever.
Greg was back at his house, with his wife, with her kids and she was left with this.

The door to his bedroom was closed as she couldn't bear to walk past it and see his things.

She turned the handle and stood in the doorway just looking. Clothes on the floor and on his chair, his books on the shelves and by his bedside, his comb and deodorants on the chest of drawers.

It looked as if he'd just popped out and would be back any minute telling her he'd tidy his room tomorrow. It was always tomorrow. But what did a tidy room matter now?

The things she thought were important faded into insignificance.

She walked in, picked up a polo shirt and pair of jeans and sat down on his bed.

She buried her face in the polo shirt as she wanted to breathe in his smell but it was gone.

She opened his wardrobe and stroked the sleeve of his favourite Ted Baker shirt. She put it to her face. No smell.

She grabbed his other clothes and held them to her face. No smell.

She was becoming desperate now.

She thought the smells would linger. It was always a bit smelly in here with his socks and trainers and clothes he hadn't got round to putting in the wash basket.

Not now.

Josh's smell had gone.

She sat back down on the bed, held his shirt and cried.

Chapter 24

Ian arrived first and got a table near the fire. It was a lovely, cosy pub with a roaring fire and no noise from gaming machines. He wondered how many pubs were called the "Brown Cow".

As he was contemplating the variety in pub names, Tricia arrived.

She spotted him and smiled in a way that changed her whole face.

'Hi, Ian. I'll just get myself a drink. Do you fancy another?'

'No, thanks. I'm on the shandy so will only have the one.'

She sat on a chair opposite him, warming herself by the fire.

'I do like it here during the week. It's quiet and warm. It's not a pub for a wild night out but it's a great place for a chat.

'So, Ian, I thought you'd have rung with an update. I found out about the charges and court hearing from the press office along with everyone else. I thought we had a special relationship.'

'I'm sorry, Tricia. It's been hectic and I've not been thinking about anything apart from the investigation and getting charges.'

She looked lovely, he thought. Her dark auburn hair was thick and the waves cascaded down her back like in some pre-Raphaelite painting. When she leaned over, he could smell her perfume and really noticed her eyes for the first time. They were such a dark brown and had a rich texture like chocolate or velvet that you could be wrapped up in and kept warm. She looked great in jeans and a chunky cream sweater like some Celtic warrior.

'I wasn't in court for the hearing but one of my sergeants was. They've been remanded in custody until next week when they're at Leeds Crown Court. I doubt there will be bail applications as it's pointless, although some of the defence might have a go to show their clients that they're working hard for them.'

'I know, Ian. I was in court, remember. What can you tell me that's not in the public domain?'

'You can't print it yet. I need your word on that.'

'You have it. I need it for my research and I'll keep it to one side till after the trial.'

'It's likely to be Z99 dealing drugs but whether it's Z99 or just these three, it's definitely drugs related.'

'Which is why he was in Fisher. What about the girlfriend?'

'She will be a prosecution witness. I can't tell you more at this stage.'

'It seems like Z99 have started dealing in Smethurst Comprehensive. They like to move into the more affluent areas as the kids there have money.'

'That's my son's school. How do you know?'

'You know I can't reveal my sources but it will be worth you having a look there. Maybe your son has heard something.'

'I'll ask him but will have to tread carefully.'

Tricia was taking him in. The pale blue eyes, the slight crinkles around them, wavy brown hair and just a bit of stubble. He had a kind face, good features without being disarmingly handsome and a lovely mouth. Tricia felt comfortable with him and had a good feeling that he was a decent person, not something she often thought about coppers.

The conversation flowed, no awkwardness, just nice and easy. She was enjoying herself and not talking much about Z99, the case or about drugs. It was the sort of conversation where you jump from one topic to another and can't remember what you've talked about, just that it's good and easy.

'Right, home time. I can't be too late with a sixteen-year-old who will hopefully be in bed.'

'So I can't tempt you to mine for a nightcap?'

'I'd love to, Tricia, but I really can't. Can I give you a lift?'

'I would say it's the least you can do for my snippets of very useful information.'

'I would say you're right.'

Outside, the cold hit him. Because he'd driven, he hadn't thought about warm clothing. It was a clear night and he could see the stars in the sky. The frost was starting and he knew tomorrow would be a morning for scraping the car windows.

'I'm parked over there.'

He unlocked his Audi and opened the door for her before wondering if that was sexist and if it somehow infantilised her by implying she was incapable of opening a car door. Anyway, too late now and she didn't say anything so hopefully it was okay.

She only lived a mile outside the town so they were there in a few minutes. She unbuckled the seat belt and turned to him.

'Thanks for the lift. It was a lovely evening even if it was supposed to be work.'

'It was. Let's do it again when it's definitely not work and I don't have to drive.'

'And we could even finish with that nightcap at my place.'

He looked at her. Those eyes were amazing. So deep and dark. He still couldn't get rid of the idea of being wrapped in soft brown velvet when he looked at her. She leaned forward and kissed him lightly on the lips. It felt like a promise of things to come.

'Night. See you soon,' Tricia said as she got out of the car and walked up her driveway without looking back.

He watched her unlock the door and sat in the car for a minute, immobilised, just looking at the door as if expecting something to happen. He wanted to run up the path, knock on the door and tell her he'd have the nightcap but he was far too sensible to give in to such impetuous desires. Maybe he had always been just that bit too sensible. He wasn't used to this strange feeling.

Was he just another useful source? Journalists in search of a good story could be ruthless but it didn't feel like she was using him. Maybe he was using her.

Christ, his head was done in trying to work it out. Still, it was a useful tip about Smethurst Comprehensive so he'd start by asking Jack.

*

'Jack, get up. If you want me to run you into school, we've got ten minutes to get out.'

Jack lumbered downstairs, opened the fridge and pondered breakfast.

'No time. Grab a bowl of cereal and a glass of juice. You can have them in the car as we haven't any time for a leisurely breakfast.'

Jack opened the cupboard. Muesli, cornflakes or coco pops. *Bloody hell, is that it*, he thought.

He poured out the cornflakes, added the milk and got a glass for the orange juice.

'Come on, Jack. Can you go any slower?'

'Get off my back, will you. I'm tired and hungry and I don't need you to have a go at me again.'

Ian was taken aback. Jack sometimes got upset or could be difficult but he didn't usually front up Ian like this.

'Hey, what's up? I'm just trying to get you to school, and me to work so don't snap at me.'

'Well, stop being a pain.'

'Right, that's enough. I don't know what's wrong but we need to get out the door now and we can have a chat about this tonight. Car, now. Bring your cereal and juice with you and you can have them in the car.'

Jack put the bowl of cereal down and went into the hall to get his coat and bag. After wrapping up, he carried his breakfast to the car and Ian started the engine. He needed to wait until the windscreen cleared up before setting off. At least the heated seats were warming them.

Jack sat there, sullen, staring out the window and eating cornflakes.

'Come on, Jack. Let's start again. I thought we'd have pizza and a film tonight.'

Jack sat there without saying a word, slowly spooning the cornflakes into his mouth.

He really could sulk, thought Ian.

They arrived at school, Jack left his bowl and glass on the seat, grabbed his bag and shouted, 'I'm at Davy's tonight,' then banged the car door shut.

Shit, thought Ian. No bonding session tonight. Sometimes work was a breeze compared with home life.

*

He arrived at the station ten minutes later. Ian was hoping to receive some forensic updates today so hopefully the day could only get better. It couldn't get a lot worse.

He ran up the stairs, dumped his coat and bag by his desk and went into the kitchen to make a coffee.

Mel was there talking to a woman he thought he recognised. When she turned round, he realised it was Ellie McVey from the forensic science service. She was

102

so short-sighted that her glasses with jam jar bottom lenses was the giveaway. He'd hoped to hear from her but didn't think he'd see her in person.

'Morning. To what do we owe the pleasure of your company, Ellie?'

'Thought I'd come and give you the update in person as well as a written report. There are a number of items I'd like to talk through.'

'Sounds ominous. See you've met Mel, our latest recruit from the Met. She left the Met to head for the bright lights of Yorkshire.'

'He'll be starting down the God's own country line before you know what's hit you, Mel.'

'He's already done that but I'm glad to be here anyway. It's a pleasant change from London and it's a great team so I think I'll be sticking around.'

'You could do a lot worse. Right, I'll get the team together and we'll see what we've got.'

Everyone gathered, drinks in hand, in the briefing room.

'Morning, everyone. Most of you know Dr Ellie McVey from the forensic science service. She's come to update us on the scientific results so I'll hand over to you, Ellie.'

'Thanks, Ian. I've been liaising with the pathologist on weapons, with Martin, our telecoms expert, and I've been having a look at clothing. If I turn first of all to the clothing. We've got clothing from the victim and the three suspects, Sutton, Brown and Price.

'We've got fibres from the victim's coat on Sutton's coat which suggests they've been in contact. We've no fibres from the victim's clothing on either Brown or Price's clothing. This means that there has been contact at some stage between Sutton and the victim.'

'Does that mean it's more likely that Sutton stabbed Josh,' asked Mel.

'No, we can't assume that. A transfer of fibres mean they've been in contact. Equally, the fact that there is no transfer of fibres doesn't mean there has been no contact. Sometimes you get a transfer of fibres and sometimes you don't. It simply supports the CCTV footage.

'Next, blood spatter. We have blood from the victim on the upper parts of the shoes of both Sutton and Price. The spatter analysis suggests a spurt of blood. It's not a smear type which you might get if someone used their foot to kick a victim and it's not on the sole which might suggest it has been walked in. It suggests close proximity to the victim when he was stabbed.

'Next, we've looked at the knives seized and I've asked the pathologist to look at them as well in relation to the wound. There is no blood on any of the knives. Lack of blood on a knife doesn't automatically mean it wasn't used as they could have been thoroughly cleaned. Having spoken with the pathologist, however, we can be pretty sure that none of these knives are the murder weapon as the blades are too short.

'The pathologist is also of the opinion, given the wound, that the knife used is likely to have had a serrated edge which none of these knives have. This means we still don't have the murder weapon.

'So, I'm afraid that we are not a lot further forward. We do have some blood and fibres to tie Sutton and Price to the victim. We don't have anything to tie Brown to the victim. All three are in close proximity to the victim when he is stabbed so it could still have been any one of them.'

'Okay, thanks, Ellie. Brown's legal team will make a lot of that. Anything on phones?'

'I was just coming to that. We've got the phones used by Sutton, Brown and Price as well as the victim. The victim's phone is full of texts, buying and selling drugs. The number he is in touch with to buy is not attributed so it's likely it's a burner phone which we haven't got. No doubt it's been disposed of. There is nothing on the phones of Sutton, Brown and Price to even suggest they knew the victim.'

'Okay, so nothing much there. We still need the murder weapon but it's looking less likely as time progresses. Still we've got CCTV which puts them there and some forensics to tie them to Josh. It should be enough for all three.'

'I agree,' said Ellie. 'There is something else I'd like to run past you in your office, Ian.'

'Fine. Thanks for that, Ellie. I can run to another coffee and some biscuits but that's about it.'

'That will be lovely.'

They walked back to the kitchen, Ian put the kettle on and grabbed the digestive biscuits.

'So what's the mystery?'

'Let's wait till we're in your office.'

Ian's office didn't have the comfy chairs and sofas like some so he had to sit behind the desk as Ellie sat on the other side. It was formal but there wasn't much he could do about it.

'So what's the big mystery that you couldn't say in front of the team?'

'It's sensitive and I'm not sure how far you want this to be known given that there can always be leaks. You might want to share it with all or just a few of the team but that's your call.

'On the victim's phone, there is a video of a young woman and, unless she's a really good actor, it looks like she's being raped by three males. Looking at the CCTV footage, it looks like the woman is Naomi. We can't tell who the males are because their faces are covered but, from the clothing, it could be Sutton, Brown and Price.'

'Shit.'

'I'm not sure how this affects the investigation but it adds another dimension.'

'It might mean nothing but, on the other hand, it might explain that the stabbing wasn't just about a drugs debt. Have you got it on you?'

'Yes, it's on my laptop.'

'Let's get Mel, Prita and John in so we can have a look at it together.'

Ian got up out of the chair faster than he got into it. As he walked around his desk, his mind was racing about the possible implications. He opened the door and scanned the room.

'Mel, John, have you got a minute. Can you also get Prita in here?'

John could see the worried look on Ian's face and looked over at Mel who just raised an eyebrow.

'I'll go and look for Prita,' said Mel as John started walking towards Ian's office.

Mel found Prita in the toilet.

'Thought you might be here. Ian wants to speak to you, me and John. Ellie is still in his office and it looks like something's come up.'

'What is it?'

'I don't know but whatever it is he doesn't look happy.'

Mel, Prita and John gathered in Ian's office. Ellie sat on one side of the desk with her laptop open. There wasn't enough space for them so they had to stand and crowd round the laptop.

'Go ahead, Ellie.'

'Thanks, Ian. I've just explained to Ian we've found a video of what looks like Naomi being raped by three men, possibly Sutton, Brown and Price but difficult to tell. It doesn't make for pleasant viewing. Are you ready?'

She started to play it.

They all watched in silence and in horror at what they saw.

'Naomi's crying and, amongst other things, says "Josh, please don't let them". It's Josh's phone so it could be that Josh is filming the rape.'

'She didn't mention it when she was video interviewed,' Ian pointed out.

'Probably because she was traumatised and wanted to forget it,' said Mel.

'Maybe, or maybe there's more to it. Let's look at Naomi a bit closer. She is present at the scene, her hand comes out to Josh's left side, the side where he was stabbed, she runs off and doesn't call an ambulance.'

'All consistent with someone who is traumatised. She panicked which is understandable,' pointed out Mel.

'She initially said she didn't really know them. She said she backed off. That's clearly not the case,' argued Ian.

'She was too frightened to name them at first. Anyway, if they raped her, it means she knows who they are but actually knowing them is a different ball game. You don't "know" your rapist. She said she backed off but she didn't say when or how far.

'She's our main witness, a young woman who has been through a lot and we don't want to alienate her. She's either a witness or she's a suspect. She can't be both, and as a witness, the case against the others is stronger.'

'There are inconsistencies in her initial account and I want to be extra careful,' said Ian. 'If Josh allowed her to be raped, or even pimped her out, she has a revenge motive. It's also possible that she is part of the gang. We have to leave no stone unturned. We can't just ignore the evidence because it doesn't fit the theory we've got. She is also on Josh's left side when he falls, the side where he was stabbed.'

'You can't be serious. Are you treating her as a suspect?'

'I'm saying we need to get her in and interview her under caution.'

'I disagree. Girlfriends of gang members are often raped by other gang members as a means of control and a rite of passage for more junior gang members. Naomi and Josh don't come under that category. He wanted more time to pay and it's likely the rape was a punishment which they made him film.'

'I'm with Mel,' said Prita. 'It doesn't add anything. We've got our three suspects and a good chance of convictions for all three. Why confuse it with pissing off our main witness who needs to get her life back on track. If she's been raped and not reported, it must be that she wants to forget it. I don't think it should be dragged up again.'

'You could be right but equally it gives her a motive and, let's face it, we can't ask Josh.'

'I think interviewing her under caution could alienate her and she's our most important witness,' argued Mel. 'No-one else on that estate is likely to come forward. We've made no progress on house to house enquiries so she's our star witness.'

'I agree with Ian,' said John. 'It needs clarifying. She has a potential motive so we need to put this to her.'

'So the men think she's a suspect and the women think she's a victim. Where does that leave us, Ian?' Mel asked.

'It's not about a male/female divide. We need to clarify in an interview and see where it leaves us. Have you had the result of the house search at Naomi's, Mel.'

'Officers are there now so we'll see what comes back.'

'I'm going to leave it to you to explain to Naomi and her parents and organise it. I think we should interview her together.'

'You're the boss,' said Mel, 'but I'm not happy with this.'

'We all have to do things we're not happy with but we need to dot the I's and cross the T's. I'll run it pass Ged at the CPS and take it from there. At this stage, I don't want it going further than this room. Okay?'

They each murmured assent and left the room.

'Fancy getting out for a coffee?' Prita asked Mel.

'Definitely.'

They went across the road to one of the few independent coffee shops left in the town.

Once they had their coffees and sat down, it was clear neither knew where to start. Mel stared at her coffee and kept stirring it as if the disappearing foam might be mirrored in a change of heart by Ian about interviewing Naomi.

'She must be traumatised and interviewing her could simply re-traumatise her.'

'I agree but I don't think the men really get it,' said Prita.

'You said he was okay and I was coming round to that way of thinking but I think he's way off on this one.'

'I also said you can disagree with him and he respects that. There's not a lot we can do unless the CPS advise against this course of action.'

'We've a meeting with the KC and junior barrister on Friday so I'm going to postpone any interview arrangement till after then.'

'Good strategy. I'd better be getting back as I've loads to do before I leave tonight.' They both stood up in no hurry to go back to the station.

Back in the station, Mel was failing to focus on anything productive when PC Jim Mellor walked in.

'Hi, Jim, did the search throw up anything?'

'Yes. I need to speak to you and the DI.'

Mel wanted to avoid Ian but knew she couldn't so walked with Jim Mellor towards Ian's office and knocked on the door.

As they walked in, she could feel the awkwardness between her and Ian.

'PC Mellor was co-ordinating the search at Naomi's and wants a chat.'

'Fire away, Jim.'

'There was nothing of interest in the house but this is what we found in the garden shed.'

The evidence bag he put on the desk contained a knife, with a serrated blade about seven inches in length. It had rusty brown marks on it.'

Oh no, thought Mel.

'Get it to forensics straight away. It might be nothing but it could be the murder weapon.'

Mel's heart sunk. If it had been found at one of the other houses, she'd have cheered but not at Naomi's.

Chapter 25

Mel decided to go round to Naomi's rather than just arranging the interview over the phone. She decided to take Sally with her again as she didn't want any misunderstandings.

As they drove out of the station, it was already dark, misty and had started drizzling. A Scottish university friend of Mel's described this type of weather as dreich. It summed it up. It was a cold, dreich day.

Sally drove the few miles out to Moss Green. Neither spoke as they weren't looking forward to this.

Sally pulled up outside of the house. They both sat there. 'Right, let's do this,' said Mel and they got out of the car. Mel thought that the short walk down the drive way felt so much longer this time.

Naomi answered the door and, although she had a worried look on her face, she had more colour in her face and didn't look quite as drawn.

'Come in. Can I get you a drink?'

She seemed more confident in herself but Mel wasn't sure how long that would last after they had this conversation.

'That would be great. I'll have a coffee with milk.'

'And I'll have a tea with milk if that's ok,' said Sally.

'Sure. I'll go and put the kettle on. Mum and dad are still at work but mum should be home soon as she said she'd try and leave early seeing as you were coming to have a chat.'

Naomi showed them into the lounge where they'd sat before looking at the same family photos.

This was not going to be easy.

'Do you want to wait for your mum to get home?'

'No, it's fine.'

Naomi returned with the drinks and sat on an armchair in front of them.

Mel decided there was no way she could make this easy so launched in.

'Naomi, there are some things we need to talk to you about down at the station and it has been decided that it's best if you were interviewed under caution.'

'What? Why? I don't understand. I thought you'd got those three locked up for killing Josh.'

'A knife was found in your shed and it's being examined to see if it is the murder weapon.'

'What? Anyone could have put it there. I don't know anything about it. Half the time the shed isn't locked and neither is the gate.'

'I don't want you to say anything now but it's obviously something we need to ask you about, particularly if it is the knife that was used on Josh.'

'Okay, I get that but I don't know anything about it.'

'Whatever you know or don't know is something you can tell us at the police station. There is something else that has come up that we need to ask you about.'

'What?'

'Josh's phone has been examined and a video has been found on it.'

Before Mel could continue, Naomi's face contorted and the colour drained from her. The girl who was starting to look more confident was gone now.

'There's no easy way to say this, Naomi. It shows you being raped by three men whose faces can't be seen. It might be that it was Josh who was filming it.'

Naomi sat still, staring at them, the tears running down her face and saying nothing.

Mel heard a key being turned in the front door and Pam walked in and took one look at Naomi.

'What's going on?'

'Hi, Pam. We've explained to Naomi that we need to interview her under caution. I think it's better if Naomi goes through it with you rather than us. I'm suggesting Monday afternoon, perhaps after college if that suits.'

'No, it bloody well doesn't suit. My husband is away and there's just me here to fit in with you lot. What are you playing at? Naomi was starting to get stronger and look at her now. Why do you want to interview her again?'

'I'm sorry but I really think it's best if Naomi explains it to you. It's also best if Naomi has a solicitor with her in interview as well. You can get the duty solicitor or choose one yourself.'

'We don't know any solicitors. We're not that kind of people. The only time I've seen a solicitor was when we bought the house for Christ's sake.'

'I know this must've come as a shock but hopefully we'll get everything cleared up on Monday. Is 4.00 okay?'

'We'll be there. Now I'd like you to leave.'

'Okay, and I'm really sorry about this.'

'Not as sorry as we are. You can see yourselves out.'

Mel and Sally stood up and walked towards the door.

'Again, I'm sorry and I'll see you Monday.'

'Just go.'

'I'm glad you gave me the heads up on that one. I appreciate it can't go any further so you've nothing to worry about on that score. Poor kid. She's been through the mill. Sounds like anyone could have put that knife there.'

'I know but the presence of what might be the murder weapon makes the interview necessary. The rape doesn't in my opinion but keep that to yourself.'

'Don't worry, I will.'

'Let's hope it's not the murder weapon.'

Chapter 26

The CPS offices occupied the top two floors of the multi-story building opposite Leeds railway station. Parking was a nightmare and ridiculously expensive so Ian, Mel, Prita and John caught the train. Mel loved being on a train, looking out of the window and just watching the countryside go by but she wasn't enjoying this journey.

Her and Ian were being polite and professional but were awkward with each other. It was amazing how the notices on trains or the pattern on the table could capture your attention when you wanted to avoid eye contact.

Mel didn't know the barristers but had heard good things about them so let's hope they'd see sense about Naomi. With the discovery of the knife it was looking less hopeful.

As they entered the glass and steel building, Mel saw the lifts opposite reception. She hadn't been here before so it was a new experience despite having had professional conferences with numerous prosecution barristers in London. She didn't suppose these two would be any different. Four silent colleagues in a lift did not bode well.

She looked at the control panel and saw the notice that pointed out the lift held a maximum of ten people. She didn't know how ten people would fit in this lift as it felt cramped with the four of them. Maybe it was like the tube and you could always squeeze more in.

Mel breathed a sigh of relief when the lift arrived at floor fifteen and they could walk out of the lift into a bit more space. Ian approached reception, gave their names and they each signed the visitors' book before Ged approached to escort them in.

'Afternoon, folks. Maria and Sebastian are already here and we can run to coffee and biscuits.'

He walked down the carpeted corridor into a room with a large table and ten chairs. There was a man and woman already sat at the table helping themselves to drinks and biscuits. Each was wearing the black suits and white shirts that made it obvious they were barristers even without the wigs and gowns.

'Ian, Prita, Mel and John, meet our KC, Maria Conroy, and junior counsel, Sebastian Wells.'

'Hi, everyone. Ian, Prita and John, I know and it's good to meet you, Mel. I hope you're enjoying Carfield CID,' said Maria.

'It's very different from the Met,' was about as non-committal as Mel could get.

Maria sensed the reserve in Mel's response. 'Let's hope the difference is positive. Right, down to work. We've got reasonable CCTV, blood and fibres which put the three of them at the scene. We've no murder weapon as yet and the only eyewitness is Naomi.

'It's more than enough to charge them. All three have previous for carrying knives and knives have been found in the house searches of the three but not the murder weapon. We will try and get their previous for possession of knives before the jury but it's a bit of a long shot.'

'Surely that's relevant,' interrupted Mel.

'I will say it is but the defence will say carrying a knife is very different to using it to stab someone.'

'Why carry it if you don't intend to use it?'

'Some will say they had it for protection, others say they had knives to make them look hard. I will make a bad character application in relation to the knives but don't get your hopes up.

'Although, they have said very little in the interviews, it is likely to be a cut throat defence with Brown and Sutton blaming Price and he will no doubt blame the others. That way we're likely to get a conviction for all three as none of them will be believable. Our approach will be it's a classic joint enterprise as they agree to meet, know that the others carry knives, know that there is an issue regarding a drugs debt and know there is going to be violence used.

'Naomi's phone recording and text is more problematic. We can't attribute the text to any phone and the recording is so muffled it will be impossible to get any positive identification. One possible scenario is that Naomi used a burner to send the text to herself and that could be anyone on the recording. This is what Sutton's team will argue if we try to get it in evidence.

'The difficulty is Naomi. We have watched the CCTV footage over and over. It cannot be seen who does the stabbing but we can see Naomi's hand come out just as Josh falls. We've also watched the video on Josh's phone so where does that leave us? We've got different potential scenarios.

'Is Naomi pressurised into stabbing Josh by boys who have pressurised Josh into filming his girlfriend's rape? Is Naomi part of that group? Is Naomi getting revenge on Josh?'

'Is she the girlfriend that put her hand out to save him? Were they both victims of this gang? If so, why run? Or is Naomi our star witness and Sutton has intimidated and threatened her?'

'I think Naomi is the victim in all of this,' argued Mel. 'She's been raped but she is still loyal to Josh. She went to Fisher reluctantly but went anyway because she didn't want him to go on his own. She ran because she panicked and didn't realise Josh had been stabbed. She was out of her depth and she could have been next.'

'So how do we explain the knife found in Naomi's shed? I know we're still waiting for forensics but if that turns out to be the murder weapon, we'll be looking to charge Naomi. When is her interview?'

'Monday and we're hoping to get forensics back by then as they're being rushed through,' Ian replied. He didn't want it to be a head to head between Mel and Maria and could feel that it might be.

'Okay. Let's see what the findings are and what Naomi has to say in interview and we can have another look at it. Now, witnesses and procedure.'

As they went through the witnesses required, the procedure for logging every piece of evidence they would rely on, as well as the material they would not be relying on, Mel couldn't help feeling down. She just couldn't see Naomi as a perpetrator.

After a couple of hours, the meeting folded, laptops were closed and they said their goodbyes.

'I'll look forward to an update on Monday and we'll take it from there. Have a good weekend, everyone,' said Maria.

'And I'm taking you for a quick drink,' said Prita to Mel.

'Thanks that would be great.'

Prita suggested a bar close to the station that served tapas and cocktails so, after a couple of margaritas, Mel suggested getting some food. The thing about tapas is you could just keep going with dish after delicious dish.

'What did you think of Maria?' Prita asked.

'Impressive, objective, clear and down to earth.'

'Great summary. I've seen her in court and juries love her because she's not one of the public school types you so often get. She is one of the few female, black KCs outside of London so she's had to work really hard to get where she is.'

'What's Sebastian like?'

'I've not seen him in action but I'm told he's very good and very thorough. He's clearly got aspirations as he works his socks off. At least we know the case will be well prepared. I suppose its watch this space regarding Naomi?'

'I don't want to think about her just now. Let's have another margarita and forget work.'

'Good idea. We've got a good few hours before the last train and we don't need to be up early in the morning so let's get hammered.'

*

When Ian arrived home, it was so quiet until he remembered Jack was at a friend's. He felt at a loose end. He put the television on but the news was too depressing. He looked around at the housework that needed doing but that was even more depressing.

He sat down with a cup of tea but couldn't settle so rang Jack to see when he'd be home. Straight to voicemail. He sent a text, "Hi, Jack. Do you need me to pick you up tonight? Just let me know. Love you xx".

He was bored and didn't know what to do with himself. Could he ring Tricia? It might seem overly keen as he'd only seen her last night. If he met up with her, he couldn't drink in case he had to pick up Jack. Jack could always get a cab but is that abandoning him. Christ, so many problems spinning round in his head. The sound of a text pinged. Jack, thank god.

"Hi, Dad. Am at Davy's. Will get lift or taxi. Don't wait up. Xx". Well, Jack was sorted so he could relax a bit but do what? Takeaway and film maybe? Early night? Christ it was only 7.00. Sod it, bull by the horns and all that. He picked his phone up again and started to type a text.

"Hi, Tricia. Free tonight? Fancy the pizzeria?" He didn't send it. Did it sound too much like a date? It didn't sound like work. He pressed send and watched his phone as if it was going to explode or morph into an alien. Ten minutes and no response. He sensed she had a life, unlike him.

The phone pinged with the incoming text. "Love to. Book a table and I'll see you there in half an hour x".

He replied immediately, "Will do. Look forward to it x". Was that too keen? He didn't care, he was bored and needed a life outside work and Jack. He was still uncomfortable about kisses on texts. Some people put them on automatically even if they hardly knew you. He was more reserved and was never quite sure about the etiquette but it was too late to worry. Book table, shower, change and get a taxi. Need to get a move on.

He arrived before her and was shown to the table. He loved this pizzeria. It wasn't fancy and with its red and white check table cloths and the Italian tenors coming over the speakers was a bit cheesy but the service and food were great. He knew she drank white wine and wondered if he should order a bottle. Is that too presumptuous? Christ, he really was out of practice, overthinking everything.

As he was wrestling with the wine dilemma, she walked in. She looked gorgeous and windswept like something out of a film. Christ, he was at it again. First, it was pre-Raphaelite and now it was a film. Maybe he was more of a romantic that he realised.

He stood up quickly and knocked his chair over then became flustered as he scrambled to pick it up. She stood in front of him and laughed. *Great start*, he thought. Once he'd recovered the chair and his dignity, he gave her a peck on the side of the cheek and was about to sit down when she kissed both sides of his cheeks which he hadn't expected and had to try and cover it up by over compensating and kissing both sides of her cheeks again.

He was completely discombobulated and she laughed saying, 'I think we're out of sync. So, is this work or social?'

'Definitely social.'

'I was hoping you'd say that.'

He was looking into those velvet eyes when she said, 'Shall we order a bottle of pinot?'

'Great. The penne arrabbiata is really good here and the pizzas are fantastic if you fancy a pizza.'

She looked him straight in the eye and said, 'I quite fancy you.'

This was going well, he thought. 'You could always have me for dessert.'

'I might just do that but in the meantime, I'll have a calzone.'

Talk about the air being charged with sexual tension, he couldn't believe he'd just said that.

His phone rang which burst the bubble. It was a number he didn't recognise.

'Are you going to get that?'

'Probably trying to sell me something. If it's important, they'll leave a voicemail.'

The voicemail message pinged.

'Sorry, I'll just listen to this and we can get back to ordering the food.'

As he listened to the message, Tricia could see his face change.

'Is anything wrong?'

'I've got to go. That was Davy's dad. Jack and Davy are at A & E. Looks like drugs.'

Chapter 27

Mel and Prita were pretty tipsy but not too far gone that they didn't know what they were doing when they walked to the train station. Leeds was buzzing with young people spilling out of bars and generally having a good time.

Mel looked at one woman and said, 'I wish I could walk in heels that high.'

Prita looked at the woman's friend. 'I was just thinking she looked cold with no coat on. I couldn't come out in this weather wearing just a dress.'

'A coat would spoil the look. Look at him with the blond hair and short sleeved very tight shirt. If he was wearing a coat, he wouldn't be able to show off his biceps and tattoos.'

People watching was a great activity in a city centre on a Friday night.

'Do you realise we haven't talked about work or about you and Ian.'

'What do you mean me and Ian?'

'Well, there does seem to be some sort of energy between you. You go from being super friendly to having a cob on with each other.'

'I thought a cob was a loaf of bread.'

'You'll have to get used to the Yorkshire sayings if you're staying up here.'

'There is no me and Ian. He's my boss and I disagree with him about Naomi.'

'Well, it looks like Maria Conroy is on page with him.'

'I know. We'll see what forensics say. Maybe it's me that's got Naomi wrong.'

'Shit, we've lasted a whole evening without talking about work. My fault for bringing up you and Ian. I thought you fancied him.'

'Definitely not. Senior officers are a no-go area.'

'Even if they're a bit hench?'

'Especially if they're a bit hench.'

*

The taxi pulled up outside the doors of the A & E department. Ian fumbled for money, gave the driver too much but didn't wait for change and ran into the hospital going to the front of the queue. He didn't care what people thought. He was looking frantically around, where to go, who to speak to. He spotted the reception desk and sprinted over.

'My son, Jack Pearce, has been brought in. Is he ok? Where is he?'

'If you take a seat, I'll get someone out to you.'

Just then someone behind him said, 'Ian, I'm Steve, Davy's dad. They're ok. My wife, Helen, is with Davy just now and Jack's with a nurse.'

'Thank God. I need to see him. What happened?'

'Let's sit down for two minutes, I'll explain.'

Ian reluctantly sat down but panic was written all over him.

'They took some MDMA, ecstasy. Davy told me they bought it off a lad in school. It's been cut with something but the doctor isn't sure what just yet and they've had a bad reaction, but they're going to be okay. Luckily, they only had half a tablet each.'

Just then, a woman in a white coat with a stethoscope slung round her neck came over to him.

'Mr Pearce, I'm Doctor Sajjad. I've been looking after Jack. He's fine but we want to keep him overnight. I'd like a quick word and then I'll take you through to see him.'

Ian turned to Steve, 'Thanks for looking after him. We'll need to have another talk about this but not now.'

'I agree. Just go and see him.'

Doctor Sajjad took him through to a room with comfy chairs and muted colours. No doubt it was a room used for breaking bad news.

'Davy and Jack have taken ecstasy but not much. They've both vomited most of it up. It's been cut with another chemical and we're still trying to work out what it is. He's going to be fine and I think he's had a scare. Is this the first time he's taken anything?'

'Yes, I think so. He's not that sort of a lad.'

'They rarely are but sometimes just want to experiment.'

'I know. I'm a police officer so I do see it.'

'So I gather. It's worth keeping an eye on him. If there is a bad batch out there, we might well be seeing many more casualties and not all as lucky as Davy and Jack.' She stood up, no doubt ready to move on to the next job. 'I'll take you through to him now.'

She took him up a corridor and pulled back a cubicle curtain. Jack was lying there looking rough but conscious and alive.

'Dad, I'm so sorry. It's the first time I've taken anything. We thought it'd be a laugh.'

'I'm just glad you're alright. I don't know what I'd do if anything happened to you.'

Jack began to cry. 'We didn't take much because we were both a bit scared but everyone seemed to be doing it so we thought we'd try it. I was starting to feel really good and we were laughing then I just puked and couldn't breathe. Davy shouted down to his mum and when she came up he told her what we'd done.

'She was trying to sort me out when Davy started to puke up so she called the ambulance. I'm really sorry. I won't do it again. I promise.'

'Shh, its okay, it's okay. We'll talk about it when you're up to it but if there's bad ecstasy doing the rounds, I need to know about it.'

'I know. I know. Can I get a drink of water, Dad?'

'Course. I'll get a drink as well and some crisps or something. Do you want anything to eat?'

'You must be joking. If I ate, I think I'd puke again. I'm okay to come home.'

'They want to keep you in overnight and that makes sense so I'm not going against that.'

'Nice shirt, Dad. Not seen you wear that in a while. Were you out?'

'Yes, I was just about to order my pizza when I got the call so need something to eat before I collapse. My adrenalin has been used up.'

'Who were you out with? Anyone I know?'

'No. I can see you're feeling better.'

'Sorry if I ruined your night.'

'You can make it up to me by promising you will never do this again. I know everyone experiments but I've seen too many lives be ruined by addiction and contaminated stuff. I've been young once and I understand it's tempting but you don't know what you're getting. I won't always be with you, especially if you go off to university, so you need to take responsibility for yourself.'

'Promise, Dad. I'll never do this again.'

Tricia looked like she'd unwrapped a birthday present only to find it was an empty box. The only person on her own in a restaurant full of couples enjoying a Friday night out. How shit was that. She didn't want people to think she'd been stood up but was starting to look a bit self-conscious, and was wondering if she should just get a takeaway when the waiter arrived with the bottle of pinot and asked her if she was ready to order. *Bugger it*, she thought.

'Yes, I'll have the calzone, no starter.'

She didn't want the makeup and the dress to go to waste after all. Nor the wine. He didn't even stop to say "goodbye" or "I'll give you a ring". Still, she supposed that's what kids do to you. She could tell he was keen so there'd be other opportunities. She wasn't entirely sure if that's what she wanted though.

Chapter 28

Naomi

They knew now. She couldn't keep it secret any longer. Her family knew and the police knew. How many more people would know? How many more would see it?

She couldn't bear the thought of it.

She was trying to forget it but the flashbacks wouldn't let her.

They just kept coming.

Maybe it was time to get some counselling?

Would that stop the sounds and the smells?

The smells clung to her clothes. She had to bin the underwear and T shirt but couldn't get rid of the jeans and coat as her mum would notice.

The stink of it all. The stench of them in the empty, smelly, tatty house. On the dirty, foul, scratchy sofa.

They pulled her hair and pointed the phone at her face filming her agony.

He ordered her to remove her clothes. All of them.

They saw her shame and laughed at her as they took it in turns.

At least none of them lasted long. Their excitement at what they were doing took over them and they came quickly.

She had to cling on to the small mercies.

And this was with her every hour of every day. She relived it over and over and over again.

It would fade. It had to.

She went through the "if onlys" time and time again.

If only she hadn't gone with him that night.

If only he hadn't got involved with them.

If only she had run.

If only she had fought back.

If only she was stronger.

But when it came down to it, she had no choice.

They liked their knives and weren't afraid to use them. They had to ensure Josh did what he was told. Filming it with the threat of exposure meant Josh would toe the line, would get them their money. And she knew Sutton would post it, that it was no idle threat. He would enjoy it.

She didn't want the exposure, the humiliation of others seeing her. Her humiliation at the time was bad enough but the thought of the added agony of others seeing it was more than she could cope with.

If only it would have exposed them but their faces were unclear with their stupid scarves pretending they were gangsters. Her face was clear enough when they put the phone right up to her and what they were doing to her was definitely clear.

At least they didn't focus on other parts of her body.

She hated them for what they'd done to her, for what they had made Josh do.

She had loved Josh, she had gone along with everything he wanted. Despite it all, she remembered hoping it would be fine when they got away and put it all behind them and he would be the old Josh, the lovely, caring Josh. They could look forward to being together at uni but it was all gone.

It was all a dream now. That was all it had ever been.

Why the fuck hadn't Josh deleted it.

Chapter 29

Ben Sutton walked towards the legal visits area where his solicitor, Charles Haig, was waiting with two others who he presumed were his barristers. As he walked in, Charles stood up and introduced everyone.

'Ben, this is Mary O'Ryan who will be the KC at your trial and this is Lizzie Taylor, your junior barrister. We will all be working together to prepare your defence. I'm going to hand over to Mary.'

Ben looked at the two barristers but it was Mary, the KC, who he focussed on. *She must be six feet*, he thought. *No makeup and short grey hair. Got to be a fucking dyke. No man would shag her.*

'Thanks, Charles. Good to meet you, Ben. As Charles said, we will be working together but we all have different jobs to do. I want to hear your initial account as to what happened on the night Josh Smithies was killed. Before you say anything, I need to emphasise that whatever you tell us is confidential but if you tell us that you did stab him, we wouldn't be able to represent you if you pleaded not guilty as that would mean misleading the court and we can't do that.'

'Yeh, Yeh, I know all that.'

We've got a real charmer here, thought Mary. *If he could slouch any more he'd be horizontal. And what was it with young men who felt a need to shove their hands down the front of their jogging bottoms?*

'Right, I know you've given a prepared statement and "no comment" interviews at the police station so I want to get your account now.'

'Well, it's what I told Charles. We met up with Josh, he owed us money and we wanted it. Simple as.'

'Did he have the money?'

'Did he fuck?'

'Did you know he didn't have the money?'

'Yeh.'

'So what was the point of the meeting if he couldn't pay you?'

'Frighten him into paying?'

'How were you going to frighten him?'

'I don't know. Just frighten him. There wasn't a plan.'

Christ, it's like pulling teeth, thought Mary.

'Well, tell me what you do in that situation when someone can't pay.'

'Don't know what you mean.'

'Right, Ben, let's not mess around here. We know it's a drugs debt, that will come out in trial and it's not a bad thing. We can point out to the court that it doesn't make sense for you to kill someone who owes you money as that would mean you wouldn't get paid. So tell me how you were going to frighten him.'

'I told him he'd got seven days to pay the money or he'd be sorry. I slapped him once, not hard, just to scare him. Harley and Luke punched him I think. I wasn't sure if I saw a knife but Luke always carries and I think there was just a flash of something in his hand when he hit out.'

'Where did you slap him?'

'Face.'

'What about Harley. Where did he punch him?'

'Stomach I think.'

'And Luke?'

'The same. It was dark and it happened so fast. I didn't see who hit where but I think Luke had a knife in his hand.'

'You think or you saw?'

'I don't fucking know. Okay, I saw. Happy now?'

'We just want your account. Don't say what you think we want to hear. When you went there, was there any discussion about causing him serious harm?'

'Was there fuck.'

'Did you know anyone had a knife?'

'No. I hadn't seen one before.'

'What was your intention?'

'I told you I just want to frighten him. Get him to pay up.'

'You're charged on a joint enterprise basis. Simply put, that means it doesn't matter who stabbed him, if there was some sort of agreement to cause serious harm or if you gave any kind of assistance to the person who stabbed him.'

'I get all that. Charles told me but I didn't do that. I slapped him to frighten him and had no idea that dickhead Luke was going to cut him. I'm not fucking guilty and I'm not going down for this.'

'What about the text to Naomi?'

'Don't know anything about it. Police have my phone so I couldn't text.'

'Are you seriously telling me you don't use burner phones?'

'Look, love, I didn't send that text and I didn't meet up with her. She's a lying little slag.'

'So the voice recording isn't you?'

'I've just told you. No.'

'And if the prosecution get a voice expert, they won't conclude that it's you.'

'How do I know what they'll conclude but it wasn't fucking me?'

'Okay, we'll start preparing your defence on that basis. Charles will take a statement from you over the next few weeks and I want a lot more detail than you've given us today.'

Mary looked at him and he just sat there with his arms crossed, legs wide apart, sulking like a two-year-old. At least he wasn't fiddling with himself now.

'We'll come and see you once the prosecution have served all their evidence as we will need to serve a defence statement, a basic outline of your defence.'

He stared at her like she was the enemy, not someone who was trying to help him. Charles knocked on the door and an officer came to collect Ben and take him back to his wing. He didn't even say goodbye or look at them.

While they waited to be escorted from the visits section, Lizzie looked at Mary and Charles.

'What a tosser,' she said. 'The jury will hate him unless he changes his attitude.'

'That's why he has such a brilliant team on side. It's going to be an uphill struggle,' said Charles. 'Don't forget it's the tossers that keep you in BMWs.'

'And it's a myth that we all drive expensive cars as well you know so don't start that one again. Most of the time I really like my clients but I'm going to have to work on this one,' said Mary.

The officer walked towards them to escort them out through the various locked doors and fingerprint scans till they got to the prison entrance where the lockers were. They didn't speak on the way to the entrance as none of them wanted to be overheard. You never knew what might get back to prisoners.

They each collected their belongings and walked into the bright sunshine.

'I suppose we need to remember he's young, it's bravado, he's not been in prison before and he's not getting to walk out into the sunshine like we are,' said

Mary. 'If we can hang on to that, we'll start to like him and see him for what he is. A frightened young man.'

'And that's why you're so good with juries,' Charles said, smiling at them both.

Ben was escorted back to the wing where it was recreation time. Harley was there and he went up to him.

'I've just met my barristers. I think the KC is a fucking dyke.'

'Who cares if she's good.'

'Suppose. I said I saw Luke with a knife and we only wanted to frighten Josh so stick with that. I don't want you saying anything fucking different at trial.'

'Okay. Don't know what Luke will be saying.'

'He'll be too shit scared to blame us if he knows what's good for him.'

*

Luke had asked to be on the vulnerable prisoner wing as he was scared of Ben Sutton and had applied to be transferred to another prison. He knew what Sutton was capable of and, although he didn't see a knife, he knew Ben had stabbed Josh. Okay, perhaps he didn't mean him to die but it must have been him. He knew it wasn't him and Harley wouldn't have done it without Ben telling him to, so either Ben did it or told Harley to do it.

Either way he wasn't going down for it. Luke didn't know how long he could hack it in here. His brief told him it could be nine months before the trial as there were loads of delays. It was doing his fucking head in. The vulnerable prisoner wing was full of nonces who made his skin crawl. He hadn't had a visit from anyone apart from his brief. His mum couldn't be arsed.

'Price, legal visit for you.'

Thank fuck, he thought. *About time.*

The officer walked him down the wing, unlocked the gate, down a corridor, through another gate and into the legal visits section containing the glass cubicles for legal visits. He supposed they had to be glass so you could see if anyone was kicking off.

The officer escorted him up to the desk.

'Price.'

'Number nine.'

Luke walked up the corridor and into the small room, numbered nine on the door, to see his solicitor and two other men who he supposed must be the barristers. One of them looked about a hundred.

The old man stood up, held out his hand and said, 'Rupert Smythe, pleasure to meet you, Luke, and this is my junior, Robert Winstanley. Frank, your solicitor, you know obviously.'

Fuck, he's posh, thought Luke. *Bet he's not from a council estate. Having a name like Rupert would be enough to get your head kicked in.* He stood there not knowing what to do. He hadn't met people like this before with their posh accents and fancy suits.

'Sit, sit,' said Rupert. It was like an order from a primary school teacher. Luke felt about five-years-old. He sat but didn't know what to say.

'Now then. I understand from Frank that you've accepted presence at the scene, denied any joint enterprise or agreement to cause Josh Smithies any serious harm and you don't know who stabbed him. Is that correct?'

'Eh, yeah.'

'So you'll be pleading not guilty then?'

'Deffo.'

'If the phone recording we've heard is authentic and it is Ben Sutton, he is likely to be blaming you, although he hasn't said that in interview. It's very unclear so I'm not sure the prosecution would be able to use it and there is no attribution for the phone.'

'It wasn't me. I didn't know anything and I didn't do anything. I hit him once in the chest or shoulder.'

'Yes, we can see that from the CCTV. Your hand goes out towards the area where he was stabbed. The footage is not clear enough to show exactly where you made contact with him. You have previous for carrying knives and a knife was found, albeit not the murder weapon, in your bedroom. That could be a problem for us. Did you see who stabbed him?'

'No, but it wasn't me. It must have been Ben. He's a right cocky bastard.'

'Well, you're all likely to be blaming each other. It's what we call a cut throat which is never good but we have no option. Frank will be taking a proof of evidence, your statement, over the next few weeks which will only be seen by us. We will come and see you again a few months down the line.'

'A few months. For fucks sake. Can't I get bail?'

'No. Because you're charged with murder, you won't get bail. I'm sorry but that's the reality regardless of what anyone else might tell you. Frank will be your regular contact. Robert and I will be working away preparing your case for trial. We will see you when we need to.'

At that, Rupert stood up and knocked on the window to summon the officer. 'Chin up, we'll do our best.'

Luke just stared, didn't know what to say. The officer opened the room and led Luke back to his wing. When he got there his pad mate, Andy was there.

'How'd it go, mate?'

'Fuck knows. He told me to keep my chin up.'

Andy just looked at him and they burst out laughing. If you didn't laugh, you'd cry.

Rupert, Robert and Frank were escorted back to the entrance.

'Did you see the cricket last night?' Rupert asked.

'Fraid not, I was at the police station till 3.00 this morning.'

'Ah yes. The joys of being a duty solicitor. Disappointing show but we're not beaten yet.'

As they made their way to their cars, Rupert called over to Frank.

'Send me a proof of evidence when you can and we'll talk then.'

Rupert and Robert carried on discussing England's poor performance in the cricket as they made their way to what he assumed was Rupert's car, a BMW 7 series. *Very nice*, thought Frank.

Frank wasn't sure about Rupert. He didn't exactly have empathy. Still, the boss said he was good and wanted him for this case so Frank was just following orders. He liked Luke and, although solicitors don't have to believe what clients tell them, he did believe Luke and didn't want him going down for something he hadn't done.

Chapter 30

Monday morning and Jack was up early. He had been on his best behaviour since he came home on Saturday. He even spent most of yesterday doing homework before him and Ian went for a pizza last night. Ian felt he'd missed out on the pizza with Tricia but going out with Jack was something they hadn't done for ages. He made a mental note to do it more often.

'Right, Jack. I'm going in for a chat with the head after I've dropped you off. It's got to be official now that we know a bad batch of ecstasy could doing the rounds.'

'I know. I just feel embarrassed and stupid.'

'We all do stupid things. The main thing is that you're okay.'

After Ian dropped him at the school, he parked up and went in to see the head.

'Mr Smethurst is busy this morning. You'll need to make an appointment.'

Ian was in no mood for a gatekeeping receptionist.

'He'll see me now. This is a police matter.'

She scuttled off and came back a minute later.

'Come this way please, Mr Pearce.'

Ian was shown in to a large office with desk, low table and comfy chairs. *Bit better than my office*, thought Ian.

'Mr Pearce, what can I do for you?'

'Detective Inspector Pearce. I'm here in an official capacity. My son and another lad, Davy Higginbotham, took ecstasy over the weekend and ended up in hospital.'

Mr Smethurst interrupted, 'I'm very sorry to hear that but the school isn't responsible for what young people do outside of the school.'

Ian was in no mood for platitudes from this smarmy git.

'It is when it's another pupil dealing. I have the names of pupils who are dealing and I'm sending officers in today to speak to them. I have a list of names here. Please make them available. It seems there is a bad batch doing the rounds and I'm sure the last thing you want is a dead pupil. That wouldn't be very good for the school.'

Smethurst went white.

'Of course. I didn't realise. You will have our full co-operation.'

'Thank you. One of my officers will be in touch this morning to make arrangements for these pupils to be spoken to. Make sure their parents are informed.'

With that parting shot, Ian turned and walked out.

Chapter 31

Mel wasn't looking forward to today. She'd see Naomi and Pam this afternoon. Apart from Josh's family, who must be going through hell, so many lives have been in a state of upheaval since Josh was murdered. Naomi was back at college determined to get the grades to get her into university and Pam had taken time off work when needed.

It was easier for her than her husband but it was obvious she was getting pissed off. A younger son, a traumatised daughter, a full-time job. Not easy at all. At least having the interview this afternoon would mean the disruption to their day would be minimal. She hoped. Not that they would see it like that.

Mel sat at her desk working through the logging of exhibits, focussing on items, lists and numbers, seeing what holes still needed to be plugged. Some considered this type of work boring but it made a welcome change looking at lists and working through them, methodically preparing the case for trial, nothing emotional or too taxing.

Just as she was wondering about the continuity of a particular exhibit, she could see Prita out of the corner of her eye talking with one of the techies. She looked very serious and followed him out of the office. Wonder what that's about. As she went back to her lists of exhibits, Ian popped his head round and called everyone into the briefing room.

As she walked into the briefing room, she saw Dr Ellie McVey. She could feel this was not going to be good.

'Thanks, everyone. I'm going to hand over to Dr McVey to give us an update on forensics.'

'Morning, everyone. As you know a knife has been recovered and we've now had the opportunity of examining it. There can be little doubt that this is the murder weapon.'

Shit, thought Mel.

'There is brown staining on the knife. We've managed to get a DNA sample from this and it is the blood of Josh Smithies. The pathologist has also examined the knife in relation to the stab wound. Although, it's difficult to be one hundred per cent certain it is the murder weapon, as you rarely can with knives, it is the right length and has the right type of serrations that makes it the type of knife used. That means that with the blood and the type of knife, we can say this is the murder weapon.'

'What about fingerprints?' Mel asked.

'None. Either gloves were worn or it was wiped clean. There are no fibres on the knife so we won't be able to link it to any clothing.'

'So it could have been used by any of the three suspects?'

'There is nothing to link the knife to a particular suspect. I just do the science, you do the police work. I know three have been charged but whether there is a fourth suspect is a matter for you and the lawyers. I wanted to come and give you this news in person but there will be a report from both me and the pathologist on the knife.'

Mel looked at Ian who caught her eye. She knew it wasn't looking good for Naomi.

Ian could see Mel's pained expression and could tell she was struggling to process this. She also knew what was coming and he couldn't make it any better for her.

'Thanks for coming and giving us the update in person, Ellie.'

'No problem. I know it's better than just getting a stark report. You've got the decisions to make now. I'll get the reports to you by the end of the week.'

'Much appreciated. Now, I'd like to run some things past John, Prita and Mel.'

'Prita's just having a word with one of the techies.'

'Okay,' said Ian, 'it'll just be you two then.'

Mel watched Ellie walk out of the office, passing the time of day with officers she knew and marvelled at how relaxed she seemed after delivering the news on the knife. She supposed Ellie was right. She just dealt with the science.

As the three of them walked into Ian's office, he looked strained. Maybe this case was getting to him more than she appreciated.

'We've got some tough decisions to make but I wanted to talk it through with you. I've not run any of this past the CPS or barristers yet but that's something we will need to do. We've now got evidence which does implicate Naomi whether we like it or not.

'She's at the scene, her hand goes out to the area Josh was stabbed; she runs away and doesn't call for help; we have the murder weapon found at her property and we have a revenge motive due to the rape.'

'I don't think it's enough to charge her,' said Mel. 'She's at the scene because he's her boyfriend, she puts her hand out, possibly to help him, she runs because she panics and the rape doesn't tell us anything apart from she was abused.'

'It's two very different scenarios. What's your take, John?'

'It's a difficult one but for me, the murder weapon being found on her property tips the balance. She's got to be considered a suspect.'

Prita walked through the briefing room and straight into Ian's office.

'David Metcalfe has been going over CCTV footage prior to the stabbing to see if there is anything else of interest. There is some footage with Josh, Naomi and the three suspects from ten days prior to the incident. Naomi slaps Josh across the face. It's from outside the shop and there's no sound but it could suggest it wasn't quite love's young dream. It's set up now so we can go have a look.'

They all trooped out and into the techies' area where DC David Metcalfe was there with one of the techies.

'It's been enhanced as much as possible,' said David. 'Okay, ready everyone, let's go.'

As the footage began playing, the five of them could be seen clearly. It was right outside the shop so the lighting was much better. Sutton, Brown and Price all seemed to be laughing as Naomi's arm went out and she slapped Josh across the face. It wasn't just a tap either.

Josh's hand went up to his cheek and the five of them stayed there talking for another minute before Josh and Naomi walked off in one direction and the other three went in the opposite direction. It seemed odd that Josh and Naomi walked off together after what had happened. They didn't appear to be saying anything to each other but it was difficult to tell.

'We obviously don't know what that's about but we're going to have to speak to Naomi. I suppose it's possible she's in it with Sutton, Brown and Price,' said Ian.

'Equally, she could be acting under duress as Josh might have been if it was him doing the filming in the rape,' said Mel.

She knew they weren't going to be able to meet in the middle on this one. Normally when you get some good evidence from forensics or CCTV, everyone is on a bit of a high. Not with this one. No-one looked happy about it. The evidence was ambiguous but even Mel knew it couldn't be ignored as it was starting to mount up.

'Mel, I'd like to be in on the interview this afternoon but, as you've been the main point of contact with her, you should take the lead.'

'Okay.' There wasn't anything more to say so Mel went back to compiling lists of exhibits. At least that didn't tax her emotions.

The afternoon dragged on. The office was quiet with everyone beavering away on their allotted tasks and Mel was clock watching. Naomi and Pam would be here soon. She really was not looking forward to this. When her phone went, her heart sank. She picked up the receiver, 'Sergeant Garvey.' After a brief pause while she listened to the person on the other end of the phone, she said, 'I'll come right down.'

Mel walked towards Ian's office. He saw her approaching through the glass fronted partition. She knocked and walked straight in.

'They're here.'

'Right, let's get her booked in and see what she wants to do about a solicitor. If you go and get her, I'll wait by the custody desk.'

'I'm not looking forward to this.'

'If it's any consolation, Mel, neither am I, but we can't ignore the evidence.'

'I know. Sometimes it's just hard.'

'I agree. Let's get this over with, see what she has to say and then speak with the lawyers.'

They walked out together, neither saying anything, and Mel turned to go to the front desk as Ian walked towards the custody area.

Mel plastered on a smile as she walked through.

'Hi, thanks for coming.'

'I didn't think we had an option,' said Pam.

'I'll show you through and we can get things started. Have you thought about a solicitor?'

'Yes.' It was Naomi speaking now, not letting her mum answer for her.

'One has been recommended to us and she's on her way. She's just rung to say she's been held up but should be here in about five minutes. Her name is Helen White.'

'Okay. That'll speed things up a bit.' She spoke to the officer on the front desk. 'When solicitor Helen White arrives, will you buzz through to the custody suite?'

'Will do.'

Nerves showed on the faces of Pam and Naomi. They looked like rabbits caught in headlights, the fear showing on their faces. *They looked so out of place,* thought Mel. *They shouldn't be here.* Neither had been inside a police station before, and it showed, unlike some for whom this was a home from home.

As Mel led them through to the busy custody area, Ian was already waiting with the duty nurse.

'Hi, I'm Detective Inspector Ian Pearce and this is Nurse Fiona Plimmer. She's going to have a chat with Naomi and make sure she's well enough for interview. First, we'll go through all the admin and get you booked in. It's all form filling now I'm afraid.'

After the personal details were taken by the custody sergeant, she went on to ask questions about drug and alcohol use, mental health and legal representation. Naomi had never been asked questions like this. It was a whole new world.

'I'd like you to sit in as her appropriate adult,' said Ian. 'It's really to make sure she's okay and that she understands everything.'

'Isn't that what the solicitor is for?'

'Your solicitor will be here to cover the legal aspects rather than the personal aspects. Who is your solicitor?'

'Helen White,' Naomi got in quickly. It was clear she didn't want her mum speaking for her.

'She will no doubt explain everything to you.'

Mel could see Ian's expression when Naomi gave the name of her solicitor. The name meant nothing to Mel but it clearly did to Ian.

When the booking in was finished, the nurse led Naomi and Pam through to the medical room for an assessment of Naomi's fitness to be interviewed.

The custody desk phone rang and the sergeant answered, 'Custody desk. Right, I'll send someone through to collect her.'

'That's your solicitor arrived. Billy, will you go and fetch a solicitor, Helen White, from the front desk?'

Billy, one of the support workers, came through from the back and went towards the door leading to the front desk.

Mel turned to Ian. 'I take it the name Helen White is familiar?'

The custody sergeant laughed as Ian grimaced.

'She's a familiar face here all right,' said the sergeant.

'Well, are you going to fill me in?'

'She's what you might describe as a "tough cookie",' said Ian. 'She can be difficult and can't resist interrupting to try and throw you off course. I'll give her five minutes before she finds something she's not happy with and I'm betting it will be a no comment.'

Mel's experience in the Met was that solicitors fell into two categories, those who didn't open their mouths and those who knew what they were doing, wanted you to know it and couldn't keep their mouths shut. At least the second group kept you on your toes and made you think.

Billy walked into the custody suite with a woman who had short, spiky hair, a sharp suit and briefcase. She couldn't have been more than five feet tall.

'DI Pearce, nice to see you again. It's been a while.'

'Nice to see you too, Helen. This is Sergeant Mel Garvey who will lead the interview. Your client is in with the nurse who's checking on her fitness to be interviewed so we can go through disclosure while we wait for that assessment. Her mum is with her and she will act as appropriate adult.'

Mel never ceased to marvel at such false niceties between police and lawyers. The formal politeness suggested to Mel that they hated each other.

'Hello. You new here?'

'Been here six months. Worked in the Met before.'

'Welcome to Carfield. Must be very different?'

'Yes, but I suppose every force is different.'

Such a non-committal, bland response, thought Mel as she said the words.

'We have some disclosure we can give you and then answer any questions you might have.'

Mel led the way through to another room, handed over the typed disclosure, as Helen extracted her laptop, pen and legal aid forms from her briefcase. She watched the expression on Helen's face change as she got to the end of the A4 sheet. She peered over her glasses perched on the end of her nose looking every inch like a headteacher about to read the riot act.

'You are joking, aren't you? The slap, hand movement during the stabbing, the running away, and the knife are all legitimate areas for questioning. A rape is not. This is a murder inquiry, not a rape inquiry so you are not asking questions about that.'

While Mel silently agreed with her, she had to back Ian so she dived straight in before he had the chance to reply.

'We have already charged three young men. These three men look like they might be the three who raped your client. We believe the footage on the deceased's phone may have been filmed by him. If this is correct, it gives your client a motive for revenge which we want to ask her about. It's not something we intend to dwell on.'

'Too right it's not. The words you are using such as "they might", and "we believe", and "if this is correct", are all far too vague. She hasn't reported a rape, you don't have a suspect and just because it's on the deceased's phone doesn't mean it's him who filmed it. It is too farfetched and too tenuous to say this could be a motive for revenge and I am requesting that no questions about this are asked.'

'We will be asking questions. Responses are a matter for your client.'

Just then, the nurse knocked on the door and popped her head round. 'All fine for interview.'

'Thank you,' said Mel. 'I will just bring her and her mum in here and we will leave you so you can have a private consultation.'

Mel returned a minute later with Naomi and Pam. Ian stood up and said, 'We'll leave you to it. Let us know when you're ready for interview.'

Mel and Ian walked out and went through to the custody area.

'You sounded almost as if you believed what you were saying.'

'Well, I could hardly go against my boss now, could I?'

'Put like that, I suppose you couldn't. Anyway, I know it's not easy for you to accept this line of inquiry.'

'It isn't and I think she is as much a victim in all of this as Josh is, but I can see your logic and you are the boss.'

'You sound as if you mean it, Mel.'

Mel could feel things starting to thaw between them. She remembered from her geography A level about freeze thaw action leading to erosion in rocks. Her and Ian seemed go from freezing to thawing to freezing again. It was exhausting.

They sat in the custody area with a cup of machine coffee. Better than nothing but not much.

*

138

Helen sat down with Pam and Naomi in the room vacated by Ian and Mel. Every interview room was the same with a table, four chairs, recording equipment and bare walls. Naomi and Pam were sitting there looking terrified. Helen had seen all types at police stations over the years.

There were the terrified kids with angry parents, the shoplifters trying to put food on the table, the pathetic looking sex offenders and the experienced criminals who knew their rights and getting arrested was just an occupational hazard. Then there were the ones who looked like they were from another planet and didn't speak the language. Naomi and Pam fitted into that last category. Helen had to try, as best she could, to put them at their ease and get them to trust her, a complete stranger.

'Hi, I'm Helen White, solicitor, and I'll be advising and representing you today. I know this must be terrifying for you but we'll take it step by step and I'll explain everything as we go along.'

Naomi took in her friendly down to earth manner and the spiky gelled hair that must have added another inch to her five feet.

Helen made them feel a bit better as she went through what had been disclosed to her and asked if Pam knew about the footage. She was vague enough in case Pam knew nothing about the rape.

'My mum knows all about it so I've nothing to hide.'

'There will be things they haven't told me as they don't have to tell me everything. You're here as appropriate adult, Pam. Interrupt if you feel Naomi needs a break, isn't coping or is not understanding what is going on. Otherwise, don't say anything no matter how tempted you might be. Naomi has to answer the questions for herself.

'They are out of order to ask questions about you being raped. You should not answer those questions as they are irrelevant. In my opinion, it is better not to answer any questions than to answer some and not others so I advise you to give a "no comment" interview throughout. If you ended up in court, and I hope it won't come to that, the court can draw an adverse inference.

'What that means is that if you didn't answer questions in interview, and you later come up with an explanation, the court might wonder why you didn't say it at the time when you had the opportunity.'

'I've thought about this but I want to answer questions. Not about the rape though. I just want to forget it. I'm not naming anyone and I'm not making a complaint. It happened and I want to move on. I've nothing to hide about what happened with Josh though.'

'It's not about having anything to hide. It's about police evidence. You're not under arrest because they've not got enough to arrest you, and in those situations it's better not to answer their questions. It's got to be your decision though.'

'I want to answer questions.'

'That's fine. As soon as they move on to the rape, I will interrupt and say you are not answering questions. They will ask them anyway but your replies should be "no comment". Are you agreeable to that?'

'Yes.'

'Right. This won't be easy for you. If you need a break or feel panicky, just let me know. I'm here to help you. Okay?'

'As I'll ever be.'

'I'll tell them we're ready.'

Helen walked through to the custody suite where Mel and Ian were waiting.

'Ready for interview, officers.'

Helen was at her most formal. She wasn't comfortable with Naomi answering questions. A young, vulnerable girl, totally inexperienced in this world, could easily get tongue tied, confused and say something that could be misinterpreted later down the line. Still, Naomi was a bright girl so here's hoping.

In the interview room, the tensions were palpable. Helen could see Naomi's hands were sweaty and to say she looked nervous was an understatement. Pam didn't look much better so would be completely useless as an appropriate adult.

The recording was turned on, date and time given, introductions were made and Mel confirmed Naomi was not under arrest but was here voluntarily. She was then cautioned.

'You do not have to say anything. But it may harm your defence if you do not mention when questioned something you later rely on in court. Anything you do say may be given in evidence.'

'What that means, Naomi, is that you don't have to answer any questions. That is your right. However, if your case were to go to court and you then gave an explanation, which you could have given us today, the court might draw an adverse inference. That means the court might wonder why you didn't tell us now when you had the opportunity. They might wonder if you've just had time to think about it and make up some explanation. Do you understand?'

'Yes.'

Helen interjected at this point.

'After taking legal advice, my client has decided she will answer questions relevant to this murder investigation.'

Ian was surprised. With Helen White he thought it would be a no comment.

Mel began by asking general questions about Josh, about their relationship and then went on to the CCTV footage showing Mel slap Josh two weeks before Josh was stabbed. She played the footage and asked Naomi why she had slapped Josh.

'Josh owed money. They threatened to beat him up but thought they'd have a bit of fun first. They told me to slap him and if I didn't, they would. I felt I had no option. Josh knew that. We walked off together so we hadn't argued or anything.'

'Are you part of Ben Sutton's gang?'

'Of course not.'

'Can you tell us about your movements after you got home from college on the evening of the 3 February?'

'I got home about 4.30. and Josh came round at about 6.00. We had a geography project to do and we were working on it together. After about an hour, Josh said he wanted to go to Fisher as he had to see some people. He wanted me to go but I didn't want to as I didn't like it there and I just wanted to work on my project. He persuaded me to go with him. He could be really persuasive when he wanted to be.'

'What was the reason for going to Fisher?'

'They were threatening Josh. He owed them money, he couldn't pay so they were going to make him pay one way or another.'

'Can you confirm their names?'

'It was Ben Sutton. The other two are called Harley and Luke but I don't know their last names.'

'Why did he owe them money?'

'It was a drugs debt. He'd been using weed and amphetamine. I think he used cocaine sometimes as well. He became a different person. He wasn't the kind Josh I fell in love with. Because he was in debt to this gang, he had to sell drugs for them but he hadn't sold much and hadn't given them much money. He wanted more time to clear the debt.'

'I'm going to play you some footage and I want you to tell me what is happening.'

Mel pressed play and Naomi watched it.

Mel could see that Pam was itching to interrupt. Neither Pam not Naomi had seen this and must have found it shocking.

Naomi started to cry.

'Do you need a break?'

'No, I just want to get it over with.'

When they'd shown the crucial part of it, Ian started with the questions.

'You told us previously that you backed off but I get the impression you haven't backed off.'

Helen interrupted. 'That's a comment, officer, not a question.'

Here we go, thought Ian. *This could be a battle.*

'You told us in your previous interview that you backed off before Josh was attacked. Are you changing your story?'

'Any previous interview was not under caution and will not be admissible,' said Helen.

Ian could see he wasn't going to get anywhere with that point.

Mel interrupted and asked in a more conciliatory tone, 'Do you think you can remember where Josh was and where you were when you backed off?'

'I can't. It all happened so fast and it's a blur now. I know I moved back at some point or was a couple of feet away when Josh was assaulted but I really can't remember.

'They all started to lay into him. You can see them moving in to him and hitting out. I couldn't see what was in their hands as it was dark and it all happened so fast. When they started to punch him, I put my hand out to protect him.'

'How could that protect him?'

'I don't know. It was instinct. I just put my hand out to protect him in some way, maybe to help him. I wasn't thinking.'

'Did you have a knife in your hand?'

'No. Of course not. He was my boyfriend. I loved him. Why would I hurt him?'

'Did you see anyone with a knife?'

'No. It was too dark. They all lashed out at him. They all wanted to hurt him. It could have been any one of them.'

'When he started to fall you ran off. Why?'

'I don't really know. I was frightened. I panicked. I didn't think he'd been seriously hurt and I just wanted to get away from there. I didn't know if I would be next. I got the bus home and went straight to bed. I didn't think Josh had been seriously hurt.

'The next morning it was on TV that Josh had died. I couldn't believe it. I kept thinking that if I'd stayed I could have done something. I will never forgive myself for not calling an ambulance.'

'No-one could have helped him, Naomi,' said Ian.

Mel thought he looked pained. You had to be made of stone not to be moved by Naomi.

Mel moved on to the knife that was found in Naomi's shed.

'It has been confirmed that this is the likely murder weapon. It has Josh's blood on it and it's the right type and length of knife. What was it doing in your shed?

'I've no idea. There is no lock on the garden gate and most of the time the shed isn't locked so anyone could have put it in there.'

Helen interrupted. 'Will you confirm there are no fingerprints or fibres on the knife linked to my client?'

'That's correct but it was found on her property.'

'And she has explained that it could have been put there by anyone.'

'I'll move on to texts and a voice recording on your phone. There's a text asking to meet you from an unidentified number and there is a voice recording on your phone. Tell us about that.'

'I received a text asking to meet. You've got screenshots of that. I assumed it was from Sutton but didn't know for certain. I met him at the end of my road. It was Sutton. He was telling me to keep my mouth shut or blame Price. I recorded it. I gave you that recording.'

'We are unable to identify the phone it was sent from and the recording is muffled so it's not clear who it is. We only have your word for it that this meeting took place.'

'That's not a question, officer, it's an observation. Stick to questions please.'

'Very well. Are you sure you met up with Ben Sutton and it's his voice on your phone recording?'

'Positive.'

The last bit Mel had to ask her about was the part she dreaded.

'I want to move on now to a video we found on Josh's phone. I'm not going to play this but it shows you being raped by three men whose faces cannot be clearly seen. Are they Ben Sutton, Harley Brown and Luke Price?'

Helen interrupted. 'At the outset of this interview, I told you my client would answer questions relevant to a murder investigation. This line of questioning is not relevant and my client will not be answering any irrelevant questions you might ask.'

'Is it Ben Sutton, Harley Brown and Luke Price?'

'No comment.'

'Is it Josh filming you?'

'No comment.'

'You're pleading with him not to make you. Was he giving these three permission to rape you?'

'No comment.'

'Did this make you angry with Josh?'

'No comment.'

'Did it make you want to stab Josh?'

'No comment.'

'Did you stab Josh and then hide the knife in your shed?'

'No comment.'

'I've no more questions, Naomi. Is there anything you'd like to add, Ian?'

'No, thanks. You've covered everything.'

'We will leave you here for a few minutes while we have a word with the custody sergeant. Can I get you a drink while you're waiting?'

'No thanks, DI Pearce. My client is keen to leave as soon as possible.'

At the custody desk, Mel gave the sergeant a brief summary of interview for the custody record and proposed to bail Naomi while they spoke with the CPS.

'Fine. How long do you need?'

Mel looked at Ian. 'What do you think?'

'Seven days should do it.'

'Okay. Back here next Monday at 4.00.'

Mel went to get Naomi, Pam and Helen from the interview room and brought them out to the custody desk while the sergeant went through the formalities about returning the following week.

After Mel showed them out, she came back to speak with Ian.

'What do you think?'

'It's all plausible but the murder weapon in her shed makes a charge more likely. I'll see if I can get hold of Ged now and we'll take it from there. You go home and we'll have a chat in the morning. Let the lawyers decide whether or not to charge her.'

Chapter 32

She couldn't believe what had just happened. This can't be happening to her.

Being interviewed at the police station like a criminal. It was unreal. It was like watching someone else in a film, an out of body experience.

She felt for her mum and dad. They haven't done anything to deserve all this trouble at their doorstep. They must be going through hell but were trying to stay calm and supportive for her.

Everything had gone to shit.

And what must Josh's parents think? Did they even know she was being interviewed as a suspect?

Once upon a time, she thought the worst thing that could happen to her was getting pregnant or not getting her grades for university but that paled into insignificance now. She was going through the very worst of it.

Josh getting involved with drugs and those scumbags had led to her rape and to his death. The connection was clear.

And now it was possible she might be charged with his murder along with the others.

Surely they wouldn't do that, they'd see sense. They'd charged the ones who were responsible for this miserable situation. Why drag her into it?

She still had the possibility of university. Were they going to take that from her as well as everything else?

She couldn't think of it, didn't want to face up to what could happen.

She'd been through the "what ifs" over Josh's death. What if they charged her?

It was unthinkable.

They would see sense.

They had to.

She couldn't begin to think of the alternative.

At what might happen if they charged her.

Chapter 33

You're not supposed to bury your child.

It was all wrong.

Anna sat by the window waiting for the hearse and funeral car to arrive, willing them to arrive so it could all be over but not wanting them to arrive because then there could be no funeral for Josh, as if they could turn the clock back and it hadn't happened.

And then it was outside.

The black cars, the black clouds and the black day.

It was like a punch to the gut when she saw it.

She couldn't do this, didn't want to do this, wanted it to go away.

Greg helped her up out of the chair, on with her coat and she was guided outside like an unwilling child. She was on automatic pilot.

She just stood there looking at the cars, the neighbours who had gathered, the bamboo coffin on display.

This can't be happening.

Bamboo seemed right, eco-friendly. Josh would have approved.

How can she think eco-friendly for her son's coffin? There was nothing friendly about it.

His name written in blue and white flowers on both sides, the colours for Leeds United, the team he loved.

A wreath of white carnations on the top. It was always white for a child. They asked her if she wanted a white coffin. How can you be expected to choose a coffin colour for your son?

She just stared. It was unreal. She was angry.

It shouldn't be happening.

'I can't do it. I can't go. I just can't. I'm not doing it.'

'You've got to, love. For Josh. You can't not go to our son's funeral.'

She clung on to Greg and wept like she'd never stop; the tears streaming down her face mixing with the snot dripping from her nose. She couldn't go. It couldn't be real.

But it was real now. This was final. Josh was no more and they were burying him, burying her baby.

Not burying but burning.

There had been asked if they wanted burial or cremation.

How can you choose that for your baby? What difference did it make? He was gone.

The funeral director held the car door open with the expectation that she would get in.

Her legs were jelly and wouldn't carry her.

She looked at Greg, unable to speak, wide eyes pleading.

'Come on, love. You can do it.'

She sniffed, wiping her nose and Greg guided her into her seat where she sat like a crumpled mess. Kit climbed in after her followed by Anna's parents and finally Greg. He got in and sat by Anna, holding her hand, joined in their grief over the loss of Josh.

They were all silent. What was there to say?

It was just three miles to the crematorium; a journey that seemed to last an eternity but, at the same time, went too quickly.

At the traffic lights before the turn off into the crematorium, she saw a young man making the sign of the cross. She wanted to scream at him that Josh wasn't religious. What's the point? Maybe she could cope better if she was religious. She could think of Josh in heaven.

If only she could think like that it might give her comfort but she didn't believe in all that stuff and neither did Josh. It would mean she had to forgive his killers and she wasn't going to do that.

When the car stopped, the funeral director got out, opened the door and helped her out of her seat as if she was elderly and infirm.

They took Josh's coffin out of the hearse and Greg, along with Anna's dad, two school friends and the funeral directors, put the coffin on their shoulders and walked into the packed hall.

It was all happening in slow motion.

She followed the coffin in, walking with Kit and her mum, all clinging to each other, holding each other up so they didn't collapse.

There was something about the sight of the coffin that made it so final, made her want to scream.

How can she be walking behind her son's coffin? It's not real. She was being guided to her seat on the front row but didn't know what was happening.

They placed him on the plinth and the funeral director stood a photograph of Josh on top of the coffin. It was taken last year when they did the college photos. He looked so happy, fuller in the face. She hadn't noticed he'd lost weight. What sort of a mother was she not to notice?

She was handed the pamphlet for the order of service. She couldn't do anything so things were being done to her as if she was some sort of invalid.

The celebrant began talking about Josh. She hadn't known him but her and Greg had talked to her about Josh so she could say the right things.

Greg spoke about Josh, about his funny side, about the good times they'd had as a family. It was almost like a father of the groom speech, all happy memories and good times.

No more.

Anna couldn't do a eulogy. She knew she wouldn't be able to hold it together, that the acting would be too much for her.

Josh's head of year and one of his friends spoke, the friend not able to get to the end of his written speech before breaking down.

Anna had asked Naomi if she wanted to say a few words but she couldn't. Anna understood that. Naomi was in pain but she was young, would move on, would get over it. Anna couldn't move on.

At the end of the service, Anna went up to the coffin, to touch it, to say her final goodbye to Josh still not believing this was happening. She wanted everyone gone so it would be just her and Josh, so she could open it and hold him.

But she knew it wasn't him inside that coffin. He was gone.

His smell had gone, his body had gone, his very being had gone. Only memories left.

Cling to the good times you've had together, the special memories, someone had said. She didn't know who. There were so many platitudes. Sometimes she just wanted to punch someone who said the wrong thing, wrong in her eyes.

The red curtains closed and Josh disappeared as they played the Robert Burns song, *My love is like a Red Red Rose*.

And she would love him for ever more or till all the seas gang dry as the song said.

Anna, Greg and Kit stayed for a few minutes and, holding hands, walked out together; a family of three now, not four.

And then they were at the golf course for the funeral tea.

How had that happened? She couldn't even remember getting there.

People she didn't know came up to her, hugged her, said nice things, said how sorry they were and to let them know if she needed anything.

All she needed was Josh back but they couldn't do that, could they?

She wanted them all to disappear.

Naomi came to sit with her and held her hand, both of them with tears streaming down their faces.

'I wish I could turn the clock back and tell you what was happening.'

'I wish that too but it's no good wishing, is it?'

There were no more words, just silence, so they sat just holding hands.

There was nothing more anyone could say.

Anna got through the day and they walked the short distance home.

The evenings had started to get lighter and the daffodils were coming up.

How can things be coming alive when Josh was dead?

It was all wrong.

She hated the people who said inane things to her, hated the flowers poking their heads above ground as if nothing had happened.

But most of all she hated his killers. She now got it why people wanted to kill in return, wanted revenge, an eye for an eye.

It wasn't her, wasn't what she thought.

But it was what she felt.

Anna felt as if all of nature should stop too, that it was somehow wrong for flowers to come alive when Josh was no more.

For the first time, she recognised the days and months of nothingness stretching out in front of her.

Chapter 34

It was gone 8.00 when Ian walked through the front door carrying the Chinese takeaway. Jack said he'd been well enough to go into school that morning and was being extremely well behaved and polite. Nothing like a bit of contrition when it came to errant teenagers.

'Okay, Jack. Can you get the plates and cutlery out? Spring rolls and chicken chow Mein as requested. Sorry, I didn't get back in time to cook us something.'

'You're cooking or a Chinese takeaway? No contest.'

'Cheeky monkey. What have you been up to today?'

'Timetable for mock exams was given out so it's head down for revision. Not much else today.'

'Did you see Davy?'

'Yeah.'

'And did you talk about what happened?'

'A bit. I don't want to think about it.'

'I know you don't but there's some bad stuff out there and we need to stop the supply before someone becomes seriously ill with it. I need names, Jack.'

'I know but I'm scared.'

'Your name might not come into it. I can't guarantee it but if you tell me who supplied you we can do a surveillance operation and hopefully catch them that way.'

'Let me think about it and speak to Davy tomorrow.'

'Okay. Tuck in now before this goes cold.'

*

Ian dropped Jack off at school and didn't get into the office till 9.00. The team was much smaller now as some had been allocated other investigations. As he walked in, he looked at them, each with their heads down, working away, dotting the i's and crossing the t's, making sure the defence couldn't say they'd messed up.

He walked into the small kitchen next to the open plan office to make a cup of tea and Mel joined him. She looked more alert than he did, that was for sure.

'Did you manage to speak to Ged last night?'

'Yes. I gave him an outline of the new forensics and CCTV footage and gave him a summary of Naomi's interview. He was going to speak to Maria and see where that took us. I'll give him a ring now and see if he's got anywhere. You okay?'

'I'm not sure what to make of it all. I think the slap and the knife makes Naomi a potential suspect but I just don't see it. We've all been around for a while and I know we can get surprised by people who do things we wouldn't expect but I don't see Naomi killing Josh. I just hope she's not charged.'

'I tend to agree with you even though you think I've gone down the wrong path. For me it's the rape. If it's Josh filming it, and she's begging him to make it stop, then stabbing him seems logical. I might be wrong but that's my take on it. The other evidence can be explained away. We're not going to agree on the evidence but we seem to be agreeing that, when it comes down to it, we don't think Naomi is involved. She doesn't seem to have it in her.'

'Bloody hell, we're almost on the same page.'

'It's called team work, Sergeant Garvey.'

She smiled at him and said, 'Whatever you say, Boss.'

He could feel the electricity between them just as Prita walked in to put the kettle on.

'Right, I'll ring Ged and let you know how I get on.'

As Prita watched Ian walk over to his office, she turned to Mel.

'What's going on between you two?'

'Nothing. Why?'

'I could almost see the sparks between you. There's definitely an attraction there and I'd say it's mutual.'

'Rubbish.'

'Are you trying to convince me or yourself?'

'I'm not trying to convince anyone. I don't fancy him and he doesn't fancy me.'

'Have it your own way but I'd say it's "watch this space".'

Mel just raised an eyebrow and took her tea back to her desk. She knew Prita was right in one respect. She did quite fancy Ian but there was no way she was going there.

*

Ian took his tea into his office telling himself he must ring Tricia. He'd left her so abruptly and not been in touch since. She'd texted him and he hadn't even replied. He wondered what made him think of Tricia now. *Right*, he thought, *ring Ged.*

'Hi, Ged. Did you manage to speak to Maria?'

'You must be telepathic. I was just about to ring you.'

'Oh yeah. And since when does anyone at the CPS return phone calls.'

'That's just a vicious rumour. And yes, I did speak to her. She's suggesting a conference here at 2.00 this afternoon if you can make it.'

'I can. Not sure about Mel, John and Prita. Do you need all of us?'

'Maybe just Mel as she's had the most contact with Naomi.'

'Okay. See you later.'

Ian popped his head around his office door and asked Mel, John and Prita to come in.

'I've just spoken to Ged and he's suggested a conference with Maria this afternoon to discuss the evidence against Naomi. He's suggested me and Mel as Mel has had most dealings with Naomi. No need to drag everyone over to Leeds.'

'Is it looking likely they'll want her charged?' John asked.

'Don't know yet. I suppose we'll be thrashing that out this afternoon. Will let you know how it goes.'

As they walked back to their desks, Prita turned to Mel. 'There's your chance to get him all on your own,' and she smiled in that wicked way she has. Some people have a dirty laugh but Prita had a dirty smile.

'You're incorrigible. Don't you ever give up?'

'Not if I can help it. I want a blow by blow account.'

*

Mel and Ian went for the 1.30 train and Ian suggested he nip over and get a couple of teas for the journey.

Mel laughed.

'I didn't think suggesting a tea was that funny.'

'Sorry, I was just laughing at something Prita said. Yes, a tea would be great.'

As he went over to get the teas, Mel imagined the conversation with Prita. 'Prita, it was so exciting. He got me a carry out tea for the train.'

She was still smiling to herself when Ian returned.

'Whatever Prita said has certainly amused you. Do you want to share it?'

'It wasn't that funny. You had to be there.'

They walked down the platform and boarded the train with time to spare. It wasn't that busy so they managed to get a table seat to themselves.

The twenty minute journey seemed to be over in no time as they talked about everything and yet nothing in particular. There were no awkward silences this time.

As they were signing in at CPS reception, Ged came out to meet them.

'Great timing. Maria and Sebastian have just arrived.'

He led them down the corridor and into the conference room.

'Hi, Ian, Mel. Grab a drink and biscuits and we'll make a start.'

Maria stood in front of the white board and divided it into two columns with headings—reasons for charging Naomi and reasons against charging Naomi.

'Let's start with reasons for charging.'

They all contributed apart from Mel.

The list was obvious.

Murder weapon found in her shed;

Arm lashes out to spot where josh stabbed;

Slap to Josh;

Ran off instead of staying with him;

Didn't call for help;

Initially said she's backed off but CCTV shows that was not the case;

Rape provides motive.

'Mel, you've not said anything. Is there a reason for that?'

'I don't think any of that is a sound enough reason for charging her. We've got our three suspects. She's a witness. I think charging her is just going to confuse the case. If we charge her we can't use her as a witness. What's her role in all of this? It doesn't make sense.'

'Okay, well let's move on to the reasons for not charging her.'

The rape makes her a victim of the gang as much as Josh;

Evidence on her phone that she's been threatened by Sutton;

Running away and not calling for help can be explained by panic;

She loved him and planned to go to university with him;

The knife can be explained as the shed was not locked;

You can't see where her hand goes to and she could equally be helping him;

Good character.

'If we charge her, we lose her as a witness and we're saying she's in on it with the other three so the evidence about Sutton intimidating and threatening her goes out the window. We can't really say he's threatening a witness and also say she's in on it with him. What about her clothing? Has it been sent off for forensics?'

'Yes, but it will take a while so we probably have to make a decision without that. In any event, she was in a relationship with Josh so fibre transfers are likely and, as she was close to him, blood is also possible.'

'Okay. Let's assume her clothing comes back clean so there are no forensics. We've still got the other pros and cons.'

Emotions were high and the discussion was heated. Maria listened to everyone but it was her call.

'Okay we're starting to go round in circles now. I doubt a judge will allow the rape to be evidence. We might say it's relevant to motive but that's just a hypothesis. We would, of course, have a go at getting it in evidence. The murder weapon, her slapping him, running away, the arm coming out to the right part of Josh's body just before he falls, not calling for help, lying about backing off are all reasons for charging her.'

'But they're all things that can be explained away.'

'I agree they could be but they need to be explained to a jury as they mount up and, together, provide a case against her. I'm sorry but the evidence points to charging her. Unusually though, I think she could be bailed out of the area which should allow her to continue at college. I understand she's got grandparents in Bradford so maybe she could go there and carry on with college.'

'I doubt she'd be in a fit state to carry on.'

'Maybe, maybe not, but we can't ignore the evidence. I'm not saying I want to do this. I'm saying it's what the evidence points to and that leaves us with no choice.'

*

As they walked out of the CPS offices, Mel and Ian were far more subdued than they had been on the way in.

'Fancy grabbing a quick drink?' Ian asked. 'I think we could do with one after that.'

'Good idea. Just one or I could get maudlin.'

'You're picking up our Yorkshire sayings.'

'To be expected. Prita took me to a bar by the station if you fancy that.'

'Perfect.'

They crossed the road and found the bar. Mel hadn't noticed the intimate atmosphere and low lighting when she was with Prita but was acutely aware of it now.

'You got the teas so I'll get these.'

'Sounds like I got the best deal. I'll have a Peroni if they've got it.'

Mel came back with a bottle of Peroni and a glass of white wine.

'Cheers. Will you break the news to her?'

'I'll go tomorrow. It'll be tough.'

'I know. Right, let's talk about something else. Have you any holidays booked?'

Mel laughed. 'It's like being at the hairdressers. Next, you'll be asking me if I'm going out tonight.'

'Sorry. I'll start again. Are you glad you made the move up here?'

'Yes. It's not been easy relocating and leaving behind a life but it was the right thing to do.'

'Why did you, if you don't mind me asking?'

Mel hesitated. Should she say anything?

'A problem with sexual harassment from a superior officer and an unsupportive hierarchy left me with no option if I wanted to continue in the police.'

'I'm sorry. It happens, I know. I keep thinking it's getting better for women and then there's another complaint or another bloke who's making comments that are just unbelievable. You might think we're all unreconstructed Neanderthals in Yorkshire but it's not the case. Might not always get it right in the police but some of us try.'

'Thanks. I appreciate you saying that.'

'I appreciate you telling me. Did you think you were going to get the same treatment from me?'

'Of course not.'

'Be honest.'

'Okay. I suppose I was just wary and wanted to keep my distance if I'm honest.'

'I had noticed. You keeping you're distance I mean. We're not all the same.'

'I didn't mean to keep my distance. I suppose I'm just a bit reserved. You're all so friendly here that it was difficult to decide if it was friendliness or if there was another agenda.'

'No agendas. It's just our Yorkshire charm.'

Mel looked at him and smiled.

Ian held her look and smiled back, neither of them saying anything.

Part of Mel was wishing he did have an agenda, although she was still telling herself she wouldn't go there. Or would she? Lovely eyes, fit body, seems sensitive, but he's her boss so no chance.

'Right, drink up, I need to get back for Jack. It was a takeaway last night and I don't want him getting used to that. Is the offer of help with maths still on the table as he's starting with his mock GCSEs next week?'

'Of course. Any time. Just give me a shout as I don't have much on.'

Now she worried that she sounded desperate and lonely.

She downed the last of the wine, put on her coat and they walked back to the train station, just two colleagues out for a companionable drink after a difficult work meeting.

Who was she kidding?

*

'Hi, Jack. Thought I'd do a chilli tonight. Sound okay?'

'Great. I'm just doing some maths revision.'

'I've got a colleague who says she's a bit of a whizz with maths and has offered to help if you need it.'

'Yes, I need it. The revision classes aren't up to much so it would help. I've also thought about what you said and had a chat with Davy. We want our names staying out of this but the person who's supplying the school is called Frankie Greenhalgh.'

'Thanks. I know that wasn't easy. Is he at the school every day?'

'Tends to be Friday and he's a she.'

Ian was taken aback. He didn't expect a girl.

'Okay. I need a description but first I'd better get on with the cooking.'

Chapter 35

Mel was in the office by 8.00. She knew Ian was in as she'd seen his Audi in the car park. She half acknowledged she was quite looking forward to seeing him. Maybe it was because he'd now admitted he couldn't really see Naomi as a perpetrator.

Tea first. She walked into the kitchen and Ian was already there.

'Hi, kettle's just boiled. Tea or coffee?'

'It's okay, I'll make it. I'm still wondering what to say to Naomi.'

She'd been going over it in her head. What is the kindest way to tell a seventeen-year-old she's being charged with murder?

'Do you want to talk about it before you ring her?'

'I think I'm better just getting on with it but will catch up with you later.'

'Okay. If you do want to run anything by me just give me a shout.'

'Will do.'

As she was making her cup of tea, she was focussing on dunking the tea bag in and out and thinking again about the words she would use. None of them made it any easier.

Right. Make that call.

She spoke to Pam as Naomi had left for college. As she was speaking, she was focussing on her post it notes, pens, cup stains and general detritus on her desk. She hadn't noticed all this crap before but it suddenly held her complete attention. Or was it just easier to keep your eyes occupied when your brain was somewhere else.

Pam couldn't believe what she was hearing.

'My daughter has been raped, could have been murdered along with Josh, is a victim in all of this and now you want to charge her with Josh's murder. You have got to be joking.'

'I'm sorry. It wasn't my decision. She will be bailed so she can finish her A levels and we thought she could live out of the area at her grandparents so she'd be safe.'

'Well, that makes it alright then, doesn't it? Do you really imagine she could concentrate on A levels when she's facing a murder charge? Are you completely stupid?'

Mel thought Pam's anger was justified and couldn't blame her for shouting at her. Let her get it out. What would she feel if it was her daughter? She couldn't imagine having kids in this job but maybe she just hadn't met the right person. Or maybe she wanted a career and didn't feel she was one of these superwomen who could have kids and career.

She didn't think superwomen existed anyway. It was an image to make other women feel shit about themselves.

Pam ranted and Mel let her. Eventually, they agreed Naomi would come in at 5.00. Pam would try and get the solicitor there as well, although solicitors didn't usually turn up for someone to be charged. She might for a murder involving a teenage suspect. There was no way she was going to arrest Naomi to bring her in for charge. At least she had some discretion over that.

When she put the phone down, she went over to Ian's office, knocked on the door, walked in and plonked herself down in front of him. She hadn't bothered with makeup and her hair was tied back in a ponytail with strands escaping over her face.

'You look exhausted and it's only 9.00.' He looked at her in a way which also managed to convey his own emotions. A look can say it all.

'I feel it. Emotions can get you that way. Even for hardened Met officers.'

'We all get involved whether we like it or not. Sometimes you just can't help it.'

'I'm not arresting her. She's coming in voluntarily at 5.00. We can bail her to her grandparents and she can carry on at college. Her courses have nearly finished anyway and it's just revision so she doesn't have to come in to Carfield until exams unless she wants to go to the odd revision class.'

'Talking of which, Jack would really appreciate your help with his maths. Fancy coming round tonight to help with homework and I'll cook dinner in return?'

'Best offer I've had in ages. Give me your address and I'll come round after Naomi's charge if that suits.'

'Great. I'll text it to you now. Jack will be pleased. He knows how useless I am.'

'Okay, see you later.'

*

Ian couldn't help but feel really pleased she was coming over tonight. Why should he feel pleased about getting someone to help with Jack's homework? Best not question that too far. He did enjoy her company but after what she'd told him about her experience in the Met, he knew he'd have to steer clear. Didn't want her thinking he was another misogynistic boss.

But what should he cook? It would seem a bit keen if he asked her.

Stick to pasta. You can never go wrong with that.

Right. Speak to DI Martha Holroyd about the drugs at Jack's school.

He rang her and filled her in about what had happened.

'Why wasn't it reported?'

'They didn't want to and were saying nothing but we've got a name now. It's obvious there's some bad stuff doing the rounds.'

'I'm gangs, Ian. How do we know its gangs and not major crime?'

'We don't but I'm giving you the option. It's not likely to be someone who's gone solo is it?'

'No. Okay, I'll put someone on it and keep you updated.'

'Thanks.'

Now Tricia. She might have given up on him so he'd start with a text and see where he got.

"Hi, Tricia. Work and home life been difficult. Fancy a meal or drink sometime?"

She picked it up and he could see the bubbles appear as she was about to reply. Then they disappeared. No bubbles and no reply. Not that he deserved anything else.

*

Bang on 5.00, Mel got the call from the front desk that Naomi, Pam and solicitor had arrived.

She rang through to Ian to let him know.

'Do you want to be in on the charge?'

'Only if you want me to be.'

'I think I'd like your support on this one. Call me a wimp but it's a hard one.'

'You're anything but a wimp. I'll join you in the custody suite.'

Mel walked down the corridor, swiped her pass to get her into the reception area and greeted Naomi, Pam and the solicitor.

'Sergeant Garvey, I have to say I'm surprised at this decision. Naomi is a victim here. She should not be treated as a suspect.'

'I respect your point of view, Ms White, but the decision has been made by prosecution lead counsel looking at all the evidence so it's out of my hands. I'm sorry.'

'Not as sorry as we are,' added Pam.

Naomi stood there saying nothing.

'Let's go through and get this over with as quickly as possible.'

Mel led the way down the corridor and into the custody suite. Ian was already there.

Helen White tried again.

'I was telling your colleague how surprised I am by this decision to charge Naomi.'

'It's out of our hands, Ms White. We are part of the team but the decisions are made by the lawyers.'

'Just what Sergeant Garvey said. Blame someone else.'

Ian decided not to engage in this. It was pointless. He understood their anger even though he knew Helen White's firm would make a tidy sum from a murder case.

Mel guided them over to the custody desk and the custody sergeant read out the charge of murder then asked Naomi if she had anything to say.

The reality hit home when she heard the charge being read to her. They believed she murdered Josh. She couldn't speak. Her eyes widened as she looked at the custody sergeant. She was expecting her to say something or do something but what?

She just stared, shock taking over and started to hyperventilate.

'I can't breathe,' she managed to say. She collapsed on to the floor gasping for breath, sobbing uncontrollably as she writhed on the floor. Her skirt was hitched up showing her knickers, all dignity gone out of the widow as she wailed and gasped for breath at the same time.

Pam fell to her knees, crying. 'Naomi, baby, it'll be okay. Just breathe, breathe.'

The custody staff just stood and stared before the custody sergeant came to her senses, ran out from behind the desk and called for the first aider.

'Now, not tomorrow,' she shouted, kneeling beside Naomi, watching her shock and pain.

A first aider ran through with a paper bag which she held over Naomi's mouth, getting her to take deep breaths.

'That's it. Concentrate on each breath. In and hold then out slowly.'

Naomi was struggling with the instructions and Pam was shouting at her.

'Call an ambulance.'

'It's ok. She's starting to breathe more slowly. That's it, Naomi, in and hold then out as slow as you can. Good. And again. Good girl, you've got it.'

Naomi gradually started to calm down and Pam pulled down her skirt, feeling she had to do something to help her but incapable of thinking straight. It was the only useful thing she could think of.

Naomi lay on the floor, crying like she'd never stop, just calling for her mum over and over again.

It reminded Ian of the accounts he'd read about boys being killed in war zones and their last words were calling out for their mums.

Pam just held her and rocked her back and forth like you'd do a distressed baby, both of them crying uncontrollably.

The custody suite was silent. Everyone who saw this was distressed. Ian felt you couldn't not be moved watching Naomi on the floor, writhing and shocked, clearly in distress, calling for her mum.

The first aider sat her on a bench and then went to get her a cup of water. Naomi gradually calmed down but looked shattered. The girl who was starting to look confident again was gone and in her place was a wreck.

'Still think you've made the right call, DI Pearce, because I bloody well don't,' said Helen White, fury written all over her face.

He couldn't reply and was starting to think they'd got it the wrong.

The custody sergeant, who'd been in that job for what seemed like forever, started to explain the procedure to Naomi. It was her job after all and the last thing she needed was some smart defence lawyer saying nothing had been explained to Naomi. She sat beside her on the bench and explained that she needed to go to Leeds Magistrates' Court in the morning and that she must live at her grandparents' address but that was the only bail condition and it was for her own safety.

Ian had never seen a whole custody suite look so distressed at someone being charged. If he was religious, he'd be praying they'd got it right, that they weren't fucking up a young girl's life.

The custody sergeant gave the paperwork, detailing the bail conditions and court date, to Naomi and a copy to Helen White who just stared at Mel.

'So much for sisterhood,' said Helen.

'I'm really sorry,' Mel said again. No-one acknowledged her.

*

Mel arrived at Ian's house just after 6.30. Nice house, nice area, nice. No character. Couldn't say much more about these executive type detached houses.

She parked her Fiesta behind Ian's Audi and was just about to ring the bell when the door opened to Ian in joggers and T-shirt. She could smell the garlic and was suddenly very hungry. You couldn't smell onion and garlic and not feel hungry.

'Hi. Let me take you through to Jack while I carry on in the kitchen. Its spaghetti bolognaise because it's one of the few things I do well. Hungry?'

'Starving all of a sudden.'

'I'll get some garlic bread to keep you going. Jack, Mel's here,' he shouted up to Jack who bounced down the stairs and greeted her with a big grin.

'Hello, Jack, I'm Mel.'

She took him in. Tall like his dad with the same blue eyes and lovely smile but gangly and hadn't grown into his height yet.

'I hope you're good at finding the values in equations as I'm hopeless.'

'I think I can remember how to do that so let's have a look.'

'I've got some past papers I've been working on so maybe we can start there.'

'Sounds like a plan.'

He led her over to the dining room table. She took it all in. Table seats eight so must be into entertaining. Or was. Abstract art on the walls and a wonderful brightly painted sculpture of two middle aged women in aprons chatting over a garden wall. It conjured up washing lines and run down terraces but was full of laughter and joy. She didn't have him down as the arty type.

A couple of school photos of Jack and one of a younger Ian, Jack aged about three with a woman who must be the ex-wife. Short, severe haircut not many women can carry off but looked good. They looked happy but doesn't everyone in photos. Just have to look at Facebook and Instagram. No-one posts a photo of themselves looking miserable.

'I see you're prepared as she took in the exam papers and notebooks.'

Jack laughed. 'Thought I'd better try to give a good impression or you might not want to help again.'

Jack wasn't what she'd expected. She wasn't sure what she did expect. The moody teenager? Sullen, uncommunicative? He was quite charming really and had a sense of humour even when it came to finding the value of x.

Ian brought in the garlic bread, fizzy water and left them to it.

After about an hour of working their way through equations, Ian came in with the bowl of spaghetti and bolognaise sauce.

'Right, help yourselves. Drinks?'

'Just water for me,' said Mel.

'You should have got a taxi so you could have had a glass of wine.'

'Didn't think but could probably do with an early sober night anyway.'

'That's what dad says every night but it never happens.'

'Cheeky.'

Just then, Ian's phone rang. He looked at it and saw it was Tricia. He couldn't not answer it.

'Hi,' he said as he got up and walked towards the kitchen.

'Must be dad's hot date. He had to cut the last date short, my fault, but she must be keen.'

Mel suddenly felt jealous. She couldn't really understand it and the feelings took her by surprise.

Ian came back in, sat down and said, 'Well, start eating before it gets cold.'

'Was that the date, Dad?'

Ian felt embarrassed but wasn't sure why.

'Never you mind, nosey. Just eat. How was the maths?'

'I'm getting the hang of these equations. It's been really helpful. Can you come again, Mel?'

'I'm sure I can if you need me but you're better than you think. It's all about confidence.'

'You just make it easy unlike my misery guts old maths teacher.'

'Well, thanks for the compliment and of course I will help you.'

'Great. Any time you're free. I'm in doing revision now so come round when you want to do the maths papers with me.'

'Well, there's an invitation I can't resist.'

All of a sudden the prospect seemed less appealing to Mel.

They chatted over dinner and Mel declined the offer of coffee so she could get away.

Ian walked to the door with her.

'Thanks for coming round. I really appreciate it and Jack does too. I can tell you've made an impression on him.'

Shit, did that come out wrong, he wondered.

'It's fine, any time. See you tomorrow.'

He watched her walk to her car, get in and drive off. He stayed watching in the doorway until she'd disappeared round the corner and then went back to join Jack in the dining room.

'She's nice and explained things really simply.'

'I'm glad it was useful.'

'So, when's the next hot date.'

'If you must know it's Saturday so let's hope it doesn't get interrupted this time.'

'Not by me. I'm staying in to revise.'

Ian couldn't help wishing Tricia had rung at a different time. He wasn't sure why. He liked Tricia, fancied her, thought she was gorgeous, sparky, sexy. So why keep thinking about Mel?

Chapter 36

Naomi got to the front of Leeds Magistrates' Court and felt her stomach churning. She looked up at the red brick façade and the groups of lads messing around outside like they were having a day out. They all looked like this was nothing to them. Most seemed to be wearing hoodies, joggers and scruffy trainers like it was the court uniform. Some of them were showing off about what they were up for and how their brief would get them off.

She had never felt so out of place.

She was dressed smartly in jacket, skirt and blouse and looked more like a paralegal than a defendant. She walked up the steps and in through the double doors to the security desk. She looked at the security guard not knowing what to do.

'Put your bag here, love, everything out of your pockets and into the tray.'

She put her bag on the table, took the mints out of her pocket and was told to walk through the scanner.

It was like being at the airport.

She walked through and it beeped.

'You must have something in your pocket, love. Keys, something metal, phone? Walk back through.'

She did as she was told and remembered her house key was in her inside pocket. She took it out and put it in the tray then walked through again. No beeping.

'That's it, love. I'll just need to search your bag.'

He took out a bottle of water.

'Is this water?'

Was he serious?

'Yes.'

'That's fine. I just need you to take a drink. Make sure it's nothing else.'

She unscrewed the top and took a sip.

'That's fine, love. Here's your bag.'

By this time, the queue had grown longer. It looked like everyone else knew what they were doing. Some people in suits just showed their phones and walked straight through. *The privileged few*, she thought.

When she and Pam were through security, she saw Helen in the distance and made a beeline for the familiar face in the unfamiliar place.

'Hello. Let's get a conference room and I can go through everything with you.'

Naomi and Pam meekly followed her along the corridor and, after trying lots of doors which were either locked or rooms were occupied, they managed to find an empty one.

Conference room suggested something grand rather that a scruffy, poky meeting room with little privacy to talk.

'Take a seat and let me explain what will happen.'

They all sat round a table that had seen better days and on chairs that had holes in them.

'We will go into court together. Your mum can sit with you and all you will need to do is confirm your name. Leave the talking to me. It will be a short hearing. Bail has been agreed and you will continue to stay at your grandparents' house. A date will be given for your first Crown Court appearance which will be in about four weeks.

'Because of your age, your name will not be reported but there will be a report to say a seventeen-year-old woman has been charged and will appear at Crown Court. I want you to stay here until we're ready to go in. I'll check that now and then come and get you. Okay?'

Naomi just nodded. She was lost for words. Should she have questions? She didn't know what to ask. She sat there with Pam staring at the table where someone had scraped their initials, PB. All she could think of was that PB was the chemical symbol for lead. She hadn't even liked chemistry.

'It will be fine,' said Pam. 'You shouldn't even be here. It's ridiculous. You're not like the others here.'

Naomi couldn't even reply. It was just too surreal.

Helen came in, 'Right, we're on.'

They followed her out of the room, like lambs to the slaughter, and into a larger room which must be the court. Naomi thought it didn't look like a court on the TV.

There were three people sat at the front, in seats that were slightly raised, and a woman sat in front, a bit below them. Helen led Pam and Naomi into the seats facing the three magistrates and she sat behind them at one end of a bench. A man sat at the other end of the bench. When everyone was seated, the woman in front of the magistrates asked Naomi to confirm her name.

'Naomi Edwards,' came the squeak from Naomi.

The man at the other end of the bench, who Naomi decided was the prosecutor, stood up and started speaking. Helen then got up to speak but Naomi didn't really understand what they were talking about. Bail was mentioned, dates were mentioned and other stuff that was meaningless.

She was asked to stand up and the woman magistrate was telling her when she had to go to Crown Court and that she had to live at her grandparents but could go into Carfield for her exams. Those were the only things she heard that made sense and Helen then ushered her out.

'Let's get another room and we can have a chat about what's happening.'

There were fewer people around now and they found a room easily.

'I know that didn't make a lot of sense. It's frightening and completely alien to you. I know that and am here for you. Ring me anytime. All you need to take from that hearing is that you are in Crown Court in four weeks for a plea and trial preparation hearing. That will be a short hearing, more dates will be set and it will be a barrister representing you. I will be there too but it's the barristers who do the speaking in the Crown Court. Have you got any questions just now?'

'Will Sutton and the others be there?'

'No, not then. They've already had their plea and trial preparation hearing but your case will be joined with theirs so you'll all be in court for the trial. In the meantime, we need to get barristers for you. Because it's serious you will have two barristers, a junior and a KC.'

'I don't want a junior barrister who doesn't know what they are doing.'

'All barrister who aren't KCs are called junior barristers even though they might have been doing it for forty years. I've got one in mind for junior who is really nice and, most importantly, really good. Together, we'll then decide on the KC. Is that okay?'

'I suppose so. I don't really understand it all.'

'I know. It's scary but I will be with you every step of the way and the barristers will be with you too. I want to arrange a meeting with them as soon as possible. Would that be okay?'

'Yes. I'm not in college now so I'm just going to work at revision. If I can concentrate.'

'I know that will be incredibly hard for you and nothing I say will make it any easier. It might just help take your mind off this though. Right, let's get out of here. I will write to you at your grandparent's address to confirm everything that has happened today. Shall I copy your mum in too?'

'Please.'

Pam wasn't saying anything. Helen could see she was trying to hold it together for Naomi.

'You'll probably think of lots of questions later. Just ring me or email me anytime.'

They walked out together, Naomi and Pam turning left to go to the car park and Helen watched them go. She was their voice now and the barristers would be Naomi's voice at the Crown Court. It must be so incredibly hard for them. Losing Josh, losing the life that was mapped out and facing the prospect of a life sentence. She didn't want to think too much about it.

She'd become emotionally involved with cases in the past and knew she was in danger of becoming too involved with Naomi which was a really bad idea. It was all such a mess, thought Helen as she turned right to walk to her office in a street filled almost entirely with other solicitors' firms.

A lawyer never knows if a client is guilty unless they confess it, the same with innocence. How do you know? In all her years of doing this, Helen had never been more convinced of someone's innocence than she was now.

Chapter 37

Back in the office, Helen felt a bit flat. She had watched Pam and Naomi walk away from court, heads weighted down in the rain. Naomi seemed to be coping better than Pam. Helen always felt it was worse for the parents. They were so used to looking after their children and sorting things out for them but now they were helpless to do anything.

The piles of files on her desk had increased to piles on the floor. It was supposed to be mainly paperless with evidence being served electronically now but it still seemed to create mounds of paper. Only a few statements had been sent through together with a police summary of the case. Not much to go on. They will have a lot more before the plea and trial preparation hearing but the full case won't be served for months.

Right. Which urgent matter should she tackle first?

Counsel. She wanted Sinead O'Casey to do this case. Digging her phone out from her bag, she rang Sinead who answered straight away.

'Hi, Helen. What are you after?'

'Why do you think I always want something?'

'Call it intuition. Or maybe it's habit.'

'Okay. I want you to take a case for me.'

'It's not another crappy street fight is it?'

'No, it's a murder. You'd be acting for the fourth defendant, a seventeen-year-old in the middle of her A levels who, if you ask me, is completely innocent and should never have been charged.'

'Wow. That's not like you. You should speak to my clerk and get it booked in at Chambers.'

'I will but I wanted to speak to you first. We will need a conference soon as. She's on bail, living at her grandparents out of the area. Three others have already had their plea and trial preparation hearing and hers is on the 28 April at Leeds. A trial date has already been set for 18 of August with an estimate of up to three weeks. We'll need a really top silk who's good with young people and not full of themself.'

'What's her defence?'

'Accepts presence at the scene but denies involvement. They're jointly charged but it looks like the other three are members of the Z99 gang on the Fisher estate in Carfield whereas she was the girlfriend of the deceased and is from a good, middle class home.'

'I've seen this one. The college student who was stabbed?'

'That's the one.'

'Ring Chambers, get the dates booked in and I'll have a think about a silk and when we can have a conference with her. Thanks for this one. I take it all back. You don't just give me crappy street fights.'

Helen ended the call, looked at her desk again and decided she'd better make a start on it as this murder was going to take a lot of her time and plenty TLC. First, ring Willow Court Chambers and make it official.

Chapter 38

Anna

She couldn't believe it.

Not Naomi.

The family liaison officer had been in touch to say a seventeen-year-old girl had also been charged with Josh's murder but wouldn't, initially, give a name. Eventually, she confirmed it was Naomi.

This was just plain stupid. Naomi was a lovely girl. She and Josh loved each other. They might have been young but they really got on well and wanted to be together, choosing the same A levels and the same universities to apply to. They stopped short at choosing the same course but they just seemed so suited.

And it was obvious Naomi was devastated.

She remembered holding hands with her at the funeral, tears running down their faces.

It had to be a mistake.

What must Pam and Phil be going through? Okay, it wasn't the same as losing a child in the most horrific way imaginable but it was still shocking and they must be going through hell.

She wondered about getting in touch but the family liaison officer advised her not to.

The emotions of everyone would be heightened and it wasn't a good idea, she said. Even with the best of intentions, arguments could start over whose fault it all was and whose pain was the worst.

Anna thought about it and, in the end, decided to do as she was advised.

It seemed callous not to get in touch, to say, 'I know she wasn't involved,' but would they welcome it?

Now that Anna knew about Josh's drug taking and dealing would Pam and Phil blame him?

Was it all Josh's fault?

When Anna found out about what Josh had been involved in, she was gobsmacked, plain and simple.

It didn't seem that Naomi had been involved when they told her about it but they must have charged her for a reason.

Was she in on it with the others?

Was she drug dealing too?

The family liaison officer wouldn't tell her why Naomi had been charged, simply that the prosecution had decided that there was enough evidence to charge her.

Sod it. She would ring Pam and Phil.

Her hand was shaking as she pressed the speed dial for Pam.

She'd see who it was. Would she answer?

A click and then, 'Hi, Anna.'

'Pam. I've just heard about Naomi. I can't believe it.'

'Neither can we. It's ridiculous. She's not involved. You must believe that. She would never in a million years have hurt Josh. She's hurting so much over his death and now this.'

'I know. I know. I wasn't ringing to blame her or rant. I'm just ringing to say I know she's not involved and you must all be going through hell.'

Pam burst into tears.

'We are, but you are too. It's just the worst situation for all of us.'

'I don't know what I can do but we need to support each other. I know Naomi isn't involved and I want you to pass that on to her.'

'I will. And thank you. It means a lot.'

Before Anna burst into tears, she ended the call.

'I'll speak to you soon. Lots of love.'

'Thank you. Bye.'

Anna stared at the phone after she ended the call as if the answers might leap out from it.

Naomi couldn't be involved, could she?

Chapter 39

Friday night and it was date night for Ian. Tricia had booked a table for them at a new bistro in town. Not too posh and not slumming it either. He had booked a taxi but was aware he was leaving Jack on his own. He was showing no inclination to venture forth after his dalliance with the drug scene.

'What are you going to do tonight, Jack?'

'Probably watch a film or go on X-box. Not nearly as exciting as your evening.'

'Cheeky. It's just a meal with a friend and I won't be late.'

'So you're not having a sleepover then even with the fancy shirt?'

'Watch it and no, I'm definitely not having a sleepover. I won't be late. You've a choice of pizzas, beef burgers or make some pasta.'

'I'll sort myself out. Don't worry. Is it Mel who's the friend?'

'Of course not, she's a colleague.'

'Just wondered. Thought you might fancy her.'

'Well, I don't. Taxi's here. See you later.'

Ian grabbed the blue jacket his ex-wife had bought him in the Boss sale. It was fitted but not formal and looked good with the blue jeans and floral shirt. He wondered if the shirt was too loud. Too late now.

Sitting in the taxi, he didn't have the same excitement as he'd had on their last abortive date but that was because he had a lot of work on. Wasn't it? It couldn't be anything else.

When he arrived at the bistro, it was the first time it had registered with him that it was still light. The days were getting longer and he felt it was like emerging from the darkness when he noticed it.

He hadn't been to this place before and when he went in he could see Tricia was already there. She was in a booth, cosy, subdued lighting and candles. An intimate setting. He clocked immediately that she had her hair pinned up which emphasised her cheekbones. He walked over and gave her a peck on the cheek noticing she was wearing a purple dress that clung to her body. He hadn't seen her in a dress before.

'Thanks for giving me another chance and sorry again for the last time.'

'No worries. I get it. Kids come first but you're here, no distractions, no work and we can just enjoy. I've already ordered a bottle of wine. Hope that's okay.'

'Perfect. And I'm starving.'

The menu had an italic typeface on parchment which looked good but, in this light, was difficult to read. Shit, maybe he needed to get his eyes tested. Growing older was a pain in the arse.

Food ordered, wine and conversation flowed. Tricia had a way of holding his gaze when she was talking which emphasised those beautiful, big brown eyes. He thought she was gorgeous, clever, witty, lots of personality. But there was a "but". Why?

Don't overthink it, he told himself, just go with the flow and the flow led her asking him to her place for a nightcap.

'That would be lovely.'

Nightcap was like coffee. It always meant something else.

She took his arm as they walked the fifteen minutes to her place on the edge of town. At her door, she got her keys out of her bag, unlocked her door and turned to him, kissing him on the lips. It went through his body and he could feel himself getting hard. It had been so long since he had felt that electricity coursing through his body.

'In you come. Living room through here, make yourself comfy and I'll get us a drink. What do you fancy, apart from me that is?'

It was an old line but the tease always worked. He took in the stylish décor, large open plan living and dining area in bright colours with lots of plants and bold art on the walls. *Nice*, he thought.

'I'll have another white wine if you have any.'

'Is the pope a catholic? Coming right up.'

She put on some Ella Fitzgerald, just the right mood, and sat beside him as she put the wine down on a table next to the terracotta coloured velvet sofa.

'Now where were we?'

She leaned into him and kissed him, gently at first, followed by a force he had forgotten existed. All his reservations disappeared as he responded with hands feeling her body through the silkiness of her dress before working his way round to the zip at the back. It was so long since he'd had sex but, like riding a bike, you don't forget and there was nothing like the excitement of the new.

He struggled with the zip and she had to help him. She pulled the dress over her head and started to unbutton his shirt, pulling it out of his jeans. She then went for his belt and, with an expert hand, unbuckled it in one easy movement before easing down jeans and boxers with one smooth pull.

Lacy black underwear against milky white skin. She was so gorgeous, so voluptuous, was all he could think.

She leaned over to her bag and pulled out a condom. He hadn't even thought of that. Shows how out of practice he was.

Tearing the packet with her teeth, she took the condom out and placed it on him, stroking him as she did so. It was electrifying.

And it was all over in a flash. Not his most impressive performance.

'Sorry, it's been a while.'

'Not to worry. You can make it up to me next time.'

He lay there on the sofa, stroking her body, her auburn pubic hair, in the hope he could go again but there was nothing happening.

'Too much to drink to go for round two I'm afraid.'

She tried coaxing him but it wasn't to be so it was just cuddles. It felt so lovely to hold someone again and to be held. He hadn't realised how much he'd missed it. He hoped his performance hadn't put her off. Didn't seem like it though if she was thinking of a next time.

'Do you want to stay?'

'Would love to but I told I Jack I wouldn't be late so should really call a taxi.'

They lay there for a bit longer, just holding each other in a way that was comfortable and familiar with no awkwardness to spoil it.

'I really had better call that taxi now.'

They dressed just as the taxi arrived. She walked him to the door and they kissed with a promise of more to come.

In the taxi, his mind was going all over the place. He felt good. He felt guilty. He was aware that his performance could have been better. He couldn't stop thinking about his ex-wife. In some perverse way, he felt he was betraying her. She was living with someone else but this was the first time he'd had sex since she left.

It revitalised him but it was weird. A new body to get used to but did he want to get used to Tricia. It made him realise how much of a wall he'd built up around himself. *Well*, he thought, *just enjoy it and see what happens.*

When he got home, Jack was still up.

'Thought you'd be in bed.'

'Watched a film and have been playing on X-box with some mates for a while now. How was your night?'

'Good. Went to the new bistro on the High street which was lovely.'

'Anything else you want to tell me?'

'No, there isn't. And I think its bed time. I'm locking up and going to bed. You should do the same.'

'I'll just finish this game.'

'Okay. See you in the morning.'

Ian climbed the stairs to bed and was asleep in five minutes.

Chapter 40

Helen was at her desk at 8.00. Getting into Leeds city centre was a bit of a nightmare so she tried to beat the traffic. Not always successfully.

Sitting at her desk, she was trying to work out which case she should tackle first. Do a list. It always focussed her thoughts and calmed her when she felt overwhelmed. Her old boss told her that when she was a trainee solicitor many years ago and she never forgot it. Some things that you learn when you're a trainee are a waste of time and some things are priceless.

Cases in the Magistrates' Court this morning, four in total; two of them were new cases, probably guilty pleas by the look of them, one was a breach of a community order and one was a sentence with a probation pre-sentence report. They should be fine. A prison visit this afternoon, one legal aid application to fill in and two briefs to counsel, one for Naomi's case and one for a robbery. With a bit of luck and no interruptions, she might just get the brief on the robbery case done before she had to leave for court.

Then her phone rang. So much for no interruptions. She looked at it before deciding whether or not to answer and saw it was Sinead O'Casey. Always time for Sinead even though she was straight. *What a waste*, thought Helen.

'Morning, Sinead. What can I do you for?'

'Thought I'd catch you before court. I've had a think about dates for a conference and, although it's not strictly necessary, I'd like to get the KC at the conference as well. I've had some thoughts about who we should have. Have you come across Lachlan Macpherson?'

'No, but something tells me he's not Welsh at any rate. Is this going to be a Celtic fest with one Irish and one Scot?'

'At least I'm second generation with a Yorkshire accent but Lachlan is the real McCoy. He's in our London Chambers and I've done one case with him. He's very thorough, great with juries as they love the slight Scottish burr in his voice, and is really good with clients as he has a very gentle manner. He's also available for the trial dates. So, what do you think?'

'If you rate him that's good enough for me. I thought you'd come up with a woman though?'

'That's just because you want some gorgeous female KC to ogle.'

'You know me only too well. Don't think the wife would like it though.'

'Promise not to tell her that you want to ogle female KCs. The other thing is the date of conference. On the assumption that you would agree to Lachlan, I've got a provisional date of the 15 April if that's suits you and the client.'

Helen checked the diary on her laptop. She would move anything she could.

'It's fine by me and I'm sure it will be fine with Naomi. Afternoon?'

'Let's say 2.00 as I'm in court in the morning. Shall we have it in Chambers?'

'Great. Will let Naomi know.'

'Don't forget to book it in with Chambers. I'm always getting told of for arranging things when it should go through my clerk.'

'Will do. You know you can rely on me. Speak soon. Bye.'

Right, back to the robbery brief. Might even get the bulk of it done before court.

*

Ian was rushing Jack out the door so he could give him a lift to school. Hurrying a teenager in the morning who had to do their hair was not always easy. He even had a hairdryer and products, whatever they were, so he could get it just so. Shame he still couldn't tie a knot in his tie properly.

'Come on, Jack. We'll be late again.'

'Coming. Just forgot to put some homework in my bag but got everything now.'

They walked out together with Ian locking the door behind them. He opened the car doors and realised this was the first lovely spring day they had. It was almost warm. Almost. It was April and Yorkshire after all. Still, the sun was shining, he'd had a lovely evening with Tricia and Jack seemed back on track. The revision session with Mel had helped and Jack had asked for another. *Must remember to ask her*, he thought.

On the drive to school, Jack was quite chatty. Revision going well, no classes after this week apart from revision classes, a new case of nasty robberies and a new girlfriend. Girlfriend? He couldn't yet think of Tricia as a girlfriend but if she wasn't that then what was she? He'd never done one night stands. It just wasn't his style.

On the drive to Jack's school, the traffic was a nightmare and he seemed to catch every red light.

'For fuck's sake.'

'Temper dad. Need to watch that road rage.'

That made Ian smile at least.

Jack got out of the car just before school so Ian could turn round and head for the station. He eventually arrived, parked up, grabbed his jacket and locked the car. As he was walking into the station, he saw DI Martha Holroyd coming down the stairs.

'Ian. Just the person.'

'Sounds ominous.'

'Just an update so don't look too worried. We arrested that young woman, Frankie, who was selling at Jack's school. Seems like she did a different day at different schools. Quite a timetable she had. She was travelling up from Sheffield each day so a county lines case and definite gang involvement.

'She seems quite a vulnerable young woman and there is evidence of trafficking by the gang for criminal gain so it's a case for the National Referral Mechanism. She has a social worker who is looking into that for her. So far she hasn't given us any names but, with a bit of support, she might. She's in a foster home just now so, hopefully, we'll get somewhere once she's settled.

'She's been charged with possession with intent to supply but that may well change depending on whether or not there's a finding that she has been trafficked.'

'So she might end up with no charges?'

'It's possible. If she gives us names, it will be worth it. There's an increasing tendency to use girls as they attract less attention. They're usually kids from difficult backgrounds drawn in with money and kind words. All the things that have often been lacking in their lives. They're sad cases.'

Martha looked tired and wasn't her usual well turned out self.

'You okay?'

'Yes. It's part of it, isn't it. Sometimes it gets to you. Maybe it's time to move away from gangs. They're all so damaged and you see the worst of life.'

'There's always sexual offences.'

181

'No, thanks. Not exactly light relief. I'm off for a meeting with the boss to explain why we haven't yet got the top dogs of the gangs. We suspect who they are but getting the evidence is another ball game. They are so careful and no-one will talk. They'd rather do the time than be a grass.'

'Good luck with the meeting then.'

She walked down the corridor to the ACC's office and Ian thought about the many times he'd been there to explain why a perpetrator hadn't yet been caught. The higher up you went in the force the more political it became and PR was what mattered.

Did he want to go higher up? Would he be any different? Anyway, nothing was on offer so no point in overthinking it.

His phone pinged for an incoming text. Tricia. He knew he wasn't good at keeping in touch despite their night of passion last week.'

"Fancy a quick drink after work x?"

He could fit in a quick one but didn't want to leave Jack all evening.

"Great. Golden Lion at 6?"

"See you then x".

It would be nice to see her again.

Right, let's have a look at this spate of robberies.

Ian climbed the stairs to his office and bumped into Mel and Prita in the corridor.

'Morning. I want to have a briefing in half an hour on those robberies.'

'Fine. See you in the briefing room,' said Prita.

Mel didn't say anything, not because she didn't want to. She just couldn't think of anything to say.

'You still pining after him then?'

'No. I never did have a thing for him. Anyway, I think he's seeing someone from what his son said.'

'Really. I wonder who that is.'

'No idea but it's nothing to do with me.'

'Have it your own way but I still think there's a spark.'

Mel smiled. 'You just want to see a spark where there is none.'

Ian popped his head round the corner. Mel blushed hoping he hadn't heard them talking about him.

'By the way, Mel, Jack has asked for more maths help if you're up for it.'

'Sure. Any time.'

'Let's fix something up later.'

He walked towards his office. Mel pulled a face at Prita.

'You don't think he heard us?'

'No. Stop worrying. Even if he did, it might spur him on to take action.'

'I don't want him to and I'm sure he's happy with whoever he's seeing.'

The briefing on the robberies didn't take them far. Street robberies, only cash taken but all were threatened with knives and a couple of them had minor knife injuries. All had been slapped or punched till they handed over cash.

Cash was the hardest thing to trace. At least with cards there was a trace and potential CCTV.

No suspects, no identifications, no CCTV.

All they had was two males, probably aged between sixteen and thirty, balaclavas, local accents. No hair colour or skin colour. One victim thought they were white but the others couldn't tell because of gloves and balaclavas.

Ian asked both Mel and Prita to widen the CCTV zones around the robberies and see if that threw up anything useful. John was tasked with going through possible M.O.s in a search for potential suspects.

Ian had a feeling this might be one of those cases where he was joining Martha Holroyd in the ACC's office before too long.

*

Tricia was in the Golden Lion with a glass of white wine when Ian arrived at ten past six.

'Sorry, I'm late.'

'Pretty punctual for you. Hard day?'

He told her about the robberies and the young girl potentially trafficked from Sheffield to sell drugs at Jack's school. It was good to talk about it at the end of the day. It was therapy, just getting it off his chest, talking about it seemed to make it that bit more distant.

The time flew by and at 7.30, Ian had to leave.

'Got to get back for Jack. Cooking steaks tonight.'

'Sounds good. Text when you fancy another liaison.'

It was loaded with meaning. Ian couldn't decide if he wanted more than just sex with Tricia. She seemed to just want sex but maybe that was a front.

'Will do. Sorry to rush off.'

She finished her drink and they walked out together. She was walking home and he was driving so she walked him to the Audi and they kissed, briefly. It didn't seem right to have more than a brief kiss in a pub car park.

Ian got in the car and waved as he started to drive off.

Thoughts went straight to the steaks. Shouldn't take more than thirty minutes for steak and chips.

When he arrived home, it was still light. He loved it when the clocks had just gone forward and it was still just about light at 8.00.

He went in the house and could see Jack at the dining room table working away.

'Hi dad. Just finishing off an English essay.'

'Good stuff. Steak and chips in half an hour?'

'Great. I had some toast to keep me going.'

'That's it. Guilt trip me. Mel's coming over to do some maths with you tomorrow.'

It felt like his and Jack's relationship was on a different level since the drugs incident. Life was starting to feel good again.

Chapter 41

Ian, Prita, Mel and John were going through the evidence, or lack of it, on the robberies when DI Martha Holroyd walked in.

'I need to speak to you now, Ian.'

No knock, no apologies.

'Okay. Carry on with what you're doing and we'll catch up this afternoon.'

Mel, John and Prita shared looks, got up and walked out.

Once they were a safe distance from Ian's office, Prita asked, 'Do you know what that's about, John? She didn't look too happy.'

'No idea but I'm sure we'll find out.'

Martha didn't begin with niceties.

'Have you leaked the story about the young woman being trafficked from Sheffield?'

'Of course not. I wouldn't do such a thing. Why would you think that?'

'There are only a handful of people who know about it. I've asked them all and I'm satisfied it's no-one on my team. That leaves you. I wouldn't even have considered it but I heard you were dating Tricia from the Carfield Post.'

'We're not exactly dating but what's she got to do with it?'

'This morning's story in the Post. It couldn't name her because of her age but the details are all there, right down to the potential National Referral Mechanism.'

'What! Let me see.'

He googled the Post and there it was on the front page.

GIRLS TRAFFICKED TO SELL DRUGS TO SCHOOL CHILDREN IN CARFIELD.

He groaned inwardly. He never thought she would do that.

'Ian, we've already done a press release but not with that sort of detail at this stage. It would have been irresponsible and it potentially puts this girl in danger.'

'Look, it's possible it did come from me but if it did it was an accident. I let it slip out and I had an agreement with Tricia that she wouldn't print anything about gangs while it was ongoing. I'm really sorry if it came from me. I will speak to her and get back to you as soon as possible.'

Martha looked furious. He couldn't blame her. He would feel the same.

'Get back to me today. I'm going to have to explain this to the ACC.'

She turned and walked out slamming the door behind her.

Ian rang Tricia. Straight to voicemail. He left a message to ring him.

He sent a text saying he needed to speak to her. He saw the message read notification but no response.

It was his turn to be furious.

Had she been using him? What an idiot he'd been. He thought he was offloading but the reality was she was just pumping him for information.

Chapter 42

Naomi worried about what to wear. She knew it was bonkers to think about appearance for a meeting with lawyers but she didn't want them to think she was like those lads she'd seen at court with their uniform hoodies and joggers. White blouse, navy capri pants, pale blue jacket and black pumps. The sort of outfit that might be described as smart casual.

She decided to straighten the waves in her long brown hair and put just a bit of makeup on. She didn't want to look as if she was going on a night out but she knew she had to look different from the rest of the people the lawyers were used to.

She was going into Leeds with her gran as her mum couldn't take any more time off work. Her gran had been great though, looking after her, feeding her up, bringing her regular cups of tea and giving her everything she needed so she could study. And talking to her. She'd always been able to talk to her gran even when she couldn't talk to her mum and dad. That little bit of distance made it easier. That's what grans are good at.

Naomi took one last look in the mirror. Like most teenage girls, she never thought she looked good. This time she felt she was creating the right image, whatever that might be. She grabbed her bag and walked down the stairs as her gran was getting her jacket and car keys.

'You look nice.'

'So do you. Helen is really nice. You'll like her. I don't know what the barristers are like.'

'Hope they're not too posh. They always are on TV.'

'If Helen has picked them, I don't imagine they will be. I've never met a barrister before.'

'Me neither. I don't think I've met a solicitor either so it's a strange world we're entering into. Okay let's get going. We've got to park up and then find it.

And I hate driving in Leeds. That loop system they have just sends you round in circles. Loop is right.'

Her gran looked at her. Her beautiful, clever granddaughter should not be in this situation. She wanted to hug her, cry and reassure her all at the same time. What do you do when your granddaughter is facing a murder charge? There was no framework for this.

She grabbed her hands and they held each other's gaze, trying to be strong for the other.

'You'll be fine. I can feel it in my bones that everything will turn out well.'

*

Helen was late out of court, legged it back to the office grabbing a sandwich on the way. When she got there her secretary collared her with messages. Urgent calls to be returned and one of her regular clients had been arrested and was asking for her at the police station.

Helen had a brief look at the messages. They could wait.

'See if Sundeep can do the police station. If not, ask him to arrange an agent to cover it. I'll return calls when I get back.'

She took the files from this morning's court work out of her bag, left them on her desk hoping she'd get to them later, grabbed Naomi's file and unwrapped her sandwich eating it as she was sorting files. A drink of water would have to do as she went to the kitchen to pour a glass.

'Okay, Michelle. I'm off to Chambers for the con with Naomi Edwards. See you in a couple of hours.'

At least it was only a ten minute walk.

*

Helen arrived at Cavendish Square with five minutes to spare. It was a square of once grand Georgian houses which were now solicitors' offices, barristers' chambers and private medical consulting rooms. Anyone entering these buildings would know they had something serious to discuss. And someone important to see.

As Helen walked up the steps, through the doorway with its Doric columns on either side and into the reception, she saw that Naomi was already sitting in the waiting room with an older woman she assumed was Naomi's gran. She waved at them, gave her name to the receptionist and then went to join Naomi.

'Helen, this is my gran, Wilma. Gran, this is Helen who I told you about.'

'Hi, pleased to meet you.'

'Hello. Naomi's told me all about you. Thank you for being there for her.'

'No problem. It's what I'm here for.'

Helen took in the elegant woman in the Barbour jacket, dark green trousers and brown ankle boots. *She doesn't look like most grans,* thought Helen.

Another woman walked into the waiting room and went towards them.

'Hello, Naomi, Helen, and this must be your gran. I'm Sinead O'Casey, your junior barrister.'

Naomi looked at Sinead. She'd never met a barrister before and didn't know what to expect. There was the inevitable black suit and white shirt which was the uniform of the barrister together with a mop of curly black hair, green eyes, pale skin and a mass of freckles. And a Yorkshire accent. Apart from the uniform, she didn't look like a barrister, whatever that meant.

'Good to meet you both. I'll take you through to meet Lachlan Macpherson, the KC who will be handling your case. Would you like a tea or coffee?'

'Not for me,' said Wilma.

Naomi asked for a tea. She decided it would give her something to do with her hands. Helen was desperate for a cup of tea after the morning spent in the Magistrates' Court.

'Sharon, would you arrange for tea and biscuits for four in conference room 1 please?'

Sinead led them up a wide staircase with dark red carpet running up the middle and held down by brass stair rods, across a landing to a door with a brass plate saying "Conference Room 1". She opened the door and led them in to a room with a large, dark wood, oval table surrounded by ten chairs. The tall windows were draped with floor length floral tasselled curtains which finished off the very traditional appearance of the room.

A man with thick salt and pepper, floppy hair, stood up and gave Naomi a lovely, warm, welcoming, slightly lopsided smile.

'Hello, I'm Lachlan Macpherson. Call me Lachlan. I'll be working with Sinead and Helen on your case, Naomi.'

Interesting, thought Helen. No "KC" and no "mister" mentioned. First name terms. She took in the piercing blue eyes under the mane of collar length hair, the well-cut nave blue suit, pink shirt and the flashy brightly coloured Jon Snow type tie. A bit flash perhaps but even Helen thought he was attractive and it was a rarity for her to find men attractive.

'Please, take a seat and we can make a start.'

Helen noticed what she assumed was the public school and Oxbridge confidence and the slight Scottish accent which had no doubt been modified by years of living in London. Well, let's see what he's like.

Naomi and Wilma sat down at the table each saying "hello" and nothing more. Wilma was thinking that Naomi's life was in his hands, literally.

Everyone took a seat, laptops and papers were extracted from bags and Sharon brought the tea and biscuits in to the room.

'I know this is terrifying,' began Lachlan, 'but we're here to explain everything to you at each stage, get information from you and give information to you. There will be a lot to take in, most of it you won't remember but you can ring Helen at any time to ask questions. Don't think any question is too silly. If you're wondering about something or if something occurs to you, just make that call. Promise me you'll do that.'

'Okay.'

'We have our first hearing in just under two weeks at Leeds Crown Court. It won't take long but it will seem pretty alien as Sinead and I will be in wigs and gowns as will the other barristers and the judge. Your co-defendants will not be there but you will all be together at the trial. As I understand it, you will be pleading not guilty, is that right.'

'Yes, of course.'

'Before we begin talking about the evidence, there is something I must say to you as it's part of my job. I need to tell you that if you plead guilty at this stage, you get a lighter sentence. You would get ten per cent off any sentence you might receive if a jury finds you guilty. It's more in other cases but that's the discount in a murder case.

'It's a sort of incentive to get people to plead guilty if they are guilty and not waste time and money by having a trial. It's a discount for an early guilty plea.'

'But I didn't do it,' exclaimed Naomi.

'That's what I understand but it's something I have to say and the judge will ask me if you've had this explained to you.'

'I'm not pleading guilty to something I didn't do.'

'That's fine. You must not plead guilty if you are not guilty. The evidence we have at this stage is a summary really and won't all be served for about another six weeks. It's just enough so we can get a feel of the case against you and advise you. Once we have all the evidence, we will have to serve what's called a defence statement.

'That is a document where we tell the prosecution and the court what your defence is and any evidence you might also be relying on. In that defence statement, we might also ask for information which might be helpful to us such as previous convictions of your co-defendants.'

Sinead saw that Naomi looked a bit glazed so she interrupted Lachlan.

'It's a lot to take in and we don't expect you to remember all of this. Helen will write to you, giving you information as we go towards the trial and, as we said, ring her any time. We will also have more conferences once we have the evidence and can discuss it in detail.'

Naomi nodded. 'I'm following you okay so far. My exams start on the 25 May and go on until the 16 June. Will I be able to sit them?'

'Of course,' replied Lachlan. 'If we needed any pre-trial hearing or conference, we would make sure it was outside of those dates. Now, let's have a look at the evidence the Crown have served so far.'

Lachlan slowly took her through the evidence, noting her comments in a blue notebook while Sinead and Helen were typing everything on their laptops and Naomi was also taking notes. *How unusual for a client to take notes at a conference*, thought Helen.

After Lachlan had gone through the evidence, what was problematic for them, what wasn't, he said, 'I now want to talk about something very difficult and that is what was on Josh's phone. Do you want your gran to be in while we discuss it?'

'Yes. She knows all about it.'

'I'm not going to ask you to go over it again. I know you've done this with Helen. It's the Crown's case that this may have given you a motive to kill Josh and they might apply to the judge so that the jury can hear about. I don't think a judge would allow this. In my opinion, a video of you being raped is too far removed from, and not relevant to, a murder charge.

191

'It's something I want to speak to the Crown's KC about and see where it takes us. They haven't served that video evidence yet and it's possible that they might not. It's something we don't know at this stage and, if the prosecution want to make it part of the trial, we will oppose this.'

Naomi looked at Lachlan and the tears welled up as Helen passed her a tissue.

'Thank you. I don't want anyone to know about it.'

'Well, that makes all of us then,' said Lachlan giving her one of his twinkly smiles.

Wonder if he's had his teeth fixed, thought Helen.

'Let's call it a day and we'll see you at court in a couple of weeks. Any questions, as I've said, give Helen a ring.'

'Thank you.'

'Thank you for what you are doing for my granddaughter.'

'We want to do her case and help in every way we can,' said Sinead. 'I'll show you out.'

Sinead took them back downstairs and, after saying goodbyes, went back up to join Lachlan and Helen.

'What do you think?'

'I think the prosecution case is all over the place. Is she a victim of rape and is getting revenge on Josh for forcing her or is she in league with the rapists and the slapping of Josh by her is evidence of a joint enterprise attack? They can't run the case both ways and I can't see a judge allowing the video of the rape to go before a jury. My money is on the joint enterprise but let's wait and see. Either of you up for a quick drink before I head back to London?'

'Not for me. I told the wife I'd be home early.'

'I'm up for it,' said Sinead.

'Great. Let me dash to the loo and I'll join you downstairs.'

When Lachlan left the room, Helen turned to Sinead and said, 'I bet you're up for it. If I was straight, I'd probably be up for it too. He's really nice, down to earth and no pretensions.'

Sinead had the grace to look embarrassed. 'He's lovely but he's a colleague so just wind your neck in, Ms White. The important thing is that he's really good and gives off this air of calm that's needed. He's posh but I won't hold that against him. That smile! Do you think he's practised it in the mirror?'

'I doubt it. He's not that self-conscious, just confident. He's not long separated from his wife and has two teenage sons.'

'Is that why you wanted to instruct him?'

'Of course not. It's because he's right for this case. The fact that he's charismatic and drop dead gorgeous has nothing to do with it.'

Helen just looked at her and laughed.

Chapter 43

Sinead arrived at court with the wheelie case that's almost part of the barrister's uniform. She had the app on her phone showing who she was, which meant she could skip the queues at security. Thank goodness for that, she thought as the queue snaked down the steps on to the pavement today. She made her way to the lift and up to the robing room, punched in the door code and saw Lachlan deep in conversation with a woman she knew was the prosecutor, Maria Conroy KC.

Helen rang her to say she was outside court 5 with Naomi and Pam.

'Right. You look after them and we'll be down shortly. Looks like we're fifth on the list so it'll be a while yet.'

She went over to Lachlan and introduced herself to Maria Conroy.

'Hi, Sinead, this is my junior Sebastian Wells.'

Everyone was terribly polite. The thing about barristers was you never knew if they despised their opponents or liked them as they used the same unerring politeness to each other regardless.

Thankfully, Sinead had been against Sebastian before and knew he was good and fair. Couldn't say that for all prosecutors.

'Shall we get a conference room and have a chat?' Maria suggested.

'Good idea.'

'I'll just get robed and sign us in,' said Sinead.

'Already signed us in,' said Lachlan.

Bloody hell, thought Sinead. KCs signing in and not expecting the junior to do it. Whatever next.

Once they'd found an empty conference room that had four chairs and a table, not an easy task, Lachlan opened the negotiations, although not exactly negotiations, each of them telling the other their case was hopeless.

It was very polite undermining but neither was backing down.

'I know the video hasn't been served yet but I'm going to raise it with the judge this morning,' Lachlan began.

'Bit premature.'

'It's irrelevant and I don't want it to be served. A young woman being raped isn't something that should be seen by any number of people. You need to decide how you're putting your case and I want to get some judicial viewpoint on it. We're in front of the Recorder of Leeds who is going to be the trial judge so, although you've not served any application, I want to see what her take is on it.'

'Your call, Lachlan, but I don't think she'll interfere at this stage.'

'We'll see. I'll go and speak to my client now and see you in court.'

'What do you think?' Sinead asked.

'She's not backing down which I think is a mistake on her part. I was hoping she might see sense. My view is that the Recorder will not like it that a rape victim has her rape used against her as a motive. If it's served, all the defendants will get to see it.'

'Ah, here's Helen and Naomi and you must be Naomi's mum.'

'Pam. Pleased to meet you.'

'Lachlan. Pleasure to meet you too. Let's try and get a conference room so I can go over what will happen today. I think it will be standing room only with the state of some of these rooms.'

Naomi's case was called on. She was led into the dock, looking round, trying to take it all in and her mum was guided to the public gallery. She looked out of place in the glass fronted dock with a burly security officer at her side.

The barristers took up their positions on the front row and Helen sat behind them, turning to smile at Naomi and check she was okay.

The Recorder of Leeds was dressed in the red robes befitting of her status as a senior judge. Her short grey hair and earrings could just be seen under the grey wig. An even greyer face devoid of makeup contrasted sharply with the brilliant red of her robes. She had a reputation for being hard on counsel and could be caustic if she thought a barrister had not covered every point.

Many thought she was one of these judges who had forgotten what life was like as a barrister with dozens of cases on the go, preparing into the early hours of the mornings and having to watch the family go off on holiday when a trial was overrunning. Still, she had a reputation as fair and wasn't just pro prosecution unlike so many judges. This was the most that could be said about her.

Maria began. 'My lady, I represent the Crown assisted by Mr Wells in this matter listed for PTPH today. The defendant is represented by Mr Macpherson

King's Counsel and Ms O'Casey.'

'Can your client be arraigned Mr Macpherson?'

'Yes, my lady.'

The charge was read out by the court clerk.

'Naomi Edwards. Please stand up. You are charged on this indictment with one count, namely murder, the particulars being that on the 3rd day of February 2022 you did, along with others, murder Joshua Smithies. Do you plead guilty or not guilty?'

A squeak came from Naomi. 'Not guilty.'

'You plead not guilty. Thank you. You may sit down.'

'My lady, this case is linked to another where three defendants have already been arraigned. A timetable and trial date has already been set for the 18 August. The Crown say this is a joint enterprise and our application is for the matters to be joined.'

'Mr Macpherson?'

'I've no objection, my lady.'

'Are you content with the existing timetable, Mr Macpherson? It seems rather tight.'

'I am, my lady. Providing there is no slippage.'

'Yes. Ms Conroy, I don't want to see an application to extend that timetable. As the evidence will no doubt be the same for all and that should be well under way by now. Bail?'

'Ms Edwards has been bailed with a condition of residence at an address disclosed to the court.'

'I can see that. Is the Crown content for this to continue?'

'Yes, my lady. There have been no breaches and there is nothing to suggest Ms Edwards might fail to surrender.'

'Very well. Bail granted on the same conditions. Is there anything else I can assist with at this stage?'

'Yes, my lady. It's a sensitive matter and I ask that the court is cleared so we can deal with the matter in chambers.'

'Ms Conroy, I assume you know what this matter is. Is Mr Macpherson's request appropriate?'

'It is, my lady.'

'Very well. Please clear the court and I will hear this matter in chambers.'

Once the court was cleared and the usher put the notice on the courtroom door that court was sitting in chambers, Lachlan got to his feet.

'My lady, this concerns evidence that the Crown seeks to rely on which the defence say is not only irrelevant but is unnecessary and does not further the Crown's case.'

'It's a bit early in the case to be challenging evidence as irrelevant, isn't it, Mr Macpherson?'

'Normally I would agree but this evidence is extremely sensitive and, in my submission, takes the Crown's case no further forward.'

Lachlan outlined the rape of Naomi which was found on Josh's phone.

'It's our submission that this should not be shown to a jury; it is purely speculative that it goes to motive and has no relevance in a charge of murder.'

'Thank you, Mr Macpherson. Ms Conroy?'

'My lady, we say this goes directly to motive. Naomi Edwards is closest to Josh when he is stabbed. Her hand comes out just as he falls and she runs off, leaving him in an alley way without calling for help. A jury will wonder what possible motive she could have for doing that when she was, after all, his girlfriend.

'The fact that we have a video from the deceased's phone where she is begging him not to make her do this means that she has a revenge motive. In addition, the murder weapon was found in Ms Edward's garden shed. The evidence points to her involvement and the video goes to motive.'

'My lady, what my learned friend is doing is asking the jury to speculate. Even if they saw the video which, I submit, they should not, it is pure speculation that this gives her a motive. If the Crown says this is a joint enterprise, and Naomi Edwards is part of it, they can do this without the need for this video evidence.'

'At this stage, I'm inclined to agree with Mr Macpherson. As you well know, often we never know what the motive is in cases, even by the end of a trial. I accept it makes it neater to have one but we can't always make cases neat and have what we want. If the murder weapon has been found in the defendant's shed and she runs from the scene, it looks like you have enough on which to base a case, Ms Conroy.

'Before I give any judgment on this matter, I would like to see the video and I also want the Crown to serve a skeleton outlining their position within fourteen days. The video can be served with the skeleton but make sure it is served securely and sent directly to me rather than being put on the digital case system for all to see. The defence shall have a further seven to reply. We can then have a further case management hearing in twenty eight days.

'Thank you for bringing that to my attention now Mr Macpherson. I will rise for fifteen minutes before the next case is called on.'

The court clerk got to her feet. 'All rise.'

After the judge had risen, everyone drifted out of court.

'Defence one, prosecution nil,' said Sinead, who couldn't help but feel smug.

'Early days and we're not there yet. She could still change her mind.'

Helen grabbed a conference room and ushered everyone in.

'Okay, everyone. I know that will have been mesmerising Naomi but it's just setting a timetable as to when we must do certain things and when the prosecution must do certain things. You will also have your trial with the other three. There's no way round that. The judge seems, so far, to be on side with the video. We're not there yet and we're back in twenty eight days to argue it but so far so good. Any questions?'

'I can't think of any.'

'Neither can I.'

'You probably will once you get home. Remember, ring Helen any time and I hope the revision goes well. See you in twenty eight days.'

Naomi got up to leave and Pam put her head in her hands.

'I just can't believe this is happening.' The tears welled up and spilled over. She looked at Lachlan.

'This is probably just another case for you but this is my daughter. This is her life. Our life. She didn't do it.'

'I know and there is no such thing as "just another case". Please believe that. We will work flat out on Naomi's case but I can't guarantee anything. No lawyer can guarantee an outcome. I can only begin to imagine what you're going through and we are here for you. We won't see you till the next hearing in four weeks' time but Helen will be in touch and if you have anything that needs running past us, Helen knows where we are.'

Helen got the tissues out. It's part of the job to carry the tissues. They're always needed in criminal cases, usually for the families.

'Mum, please don't. I'm sorry this is happening.'

'It's not your fault. It's Josh's fault for getting you into this and the fault of those bastard drug dealers who destroy lives.'

Pam, the one who had remained calm and together for Naomi, was starting to lose it and who could blame her. Her happy family life was falling apart. The professional jobs, the children doing well at school and going to go on to university was all nothing in the face of a murder charge where her beautiful, clever daughter could face a sentence of detention for life and be in prison for maybe fifteen years.

It couldn't be happening. It was unreal. How did they get here? She was now inconsolable. The tears flowed and then Naomi started.

'I'm sorry Mum. I'm so sorry. I didn't do it.'

'I know love, but I just can't believe we're here, that I had to look at you in the dock behind that glass screen with a security guard. I wish you'd never got together with Josh.'

'Me neither. But I did. It'll be okay, Mum, I know it will. Gran says she can feel it in her bones and you know she's always right.'

Naomi was trying, unsuccessfully, to lighten the mood.

'We have to try and take this one small step at a time, otherwise you will just keep imagining the worst case scenario. So far I think the judge is with us on the question of the video. That's the next step. Don't focus beyond that,' said Lachlan. 'I know it's hard but it's the only way you will survive this.'

Helen was starting to fill up. She had spent so much more time with Naomi and Pam than the barristers had so she knew them, their hopes, their lives, and it was hard watching them fall apart. The reality of Crown Court sometimes got people like this. The formality, the dress, the words used. It was another world, a world that was seen on television for entertainment but a world that was far from entertaining for those involved in it.

'Come on, Mum, let's go, remember I've got lots of revision to do.' Naomi tried smiling. It was as if she had become the parent and needed to take care of Pam.

Pam pulled herself together. She visibly straightened, wiped her eyes and took Naomi's hand.

'I'm okay, love. It's me who should be apologising. I should be supporting you.'

'Mum, you've been brilliant. I love you and I just know everything will be okay. Come on, I need to get back to gran's and get to work.'

Naomi put her arms round her mum. Sinead felt that watching the emotion between a mum and her daughter was somehow intrusive and was just about to suggest they leave when Pam stood up and said to Naomi, 'Come on then. Let's get you get back to your gran's.'

She turned to all three lawyers. 'Thank you for what you're doing and also for believing in Naomi.'

'It's not a problem, believe me,' said Lachlan and smiled.

'I'll walk out with you,' said Helen.

They left Lachlan and Sinead in the conference room. Sinead turned to Lachlan saying, 'This is going to be one of those emotional ones.'

'I know. Let's hope we can win it but we've a long way to go and, even without the video, we've got problems with the assault and the murder weapon. You don't need to tell me but she will come across well and that's half the battle.'

'Yes, but it's the other half I'm worried about.'

Chapter 44

Harley couldn't eat, couldn't sleep and, although the tremors had stopped, he needed something to calm him.

Getting to see a nurse or doctor in here was fucking impossible. Half the wing was climbing the walls as they were either coming off something or were high on spice. He was trying to stay clean now but didn't know how long it would last.

And no-one had been to visit him apart from the lawyers and they didn't have much to say. He thought his mam would have got her act together to come but she couldn't be arsed. He phoned her every couple of days but didn't get a lot of sense out of her. She was always pissed. She kept promising to come.

He'd send her visiting orders but then she didn't turn up. He'd ring and she'd say she didn't have any money for the bus fare. Liar. She spent it on booze.

'A'right, mate.'

'A'right, Ben.'

'What you up to?'

'Nothing much. Going for a game of pool. Fancy it?'

'Nah. Me mam's coming in a bit. Last time she came, the screws told her I didn't want to see her. Lying bastards. They couldn't be bothered to come and get me out of the rec room. Yours' been to see you yet?'

'Nah. Hasn't got the bus fare.'

'Lying bitch. She drinks her money as soon as she gets it. You're better off without her.'

'Yeah, I know.'

'Right. See you later. Off to my pad to wait for them to come and get me.'

'Yeah. See you.'

Ben didn't know how lucky he was. At least his mam cared enough to visit which was more than he could say.

Chapter 45

Naomi was with her gran this time and they went into the court building together. The hearing was listed at 10.00 before the bulk of the cases started so she hoped they wouldn't have to hang around for too long. She hated these places.

Helen met them when they arrived at court. Sinead and Lachlan were already there and Helen was surprised to see DI Pearce and Sergeant Garvey outside the court. They each nodded an acknowledgment but no-one was going to pass the time of day with the other.

Maria Conroy and Sebastian Wells walked swiftly along the corridor, laptops in hand. Maria greeted Ian and Mel. 'Didn't expect to see you here today.'

'I wasn't sure I'd be able to make it but things are a bit less hectic. I know I was the one pushing that the video gave her a motive and Mel was unconvinced so we wanted to be here.'

'Well, it's always good to see you. There's Lachlan. Excuse me, I want a quick word with him.' She walked purposefully over to Lachlan, leaving Ian and Mel with Sebastian, black patent high heels clicking on the wooden floor.

'What do you think?' Mel asked.

'We've worked on the skeleton argument. It clearly goes to motive but it could go either way today. The judge didn't seem keen the last time we were here but she might have changed her mind. Even if it doesn't go our way, we've still got the assault and the murder weapon so, in my opinion, we've still got a case. Not sure how strong it would be though.'

'But without the motive, why would she do it. That's the big question,' pointed out Mel.'

'I know but we rarely get a case before a jury with all the ducks in a row so we'll do what we can. Anyway, fingers crossed the judge will see sense and let it in. I'd better see what Lachlan's saying. See you later.'

For the first time since the discovery of the video, Ian wasn't sure about anyone seeing it. He turned to Mel, 'What do you think?'

'I still think she shouldn't have been charged and it's rare for me to say this but I hope the defence wins today.'

'I'm beginning to come round to your way of thinking. I just can't see her being involved.'

Mel looked at him open mouthed.

'I can't believe you've just admitted that. How come you've had a change of heart?'

'I've just been mulling it over. I can't see her being in on it with the other three and I can't see this as some sort of revenge attack so it's starting not to make any sense.'

'Bloody hell. Does this mean we're on the same page?'

He looked at her and grinned, 'Looks like it, Sergeant Garvey.'

'Morning, Lachlan, Sinead.'

'Morning, Maria, Sebastian. Good to see you. Ready for defeat today?'

'In your dreams, Lachlan. Let's see what she says. She'll have made up her mind by now. I understand that the prosecution case papers were served yesterday. I take it you've seen it.'

'I've not had the chance to look at it but I believe Sinead has.'

'Yes, I've had a quick look. Nothing unexpected.'

'Good. So there won't be any applications to put the trial back.'

'Not from us providing we get full disclosure of everything we request in our defence statement.'

'I'm sure there won't be any problems but Sebastian is dealing with that. Did you come up this morning?'

'No, had to come up last night and stayed in a hotel near the station. We should be on soon so I'm hoping to get back to London mid-afternoon.'

'It's always a pain when you're doing a case out of town. This shouldn't take the full hour it's listed for.'

'We'd better get into court and hope it starts on time.'

Lachlan, Maria, Sebastian and Sinead walked towards the courtroom almost bumping into Helen and Naomi.

Maria spotted them and said tactfully, 'I'll leave you to your client then.'

'Morning, Naomi. How are you today?'

'Nervous, partly because I've got my first A level exam in two days.'

'Well, fingers crossed we get some good news then. Let's get into court.'

Walking into court was no easier this time but at least Naomi knew where the dock was. She was led towards it and the dock officer unlocked the door to let her in then locked it behind her.

She sat down and wished today was over. The thought of people seeing that video was just unbearable. She looked over and smiled at her gran. She's got to be strong for her family and she had to get through these A levels if she had a hope of a better life. A hope of any life. That was providing everything went well. She couldn't even begin to think of it not going well.

'All rise.'

The judge walked in looking no less grim than she did the last time.

The court clerk began by identifying Naomi.

'Are you Naomi Edwards?'

'Yes.'

'You may sit down.'

Maria opened her laptop, got her papers in order, stood up and began the proceedings.

'Your ladyship knows the representation having dealt with this matter on the last occasion. Today is listed for your ladyship to determine whether video evidence of the defendant should be put before the jury. Has your ladyship seen the video, the prosecution skeleton and the defence skeleton?'

'I have, Ms Conroy. Thank you both for your detailed skeleton arguments which I have had time to consider. You may of course make further oral submissions but you can be brief.'

'Thank you for that indication, my lady.'

Sinead turned to Lachlan. 'That means she's already made up her mind.'

'And her face is even more thunderous than usual so someone is in for a roasting.'

Maria began, outlining all the reasons why the video of Naomi being raped should be seen by a jury as it gave her a motive which, without it, a jury might struggle to understand.

When she finished, she sat down and Lachlan stood up.

He went through his points with a slow, clear delivery managing to make everything sound simple and obvious.

Sinead was looking at the judge. She was giving nothing away so it was impossible to decide which side she was on.

Lachlan finished and sat down.

The judge launched straight into her judgment without pausing. It was already prepared and written.

She was on the side of the defence and ruled in favour of Lachlan and Sinead.

When she finished, she looked at Maria Conroy.

'Ms Conroy.'

Maria stood up.

'I am surprised that experienced counsel would want this video to go before a court. A video of a young woman apparently being raped and begging for it to stop is not, in my opinion, evidence that should be seen. To say it goes to motive is stretching matters and asks a jury to speculate into the realms of fantasy.'

'I understand your ladyship's ruling. Thank you.'

Maria sat down thinking that thanking the judge was the last thing she wanted to do. It was always touch and go whether such a video would be allowed in evidence but, not to worry, they still had a case against Naomi. Maria wasn't convinced by the grieving girlfriend act.

Helen turned round and winked and smiled at Naomi. She hoped that Naomi understood all of that as it was dressed up in legal jargon.

'Will this case require a further case management hearing?'

'It is not anticipated by the Crown.'

'Nor by the defence providing full disclosure is made. My learned junior is dealing with disclosure matters and will make an application for disclosure should one be necessary,' said Lachlan.

'Very well. If you need my assistance on matters, I will be happy to deal with it. Otherwise, I will see you at trial in August.'

The next case was called on as they left the court.

Helen turned to Sinead and Lachlan and said, 'I don't think "happy" is in her vocabulary.'

'I think you're right but she made the decision we want today.'

Maria said, 'Well done, Lachlan. It was always touch and go that we'd get that in.'

'Thank you, Maria.'

Helen was starting to get the impression they really disliked each other despite the veneer of politeness.

Helen spotted a barrister with his client coming out of a conference room and grabbed it before anyone else could get it. *There really should be more rooms for private discussions*, thought Helen.

They all went into the room which had three chairs around a low table which was pretty useless.

'Please sit down,' said Lachlan to Naomi and her gran.

The one remaining chair was left vacant as everyone insisted someone else should sit down. Eventually, Helen sat down simply so they could get a move on with this.

'I hope you followed that. Basically the judge has said the video will form no part of the evidence so no-one else will see it which includes the other defence teams and defendants. Without a motive your case is stronger. You had nothing to do with Josh's murder and no motive to kill your boyfriend.

'Now, the next step is for Helen to take a full statement from you about your relationship, events leading up to Josh's murder and the murder itself. This will only be seen by us but it will form part of what is called your defence statement which we need to submit in twenty eight days. After that, it's the trial in August but we will see you before then.'

Naomi burst into tears with relief.

'Thank you. Thank you so much.'

'I'm sorry this is so difficult for you.'

'It's not that. I'm just so pleased about today. It's the first good news I've had in months. Everything has just been getting worse and worse. I was dreading anyone seeing this so I feel I can breathe a bit.'

'That's great. Let's hope it continues to get better and better. Now get your head down and crack on with that A level revision.'

'I will. And thank you.'

Naomi and her gran walked out both looking taller than when they entered the court.

'Right, next up is her statement of evidence and then the defence statement. Sinead, can I leave that with you and we can communicate by email about it.'

'Fine by me. What we haven't had yet are the co-defendants previous convictions but I imagine the prosecution will want those in if they've got anything relevant.'

'I would think so but if they don't do a bad character application we most certainly will. Now, I've got a train in twenty minutes so I'm going to dash. It's good working with you again, Sinead. Mustn't leave it so long until the next time. Speak soon.'

Lachlan grinned at her in that winning way and out he went.

'I think that was him flirting with you,' said Helen. 'And what a sexy smile. I think it's because he's had his teeth fixed.'

'You cynic.'

'No drinks for you today then.'

'No, but there's always a next time.'

They opened the door to leave the conference room and a barrister grabbed it.

'Finished in here?'

'Yes.'

'Thanks,' he said, beckoning his client over indicating he's got a room.

'Like gold dust,' said Helen. 'Fancy a cuppa before we head back to the grindstone?'

'Love one. Let's get out of here and go to Amy's. Best coffee in Leeds.'

Maria, Sebastian, Ian and Mel went down to the CPS room to have a chat.

'Could have gone either way but I didn't think she'd be so critical. Without a motive, it's not as strong.'

'Do you think we should continue the case against her?' Ian asked.

'Yes definitely.'

'I'm not as sure as I was,' said Sebastian. 'She'll be presented as the grieving middle class teenager who has no doubt been coerced into drugs and into slapping him by these horrible, scummy drug dealers.'

'You're going soft, Sebastian. You must be doing too much defence work. We've got her slapping her boyfriend, she's the closest to him when he falls which makes her most likely to have stabbed him and we know duress is no defence to murder. She runs off at the scene without calling for help and we've got the murder weapon in her shed.'

'A shed that is open and could have been put there by anyone,' added Mel.

'But it is still in her garden. On top of that, we've not identified the phone that the text came from that she says is Ben Sutton and the recording is too poor to even try any form of voice identification. She could have bought a burner phone and sent the text to herself and the recording could be anyone. We've definitely got a case against her, nice middle class girl or not.'

'Okay, you're the boss.'

'I know I was up for charging her but I'm just not sure now that we have no motive.'

'And I'm with Ian on that.'

'Well, that's for a jury to decide. We've got evidence to go before a jury and that's what we're doing.'

With that, Maria turned on her stilettoes and walked out.

'She's not happy.'

'Well, she was criticised by the judge and no-one likes to lose and then be criticised on top of it. She's right about the evidence and she has good instincts so we've got to trust she's making the right call,' said Sebastian.

'I hope so.'

'Any holidays planned?'

'A week away with my son at the end of July.'

'Only your son? A little bird told me you were seeing that journalist. Not going away with her?'

Mel looked embarrassed and Ian bristled. 'Word gets round. No, that's over. She's got a job in London now. She's making a name for herself on gangs and county lines stories.' Ian was not happy that he had been the subject of gossip and even unhappy that he felt he'd been used. He wanted to hide in a corner and lick his wounds not be discussed by all and sundry.

Mel hadn't realised that it was all over but was trying not to show how pleased she felt.

Ian changed the subject. 'You going away?'

'Not unless a trial cracks. My wife is taking the kids to Italy for two weeks and, fingers crossed, I'll get to join them for some of the time but we'll see.'

'Well, good luck. We'd better get back to the station to our outstanding spate of robberies.'

'See you in August then if not before. And thanks for your thoroughness on this one.'

'It's what we do.'

'I wish all police departments were as thorough as yours.'

Mel and Ian walked out into the fog that was hanging around over Leeds.

'It's a bit early for lunch but fancy a coffee before we head back?' Ian asked.

'Would love to. We can celebrate the defence victory.'

'Can't make a habit of celebrating defence wins. We'll forget whose side we're on. By the way, Jack has asked for another maths session if you don't mind.'

'Would love to. I can come over tonight.'

'Great. I'll cook again.'

As they walked off for a coffee, Ian was feeling more positive about being duped by Tricia. What is it they say about every cloud?

Chapter 46

This was the first bit of good news Naomi had had in a long time. She felt she was emerging from the darkness into the light.

It was good to stretch her legs on the walk back to the car even if it was in the fog. Things were starting to go her way.

And she'd managed to get her head down for revision as there were no distractions. Apart from the dark thoughts of "what ifs?" but she was trying not to go there. She was amazed that she could focus on her work. It was actually a distraction from all the crap in the rest of her life.

And gran and granddad had been great. They cooked some amazing food. Her mum had obviously not inherited the cooking gene from her parents and her dad had always been pretty useless in the kitchen.

She was starting to see how Josh had taken up so much time, had distracted her from her studies and isolated her from her friends. She hadn't seen it at the time, had thought she'd wanted to be with him, didn't think she'd missed her friends but could see things more clearly now with that bit of distance.

He'd involved her in some horrible stuff, had taken all her time, had pressurised her into doing stuff she didn't want to, and then there was the rape. She didn't even want to go there.

Just now, her head was full of Shakespeare which was at least a good thing. She knew she'd been thorough in her revision. There was no question she could be asked on King Lear that she couldn't tackle. She never thought she'd be able to concentrate with this trial hanging over her but she had. She was determined to ace these exams.

The next few weeks it was all exams so, with the lightness she felt about the rape evidence being excluded, she could give it her all.

She had to. If she had a chance at a new life after this horror the exams were a huge part of it.

The rest was up to the lawyers.

Chapter 47

Sinead was so excited she had to speak to Lachlan. Had he seen it?

She phoned him and he answered immediately not that she thought he was sitting by the phone waiting for her to ring.

'Sinead, lovely to hear from you. How are you?'

'All the better for speaking to you, Lachlan.'

'You say the nicest things.'

She launched in, 'Have you seen the bad character applications? They've just gone on the system today.'

'Sorry, I've been tied up with a murder at the Bailey. Jury out tomorrow so pressure will ease off then. Tell me more.'

'Bad character applications for all three co-defendants. All three have previous for carrying knives, two of them have previous for possession with intent to supply, Sutton has previous for a section 18 grievous bodily harm and both Brown and Price have section 47 actual bodily harms. So we've got knives, drugs and violence. Should we put in an application as well?'

'Great. Not sure if it will all go in though. Anything for violence with a knife?'

'Unfortunately not.'

'Let me have a look at it and we can chat again once my jury goes out. I've seen Naomi's statement of evidence. Very long and thorough. Includes everything but the kitchen sink.'

'Helen is like that. No stone left unturned. I've done a first draft of the defence statement which I can send through to you today.'

'Great stuff. I'll have a look at it all tomorrow and get back to you.'

'Thanks. Speak soon.'

The jury might not all get to hear about all of it, thought Sinead, but surely the knives just had to be relevant. Fingers crossed. If the jury heard about the co-defendants' previous convictions, it would help to show Naomi in a totally different light from them.

*

Lachlan's jury retired to reach their verdicts. He didn't think they'd be long as the evidence against the two defendants, particularly his client, was overwhelming. Still, you never knew. It should give him at least a few hours to look at Naomi's case.

First the defence case statement. He was contemplating Naomi's statement and thinking about everything the defence statement needed to cover without giving too much detail. The defence statement was the one document the prosecution and court would have, apart from Naomi's police station interviews, so it had to be right. He scanned his eyes over it.

It covered all the basics in a point by point way of Josh getting involved in drugs, reasons for the slap, Naomi putting her arm out to help Josh and the open garden gate and shed. It told a story of a young girl in the wrong place at the wrong time. *Hits just the right note*, thought Lachlan. He was bothered about the timing of the arm going out to Josh though.

Is it before he falls, as he falls or just after? Difficult to tell. Must watch the footage yet again, he thought, as this was crucial. It was difficult to tell as the video footage, despite the enhancement, was not great.

He didn't need to tweak it as Sinead had done a good job of giving Naomi's defence without giving too much detail that might trip her up if she gives evidence in court. *It was good to work with Sinead again*, he thought. She knows what she's doing and she's fun to be with. He was looking forward to being in Leeds for a couple of weeks when they did the trial.

Lachlan also felt this was a case where Naomi really had to give evidence to explain what was going on and what she was doing. Sometimes you didn't want to let a client anywhere near the witness box.

Now to disclosure. Sinead has requested co-accused's previous convictions which we've now got, Josh's medical records which is standard and phone downloads of co-accused's phones and Josh's phone. Everything else was pretty standard. The prosecution might be reluctant about the phone downloads but we'll see. Chances are the phones won't show up anything as they'll have used burners but you never know as sometimes they slip up and use their own phones.

Well, the stupid ones do anyway. Let's add a request for all CCTV footage seized and previous convictions for all civilian witnesses and see where it takes us. Don't suppose there will be anything but it's a possibility.

He thought the bad character applications were interesting. The prosecution want the jury to hear about their convictions for drug dealing, assaults and for carrying knives. What the prosecution want to do is say they are violent, knife wielding drug dealers and he couldn't see that happening. Lachlan looked at the details of their drugs convictions and thought they were a non-starter.

Dealing drugs doesn't exactly mean you're a murderer but the jury will probably hear about their activities as it explains the relationship between Josh and the others. After all, why was Josh there in the first place? That couldn't be explained without the jury hearing about drugs.

Thank goodness Naomi would appear so different from the others in this. That would form part of their strategy. Nice middle class student, heading for university, boyfriend gets mixed up with drugs and is murdered by his dealers for non-payment. Let's hope the jury buy it.

He heard the tannoy. All parties in his trial to court one. Probably a verdict. Quick but not really a surprise.

Chapter 48

Sinead ended the call. Shit. God knows when Lachlan would get here and Naomi was due in less than an hour.

She dialled Helen.

'Hi, Helen, it's Sinead.'

'I can see it's you. Everything okay?'

'Lachlan's been delayed. There's an obstacle on the line and his train is stationery.'

'How far away is he?'

'Not far out of Kings Cross so we'll have to start without him. We can't postpone it as the defence statement needs to be served and we've got to go through it with Naomi and get her to sign it.'

'I'm sure we can manage without him. He'll hopefully get here before we finish and he can sweep in, be charming and say all the right things.'

'You're getting to know him well. I'll see you soon then.'

Sinead looked again at the defence statement. It should be fine. They'd already gone through the prosecution evidence with Naomi and there were no surprises so this should be straight forward.

She got distracted by her broken nails and then noticed the ladder in her tights. How was it that some barristers managed to look impeccable with their polished nails, which she never had time for, and their immaculate makeup which she had never mastered? She couldn't manage more than pulling a brush through her thick, unruly hair each morning, and adding a bit of eyeliner, mascara and lipstick.

She told herself it was a natural look but she couldn't help but feel a bit grubby next to some of the more polished barristers with the immaculate makeup and nails.

Right. Concentrate. Defence statement. Need to make sure Naomi understands it and is happy to sign it so it can be served. At least it will be only the prosecution and judge that sees the defence statement although its contents could come out at trial.

She decided to grab a coffee before they got here. No time for lunch. Again. She walked through to the kitchen in chambers to make a coffee and saw a tin of biscuits with a "help yourself" note next to it. This would keep her going. She grabbed a few Belgian chocolate ones, made the coffee and went back to her room to check over the defence statement one last time.

Her phone rang and Debbie from reception told her the client was here.

'Thanks, I'll be right down.'

She stood up, grabbed her laptop and papers before noticing the crumbs down the front of the black jacket. *It doesn't get any better,* she thought and brushed them away.

Walking down the staircase, she could see Naomi with Helen and a man she hadn't seen before.

She walked into reception and Helen stood up.

'Hi, Sinead, this is Phil, Naomi's dad. I don't think you've met. Phil, this is Sinead, the junior barrister.'

'Hello. Pleased to meet you,' said Phil. 'I'm sorry this is the first meeting I've managed to get to with you. I work away a lot and it can be difficult.'

'Pleased to meet you too. Don't worry about that. We understand how hard it is to drop everything. Lachlan's train has been delayed but we can make a start. I've got a conference room reserved on the first floor. Would you like a tea or coffee?'

'Tea would be great,' said Phil.

'Me too,' added Naomi.

'Make that three,' added Helen.

'Right. Debbie would you mind organising tea for four and some biscuits as well please.'

Sinead thought she might as well get some biscuits as she could do with more even if the others didn't want any. Sometimes conferences had their perks. Must remember the crumbs though.

Sinead led them into the first floor conference room where they sat round the large oblong table, Phil and Naomi facing Helen and Sinead.

She handed Phil and Naomi hard copies of the defence statement as she and Helen opened their laptops to view their saved copies.

'This is a brief outline of your defence. We need to say enough in it so there are no surprises at trial. If something did come out at trial that we hadn't mentioned, the court might think you've just thought of it or made it up and wonder why you hadn't mentioned it before. We don't need to tell them everything as it's just a summary as you will see under the heading of "general nature of the defence". Give it another read through and we can discuss it.'

Sinead and Helen read through it again, although by this time it was etched on Sinead's mind.

1. The defendant denies stabbing the defendant.
2. The defendant denies knowing of any plan or agreement to stab the defendant. She was not party to any agreement if there was one.
3. The defendant accepts she was present at the scene when the deceased was stabbed.
4. The defendant went with the deceased, who was her boyfriend, to a prearranged meeting with the co-defendants. The deceased asked the defendant to accompany him as he was nervous about going on his own. The deceased had been selling drugs on behalf of the co-defendants and owed them money which he did not have as he had been unable to sell very much. The defendant understood that the meeting was to discuss what the deceased owed them.
5. The defendant and the deceased arrived at the meeting place which was outside the Fisher estate local shop. There was no sign of the co-defendants so they entered the shop to see if they were there and bought a drink. When they left the shop a boy aged about ten told them to meet the co-defendants up an alleyway that ran alongside the shop.
    The defendant and the deceased walked up the alleyway and the co-defendants were waiting towards the other end of the alley. There was an argument about the debt and the deceased asked for more time to pay.
6. Ben Sutton punched the deceased and the two others then joined in. The deceased began to stumble and the defendant put out her hand to steady him. As the deceased fell, the defendant became frightened that the co-defendants might attack her so she ran off at about the same time as the co-defendants ran. She ran in a different direction at the top of the alleyway and caught a bus home.

7. She was frightened of the co-defendants as she had seen them use violence against the deceased and had been present on a previous occasion when they had threatened the deceased. On one occasion, they told the defendant to slap the deceased and if she refused they would assault him. She felt they had control over her as well as over the deceased. On that occasion, she did slap him as she felt she had no choice.

8. When she was on the bus, she rang the deceased but there was no answer. She rang him when she arrived home but there was no answer. She assumed he was angry with her for running off and leaving him.

9. The defendant did not think the deceased was badly hurt. She did not see a knife and did not see the deceased being stabbed. Had she done so she would have called for help. The defendant believed the deceased began to stumble because he had been punched.

10. The defendant found out the following morning about the death of the deceased.

11. A knife with the deceased's blood on it, believed to me the murder weapon, was found in the garden shed of the defendant's home. There is no lock on the garden gate leading to the back garden and there is no lock on the garden shed. The defendant knows nothing about this knife. She has not seen it before and has not touched it. Her fingerprints are not on this knife. Anyone could have placed this knife in the garden shed.

'There's no mention of Sutton texting me and meeting up with me to threaten me to keep quiet.'

'That's because we have no evidence to support it. We have your phone download but the text has come from a burner phone so anyone could have sent it. Sutton's team will say you sent it to yourself. The voice is too muffled to be recognisable so could be anyone and we have no CCTV to show him either there or going there even though we have requested it. Plus, Sutton has an alibi. His mum is saying he was at home.

'It's better not to mention something that can be easily attacked. We've told the prosecution about this meeting when we've requested CCTV and phone downloads but without evidence of the meeting it leaves you more open to attack by Sutton's defence team. If, by some miracle, we did get evidence of this, we can bring it in and show that we've already informed the prosecution about the meeting and the threats.'

'Okay, you know best.'

'Will the others be putting the blame on Naomi?' Phil asked.

'It's possible but it's more likely they will blame each other. We think that Price will blame Sutton and Brown so they might, in turn, blame him. That would be best for us as it keeps you out of it.'

'I still don't get it. If they are blaming each other, why has Naomi been charged? It makes no sense to me.'

'The prosecution are saying that they were in it together. We will know more when we get their opening speech but it seems that their case is Naomi, even if she was pressurised into doing it, had assaulted Josh previously and was part of the group even if she was an unwilling part of it. Plus the murder weapon was found in her shed.'

'If she had been pressurised and was unwilling, how can she be charged with murder?'

'Because being pressurised into something, even where you fear serious violence, can be a defence to some crimes but it's not a defence to murder. You can't say to a jury "I'm not guilty because he made me do it".'

'Well, you know what you're doing but it seems crazy to me. How can they lump her with those drug dealing scum? Anyone can see she's not like them.'

'And that's what we'll be emphasising. Naomi is from a good home, an A level student, with dreams of going to university. The jury will see how different she is. That's the plan.'

'I hope you're right.'

The door opened and Lachlan walked in carrying the confidence and smile as part of his uniform.

'Hello, everyone. Sorry I'm so late. There was a suicide on the line and many of the trains out of Kings Cross were delayed. You must be Phil, I'm Lachlan Macpherson. I'll be representing Naomi along with Sinead. Have you had a chance to go through the defence statement?'

'Yes. We've just been going through some questions and I've explained that we'll be doing everything to separate Naomi in the eyes of the jury from the co-defendants. I've also explained why we won't be using the text and meeting with Sutton.'

'Great stuff. We don't know what the co-defendants will be saying but we assume they will be putting the blame on each other rather than Naomi.'

Lachlan went on to describe how the trial would work, who went first and who all the participants were.

Phil sat and listened as if he was describing a television courtroom drama rather than his daughter's murder trial.

'Do you want to ask anything, Naomi?'

'No, thanks, I can't think of anything. I just want to get it over with now. My last exam was last Friday so all I can do is think about it.'

'How did the exams go?' Lachlan asked.

'Okay I think. At least I had no distractions at my gran's. Apart from this of course.'

'It can't have been easy. You'll get the results a few days before the trial starts. One of my sons has just sat his A levels too.'

'Yes. It might all be pointless if I'm convicted.'

'We will do everything to make sure that doesn't happen.'

'I know. I trust you. Will I see you before the trial?'

'If you want to. We can have a conference to go through the trial process and what to expect.'

'Yes. That would be useful.'

'We'll do it just before the trial so it will be fresh in your memory.'

'Thank you.'

'I know it seems ridiculous to say try and put it to the back of your mind, but you need to do that for your sanity. You've got just under two months till the trial. We will be working hard on your behalf.'

'I know.'

'Right. I'll show you out and you can try and forget about it for a while.'

Lachlan got up and led them downstairs leaving Sinead and Helen there.

'I've got a note of everything,' said Helen.

'Glad you can type fast. Told you Lachlan would sweep in and be charming.'

'But he does it so well. He comes over really relaxed and confident, like a granddad telling you everything will be okay.'

'He doesn't look like any granddad I've seen.'

'You know what I mean. He has a knack of comforting you. And don't forget that twinkle in his soulful blue eyes and the ever so sexy smile.'

'Careful now.'

Just then, Lachlan walked in. Sinead blushed and Helen laughed.

'What's so funny?'

'Nothing. It's just you walking in at the eleventh hour and being charming.'

'That's what KCs are for, didn't anyone tell you that.'

'Do you think she will be convicted?'

'I don't know is the honest answer. She has a good run but the slap and the murder weapon, even if we can explain them, are problems. I'm also worried that the other three will blame her now they know the murder weapon was found in her shed. They will no doubt have got their heads together.'

'They're not in the same prisons, are they?'

'Not now, but it doesn't stop them. Anyway, we will just have to wait and see but be prepared for it. The last thing we need is for them to be saying they saw Naomi with the knife.'

Chapter 49

DC David Metcalfe had the unenviable job of going through the rest of the CCTV that wasn't going to be used in evidence but had to be disclosed to the defence in case it helped them. He hated this task. The defence asked for everything in the hope that something might help them, that there might be a gold nugget somewhere. There rarely was.

He'd already been through all the council CCTV but there was some that had been collected from houses near the scene and near the defendant's homes that he had yet to go through. It would take him days.

After several hours he was getting a headache and decided to go for a walk, rest his eyes and stretch his legs. The room was airless and he was developing a headache. A wander round the town centre and a cup of coffee was what he needed. He got up and walked towards the door when he bumped into Prita.

'Hi, David, how's it going?'

'I hate being disclosure officer when there's loads of CCTV to go through. I need some air before I go boggle eyed so I'm going for a coffee and a leg stretch. Fancy joining me?'

'Would love to but can't. Got to do an interview on a GBH.'

As David left the building, the wall of heat hit him. There was no breeze. White bodies wandered round in strappy tops and shorts with a good few beer bellies on show. *Some people should really keep the bellies hidden no matter how hot it gets*, he thought. The early summer heat wave wasn't due to last much longer but it wasn't helping his concentration sitting in a cramped and airless office. He didn't know which was worse, the lack of heating in winter or the lack of air conditioning in summer.

The coffee shop was unusually quiet. Too hot for coffee, although there were plenty of iced drinks on offer.

'I'll have a Frappuccino please.'

'Anything else?'

Not at these prices, he thought.

'No thanks. That's all.'

He paid and left with his iced coffee. Not that long ago it was either coffee or tea. Now it was a countless variety of each at three times the price. And if you stuck "artisan" on the front of something, you could really hike the price. God, he was sounding like his dad.

He couldn't face going back to his airless office yet so he wandered around the town square where people were sitting out in cafes and on benches with cold drinks enjoying the sunshine. The fountain was even working.

He sat down on a bench to drink his coffee, take his jacket off and watch the world go by. A ten minute break to sit and do nothing was needed to clear his head. He might not be cooling down but at least he could enjoy the sun even if it was only briefly.

He could sit here all afternoon but work called, so he reluctantly got up and walked slowly back to the office.

He was dragging his body through the large double doors and noticed a bronze coloured Golf parked on double yellows. He thought it looked vaguely familiar as you didn't get many that colour. A youth in joggers came out of the station, brushed passed him and got into the Golf. It took a bit of nerve parking on double yellows outside a police station.

Paul was on the front desk.

'What did he want?' David asked.

'Broken tail light and got a producer.'

'What's his name?'

'Mark Sutton. I've got all his details if you want them.'

'Great. Could just be a coincidence but I need to check him and the car out.'

'Here we go. Name, address, vehicle make and registration number. Car is taxed and insured so that was all legit.'

'Lovely. I owe you one.'

The heat lethargy had left David as he ran upstairs to the stifling office carrying the printout Paul had given him. He wasn't noticing the heat as he sat down to have another look at some CCTV footage he'd previously been through. That car was such a distinctive colour, even in the dark, it could probably be seen passing lampposts and garages. He was sure he'd seen it somewhere.

After about an hour, he saw it. Bingo. Mark Sutton's car going on to the estate where Naomi lives on the night she said Ben Sutton threatened her. Mark and Ben Sutton lived at the same address.

He got straight on the phone.

'Boss, I think we've got something else on Sutton that might help Naomi Edwards. I think you should have a look at it.'

'Be right up.'

Ian beckoned Mel over. No sign of Prita or John.

'David Metcalfe's found something he wants us to see. Don't know what it is but have you got some time?'

'Sure.' Mel knew David was the disclosure officer so he must have found something that helped the defence. *Shit*, she thought, and hoped it wasn't going to blow the whole prosecution wide apart. That just couldn't happen, not after all their hard work.

The door to David's cramped room was open and a couple of monitors were on the desk with boxes of lever arch files on the floor. It was stifling with the monitors pumping out heat.

'Have a look at this. I'd offer you a seat if I had some.'

'Don't worry. Working here has made us used to slumming it.'

David played the footage which showed the car going on to Naomi's estate at the right time.

'That's Mark Sutton's car, Ben Sutton's older brother.'

'Okay, it's an unusual colour which you can see as it passes that lamppost but you can't see the plate.'

'Hang on. Have a look at this.'

David played a separate piece of footage where the car passed a garage and then signalled to turn in to Naomi's estate. The plate can be seen.

'How did you find that out?'

David told them about his stroke of luck.

'It supports Naomi's story about Sutton threatening her,' said Mel. 'Her team will be happy with this.'

'Sutton's won't. The thing is we can't see who is in the car. It looks like it's just the driver. There are no cameras closer to Naomi's which show anyone getting out of the car so he'll just say he wasn't there.'

'He might but we've got enough to bring Mark Sutton in on suspicion of assisting an offender. As you know your way around this footage perhaps you and Mel can interview him?' Ian asked.

'Fine by me.'

'Okay.'

'Thanks. Let me know how you get on.'

Ian went back down to his office and thought about it. Mark Sutton's car near Naomi's house doesn't prove anything. Mark Sutton will no doubt deny he was going to Naomi's but will he deny Ben was in the car with him? It might help Naomi throw a bit of mud but it doesn't go much further than that as there is no positive sighting of Ben Sutton.

Right, onwards and upwards. He needed to go through some budget figures that were doing his head in. Not what he joined the police for but can't be avoided these days. He was finding it difficult to concentrate as he kept thinking of Jack. His last maths exam today.

He was a different person after that drugs scare and Mel had no doubt helped with the maths tuition so all was good. Apart from his love life which was non-existent since Trisha dumped him and moved to London once she got a scoop out of him. A learning experience but one he could do without.

When Mrs Sutton answered the door, Mel and David held up their ID.

'What do you lot want? You know where Ben is. You put him there.'

'It's Mark we'd like to speak to.'

'For fuck's sake. Are you planning on arresting the whole family? It'll be me next. He's not done owt.'

Despite the bravado, she couldn't help wondering what Mark had been up to. She couldn't cope with another one banged up. Besides, Mark brought in some money and she needed that.

'Is he in?'

Eileen Sutton looked at Mel as if she was going to punch her. She took her time before turning round and shouting, 'Mark, down here. It's the bizzies.'

Mark took his time and sauntered down the stairs with an exaggerated swagger as if he was in some sort of gangster film.

'What do you lot want? I've produced my documents and everything was legit.'

'Mark Sutton, I'm arresting you on suspicion of assisting an offender. You do not have to say anything but it may harm your defence if you do not mention when questioned something which you later rely on in court. Anything you do say may be given in evidence.'

Mark was open mouthed. 'What you on about? I haven't done anything.'

Mel asked him to turn round and place his hands behind him then handcuffed him at the back.

'You stuck up cow,' added Eileen Sutton.

If that was the best she could come up with Mel wouldn't worry. She'd had a lot worse in London.

*

Back at the station, he was booked in by the custody sergeant, asked for his solicitor and was then placed in a cell to wait.

They didn't have to wait for long. Charles Haig arrived. Same firm of solicitors as the three already charged. They must be doing a roaring trade with this lot.

Mel and David showed the solicitor the footage and gave him a page of disclosure before he went in for a consultation with Mark Sutton.

After ten minutes, he was out again telling them he was ready for interview.

That was quick. It was nearly 6.00 and he probably wanted to get home, Mel thought cynically.

The interview didn't take long either. No comment but a prepared statement saying the footage shows him on his own in the car and, as it was so long ago, he can't possibly remember where he was driving to.

They had no choice but to bail him and then have a think about it.

It looked like another dead end but they'd send it to the defence in case they wanted to make something of it.

She went up to see Ian but he'd already left. Of course, Jack's maths exam so he'd want to get home. Should she ring him?

She dialled and he answered straight away. After filling him in, Ian suggested she join him and Jack for a pizza in town if she was free. Jack's exam had gone well and it was down to her.

Well, she thought, it wasn't as if she had anything else on so she arranged to meet them there in half an hour. Time for a quick change and a bit of makeup. She couldn't do more than that in half an hour.

She was home in ten minutes. As she rifled through her wardrobe discarding clothes that were either too tarty or too severe, she settled on a red dress that emphasised her curves, was flattering but not revealing and a pair of black heels, not too high or she wouldn't be able to walk there and back. Christ, she didn't think Ian would be worrying about what to wear.

They were already there when she arrived and it was obvious Jack was really pleased to see her.

'Mel, thank you for everything,' and gave her an unexpected hug.

'You're welcome. I hope you get the grades you deserve. It's you that's put the work in.'

'Looking good, Mel. And this is on us,' said Ian. You've been a star and we're both very grateful.'

She smiled. 'Thank you,' her eyes crinkling, beautiful laughter lines, and he held her look for longer than a boss should.

'And I think you've had enough of my cooking so it's about time we had a meal out.'

She couldn't help but hoping this was just the first of many more to come.

Part Two
The Trial

Chapter 50

Day One

Naomi felt sick. There was no getting away from it. This could be the end of her life or the start of a new life. There was no halfway house. She could have all the A levels in the world but if she was found guilty all her dreams would be over.

Her dad parked in a multi-storey just off the Headrow. Parking was a nightmare in Leeds but at least they got a place. She knew they were too early but her dad kept saying that you never knew what the traffic would be like.

It was just a five minute walk to the court but her legs felt like lead and she wasn't sure she would make it there.

'Shall we get coffee to take in with us?' Phil asked.

'If you like.'

She was trying to hide her nerves but fooling no-one. Her stomach was doing somersaults and she felt like she was about to vomit. Yet again. She was fed up with all the puking she had done. Coffee churning in her stomach was the last thing she needed.

'You've not eaten anything so maybe a coffee and Danish would do you good. You'll be collapsing with hunger if you're not careful.' Pam was concerned.

'Okay.' She knew this was hard for her parents and they were really trying. She looked at her dad and saw the helplessness written all over his face. She just wanted to scream. She shouldn't be here. This shouldn't be happening. She could tell from his look that his feelings mirrored hers.

Pam spotted a café. 'Let's go in there, it looks quiet.'

They crossed the road and went into a small independent café. The guy behind the counter was unbearably friendly and cheerful.

'Hi. What can I get you this lovely sunny morning?'

Naomi wanted to hit him. She sat at a table while her mum and dad ordered coffee, toast and croissants. On the surface, it was all so normal but it was far from it. She was on trial for her freedom and her sanity.

'Take a seat and I'll bring your food and drinks over.'

Phil and Pam sat down with Naomi. No-one really knew what to say. Small talk didn't really cut it today.

'You look nice,' said Pam. 'It was worth getting a suit. The jury will see you're nothing like the rest of them.'

Naomi was wearing a navy suit, navy shoes with a small heel and a white blouse buttoned up to the neck. Her hair was tied back and she was wearing small pearl earrings and just a little bit of makeup. Helen had talked to her about the way women on a jury often judge other women harshly so go for smart but avoid anything too tarty. She didn't do tarty anyway.

'There you go. One Americano with cold milk, one cappuccino, one skinny latte, one toast and two croissants. Enjoy.'

As if she would. She nibbled at the toast to please her mum and dad so that would be one less thing they'd have to worry about.

'Gran and granddad will hopefully come tomorrow.'

'I know. They told me.'

Small talk, thought Naomi, but everyone's nerves were strained to breaking point.

'I think we should be getting over there now,' suggested Phil.

They got up to leave and Pam brought the cups and plates over to the counter.

Mum always has to clear the crockery. Why do women do that? Her dad never did. She wouldn't do it, wouldn't be the stereotypical female that cleared up after everyone else. If she got the chance of a different life anyway.

'Thanks, folks. Have a great day.'

The urge to punch him was getting stronger. Naomi knew he was just being friendly but she couldn't handle it.

They walked slowly over to the court. Naomi thought this must be what it felt like to walk to a scaffold.

When they got to the entrance, they were still early and the queues hadn't formed yet. They went through the scanners individually, emptying pockets and offering up handbags for inspection. When they got through, Naomi looked for a friendly face. No sign of Helen, Sinead or Lachlan.

Phil went over to look at the list on an electronic board. He didn't want to ask at reception, didn't want the receptionist to know it was his daughter up for murder. Not that she'd care, he supposed. Must be used to seeing all sorts here. He saw Naomi's name. Court One. How could his daughter's name be on a court list? None of it made sense.

He turned away and saw Josh's parents come through security. He caught Anna's eye as she walked over to them.

Anna looked at Naomi. 'Hi, Naomi. Is it okay if we have a word in private?'

'Of course.'

'We could just sit over there on our own,' said Anna pointing to an empty row of seats.

They walked over and sat down.

Naomi didn't know what to expect. Was Anna going to hit out at her? Was she going to blame her? Was she going to rant and start shouting? She'd been supportive before but that was months ago and Naomi was betting the police had poisoned her mind about her.

Naomi couldn't take it if she did. Her nerves were like wires jangling and her stomach was in overdrive.

'The family liaison officers have been keeping us up to date with the case and the evidence, and I just want to say that I know you had nothing to do with Josh's death. I know I've said it before but nothing has changed about the way we all feel about you.'

Naomi couldn't imagine what it was like for them losing Josh and being here.

'Thank you. That means so much,' said Naomi.

Anna gave Naomi a hug.

Pam watched from a distance and her eyes filled up with tears.

'Thank you. I didn't do it. I don't know who put the knife in our shed but it wasn't me. I can't believe I'm here. I'm so frightened. I know I should have stayed with Josh but I was just scared.'

Naomi's tears started but she managed to hold it together because she had to. They held on to each other, both of them trying to stay in control, as their families looked on.

Anna pulled away first. 'I'll be with you all the way. And I heard about your results. Well done. Josh would have been proud of you. Is it still Birmingham?'

'No. I've decided to go to York as it was one uni that we hadn't thought about and I felt that would be better for me.'

'Good thinking. Think of it as just being a few weeks away and you can put all this behind you like a bad dream.'

'I hope so but I keep thinking, "what if they find me guilty? What if they don't believe me?" What if I spend fifteen years in jail and have no life? I can't stop those thoughts. The worst bit is in the night when I wake up and the thoughts won't stop.'

Anna grabbed hold of her hands and held them tight.

'That's not going to happen. We know you shouldn't be here and the jury will see that. The next few weeks are going to be really tough for all of us. We just need to get through it. I don't know how but we've got to. Stay strong and remember we're behind you all the way.'

'Thank you. You don't know how much that means to me.'

Anna kissed her forehead, got up and walked towards Greg and the family liaison officers as Naomi walked back to her family.

Pam watched Anna go and felt her heart would break for her but she didn't want her pain and Naomi just had to be acquitted. She had her whole life in front of her.

Helen approached her.

'I saw that. It must have been very hard for you. For all of you.'

Naomi nodded. Pam and Phil didn't say anything.

'It's going to be hard to focus on the trial now but that's what we've got to do. We've got a room and Lachlan and Sinead are already there. It's better that we use the stairs as it might be a bit awkward in the lift if we bump into any of the other families.'

Helen took them to a room that had a laminated sign on it saying, "In Use". 'Lachlan charmed them at reception into giving us a room for the duration of the trial. It's one of the benefits of being a KC.'

'At least we won't bump into the other families.'

Helen opened the door and led them in. Lachlan and Sinead were already there, sat at the table deep in discussion.

'Good morning, Naomi,' said Lachlan. 'Helen told us about your fantastic results and that you're going to York. Well done.'

'Depends what happens here, doesn't it.'

'Well, it's our job to make sure you can take up that place and we're going to do everything we can to get you there. I'm going to do an opening speech. It's something the defence don't usually do but I want to separate you out from the others right from the start of the trial. You look very smart by the way. Just right.'

Naomi couldn't help but think that it was partly about how you looked and presented. Almost as if it was a game. Well, she was prepared to play it if it would get her off.

'There has been one development. There is footage of Ben Sutton's brother's car turning into your estate on the night you say Ben Sutton met you. The problem is there is no evidence that Ben Sutton was in the car so I'm afraid it takes us no further forward.'

'But surely it shows I'm telling the truth.'

'We think you are but it's what a jury thinks that's important. Footage of Mark Sutton's car driving onto your estate, no-one in the passenger seat and, let's face it, it's a big estate and he could have been going anywhere. We can't use it.'

'Well, they're lying. He was probably hiding in the car but I suppose you know best.'

'You've got to trust us on this one. It's better not to use something which can so easily be shot down.'

Lachlan just hoped he was making the right call on that one.

*

'All parties in the case of Sutton, Brown, Price and Edwards to Court one,' was heard over the tannoy.

'Right, that's us. Pam and Phil, you'll be in the public gallery. You will see the defendants for the first time and I know that won't be easy. I get it. Try and sit as far apart as you can from any of the other defendants' families. Naomi, you're in the dock with the others but you'll be sat at the end and there will be two officers in the dock so don't worry about the other defendants.

'I understand how hard it will be for you being in that confined space with them. It will be emotional and, no doubt, frightening. If there is a problem, you need to make the dock officer aware of it. Helen's given you pen and paper so if there's any issues, or anything occurs to you or if you need anything at all, just scribble a note and bring it to the attention of one of the dock officers. Okay.'

'Yes. I know you'll all do your best for me.'

The usher showed Naomi into the dock when the security officer unlocked it. The other three hadn't yet been brought up from the cells. She was shown where to sit by the woman security officer who smiled at her warmly and called her love.

Helen turned round to smile at Naomi. Sometimes lots of reassuring smiles throughout the day was the best you could do.

The other barristers trooped in, chatting and smiling like it was an ordinary day. She supposed it was for them.

Weren't they taking this seriously? Wondered Naomi.

They all took their positions with four on the front row and six on the second row. Helen was sitting on the third row just in front of the dock and there were two other men who Naomi assumed were solicitors.

Laptops were opened and blue notebooks emerged along with ring binders and pens.

There was a knock on the door at the front of the court, 'All rise,' said the court clerk and the judge walked in and sat down in her chair high above everyone else, looking down on the players.

She looked as miserable as she did before. The rays of sun had definitely not reached her face as she looked as grey as ever.

'Bring up the other defendants,' said the judge.

Ben Sutton, Harley Brown and Luke Price came through, one by one and were shown where to sit. Naomi was closest to Luke Price and Ben Sutton was at the far end. That was something at least. Ben and Harley were wearing white shirts and black trousers. They looked like waiters.

Luke was in the usual joggers and sweat shirt. Naomi assumed his parents hadn't bothered to get him anything decent to wear. At least being next to Luke showed a marked contrast in appearance. Let's hope the jury thought the contrast didn't stop there.

*

Phil stared at them. He was seeing them for the first time. They were nothing. These ugly little scroats were the lads who'd raped his beautiful, precious daughter. He couldn't bear to think what they'd done to her, what they'd put her through.

A gang rape for fuck's sake. That's what it was.

Why the hell didn't she report it? She'd told them why but he still didn't get it.

If she'd reported it, they would've been arrested and none of them would be here now.

He wanted to be angry with her for not going to the police but how could he be angry with her? She was the victim. None of it was her fault.

He wanted to get his hands on them and batter the living daylights out of them. He could strangle them with his bare hands.

He wanted justice for her.

Didn't she want justice for herself?

And now she was standing next to them. It was all wrong.

What must Naomi be going through having to share that small space with them, breathe the same air as them? He couldn't get his head around it. Having to stand next to these inadequate little tossers remembering what they'd done to her.

She must be going through hell. She must be re-living it.

How could she just stand there? It must be beyond agony for her.

How can the prosecution make out she's one of them?

And the prosecutor is a fucking woman.

He'd heard about being traumatised by events. Being next to them must be traumatising her. He wouldn't be surprised if she ended up needing psychiatric treatment after this.

Would the prosecutor care?

Had the judge even thought of that?

Surely the court could have separated them after all she'd been through?

The judge knows about the rape. She's a woman. Doesn't she get it?

Lachlan told him why they had to be in the dock together but it wasn't his daughter that had been raped and had to stand for weeks next to her rapists.

How could the court just lump them together?

Pam grabbed hold of his hand and their eyes locked, both thinking exactly the same thing and nothing needed to be said.

He hoped they'd rot in prison for a very long time.

And that Naomi wouldn't be joining them.

He wasn't religious but prayed every day that she'd get off.

And they wouldn't.

Please God.

*

The court clerk asked the defendants to stand and identified each one of them before asking them to sit.

The judge addressed the prosecutor. 'Before a jury is empanelled, are there any preliminaries I need to be aware of, Ms Conroy?'

'My lady is aware of the representation. There will be one defence opening speech as I understand, from Mr Macpherson King's Counsel, on behalf of Naomi Edwards. There will be no other defence opening speeches. There is a bad character application by the Crown, supported by Mr Macpherson and Ms O'Casey. We invite your ladyship to deal with this at the close of the prosecution case.

'The drug dealing by the defendants and the deceased will be referred to by both the Crown and the defence. This has been agreed between all parties as it has to do with the alleged facts of the offence. Unless my learned friends have anything to add, a jury can now be empanelled.'

There was a chorus of "no thank you" from the barristers and the judge nodded to the usher who went out of a door at the back of the court.

Naomi knew she was a clever girl but this was like being in a parallel universe where an elite core dressed differently, spoke in a code and only they knew what was going on.

The usher came back a few minutes later with a group of people who looked bewildered.

The court clerk had cards, presumably with names on, which she kept shuffling like she was about to play a game of poker. A name was read out, a hand was raised and the person was asked to take a seat in the two rows reserved for the jury. The cards were shuffled again, another name read and so on until the jury rows were filled with twelve men and women.

The remaining ones whose names hadn't been called were led back through the door. The jury, seven men and five women, were then sworn in. Some swore on the Bible, one on the Quran and some affirmed. Some of them stumbled over the words in their nervousness at speaking so publicly in such a strange place with men and women dressed in odd costumes.

The judge spoke to them. She was all smiles now as she explained what her role was, what their role was and that the case will be opened by prosecuting counsel, Ms Conroy, King's Counsel. She turned and nodded to Maria Conroy who got to her feet.

'Members of the jury, the defendants who you see in the dock, are Ben Sutton, Harley Brown, Luke Price and Naomi Edwards who we say, together, on the night of the 3 February, stabbed Josh Smithies, a seventeen-year-old A level student. Josh did not die right away. He was left in an alley as all four ran off, not tending to him or calling for help. It was left to a passer-by to call an ambulance. You have in front of you a sheet of paper, called the indictment, which is the charge that they each face, that of murder.

'At the time Naomi Edwards was the girlfriend of Josh Smithies and also an A level student. She had become embroiled, along with Josh, in doing what the others in the dock bid them to do and, you will hear, on a previous occasion she had assaulted Josh. Just because someone else tells you to stab someone, or even threatens you to get you to be part of a plan to stab someone, it is not a defence to murder.

'And this was all because of a drugs debt. Josh Smithies had started using some drugs and began selling drugs for this group. We say there was a plan to punish him because he failed to pay up on time.

'Much of the evidence is on CCTV. The evening was cold and dark but the figures can each be seen, some assaulting Josh and all reaching out towards him. One of those reaching out had a knife which was used to fatally wound Josh. It cannot be clearly seen which one of them struck the fatal blow but we say they were in this together. Josh was to be punished. You will also hear that the knife used to stab Josh Smithies was found at the home address of Naomi Edwards.

'Now, let me introduce the representation. I prosecute this case on behalf of the Crown along with Mr Wells.

'Ben Sutton is represented by Ms O'Ryan, King's Counsel, and Ms Taylor.

'Harley Brown is represented by Mr White, King's Counsel, and Ms Harris.

'Luke Price is represented by Mr Smythe, King's Counsel, and Mr Winstanley.

'Naomi Edwards is represented by Mr Macpherson, King's Counsel, and Ms O'Casey.'

Each of the barristers nodded towards the jury when they heard their names. *As if the jury would remember them*, Naomi thought. They all looked much alike in their wigs, white collars and black gowns.

Maria Conroy carried on talking about the evidence and what the prosecution had to prove.

After about forty minutes, she finished and sat down.

The judge thanked her and turned towards the jury.

'Members of the jury, it is the right of each defence team to make an opening speech. Many choose not to do so. In this case, Mr Macpherson will address you on behalf of Naomi Edwards.'

*

Lachlan stood up and smiled at the jury making sure he made eye contact with each one.

Naomi held her breath. *Please be brilliant.*

'Ladies and gentleman, I'm going to tell you a little bit about Naomi Edwards and you will hear more about her and her relationship with the deceased in the evidence over the coming days.

'Naomi was seventeen when Josh Smithies was stabbed. They were what you might describe as childhood sweethearts, an old fashioned term, but they'd been friends having gone to the same primary school, secondary school and then sixth form college before becoming closer when they were sixteen. They were studying for their A levels, spent most of their time together, were in some of the same classes, planned to go to the same university, planned to be together. In short, they were two young people in love with their whole lives in front of them.

'And then Josh started to take drugs, initially you will hear, to calm his anxiety and then to keep him awake while he studied. It became more of a problem and, to pay for these drugs, he began to sell drugs for this group of three young men. But he didn't have many buyers and still owed money so he had to be taught a lesson. A lesson that perhaps went a bit too far.

'You will hear how Naomi supported him, reluctantly, went along with him when he was meeting this group and that she was with him on the night he was killed. Ladies and gentlemen, what we say, is that being with her boyfriend, being in the wrong place at the wrong time does not make Naomi a killer or part of any plan to kill Josh, nor does the fact that the police found the knife that killed Josh in Naomi's unlocked garden shed, make Naomi a killer.

'Naomi Edwards is a victim of the three defendants who sit in the dock beside her, a victim of circumstances.'

Lachlan carried on talking about the evidence.

Naomi could see the jurors looking at her and then looking back at Lachlan.

*

Sinead was watching the jurors' faces. No reaction. But you wouldn't expect it at this stage. Lachlan was using Naomi's name a lot, getting the jury to see her as a person, an individual, separate her from the others. It was a good tactic.

After about fifteen minutes, Lachlan smiled and thanked the jury for listening to him then sat down.

He had such an easy, relaxed style as if he was just having a chat with the jury but Sinead knew how he'd agonised about what to say in his opening, making it long enough to give some detail but short enough to hold their attention. Sinead had seen too many barristers lose a jury by droning on and on.

The judge turned to the prosecutor. 'Ms Conroy.'

'My lady, the first witness for the Crown is Chelsea Brittan.'

The usher went outside the courtroom and brought Chelsea into the witness box where she was sworn.

She was clearly nervous and could hardly be heard.

The judge turned to her.

'Mrs Brittan, you are quite softly spoken and it's important that the jury hear what you have to say. Imagine you are speaking to the jurors on the back row, look towards them and keep your voice up please.'

Maria Conroy began by confirming Chelsea's name and then took her through what she was doing on the evening of the 3 of February.

Sinead saw that she kept glancing towards the dock. She was scared of those three.

She said she didn't recognise who was there, just that there were noises and people running. She hurried up the ginnel and found the deceased then called an ambulance. When she described finding Josh and staying with him till the ambulance came she became visibly upset and the usher handed her a glass of water and some tissues.

It must have left her quite traumatised but there was no way she was going to say who else was in that alley or if she could see who had struck the fatal blow. There was no way she could remain in Fisher if she did give that sort of evidence. It was more than her life was worth.

239

The context was now established. One of the jurors looked pretty emotional. It was hard not to be emotional in a trial involving the death of a young person. Sinead had seen many jurors in tears when listening to evidence and even when delivering verdicts. It was not an easy task for them.

None of the defence barristers had any questions for Chelsea Brittan. She described the scene, didn't identify any of the defendants so there was no need to ask her any questions. It was as if she was there to describe the opening scene of a play, a play with tragic consequences.

*

Next came the pathologist, Doctor Montgomery.

Maria Conroy took him through his findings and established the cause of death was massive blood loss due to severing the mesenteric artery. It was a single stab wound caused by a knife with a serrated blade at least six inches in length.

'How can you tell the blade was at least six inches, Doctor?'

'It has gone six inches into the deceased's body. This means it could be longer than six inches. If it was longer, it means the blade has not gone all the way in. It could not have been shorter than six inches otherwise the blade would not have been able to pierce the body as far as it did.'

'And how can you tell the blade is serrated, Doctor.'

'The cut is not clean. A blade entering a body has to first pierce the skin. That is the biggest barrier for it. Once it manages to pierce the skin it goes in to the rest of the body much more easily. The skin is slightly ragged where the blade has pieced it giving the indication that the edge of the blade is serrated.'

Maria asked that the pathologist be shown exhibit IA/1. DC David Metcalfe was in court dealing with the exhibits. He took the knife from a box next to him. It was inside a sealed exhibit bag with a yellow label marked exhibit IA/1, the initials being those of the officer who sized the exhibit, PC Idris Ahmed, and the number being the first exhibit he seized.

'Could this be the knife that was used to stab the deceased?'

'It's the right sort of length and has the right type of serrations so yes, it could be.'

'Thank you. Can the knife be shown to the jury please?'

The usher took the knife along the two rows of the jurors and they all stared at it in fascination.

There was always something powerful about showing a jury a murder weapon.

When they had each had the opportunity of getting a good look at the knife, it was passed back to DC David Metcalfe who put it back in his box of evidence.

The pathologist continued with diagrams which were shown on the monitors in court and in front of the jurors. Maria Conroy took the pathologist through the diagrams showing the passage of the knife, the injuries which could be due to falling, bruising and the mesenteric artery.

'Can you tell us about the toxicology findings, Doctor?'

'Blood analysis showed that the deceased had low levels of both cannabis and amphetamine in his system?'

'Is it possible to tell when these substances entered his system?'

'It's difficult to tell and depends on a number of factors. Cannabis can stay in the system for three days, longer if someone is a regular user. It is similar with amphetamine. We can't, therefore, be precise about when the substances were taken or if they were taken at the same time although that is less likely.'

'Why is it less likely that they were taken at the same time, Doctor?'

'Cannabis is more likely to be taken to relax someone, perhaps calm them. Amphetamine is often used to keep someone awake which is why it is a popular drug at all night raves. The two drugs tend to have an opposite effect which is why it is unlikely that the drugs would be taken at the same time.'

'If a student was using these drugs to assist with study, what would they be used for?'

'The cannabis might be used to help with sleep and anxiety whereas the amphetamine might assist with staying awake to study.'

Juries can turn off when it came to scientific evidence but this one was good. He described everything in layman's language and it was obvious that the jurors were really paying attention.

Helen turned round to check that Naomi was all right. Although, Naomi had her head bowed, Helen could see the tears so nodded to the usher to pass her a tissue.

When the pathologist finished, there were no questions from the defence barristers. No need as no-one disputed the cause of death.

It was just after 1.00 when the pathologist was released from court.

'We will adjourn for lunch. We will start again at 2.15,' said the judge.

The jury was led out of the door at the back of court.

The judge stood and the court clerk said, 'All rise.'

Everyone stood up as the judge walked out.

Naomi could not get over all the ceremony and performance that went with a trial.

Sinead whispered to Lachlan, 'Great opening. Hit just the right tone.'

'Thanks. That was the aim. Keep the message simple is my motto. Juries don't want anything complicated.'

Helen waited for the dock to be unlocked and for Naomi to be let out after the other three passed behind her and were taken out of the back of the dock and down to the cells.

Helen realised how hard it must be for her to be in a confined space with them after what they'd done to her.

'Right, go and get some lunch,' instructed Lachlan to Naomi, Pam and Phil.

Sinead watched them walk towards the stairs looking more hunched than when they arrived this morning.

'How do you think its going?' Helen asked.

'Nothing unexpected or contentious yet. That will come later,' said Lachlan.

'Naomi was crying when the pathologist was describing Josh's injuries.'

'To be expected I suppose but certainly no bad thing. Time for a sandwich. I'm buying.'

After lunch, Naomi was sitting in the dock and watched the same pomp and ceremony when the judge entered the courtroom and sat down. She nodded to the usher who went out to bring the jury up. *Nods obviously meant different things at different times*, thought Naomi. There was a code which she hadn't yet broken.

Next up was the forensic scientist, Doctor McVey.

Maria Conroy took her through the findings on phones. Texts on the phone of the deceased indicated drug dealing but it was established that the phone numbers which the texts were sent to had not been identified.

'What does this indicate?'

'The phones are not attributed to a user. They are likely to be what is known as burner phones. This means that they are bought cheaply, cannot be identified with a particular person, no contract and are pay as you go phones.'

She then asked that Doctor McVey be shown exhibit IA/1, the knife.

'Have you carried out a forensic examination of this knife, Dr McVey?'

'I have.'

'And can you tell us what you found.'

'There are brown marks on the blade of the knife which, when analysed, show they are dried blood.'

'Did you identify the source of this blood?'

'I did. DNA analysis was carried out. The findings were that this is the blood of the deceased, Josh Smithies.'

'Can you tell us if this is the murder weapon?'

'I cannot categorically say it is the murder weapon. The blood has been deposited on six inches of the blade and the blood is that of Josh Smithies, so the conclusion is that this is more than likely the knife that was used to stab Josh Smithies.'

'Thank you, Doctor. Please wait there as there are likely to be some more questions for you.'

Monica O'Ryan stood.

'You analysed this knife for fingerprints, did you not?'

'I did.'

'Did you find the fingerprints of Ben Sutton on this knife?'

'I did not.'

'Thank you. I have no more questions.'

Next came Fitzroy White with the same question.

No fingerprints belonging to Harley Brown.

Then the turn of Rupert Smythe.

Same question and same answer.

And last, it was Lachlan with the same question and the same response.

They had the murder weapon but nothing to link it forensically to any of the defendants.

*

I'm not going to cope with weeks of this.

Them walking in and out behind me, brushing past me, being next to them.

Everything tenses up when they come in and go out. Every sense is heightened when they move, when they speak.

I want to vomit.

They make my flesh crawl as if there are insects in my clothes.

They are insects. Lice.

I can't bear being so close to them.

I can smell Luke Price. He was the smelliest that night. A grotty, smelly no mark. He'd always looked dirty but you'd have thought he'd have made an effort for court.

I want to get away from here.

At least two weeks of this, having to be near them, holding my nose so I don't smell them.

I want to go home to my own house and my own bed.

I want to leave Carfield and never come back.

I want to go to uni.

I want to run away.

I don't want to come to court tomorrow.

What I want is in someone else's hands.

Chapter 51

Day Two

At least getting through security was becoming familiar, thought Naomi, as she automatically put her bag down to be searched. She was wearing the same suit with a blue and white flowered shirt which her mum assured her looked good.

She went up the stairs with her mum and dad to the room near court one which Lachlan had commandeered for the duration.

Lachlan, Sinead and Helen were already in there so she knocked on the door.

'Come in, come in. No need to knock. Take a seat. Hope you slept as well as you can in these situations.'

'My mum's got me on the valerian tea so that's helping a bit.'

'Good. Mum's always know best,' Lachlan said as he grinned at Pam.

He was always smiling, thought Naomi. He looked so relaxed. Is he not going through the same stress as the rest of us?

'Josh's mum, Anna, is going to be giving evidence today. Given how she was with you yesterday, I think this will be good for us. Will you be okay with that?'

'I'll have to be, won't I?'

'Well put. Yes, you will, but I still wanted to check with you. We have no say in who the prosecution calls to give evidence unless it's irrelevant. The evidence of Anna Smithies is obviously not irrelevant and the prosecution want to evoke as much sympathy as possible for Josh. It could help with sympathy for you as well. Now, I just want to go over some tactics with Sinead so do you mind waiting outside the court with Helen?'

Naomi knew when she was being dismissed. Still, better they prepare the case than chat with her.

Naomi, Helen, Pam and Phil left the room and went to sit outside court one. There was a woman already sitting there who had to be Ben Sutton's mum as they looked so similar. She had more tattoos though.

She gave Naomi a filthy look which Helen clocked so led them away to sit around the corner.

'Better to avoid the other families,' said Helen.

After about fifteen minutes, Naomi heard the now familiar tannoy.

'All parties in the case of Sutton, Brown, Price and Edwards to court one.'

Pam and Phil went up to the public gallery as Helen led Naomi into court.

The security officer unlocked the dock and Naomi walked in to her usual seat. It was becoming too familiar. She didn't want to get used to this charade. The other defendants came up from the cells and took their seats. They were all wearing the same clothes as they had on yesterday.

There was the knock on the door close to the judge's throne and everyone stood. It wasn't a throne but Naomi felt it was like one and the judge was the queen of the court.

The jury was called up and took their seats. They sat in the same places they were in yesterday as if the familiarity of the seat was important to them in the unfamiliar world of the court.

When everyone was settled, Maria Conroy stood up and said, 'Call Anna Smithies.'

The usher went out and brought Anna into the court leading her to the witness box.

Anna took the oath and Maria asked her to give her full name and relationship to the deceased.

'Josh was my son.'

The sympathy coming from everyone in the courtroom was palpable.

Maria continued. She asked about Josh as a young child, how he'd done at school, friends, family and then went on to ask about what he was like as a person.

Anna started to describe Josh, how he helped with shopping, did the garden for his grandparents and then she faltered. She tried to continue and broke down, sobbing.

Naomi wanted to hug her and comfort her and just be next to her. Poor, poor Anna.

You could hear a pin drop.

'We'll take a twenty minute break,' said the judge.

Anna was led out of the courtroom by the woman from witness support.

'Ms Conroy, just let me know if your witness requires more time. There's no rush.'

'Yes, my lady.'

After about twenty minutes, the woman from witness support told Maria that Anna wanted to continue so it was back into court for everyone.

It never ceased to amaze her how long it took to get everyone in and out of court so a twenty minute break could stretch to forty minutes before they were ready to start again.

The usher gave Anna a drink of water and box of tissues.

Maria continued by asking about Josh's personality, his hopes and dreams and about her knowledge of the defendants.

Anna described how she knew Naomi as they lived a few minutes away and Josh and she had grown up together, going to the same schools and college and hoping to go to the same university.

Maria didn't want to get into that as she didn't want sympathy for Naomi. No doubt Lachlan would try and milk that.

Anna said she'd never heard of the other defendants.

Maria then had to ask about his drug taking and selling.

'I didn't know anything about it. He had been a bit short with us but I just put it down to nerves about assignments and the upcoming exams. I never in a million years suspected he was taking any drugs or selling them, and I didn't know he was going to Fisher. When he was out in the evenings, he usually said her was going round to Naomi's.'

Maria finished up and was about to hand over to the defence when the judge decided to break for lunch.

She obviously didn't want to exhaust Anna too much.

After lunch, the judge handed over to the defence. Counsel for Sutton, Brown and Price all asked the same sort of questions.

No mention of their client's name.

No reason to assume there was any animosity between them.

Then it was the turn of Lachlan.

Sinead stood up. They had decided between them that Sinead would deal with the cross examination, woman to woman.

Sinead asked about the relationship between Naomi and Josh.

'It was like love's young dream. We knew they were young but they seemed really suited, wanted to go to the same university and seemed really happy together.'

Sinead probed about who wore the trousers in the relationship. It wasn't a term she would normally use but she knew everyone would get what she meant.

'I suppose Josh could be a bit bossy but not in a horrible way.'

'Would you say Naomi was easy going?'

'I suppose so.'

'Whose idea was it to go to the same university?'

'I'm not sure. Josh had always wanted to go to Birmingham so maybe it was his idea but I just assumed Naomi wanted to go there too.'

'Would Naomi go along with most things Josh wanted?'

'She was probably the more passive of the two. On the surface anyway. It seemed like she just wanted to make Josh happy. They wanted to make each other happy.'

By the end of Sinead's cross examination, the jury must have been left with the impression that Josh was the dominant partner and Naomi was a bit of a mouse, just going along with what Josh wanted.

That was the intention anyway.

When Sinead finished, it was 4.00 and the judge decided to break for the day.

One witness in a whole day. This was certainly slow going.

*

I couldn't bear to look at Anna, to look at her tears, to see her pain.

She'll never get over the loss of Josh, her baby.

It made me cry too.

Lachlan keeps saying 'tears are no bad thing.' I wish he'd stop saying it. I know he means well but it's not as if I've any choice about crying or not crying. I can't just turn it on and off, not after what I've been through, what I'm going through.

Will I be going through this forever?

Will I have to relive it all forever?

Will it ever go away?

It won't for Anna.

I'm crying for me now, for my family, for my pain and the life that I might not have.

At least Anna believes me.

Chapter 52

Day Three

Maria Conroy called Prita Patel. She wanted her to take the court through the CCTV evidence.

DC Metcalfe played the footage with Maria asking him to stop and start at different points then asking Prita to explain what could be seen on the footage.

Prita described how a different coloured arrow was used for each defendant and for the deceased. Josh could be identified with the blue arrow. That way you could play and replay the footage focussing on each one at every playing.

Maria started with Sutton who had a green arrow. She asked the jury to focus on the green arrow. She then asked Prita to describe what Sutton could be seen doing starting with him coming from the top of the alley to about half way down. He had his hands in his pockets. As Josh and Naomi walked up the alley to them, Sutton moved forward and can be seen punching Josh who just stood there.

Sutton moved back and Brown and Price moved forward. Sutton then moved forward as did Naomi. The bodies were so close together it was really hard to tell what was happening.

Sutton's right arm went out towards Josh.

'Did he have anything in his hand?' Maria asked.

'It's impossible to say. What we can say is that his right hand goes out towards Josh, looks like it makes contact with Josh who stands there initially and then after three seconds, begins to stumble and fall.'

'Where about does his hand make contact with Josh?'

'It looks like it makes contact with his chest area but, because of the crowding of the bodies, I cannot be certain about this.'

Maria then moved on to Brown. Same drill with the red arrow now for Brown.

Prita described what could be seen.

'After Sutton punches Josh, Brown moves forward and punches him. Josh's head goes back. All of them come together and Brown is behind Josh. His arms cannot be seen so it's impossible to say what he's doing at the point Josh begins to fall.'

'Does he have anything in his hands?'

'As his hands cannot be clearly seen, I cannot say whether he does or does not have anything in his hands.'

Next came Price who was identified with a yellow arrow. Prita described how Price can be seen on the left of Josh. When Sutton punches Josh, Price stays at a distance then moves forward. His right hand goes out in a punch to Josh's face. He pulls his hand back then it goes out again just as the bodies come together and just before Josh falls.

'Is there anything in his hand?'

'It's difficult to see. All we can say is that his hand comes out. We can see the first hit is a punch to the left side of the face. Everyone crowds round and we can see Luke Price's arm come forward towards Josh but cannot see if there is anything in his hand.'

'Where is his arm when Josh falls?'

'It's towards Josh's left side.'

'Remind us where the stab wound on Josh's body was.'

'It was on his left side.'

Now it was Naomi's turn.

'Naomi can be identified with the orange arrow. Can you describe to us what can be seen?'

'Naomi walks towards the top of the alley with Josh. She is on the left and Josh is on the right. When they reach the others, Naomi is stood slightly back, about two feet away from Josh. The others come forward and Naomi stays where she is initially. After punches from the other three, Naomi moves forward to Josh. Her hand goes out and Josh falls.'

'Does Josh fall before or after Naomi puts her hand out?'

'He falls one second after.'

'Where does her hand go to?'

'To the left side of Josh's body.'

'And where was Josh stabbed?'

'On the left side of his body.'

'Whose is the last hand to go out towards Josh?'

'Naomi's.'

Sinead watched the jury. A couple of the women looked over at Naomi at that point but she couldn't tell what the looks meant.

The judge decided to break for lunch at that point. Concentrating on CCTV footage was exhausting for everyone.

*

After lunch, Maria moved on to what happened after Josh fell, where everyone was and what they did.

Again, Maria took it by each defendant, or each arrow, in turn.

Blue, green, red, yellow, orange. You could almost sing a rainbow.

Sutton leaves at the same time as Brown. They get to the top of the alley together and run to the right. Nothing can be seen in any hands.

Price leaves one second later. He runs to the top of the alley and follows them to the right.

Naomi is close behind and at the top of the alley she runs to the left.

'Anything seen in any hands?'

'No. The only things that can be seen is a brief flash of something in Naomi's hand.'

'Could this be a knife?'

Lachlan leapt to his feet.

'My lady, my learned friend is asking the witness to speculate what a flash might be. It could be a reflection, it could be a phone, it could be nothing at all.'

'I agree, Mr Macpherson. Please stick to what can be seen rather than inviting speculation, Ms Conroy.'

'Of course, my lady.'

Maria didn't mind being stopped. At least it was in the minds of the jury that Naomi might have something in her hand and that something could just be a knife.

The CCTV was played over and over till everyone was bored with it. Sinead was bored with it and had lost count of the number of times her and Lachlan had watched it, frame by frame, trying to see something that couldn't be seen.

Sinead thought it was always so sad when you could see someone on CCTV whose life was about to be cut short. One minute they're alive and the next they're dead. You want to go back and change the course of history.

What could be seen was so unclear. What each might be doing was really a matter of guesswork and guesswork wasn't enough to convict someone. Or was it?

After the alleyway footage was exhausted, Maria asked Prita about footage from approximately two weeks before the incident where Josh was stabbed.

DC Metcalfe retrieved the piece of footage and the date was identified as the 21 January beginning at 6.38 pm.

The same four defendants and Josh can be seen. They are stood in a circle. Naomi can be seen slapping Josh in the face. Josh's hand goes up to his face. The other three stand and do nothing. Although, it's dark, Sutton can be seen laughing. He then points aggressively at Josh in a stabbing motion, although doesn't make contact with him.

They all stay there for another three minutes, apparently talking. Josh and Naomi turn and walk off together. The other three remain there.

That's where Maria ends.

It's a powerful ending and not a good one for Naomi.

*

They played it over and over.

That bitch of a prosecutor has it in for me.

Why?

It doesn't make sense.

She's got these three drug dealing scumbags punching Josh so why drag me into it.

Lachlan says it was because I was raped.

That's right. Kick me when I'm down.

Chapter 53

Day Four

They were all well into it now.

Naomi watched them all from the dock, her life playing out in front of her. She wanted to scream at the barristers, the judge, the jury. She wanted to scream at the world.

She wanted to punch the prosecutor.

She was a woman. Didn't she get it? Was it just about winning?

It was all so unreal but at the same time, the reality was hitting her in the face.

Sergeant Mel Garvey was called.

Mel was asked about house searches. Knives were found in each house. In the houses of Sutton, Brown and Price the knives were found in their bedrooms. None of these knives were the murder weapon as the blades were all too short, not serrated and the deceased's DNA was not found on the knives.

Next the search of Naomi's house.

The knife found to have stabbed Josh was found in Naomi's shed.

Some of the jurors looked over at Naomi.

Naomi looked at one older woman who was clearly not on her side with the look she gave her.

Maria then asked Mel to read the interviews of all the defendants.

Even though no comment interviews were given, for the most part, the questions were read out so the jury could hear what they were asked and then Mel said at the end of each interview, 'The defendant answered no comment to all questions put to him.'

Then came Naomi's interview.

It wasn't just Naomi that breathed a sigh of relief that she'd answered questions. All her lawyers were relieved. It was a risky call advising her to answer questions but it turned out to be the right one.

She explained how Josh got into drugs and was in debt and, most importantly, she sounded reasonable and articulate. She had then gone on to describe how she hit him on the 21 January as the others thought it amusing to get her to do it. If she hadn't hit him, they were going to really lay into him.

By this stage, Naomi could feel the eyes of the other three defendants boring into her.

Let them stare at her. Let them hate her. At least no other part of their bodies would ever bore into her again.

In her interview, she had gone on to describe the night Josh was killed. It was clear Naomi was emotional in her interview. She described her fear, her panic, why she ran and how she could never forgive herself for not calling an ambulance.

They all listened to Mel reading out the questions and answers. It was a good interview and explained it all.

But Lachlan worried that it would not be believed.

Then it was the turn of the defence barristers.

They were all brief.

The barristers for Sutton, Brown and Price all reinforced that the knife found in their client's house was not the murder weapon.

It was overkill as that had been made clear. They just wanted to hammer it home though.

Next, it was Lachlan's turn. He couldn't exactly say the knife found in Naomi's shed wasn't the murder weapon.

He concentrated on the search.

'Tell us where exactly this knife was found?'

'It was on a shelf in the garden shed.'

'Had an attempt been made to hide it?'

'It was next to some shears and a trowel.'

'Could it be easily seen in the shed?'

'The shed and the shelves in it were very full so no relatively small item could be easily seen. However, it was not behind anything or underneath anything so I would say it did not appear that an attempt had been made to hide it.'

'And was the shed locked?'

'No, it was on a latch and there was no lock on it.'

'How did you get to the shed?'

'There is a gate at the side of the house that leads to the back garden. The shed is at the rear of the back garden.'

'Is there a lock on the gate?'

'No.'

'So, hypothetically, anyone could go into the back garden, go into the shed and put the knife there on display to be found?'

'Yes, that's possible.'

'And no fingerprints were found on this knife?'

'No.'

'So the only evidence to link Naomi Edwards to this knife is the location where it was found, a location that could have been accessed by anyone?'

'Yes, that's correct.'

Lachlan sat down.

Sinead leaned over.

'That went well.'

He grinned. 'Well, you know you only ask the questions you know the answer to.'

*

I think Mel believes me. I know she said that charging me hadn't been her decision but I didn't believe her.

I do now.

I could feel her rooting for me.

Even the way she read my interview was different. I know the others hadn't answered questions but she seemed to read mine as if she believed it. Or was that wishful thinking?

Please, please, please believe me.

Chapter 54

Day Five

The prosecution case was nearly finished.

Naomi was stood in the dock as the other three came up from the cells. She didn't look at them. Whenever they came in or went out, she fixed her eyes forward and pretended they weren't there.

Sutton passed her on the way to his seat and hissed at her, 'Skanky slag.' She froze and said nothing but one of the dock officers heard him.

'That's enough. I'm going to have to report this to the judge.'

'Fuck off, bitch.'

Helen could hear something so turned round and the dock officer signalled her over.

'He's intimidating the female defendant. Called her a "skanky slag" and then told me to "fuck off bitch".'

'Okay. Thanks for letting me know.'

Helen leaned over the desk, tapped Lachlan on the shoulder and told him what had happened.

Lachlan stood up.

'My lady, I regret to say that Mister Sutton is attempting to intimidate my client. My instructing solicitor has been informed by the dock officer that he referred to my client as a "skanky slag", and, when told by the dock officer that the matter would be reported, he told the dock officer to "fuck off bitch". If my client should decide to give evidence, this sort of behaviour could affect her evidence and ultimately could affect her right to a fair trial.'

Lachlan knew the last thing judges wanted to hear was that someone in their court might not get fair trial. It could all blow up.

'Thank you, Mister Macpherson. Mister Sutton, stand up.'

He stood with an exaggerated swagger and as slowly as possible. He was still trying to look hard.

Naomi couldn't decide if it was pathetic or sad.

Pathetic, she decided.

'Mister Sutton, I will warn you just once. Repeat this type of behaviour and you will stay downstairs for the remainder of the trial. I will not tolerate such behaviour in my court. Ms O'Ryan, I would be grateful if you would reinforce this with your client when we have a break.'

Monica O'Ryan stood and nodded.

'Certainly, my lady. I will explain the possible consequences to my client.'

'Thank you.'

The judge nodded at the usher. 'Jury please.'

And off she went to fetch the jury up.

Naomi was getting used to the nods and what they all meant. The masons had nothing on this lot. She kept her face blank but inside she was rejoicing at Sutton getting a bollocking. She could see his KC whisper something to his other barrister. She wished she could hear.

Lachlan could hear though.

'What a dickhead,' were the words uttered by Monica O'Ryan.

Maria Conroy stood up and spoke directly to the jury.

'Members of the jury, there are a number of ways you can hear evidence. It can be from a witness in the witness box, it can be statements read to you and it can also be what are called "agreed facts". This is where the prosecution and defence agree certain facts, or evidence, and these are given to you in writing. Mister Wells will now read these to you.'

Sebastian Wells stood up and began to read.

There was nothing controversial. The facts covered dates of birth of defendants and deceased, date of death and, most importantly, the fact that Naomi had no convictions or cautions.

There was no entry for the other three. That said it all. The jury would know they had convictions but wouldn't know what. Not yet anyway.

After Sebastian had finished, Maria stood.

'There is a legal matter that needs to be dealt with now, my lady.'

More code, thought Naomi.

The judge turned to the jury.

'Members of the jury, I need to deal with a point of law with counsel. You will, therefore, be getting an early finish today and I will see you at 10.30 on Monday morning. Remember you must not speak about this case to anyone. Put it out of your minds over the weekend. Thank you.'

And another nod to the usher to take the jury out of the back of the court.

Once the jury was out, Maria Conroy stood.

'Has my lady seen the bad character application in respect of the three defendants, Ben Sutton, Harley Brown and Luke Price?'

'I have and I have had time to consider them but I would like to hear oral submissions from counsel.'

Maria went first.

'The Crown seek to admit the previous convictions of these three defendants for offences of violence and for possession of knives. The details of each conviction are set out in the application. Sutton has a conviction for section 18 grievous bodily harm, Brown for a section 47 actual bodily harm and Price also has a conviction for section 47 actual bodily harm.

'These offences of violence together with each having convictions for possession of knives go to the heart of the offence with which they are charged. While the offence of murder is far more serious, it is a violent offence where a knife has been used. The jury ought, therefore, to be aware that they have a history of using violence and possessing knives.'

'Thank you, Ms Conroy. Mr Macpherson, I believe you support this application.'

'I do, my lady. These three young men have a history of drug dealing, not immediately relevant to the offence with which they are charged, but the jury has heard about it because it gives them the context regarding the deceased and explains why he had a relationship with them.

'Knives and violence go hand in hand with drug dealing. These are young men who are no strangers to using violence and carrying knives. They might not have convictions for actually using knives in the past but one must ask oneself, why carry knives in the context of drug dealing if there isn't the possibility they will be used.'

'Thank you, Mr Macpherson. Ms O'Ryan.'

'Ben Sutton has a conviction for causing grievous bodily harm with intent. The facts are set out in the Crown's application. Briefly put, he assaulted a young man by kicking and punching causing broken ribs and a broken jaw. There was no weapon, no knife used in this assault and, when he was arrested shortly after the offence took place, he was not in possession of a knife. Although an offence of violence, it is of a completely different character from the one with which he is now charged.

'He has a conviction for possession of a knife. This was discovered on him when police undertook a random stop and search. He has no history of actually using a knife. My lady, to allow these convictions to go before the jury would be extremely prejudicial. It is possible that the jury will jump to the conclusion that, as he has used violence and possessed a knife in the past, he must have used a knife on the deceased.'

'Thank you, Ms O'Ryan. Mr White.'

'My lady. Our objections mirror those made by my learned friend. Harley Brown has a conviction for an offence of causing actual bodily harm. During the commission of this offence, he used his fists and caused a cut above the eye, requiring four stitches, together with some bruising. This is an offence of an entirely different character to the one he faces before this court.

'He has one conviction for possession of a knife and, as in the case of Ben Sutton, this was discovered during a random stop and search. He has no convictions for actually using a knife. To repeat my learned friend's submission, to admit these convictions would be prejudicial and could distract the jury from the evidence before it.'

'Thank you, Mr White. Mr Smythe.'

'My lady, I'm not going to repeat the submissions made so eloquently by my learned friends who represent Sutton and Brown. My lady has the details of the convictions. In respect of the actual bodily harm, Mr Price used fists which caused bruising and a chipped tooth. The knife was found in a random stop and search. The admission of these convictions would cause severe prejudice to my client and prevent him from having a fair trial.'

Sinead leaned over and passed a note to Lachlan.

'Comes across as a tosser,' said the note.

'My thoughts exactly,' wrote Lachlan.

If the jury clocked the note passing, they probably thought it was some weighty legal point, not just insults against their fellow counsel, thought Sinead.

Light relief was needed where you could get it.

'Thank you. I will give my judgment at 2.15.'

'All rise.'

'I have considered the application and am grateful for the oral submissions made both in support of the application and in objection to it. It is probative that the jury hear of the convictions for carrying knives even though those convictions did not involve the use of knives. I agree that it would, however, be more prejudicial if the jury were to hear of the offences of violence given that these were essentially fights and did not involve the use of weapons.

'My full judgement will be uploaded on to the system. I intend to rise early today to enable counsel to have conferences with their clients prior to next week. Have a good weekend and if you need my assistance over the weekend please email me.'

Everyone stood. It reminded Naomi of when she used to go to church. All that standing and sitting and everyone an actor knowing what to do when.

They all filed out of court.

Rupert Smythe could be heard giving out loudly, 'We've an appeal point there.'

In your dreams, thought Sinead.

What was it about these posh types, wondered Sinead. They were so much louder than everyone else and came across as supremely confident, or was it that they were just more arrogant than those around them. Sometimes juries liked that. Perhaps that was the image of a barrister they'd seen on TV. Sometimes juries hated their arrogance though. Still, it's about the evidence and at least today was going in their favour.

*

Rupert Smythe and Robert Winstanley went down to the cells to see Luke. Rupert had hoped for an early finish and he could still beat the rush hour if they were quick with Luke. At least he got down there before Sutton and Brown's teams. You could wait an age to get into the cells if there was a queue.

'Much on this weekend, Robert?'

'Barbecue with the relatives tomorrow but that's about it. You?'

'Relaxing in the garden with a few drinks. Nothing too taxing. Ah, here we go. At least we've not had a long wait. I'm concerned about our chap. Not sure he's all there despite what the doc said.'

'Know what you mean. And I wish he would wear something else.'

'Yes. Better mention that to him.'

After signing in, Luke was brought through.

'Sit down, Luke. Wanted to explain just a few things to you. The jury will be told you have a conviction for carrying a knife. Not the end of the world as it was a random stop and search, and I want you to think about whether or not you want to give evidence. I know we've discussed it but think about it over the weekend, old boy.'

Luke just stared at him.

'Are you following most things?'

'I don't know.'

'Well, I suppose it's a bit mesmerising but just now all you need to think about is whether or not you want to take the stand. Okay.'

Luke just nodded.

'And it would be a good idea to wear something else. Smarten up a bit. Did your parents bring in any clothes?'

'There's only me mam and she's not been to see me since I've been banged up so I don't have any other clothes.'

'I see. Ask your wing officer. The prison will have some suitable court clothes for people in your situation. Try and get something from him. Okay?'

Luke just nodded again.

'Fine. We'll see you Monday.'

Rupert knocked on the glass door and waited to be let out. He waited till they were out of earshot before saying, 'Can't help but feel sorry for our boy. No parent to visit him, obviously no father on the scene.'

'I know what you mean. It's no wonder he's ended up here. What chances has he had?'

'Not a lot, old boy, not a lot.'

*

Harley sat in the cell and waited for his barristers. He had seen Luke be taken out of his cell so he must be seeing his now. What a fucking shit show.

He heard a shout down the corridor, 'Visit for Brown.'

About fucking time.

His cell was opened by one of the security officers that Harley liked. She was always nice to him which was more than his fucking wing officer was. She walked him down the corridor and into the room where Fitzroy White and Pamela Harris were waiting for him.

'Hello, Harley,' began Fitzroy.

Harley thought he looked like he'd rather be anywhere than here.

'I'm sorry we've not managed to get down to see you much but I just wanted to explain what happened today.'

'I know what fucking happened. That bitch of a prosecutor is going to tell the jury I've carried a knife. I've never used a fucking knife.'

'I know and the jury will also be told that.'

'It's all going to shit, isn't it?'

'No, it's not. You need to stay positive and I want you to think about whether you want to give evidence next week. It's got to be your call. I think you should tell your side of the story, tell what happened that night, what was going through your mind. If you do decide to give evidence you need to stay calm.

'It's emotional, it's frightening and people can get easily tongue tied, say things they didn't mean to say or get angry if they feel they are being wound up by the prosecutor's questions. If you don't think you can cope with it, then don't do it but I think it's your best chance as all the jury has so far is the video showing you all laying into Josh Smithies which isn't good.'

'Yeah, I know. I'll have a think about it. How's it looking?'

'Difficult to tell just now but the knife isn't linked to you so that's one piece of evidence in your favour.'

'Okay. I'll have a think.'

'Good. We'll see you Monday.'

Pamela knocked on the window and the security officer came to take him back to his cell to wait for the prison bus.

After he was led out, Fitzroy and Pamela were led in the opposite direction to the locked door which led to the outside world.

Once they were on the other side of the door, Pamela turned to look at him. 'You know that the fact the knife can't be directly linked to him isn't enough to get him off?'

'Yes, but what's the point of rubbing it in now. Anyway, we've all seen juries come up with surprise verdicts so fingers crossed. He seems like a nice lad underneath all that bravado.'

'Being a nice lad isn't enough.'

*

Ben Sutton passed Harley as he sauntered down to corridor to where his barristers, the dyke and the small one, were waiting for him in the consultation room.

'I'm fucked off about that knife. I didn't even use the fucking thing.'

'We know and the jury will know it was just a random stop and search. The important thing is that the knife that was used to kill Josh Smithies was not found on you or on your premises and there is nothing to link you to it.'

'Fucking Luke must have put it there.'

'Or was it Naomi.'

'How the fuck should I know. I just know it wasn't me.'

'Okay. You need to decide if you're going to give evidence. What's important is how you come across. If you're going to act cocky or swear, you might as well not bother. It's up to you. If you think you can tell your version of events calmly and without losing it, then our advice is for you to give evidence. If you can't manage that then don't do it. Think about it over the weekend.'

'I've thought about it and I want to.'

'We can make a final decision on Monday so just mull it over.'

'I've decided. End of.'

'Very well. I will ask you again on Monday so don't be hasty.'

With that parting shot, Monica stood up and rapped on the window to attract the attention of a security officer.

Ben decided he couldn't stand either of them but he knew he had to play the game. He was going to make sure he got off.

*

Mel got out of court where Ian was waiting for her.

'Hi. Thought I'd pop over to see how it went. Giving evidence is never easy.'

'Thanks, I appreciate that. It was fine though. No surprises and no mauling by the defence.'

Just then, Naomi came out of court and Mel caught her eye and smiled.

'Should you be smiling at defendants?' Ian asked.

'Only this one. I'm rooting for her.'

'Me too but don't tell anyone or it will ruin my street cred. Fancy going for a drink and something to eat? Hope you don't think I'm being too presumptuous.'

'That would be lovely and no, I don't think you're being too presumptuous.'

*

At last. The jury will hear about them carrying knives.

They've got to believe they stabbed Josh.

Or that one of them did.

I'm the good girl, the student, the one who should be going to university.

And what are they? Drug dealing, knife wielding scumbags.

And now there is a whole weekend to wait till we start again.

A weekend where all I can think of is what might happen.

A weekend of waiting.

A weekend of terror, of not being able to sleep, of nightmares, of remembering.

And worst of all a weekend of "what ifs".

I know the lawyers are great but they don't really get it. They've seen people go through it but they don't know what it feels like to be in it.

They don't know what it's like to live it, to be in my shoes, to be next to them in the dock.

They're onlookers in this horror film. Important onlookers but onlookers nonetheless.

No-one knows what it feels like unless you live it.

And I can't live it much longer.

Chapter 55

Day Six

Once everyone was settled, Maria Conroy stood and faced the jury again.

'Members of the jury, Mr Wells has some additional agreed facts to read and then distribute to you.'

Sebastian Wells handed the papers to the usher who gave a copy to each of the jurors.

He then read what was on the paper.

1. On 15 March 2020, Ben Sutton pleaded guilty to possession of a bladed article.
2. On 12 December 2019, Harley Brown pleaded guilty to possession of a bladed article.
3. On 29 October 2018, Luke Price pleaded guilty to possession of a bladed article.

The bare facts, thought Lachlan. It didn't sound that bad when it was read like that but at least we've got them carrying knives. Pity the assaults didn't go in though. And, more importantly, Naomi is separated out from them.

Sebastian sat down and Maria stood up.

'My lady that is the case for the prosecution.'

'Thank you, Ms Conroy. Ms O'Ryan.'

Monica stood. 'Call Ben Sutton.'

She knew she was taking a risk putting him in the witness box but it had been his decision. He was a loose cannon and there was no way of knowing how this would go. Not well, she suspected.

Ben Sutton was led out of the dock and into the witness box. Even now he was swaggering.

Monica was starting to regret this as he took the oath still looking cocky.

She guided him through his evidence and let him tell his story.

'I first used weed, cannabis, when I was twelve. Then I got into ecstasy and speed. Then I had to sell it to pay for it.'

'And were your parents aware of this?'

'Dad was never around and mum had her hands full with the younger kids so I just got on with stuff. She wasn't bothered what I was doing.'

'We've heard you have a conviction for carrying a knife. Tell us about that.'

'When you're selling, you need to make sure your stash doesn't get nicked. Lads might come up to you, get their knives out and try to rob you. So you have to carry a knife. It's for protection.'

It carried on as he described his drug dealing career, his lack of parental input, lack of educational qualifications, lack of any warmth and affection from anyone.

Even he could get the sympathy vote, thought Monica.

'Tell us what happened on the night of 3 February.'

'Josh was meeting us as he owed us. He was just coming to pay up. He said he didn't have the money so I hit him. That's all I did. I wanted to frighten him a bit so he'd pay. I didn't want to skank him, er stab him, just frighten him into paying up. If I stabbed him, I wouldn't get my money. I told him he'd got two days or he'd get another beating.'

'Did you talk with the others about stabbing him?'

'Course not. Why would I? I just wanted my money.'

'Did you see who stabbed him?'

'It was too dark. I think Luke Price had something in his hand so it might have been him.'

Luke stood up in the dock and shouted, 'Liar.'

'Mr Price, sit down or you will be removed from the court,' said the judge.

Luke sat. His face was like thunder.

Monica knew he'd get his own back but there was nothing more for it.

Luke and Ben stared each other out, neither willing to look away.

Ben was cross examined by each of the other KCs. The defence barristers were each blaming him rather than their client. He stuck to his guns and batted it back. Luke was the one who was getting the blame.

Maria Conroy took a different tactic.

'You didn't mean for the knife to go in so deeply.'

'I didn't have no knife.'

'You agreed with the others you'd do this, didn't you.'

'No, we just wanted our money. If Luke skanked him, it was down to him but we didn't talk about it.'

'You wanted a flesh wound, a few stitches, a serious injury but not life threatening. That way you'd make sure he'd pay up.'

'Look, love, I didn't have no knife and I didn't talk about skanking him. Nothing to do with me.'

Monica thought it was going better than she'd expected. He was standing up to the cross examination but he still didn't come across as likeable. That was half the battle with juries. She'd done enough rape trials to know that if a jury liked the defendant, particularly if he was good looking, he'd be found not guilty. Did they like Ben Sutton? She doubted it.

*

They'll have hated him like I hate him.

Swaggering up to the witness box, his shirt and smart trousers fooling no-one.

Lachlan said they'd blame each other. At least that meant they left me alone. Hopefully.

With his pink skin and freckles, he was revolting. Everything about him makes me want to vomit.

I remember what he did, the threats from him, the laughter.

That night he made me meet him at the end of the road when I couldn't stop shaking. Shaking with revulsion.

That meeting that left me shaking, frightened and in tears but the jury wouldn't hear about it.

It all seemed so unfair.

Being that close to him.

Having him laugh at me liked they'd all laughed that time.

In that house.

Shaking at the memory of what he'd done.

After everything he did to me, I just hope he suffers for a very long time.

Chapter 56

Day Seven

It was Harley Brown's turn.

Lachlan watched his barrister take him through his evidence.

He was more likeable than Sutton but his story mirrored Sutton's and he too was blaming Luke. Sutton was obviously the ringleader and Brown, the follower.

He was nervous. None of Sutton's cockiness. He couldn't keep his hands still and was constantly drinking from the glass of water put in front of him. Each time he picked the glass up, you could see his nails were bitten to the quick, fingers gnawed, blood visible on some of them.

Would the jury put the nerves down to lying or to an innocent young man found in a position no-one would want to be in?

Lachlan looked over at the jury. He couldn't work out what they were making of Brown. Sometimes you could tell when a jury just loathed a defendant but sometimes juries gave nothing away. And now they were giving nothing away.

Brown stuck to the story, although he was a bit hesitant in parts as if he'd forgotten his lines. The jury would pick up on that.

Then came the cross examination.

And the nerves really came through. He couldn't answer without biting his fingers first or slurping at the water.

Luke Price's barrister was having a field day with him.

'You were in on it with Sutton and Edwards, weren't you?'

'Yes. I mean no. No.'

'Did Sutton tell you to put the blame on Luke Price?'

Harley hesitated and looked over at Sutton in the dock. It was enough for the jury to see so it hardly mattered what his answer was.

'No, course not. Luke had a knife so it must've been him. I hardly know Naomi so why would I be in on it with her?'

'So is it just Sutton you were in on it with?'

'What? No. What you on about? I'm not in on it with no-one?'

'Are you saying it was just you then, on your own?'

'No, I didn't do it. It were nowt to do with me.'

'Well, who was it to do with?'

'I don't know. It were Price.'

'Are you saying you don't know or are you saying it was Price?'

'I don't know.'

'You're saying you don't know who it was?'

'I don't know.'

'You don't know what you're saying?'

'No.'

'You do know what you're saying?'

'No.'

'So which is it?'

'I don't know.'

It was getting embarrassing now, thought Lachlan. Brown was not coming across well and was sinking himself. As long as he wasn't sinking Naomi that was fine with him.

By the time all the barristers had finished with Harley Brown, he looked like a wet rag rung out to dry. He'd been through the mill and not much could save him now.

*

What a pathetic specimen.

Harley Brown isn't going to win any prizes for brain of Britain.

He was shifty and it was clear he was under Sutton's thumb as well as being a lying little shit.

Some of the jurors were smiling when he was getting himself all twisted up in knots. I bet they wanted to laugh out loud at him.

I bet they'll tell their friends about this one.

It would be funny if it wasn't so serious.

Well, at least they're both blaming Price and not me.

I was terrified they'd stick together and gang up on me.
Like they ganged up on me before.
But why should they?
I'm innocent.

Chapter 57

Day Eight

Luke made his way to the witness box and tripped as he stepped up into it.

Lachlan supposed that Luke felt foolish but tripping up do Luke probably got him the sympathy vote. Never underestimate the power of the sympathy vote.

Anyway he'd need a lot more than just sympathy if he was going to be acquitted.

As Luke's barrister took him through his evidence, it was obvious Luke was furious. He was getting the blame by Sutton and Brown and he wasn't having it.

'Did you see a knife?'

'No. It was too dark to see anything but Ben Sutton carries knives all the time and likes kicking the shit out of people. Harley Brown will do just as Ben says.'

'Why do you think Sutton would blame you?'

'How the bloody hell should I know. They're both trying to blame me to get themselves off the hook. They're fucking liars. I didn't do it and I didn't talk to no-one about doing it. End of.'

As he carried on he was getting angrier by the minute.

He's going to explode, thought Lachlan.

The cross examination started.

Lachlan didn't ask too many questions. Price didn't want to land Naomi in it in case she did the same with him when it was her turn. He hadn't seen Naomi with a knife and hadn't seen her do anything.

It wasn't long before the fireworks started with Sutton's barrister.

'He's a fucking liar. I didn't have no knife and he didn't see no knife because there was no fucking knife.'

'So what did you have in your hand?'

'Look, mate, I didn't have nothing in my fucking hand.'

The judge had had enough.

'We're going to take a fifteen minute break there.'

As the jury was led out, she turned to Luke Price.

'Mr Price, I understand that emotions are running high.'

'Too fucking right.'

'That's enough. You will curb your language and you will answer the questions put to you in a polite way. You now have fifteen minutes to calm down. I suggest you have a drink of water and collect yourself.'

He looked at her with confusion written over his face.

'Collect myself from where?'

She was getting exasperated by now.

'Calm down and stop swearing. Understand?'

'Okay.'

He waited in the witness box as everyone else walked out of court. He'd been told his barrister couldn't speak to him as he was in the middle of his evidence, nonetheless his barrister looked at Luke in a way that shouted, "Shut up and behave".

It was alright for him, thought Luke. *He'll be going home tonight and I won't.*

After the break, Luke had calmed down, stopped swearing and just kept denying he had a knife, knew anything about a plan to stab Josh or cause him serious injury.

He wasn't coming over well. He was angry. Sutton and Brown were blaming him and he was blaming them. A typical cut throat meant they were all likely to be convicted. Hopefully, that will get Naomi off the hook, thought Lachlan. Although, you never could tell.

*

What a tosser.

He lost it completely and couldn't string a sentence together without the word "fuck" in it.

I had a sneaky look at Sutton when Luke Price was blaming him.

Not that I really wanted to look at him.

He looked furious. His pink face had gone purple with anger. He looked like he wanted to stab Price. Well, they do like their knives after all.

The best bit of today was having space between me and Brown, not having to stand next to smelly Luke. I felt I could breathe without being reminded of his smell and what he and the others had done to me. Lachlan said he understood it would be difficult being in the dock next to them.

He didn't know the half of it. No-one did. How can I explain the smells that are with me all the time as if they've been stamped inside my head with indelible ink?

He was the smelliest though and his smell took me back to that night, their hands all over me. That awful night that will never leave me.

The only chance I've got of forgetting it all is in the hands of those twelve men and women.

My turn tomorrow. The thought of having to stand there, in front of everyone and go over it again is making me feel sick. Feeling sick is a constant state now. I don't know how much weight I've lost but I wouldn't recommend this as a way of dieting.

I just need tomorrow to be over.

Chapter 58

Day Nine

It was Naomi's turn. She just hoped she wouldn't lose her breakfast.

Lachlan had told her what to expect but it was different actually having to do it.

She was led out of the dock towards the witness box. Her legs were propelling her forward irrespective of any intention by her.

She took the oath barely able to speak. Her tongue was sticking to the top of her mouth and a sound barely above a squeak was escaping through her lips.

The judge asked her to speak up and direct her answers towards the jury as they needed to hear her.

She just nodded in response.

'And try not to nod. The microphones need to pick up your words for the recording.'

She nodded again then remembered.

'Yes, my lady.'

Lachlan had told her what to call the judge and to remain calm and polite at all times.

He stood up and the questions began.

He said it was going to be all straightforward stuff to create an impression. And it was.

Her age, her ambitions, A levels, family life, how she met Josh, how they wanted to go to university together, how Josh got into drugs and how he'd changed.

Then it got harder.

'Tell us what you did when you returned from college on the evening of the 3 February.'

'I went home after college, had my tea and started doing my homework. It was my geography project which was going towards my A level exam. Then Josh rang. He said we had to go to Fisher. I didn't want to go but he said he had to and wanted me to go with him because he thought it would be better for him if I was there. He came round to my house and then I told my mum and dad that we were going round to his to work on our geography projects.'

'What happened when you left your house?'

'He was worried that he owed Ben Sutton and the others money for drugs. He was scared what they'd do to him. He wanted me to come so he'd be safer.'

'Why did he think he would be safer if you were there?'

'He thought that they wouldn't hurt him if I was there.'

'Is that what you thought?'

'I didn't think it'd make any difference. If they were going to hurt him, they'd do it whether or not I was there.'

'And we've seen from the CCTV footage that you went. Tell us what happened when you got there.'

'Josh said he was supposed to meet Ben Sutton, Harley Brown and Luke Price outside the shop on the estate. That seems to be where they hang out. We've met them there before. A kid of about ten came up to Josh and said Ben and the others were in the ginnel so we walked up. It was dark but we could see them at the end.

'They were asking Josh where the money was. He said he didn't have it but he'd get it. Ben Sutton punched him. The others joined in. It was dark and it all happened so fast. Josh seemed about to stagger and I put my hand out to steady him. I didn't want him to fall. He started to fall and then I ran and they ran.'

'Why did you run?'

'I thought they'd start on me. I wasn't thinking. I just wanted to get away. I thought Josh had just fallen over. I should've stopped to help but I wasn't thinking. I just ran and ran till I saw a bus. I couldn't think. I was scared. I keep thinking I should have called an ambulance. Maybe if I'd called an ambulance, he wouldn't have died.'

The tears rolled down her cheeks and the words wouldn't come out.

'If only…'

She couldn't go on. She fell down in the witness box and couldn't control the sobbing.

The judge intervened and very gently said, 'Would you like a break, Ms Edwards?'

'No. No. I just want to go on. Can I have a drink?'

The usher brought a glass, a jug of water and a box of tissues. Naomi took a drink then wiped her eyes and nose.

'I'm okay now.'

'Did you see a knife?'

'No. It was too dark but one of them must have had a knife or he wouldn't have got stabbed.'

'Did you have a knife?'

'No! Why would I? Josh was my boyfriend. I loved him. We were going off to university together.'

'Can you explain why the knife that killed Josh was found in your garden shed?'

'There isn't a lock on the garden gate or the shed. Anyone could walk in. Any of them could have put it there but it wasn't me.'

She could feel their stares but didn't care now. She wasn't going to look at them but she would blame them.

'We've seen some CCTV footage from two weeks before Josh was stabbed. You've seen that footage. You can be seen slapping Josh. Why did you do that?'

'Ben Sutton said that if I didn't slap him then he would. I knew he'd do it harder than me so I slapped him hard enough so that Ben wouldn't want to hit him. I didn't have any choice. Once I slapped him, me and Josh walked off together. Josh knew I had to do it. He knew I didn't have a choice.'

'Thank you. I've no more questions but please wait there as the other barristers will have questions for you.'

Lachlan smiled at Naomi and sat down.

She knew the smile was to tell her it went well and keep it up.

She took a deep breath and waited for the onslaught from the other barristers.

Sinead passed Lachlan a note. He opened it and read, 'That went well and the tears were genuine.'

He smiled and nodded at Sinead. It said enough. He was pleased. Tears never did a witness any damage and it will have done Naomi a lot of good.

*

They got up to question her in turn. She didn't budge from her story, although Maria Conroy shook her up a bit.

'What did you have in your hand when you went towards Josh in the alley?'

'Nothing.'

'Let's have another look at the CCTV.'

She played the CCTV footage again. There was a split second flash as Naomi's hand went out.

'Let me ask you again. What is that in your hand?'

'Nothing. I might have been holding my phone but I had nothing else in my hand.'

'Let's move on to the discovery of the knife in your shed. You have a security light in your garden?'

'Yes.'

'Yet you didn't notice anyone setting it off?'

'No, but it could have been when we were all in bed?'

'Didn't hear anyone opening the metal gate to the garden?'

'No.'

'It squeaks, doesn't it?'

'Yes.'

'Didn't hear the shed door being opened?'

'No.'

'The shed door sticks, doesn't it?'

'Yes.'

'So you need to give it a good tug to open it?'

'Yes.'

And that makes a scraping noise, does it not?'

'Yes.'

'And again you didn't hear anything.'

'No.'

'And didn't see anything?'

'No.'

'Isn't that because you put the knife in the shed?'

'No.'

'You told the jury how Sutton, Brown and Price got you to slap Josh approximately two weeks before he was murdered, didn't you?'

'Yes.'

'Did they also get you to stab him?'

'No.'

'You panicked and left the knife in the shed, didn't you, never thinking it would be searched.'

'No. That's not true. I didn't. I don't know how it got there.'

'You intended to dispose of it later, didn't you, but the shed was searched before you had the chance. That's right, isn't it?'

'No, it's not right. I don't know how it got there. I just know I didn't put it there.'

At the mention of the discovery of the knife, Naomi started to cry again.

More water.

More tissues.

More sympathy hoped Lachlan.

Naomi wasn't for shifting.

The barristers for Sutton, Brown and Price didn't have much of a go at her. They were too busy blaming each other to blame Naomi. She didn't exactly relax but the tension eased a little, her voice became stronger and more confident.

Not too confident.

At last it was over and she was led back to the dock. She didn't look at the others as she took her seat. Her heart was thumping and she just hoped she had come over well enough.

Next, it was the turn of her character witnesses.

Unlike the others, Naomi's legal team were calling witnesses on her behalf to describe her good character. *Well, the others couldn't exactly call witnesses to talk about their bad character, could they*, thought Naomi.

First was her year tutor, Elisabeth Cunningham, who spoke glowingly about her.

'She is such a hard worker and model student. Her grades are excellent and she's a very good role model for the students in the year below. We all hope she will be starting university next month. She deserves to do well.'

'Any extra-curricular activities?' Lachlan asked.

'Yes. She helps out at a residential care home on Wednesday afternoons. The residents love her as she is such a kind and giving person.'

Sinead was making a note as Lachlan carried on with the questions. Helen had taken a statement from Elisabeth months ago so there was no surprises in what she was saying. It was all good stuff. She sneaked a look at the jury and could see one woman taking notes. Another good sign.

None of the co-defendants' barristers had any questions for her. What was the point; it would simply reinforce how highly she thought about Naomi.

Maria Conroy stood up.

'Did you know Josh had been using drugs?'

'No.'

'Did you know he had been selling drugs?'

'No.'

'You don't know what your students get up to out of college, do you?'

'Not unless something is brought to my attention, no I don't.'

'So you can only speak about what Naomi gets up to in college. Is that correct?'

'Yes, but I can also say what she's like as a person and how she is regarded by the staff.'

'I'm talking about other activities, Ms Cunningham. You would have no idea what Naomi did outside of college, would you?'

'No, I suppose not.'

'Just like you had no idea what Josh was doing outside of college?'

'No.'

'Thank you. No more questions.'

Although, she tried to cast doubt on Naomi, it didn't really work thought Sinead. The jury must surely be left with a good impression of her.

Next came a neighbour, Arthur Smethurst.

Lachlan began.

'Mr Smethurst, I don't usually ask this question but would you mind telling the court how old you are?'

Arthur Smethurst pulled himself up to his full height, all five foot six inches, and answered proudly.

'I'll be eighty six next month and I've still got all my wits about me even if the legs don't work too well.'

That raised a smile from some of the jurors. Great stuff.

'And how do you know Naomi Edwards?'

'Naomi and her family live three doors away from me. When my wife died two years ago, Naomi offered to do some shopping for me. Her dad helps me with odd jobs. They're a lovely family. I don't know what I would have done without them.'

'Is this grocery shopping she helps with?'

'Mainly, but if I need anything else I know I can just ask her. She's such a lovely, helpful girl. I can't get around like I did and she will help me choose presents for my grandchildren as I don't have much of an idea what youngsters like these days. It's all a bit technical for me.'

'Anything else Naomi helps with?'

'I've got a cleaner who comes in once a week but if there are any other little jobs, I know I can ask Naomi and her family.'

'Thank you, Mr Smethurst. I've no more questions.'

And no questions from anyone else.

Maria Conroy obviously thought it wasn't worth it this time.

She thought Naomi should be auditioning for a drama degree and that the tears were all put on.

'I have no more witnesses. That is the case for Naomi Edwards,' Lachlan smiled at the jury as he said this.

Sinead could see one woman smiling back at him. *He's a bit of a flirt*, she thought, *even with a jury*.

'Thank you, Mr Macpherson.'

The judge turned to the jury.

'Members of the jury, you have now heard all the evidence in this case. Tomorrow, I will give you legal directions and then we will begin to hear the speeches from each of the barristers. After that, I will remind you of the evidence before you retire to reach your decisions. Thank you for your attention. We will begin tomorrow at 10.30 for this final part of the proceedings.'

As the jury stood up to be led out of the court, Naomi couldn't help but wonder if Lachlan and Sinead had done enough to persuade them that the knife in the shed was nothing to do with her.

*

That's it then. There's no more that can be done.

How did she know about the security light, the squeaking gate and the sticking shed door? I suppose the police will have clocked that and told her.

281

You wouldn't notice any of that during the night though. I just hope the jury realised that.

I thought taking exams was nerve racking but it's got nothing on giving evidence in a trial. It's surreal. It's like you're on a stage and you're the main actor. Did I carry it off?

Arthur and Elisabeth were great. The jury just has to see the difference between the others and me. They just can't lump me in with them.

I look different, I sound different, different backgrounds, different futures. They must surely see that.

Let's hope it was enough for me to have that different future, otherwise I will be going down like them.

Chapter 59

Day Ten

'For some reason, Maria Conroy is out to get you as well as the others. I don't really understand why but that's the reality. She's not satisfied with the other three and wants you as well. I think it's since she saw the phone footage taken from Josh's phone. She's convinced that you have the motive and she's cherry picking the evidence to fit that.'

Naomi was aware how Lachlan referred to her rape. The word was never used. It was wrapped up in terms like "phone footage" or "material found on Josh's phone".

It sanitised it and didn't refer to the horror that it was.

'In her closing speech, she will focus on you slapping Josh, you willingly going along with Josh to Fisher on numerous occasions and, most importantly, the knife being found in your shed.'

Naomi nodded.

Lachlan continued.

'The important thing is that you created a good impression for the jury. It was more difficult for me to look over at them but Sinead did.'

That was Sinead's cue to step in and try to bolster Naomi. The closer to the end of a trial you got, the more tense it became.

'There were a few of them taking notes when you were giving your evidence. That's a good sign. They were really paying attention and hanging on every word. Mr Smethurst and Ms Cunningham were great too. None of the others had character witnesses so it sets you apart from them. She will point to the evidence against you but Lachlan's speech will be the last one so, hopefully, that will be the impression they are left with.'

'First of all, it's the judge's legal directions. She will explain the law in simple terms and then it will be on to speeches.'

*

The judge began. She was droning on. What a boring voice. Naomi was sure the jury wasn't listening. She looked over at them. One man had his eyes closed. It was hot in the court but it was her voice that was sending them to sleep.

'The prosecution have to make you sure. If you are not sure you must find the defendant not guilty.'

Naomi would hang on to that. They couldn't be sure. Could they?

'Let me turn first to character. Ben Sutton, Harley Brown and Luke Price have previous convictions for carrying knives. How should you approach this? Do not place undue reliance on this. Whether this shows a propensity to actually use knives is for you to decide. It is a matter for you as to how much weight you give this.'

Naomi thought she'd stick the boot in when it came to the knives but she hasn't.

'Naomi Edwards has no previous convictions. She is of good character. You should take this into account when assessing the weight of evidence against her. However, what weight you give this is a matter for you. You should take into account everything you have heard about her.'

All that fuss about bad character and good character has boiled down to nothing, thought Naomi. It angered her. She wanted to shout at the judge. Not advisable, she knew, but she couldn't help it.

'Naomi Edwards became distressed when giving her evidence. The other defendants did not show signs of distress when they gave their evidence. Signs of distress does not confirm the truth or accuracy of what you are being told. Conversely the fact that a witness does not show signs of distress does not mean they are lying. Demeanour does not confirm the truth or accuracy of a witness's account.'

Has the judge got it in for me, she wondered? Lachlan said that crying would be good. It wasn't as if she could control the tears though. You can't be on trial for your life and not cry.

She droned on for another half hour. Were the jury listening?

When at last she finished, Naomi breathed a sigh of relief. It couldn't get any more boring or could it?

Now it was the prosecution speech.

Everything Lachlan warned her about was there. The knife, the slap and going to Fisher.

And joint enterprise.

'Where two or more people join together to commit a crime. It's not a written agreement, it's informal. One might know that another has a knife and suspect it might be used. One person might be there lending support to the attack by their presence, perhaps goading the others on. One person might not have a knife and might not have committed any assault.

'The issue is whether they knew or suspected that an attack might take place and they were supportive of that. It does not matter who used the knife. If they all knew or suspected an attack on Josh might take place and serious injury might result, then they are as guilty as the one who used the knife.'

'Bollocks,' shouted Ben Sutton and stood up.

'Any more of that, Mr Sutton, and you can go downstairs.' It was obvious the judge was angry now.

'Well, it is.'

'This is your last warning.'

He sat down looking a bit chastened, watching the jury watching him. He couldn't believe this was happening to him. All the things he'd done and not been arrested for and now this. Murder. And he hadn't done it.

And now she was trying to get Naomi as part of it whether she used the knife or not.

'Was the knife planted there or was she hiding it for the others? In other words was she in on it with them?'

No fancy legal terms, thought Naomi. She put it in a way everyone could understand. And it was possible everyone could conclude she was in it up to her neck.

*

Lachlan and Sinead said it went well this morning but today was shit. I think the judge has it in for me and that cow of a prosecutor definitely has it in for me.

Why?

She's seen the video.

Hasn't she heard of sisterhood?

She can see what they're doing to me and she thinks that's enough for me to be a murderer.

She must have prosecuted loads of rape cases, know what it's like for women, what we go through.

Why doesn't she get what I've been through?

What I'm still going through.

And now I've a whole weekend of nothingness.

This could be my last weekend of freedom.

Please, please, please don't let the jury think I did it.

Chapter 60

Day Eleven

Sinead was all smiles on Monday morning. Naomi didn't know what there was to be so happy about. She'd had a terrible weekend, hardly slept and snapped at her gran and granddad. All these months she just wanted it to be over and now it nearly was. She couldn't stand it.

'With a bit of luck the jury will have forgotten most of what the prosecutor said. Barristers always hate having to do their speech on a Friday afternoon when the weekend just lessens the impact of it. It should be speeches for Sutton, Brown and Price today and Lachlan will do his in the morning when the jury is wide awake and hopefully paying attention.'

The three speeches were much the same.

Lack of evidence on the knife, not found in their possession, no motive because they wanted their money.

And a dead boy meant they wouldn't get paid.

Luke's barrister finished and sat down looking pleased with himself.

He was so smug. As her granddad used to say, 'A face you'd never tire of slapping.'

'Thank you, Mr Smythe.'

The judge turned to the jury. She was all smiles to them but not to anyone else.

'Members of the jury, concentrating on three speeches in one day is tiring so I will leave Mr Macpherson's speech till tomorrow. Thank you.'

And that was it. Another day closer to the verdict.

*

No mention of me today. Thank god.

I could see the jury looking over at us all. Maybe they weren't looking at me. It's hard to tell and I didn't want to catch anyone's eye.

Were they looking at the other three and thinking there's no evidence against them?

Were they believing the speeches and thinking they had no motive?

Why would they stab him if they wanted their money?

I'd slapped him after all.

I had the murder weapon in my shed.

Were they thinking that was enough?

Were they looking at me and thinking I'd done it?

Chapter 61

Day Twelve

Lachlan rose slowly from his seat. He looked at each of the jurors and enveloped them in his smile. He was in no rush. This was the drama that Naomi had supposed it would be. There had been the dramatic moments which were a disaster. She hoped this would be one of those dramatic moments that would be good for her.

'Members of the jury, I'm going to begin with one of those phrases you've heard many times. You will have read it in books, heard it on films and on television. And that phrase is "Beyond reasonable doubt". But what does it mean? It means that you must be sure.

'Not, maybe Naomi Edwards was involved in Josh's murder, not possibly, not even probably. In order to find Naomi guilty, you must be sure that she either stabbed Josh or was part of a plan to cause him serious injury. And I'm going to suggest to you that the evidence against Naomi is simply not there. Let's have a look at it.'

Naomi listened closely to what Lachlan was saying and she could see the jury were hanging on his every word. He was slow and every word seemed to be carefully chosen. It was a great start. He put it so simply and it seemed so obvious that the evidence against her was so contradictory. They just couldn't find her guilty.

It was all she could think about. They couldn't. They mustn't.

'And think about this. Why? Why would she want him dead? Why would she want him harmed? Why would she stab him? He was her boyfriend. She loved him. They were going off to university together, their whole lives before them. It simply does not make sense.

'And finally, ladies and gentlemen, I ask you to try Naomi Edwards as you would wish a member of your family or a friend to be tried. And that is with reference to the evidence. And when you look at that evidence in detail, I suggest that you come to the only conclusion possible and that is, Naomi Edwards is not guilty of murder. Thank you for listening.'

Another pause, another all-encompassing smile and then he sat down.

Naomi wanted to clap. She looked at the jury and could see a couple of the women smiling at Lachlan. For an older man, he was definitely a flirt.

*

'Members of the jury, now that you have heard all the speeches I am going to remind you about the evidence you have heard.'

She started with Chelsea Brittan, the woman who had discovered Josh on the floor in the ginnel and went through the evidence of each of the witnesses.

Naomi could see some of the jurors glazing over. This judge really was the most boring. She wondered how she could have won any trials when she was a barrister if she was so boring. She had one of those monotone voices that sent you to sleep. A boring voice to go with the boring face.

On and on she went.

They stopped for lunch.

And on she went after lunch.

At last she was finished.

The jury bailiffs were sworn and led the jury out of court. Some of the jurors looked over at the dock. One of them smiled. Was she smiling at her or one of the others? Naomi couldn't tell. Most of them looked down at their feet as they were led out, avoiding eye contact at all costs. Is that a bad sign?

She was desperate to look for clues. Which way were they going to go? No clues. No way of telling what any of them were thinking.

*

The defendants were led downstairs and the dock was then unlocked to let Naomi out. Each of the barristers gathered up their files, notebooks and laptops and made their way along the benches and out of court.

Naomi waited outside the court room on the main concourse. Lachlan and Sinead walked out, their heads close together in a confab.

Sinead spotted Naomi and her parents and swooped down on them. Her robe was like a bat cape, billowing out as she came towards them.

'Let's go into our room and have a debrief.'

Lachlan, Sinead, Naomi, Pam and Phil gathered in the small, tatty room they were now used to. No Helen today.

'That was a brilliant speech,' gushed Pam.

'Yes. The jury surely can't convict her. You just made it so obvious that she's not guilty,' added Phil.

'Hopefully, but there really is no way of knowing. I wasn't getting any clues from the jury. Sometimes you get nods when they agree with you but there really wasn't anything apart from a couple of smiles.'

'That must count for something.'

'Maybe, but we'll have to wait and see.'

'How long will they be,' asked Naomi.

'I don't want to sound flippant but how long is a piece of string? They could be a couple of hours or they could be days. It depends if they agree amongst themselves or not. In many ways, this is the worst bit of the trial, the waiting. It's out of our hands now and in the control of those twelve men and women.'

*

Another day over.

Is tonight my last night of freedom?

They wanted to go out for a meal tonight but what's the point?

It felt like they were suggesting the condemned man's last supper. Not that I can eat anything anyway.

How can they be taking so long?

They've had all afternoon. I know Lachlan said it could take days but I can't stand this waiting. Wanting the verdict and dreading it at the same time.

It's obvious I didn't do it. Isn't it?

Chapter 62

Day Thirteen

As Pam, Phil and Naomi were walking towards the court, Naomi spotted one of the women jurors. Their eyes locked and then the woman looked at the floor and hurried on towards the court.

Was that a bad sign? Was she avoiding eye contact because she'd decided Naomi was guilty?

She pointed it out to her mum and dad.

'Do you think she's looking away because she's made up her mind I'm guilty?'

'She probably just feels awkward,' pointed out Phil.

Naomi wanted to scream "this is killing me", but she had to stay calm for her parents. She thought they probably wanted to do the same. Lachlan was right when he said this was the worst bit of the trial. She hoped there would be a verdict today but only if it was the right one. At least now she still had some hope. Maybe later today that hope would be dashed.

Lachlan and Sinead joined them for a coffee in the court cafeteria.

'I'm not sure I could drink any more coffee,' sighed Pam. 'My stomach is churning with coffee and anxiety. I know you said this was the worst bit but every minute is dragging and every time there's a tannoy, my insides flip.'

'There's nothing either of us can say to make it better,' said Lachlan. 'It's just the agony of waiting.'

Naomi examined Lachlan's face. The shared anxiety seemed to be written all over it. No-one knew what to say. What more was there to say? Just wait. And wait.

Another tannoy.

'Will all parties in the case of Sutton and others please return to court one.'

Pam's hand went to her mouth. 'Is this it?'

'Maybe not. It could be a verdict or it could be that the jury has a question. We won't know until we get up there. If it is a guilty verdict, remember you will be taken down to the cells and we will then come and see you.'

'Great. I didn't need you to remind me of that.'

'Sorry, but I just need to be sure you are aware of it.'

'I love you,' said Phil as he grabbed hold of Naomi's hand, fighting back the tears.

Naomi's eyes filled up. Her dad never said "I love you". That was something her mum said. It was all feeling too real.

The five of them walked up the stairs to the courtroom. Naomi's legs were like jelly. She wanted to run. But where to? Her legs were going on automatic pilot.

When they got to the courtroom door, the usher was there to meet them.

'It's a note.'

Lachlan turned to Naomi. 'It's not a verdict, just a query from the jury, so you can relax and stop holding your breath.'

Relax? Who was he trying to kid?

No doubt he was used to seeing people going through this but for her and her family this was a first.

Talk about an emotional roller coaster.

Everyone took their usual places and the judge passed the note to the prosecutor who then passed it to the other barristers. They each read it and it was passed back to the judge.

'The jury are struggling to come to unanimous verdicts. They have been deliberating for four hours twenty minutes. It is a bit early to give a majority direction in a case as serious as this but I am content to do that if it is the opinion of the Bar that the time has come to do so.'

There was some whispering amongst the barristers as they all conferred with each other and a couple of nods.

Maria Conroy stood.

'My lady, I can address you on behalf of us all and we are agreed that, as the minimum time of two hours and ten minutes deliberation for the jury has passed, the majority direction should be given.'

'Very well. Jury please.'

The jury trooped in, none of them looking at anyone in the dock. Sinead looked at Lachlan. They knew what it meant when a jury can't look at the defendants.

'Members of the jury, the time has now come when I can accept a verdict on which a majority of you are agreed, that is, at least ten of you. Please continue with your deliberations.'

The jury was led out again, each of them looking at their feet.

*

Outside the courtroom, Lachlan beckoned Naomi, Pam and Phil over and led them to the room they had been occupying. Naomi ran off.

'Where are you going?' Sinead called. She then saw Naomi run into the toilet at the end of the corridor.

Pam ran after her.

At least she wasn't doing a runner out of court, thought Sinead.

Phil walked over to the ladies' toilet and waited outside for them.

'For an awful moment I thought she was doing a runner,' said Sinead.

'Me too. Still, I suppose the tension is getting to everyone. Even an old lag like me.'

'You're not an old lag, Lachlan. Stop pretending you don't care.'

'I know. I've never been more convinced of a defendant's innocence which is why I feel so much pressure.'

'Here they come.'

Pam, Naomi and Phil were gathered together outside the toilet. Pam cuddled Naomi who was crying.

Lachlan and Sinead waited till they came over and then all of them walked towards their room.

'How are you?' Lachlan asked.

Naomi couldn't respond. She was still trying to breathe.

'She's had a bit of a panic attack and vomited,' explained Pam.

'It's understandable. I know I can't feel it in the same way you do but I do understand how difficult it is for you.'

Naomi nodded. 'Thanks,' she whispered.

'Now that the judge has given a majority direction, it means that at least ten of them must agree, either ten for guilty or ten for not guilty. It usually doesn't take long after they have been told this. I think you should get some fresh air and water but please don't go beyond the court steps as they might call us back very soon.'

'Good idea. I think we all need this,' agreed Phil.

'I've got your phone number so if there is a tannoy while you are still outside, I will give you a ring.'

'Thank you.'

The three of them walked out together with heads bowed as if they were facing the gallows.

*

When they were alone, Sinead said, 'I didn't get a feel from the jury, did you?'

'No, but I've long since given up trying to read a jury. You just can't tell.'

'Well, if they look and smile at the defendant then you know it's in the bag.'

'Yes, but don't forget there are three other defendants so they might be decided on some and not others. If they have decided that one or more are guilty then they aren't going to look and smile.'

'Yes, you're right. All we can do is wait. I've never had this much tension waiting for a verdict.'

'Me neither. Well, one way or another it looks like it will be over today.'

*

It was only another thirty minutes before the tannoy went.

'All parties in the trial of Sutton and others please return to court one.'

'This is it.'

Sinead and Lachlan left the barristers' robing room and walked towards the courtroom where Naomi, Phil and Pam were waiting.

'I imagine this will be a verdict but can't guarantee it.'

'Whatever happens, thank you both for everything you've done,' said Pam.

'That's kind of you,' said Lachlan.

There was nothing more he could say at this stage. The colour was drained from Naomi's face which was hardly surprising as she'd lost her breakfast down the toilet.

They took their regular, familiar places yet again. Naomi never thought a few weeks ago that she'd automatically know where to go, where to sit and what to do. How the alien can become so familiar.

She could see that there was a whispering between the usher and Sinead who in turn looked at Lachlan and nodded.

Lachlan turned round to look at Naomi and nodded. She knew it was a verdict. Even Lachlan looked grey. Probably not as grey as she looked though.

The jury filed in and took their seats.

The court clerk stood.

'The jury has been out now for five hours and twelve minutes. Will the foreperson please stand.'

The woman who had avoided eye contact with Naomi outside court stood up.

Naomi's heart sank.

The clerk continued.

'Madam Foreperson, have you reached verdicts upon which at least ten of you are agreed?'

'Yes.'

'On the count of murder, do you find the defendant Ben Sutton guilty or not guilty?'

'Guilty.'

Sutton stood up and shouted, 'You fucking tossers, I didn't do it.'

Sutton's mother was in the public gallery. She'd been there every day. No-one had been there for Brown or Price. She just screamed.

'Take him downstairs,' ordered the judge.

After a tussle, he was removed from the court sticking two fingers up at the judge.

'On the count of murder, do you find the defendant Harley Brown guilty or not guilty?'

'Guilty.'

Harley looked shocked. He didn't move.

'On the count of murder, do you find the defendant Luke Price guilty or not guilty?'

'Guilty.'

Luke burst into tears.

'No, no, no. I didn't do it.'

The dock officer passed him a tissue but he couldn't stop crying.

'On the count of murder, do you find the defendant Naomi Edwards guilty or not guilty?'

Naomi held on to the wooden rail in front of her to stop herself from falling.

The chairperson looked at Naomi, smiled and said clearly, 'Not guilty.'

Phil punched the air and shouted loudly, 'Yes.'

Naomi collapsed in tears of relief.

'Ms Edwards, you are now discharged and may leave the court. Sentence in respect of those who have been convicted will take place on the first of October if that is convenient. In the meantime, you will remain in custody.'

Nods from the four barristers involved in the sentence.

Lachlan looked over at the jury. He smiled and mouthed a "thank you" to each of them. Sinead could see them smiling back and one woman winked at him. That was a first.

Harley Brown and Luke Price were taken down to join Sutton. Luke Price was still in tears.

Once they were gone, the dock was unlocked. The dock officer shook her hand and wished her good luck. That wasn't something you often saw.

She ran out of the court into the arms of her mum and dad as they had a group hug, each of them crying uncontrollably.

Lachlan and Sinead followed them out and stood to one side to give them a few minutes with each other.

Anna and Greg came out of the public gallery holding each other and looked towards Naomi. Sinead held her breath. You never knew what was going to happen once they'd heard the evidence against Naomi.

It was obvious Anna had been crying and still had the tissue in her hand.

She ran towards Naomi, hugged her and the tears wouldn't stop for either of them.

'We just wanted to say that we're really pleased the jury found you not guilty. We knew you weren't involved and you should never have been here with the others. At least we've got justice for Josh. He would want you to go off and have a life.'

Naomi held on to Anna, tears streaming down both their faces.

'Thank you and I'm so sorry for everything.'

'It's not your fault so you just get on and live your life. Josh can't do that so you must. It's what Josh would have wanted.'

'Thank you. Thank you so much.'

Anna couldn't stop crying, the pent up emotions of the last couple of weeks being released. 'We'd better go and leave you to it,' she sniffed through the tears. She and Greg turned and walked towards the stairs, backs bowed like Atlas with the weight of the heavens on their shoulders.

Naomi looked over and, through her tears, saw Lachlan and Sinead standing there and rushed over. She hugged Lachlan.

He didn't usually hug clients but he returned the hug and the wide grin was so genuine. Sinead even thought he looked a bit emotional.

'Thank you so much. You've both been brilliant. I can't believe this nightmare is over.'

'It is. There is no stain on your character, you have no criminal record and you can start university in a couple of weeks' time, putting this behind you as much as you can.'

She let go of him and wrapped her arms around Sinead.

'You will tell Helen, won't you?'

'Of course. I'll ring her when we get downstairs. Just now you should go and have a celebratory drink. You deserve it.'

Phil shook Lachlan's hand in that awkward manly way that some men have. He did the same with Sinead, thanked them and couldn't stop grinning through the tears.

'You're welcome. I'm glad we could help.'

Pam hugged them both. No emotional awkwardness on her part.

'Thank you both so much. You've been brilliant. I didn't even want to think about celebrating in case it was tempting fate but now that we can I'm not sure what to do.'

'Well, I know,' said Naomi. 'It's a pizza and cocktails. Just what I need. And I'm pretty sure I won't be vomiting it up. Unless I have too many cocktails.'

'Let's ring your gran and granddad, tell them the good news and get them over to join us. They'll be on tenterhooks waiting to hear,' said Phil.

'Good idea,' added Pam as she got her phone out to ring them.

'Off you go and have a good evening and great time at university. You deserve it after what you've been through.'

The three of them walked off all smiles leaving Lachlan and Sinead standing alone on the concourse.

'Did you notice DI Pearce and Sergeant Garvey in court?' Sinead whispered, just in case they could be overhead.

'I did. Their faces weren't giving anything away so who knows if they were pleased or disappointed.'

'Well done, Lachlan,' uttered Maria Conroy through gritted teeth as she walked past them with Sebastian and the police officers.

'Thank you, Maria. Always a pleasure.'

Ian and Mel passed them, smiled and nodded. Mel added her congratulations. Not usual from a police officer.

'Always a pleasure. You definitely don't mean that, Lachlan,' said Sinead.

'I know but you have to play the game. She should be happy at getting three of them. The officers seemed okay though.'

'Maybe. I still think she shouldn't have been charged.'

Lachlan turned to her, grinned and said, 'Anyway, after all that emotion, I think we deserve a celebratory drink, Sinead.'

'You're on.'

*

Mel and Ian left the court together.

'It was the right result,' said Mel.

'I agree but I don't think Maria Conroy is happy.'

'Well, I am. And its obvious Josh's parents are so that's what matters.'

'Me too, and I agree with you.'

'Gosh, we'd better not make a habit of agreeing.'

'I think you should do a bit more of it, Sergeant Garvey. You must have realised by now that I'm the type of boss who requires absolute obedience from my team.'

Mel laughed. 'And you know you won't get it from me.'

'I wouldn't have it any other way. Jack has some friends round tonight celebrating results so we could go for a drink and something to eat if you like?'

Mel's stomach did a little somersault as she said, 'I'd like that very much.'

'Great. Bar by the station and maybe get something to eat?'

'Sounds lovely.'

*

Sinead and Lachlan walked to one of the swish bars near the station where Lachlan ordered a bottle of champagne.

'I thought you were a bit of a flash git. It was the tie that did it at first but now that you've ordered the champagne, I've had my opinion confirmed.'

'Well, I'd hate to disabuse you of that notion so we'll just have to get another bottle after this one. Pizza sounds good as well if you're up for it.'

'Champagne and pizza. How could I refuse such a classy invitation?'

'Exactly. I have a way with words.'

'You certainly have.'

'And here's to us working together more.'

'I'll drink to that. You're my favourite silk.'

'Flattery will get you everywhere.'

As the cork popped, two figures approached them. Ian Pearce and Mel Garvey.

They were both smiling as Ian reached out to shake Lachlan's hand.

'We don't want to interrupt your celebrations but we spotted you as we were walking past. You did a good job. We just wanted to say that we both think it was the right result.'

'Yes. We're pleased she was acquitted and hope she can move on,' added Mel. 'She's been through so much.'

'Thank you,' said Lachlan.

Sinead was not going to be so polite.

'You should never have charged her in the first place. This will always be with her. It's not something you can easily forget about.'

'I know. It wasn't our decision to charge her.'

'But it was your decision to treat her as a suspect and investigate her.'

'We didn't have an option,' said Ian.

Mel was silent. She agreed with Sinead but couldn't say that.

'Well, we just wanted to add our congratulations. We'll leave you to our celebrations. I think it will be celebrations all round tonight.'

Lachlan stood up. He looked like he was going to ask them to join them. No chance, thought Sinead as she put her hand over Lachlan's.

He got the message, sat down and simply said, 'Thank you,' as he then watched them walk away, hopefully to their own celebration. After all, they've got murder convictions.

'I didn't realise you wanted to hold my hand. You should have said.'

'I've been wanting to do it for weeks. Never thought it would be a police officer who forced me to take your hand.'

'Well, I'm certainly not complaining. Let's pour that champagne and think about where we're going after here. I'm not in a hurry to get back as my hotel room is booked for another night.'

'You smooth talker you.'

They raised their glasses.

'Here's to us working together more often,' said Lachlan.

'I couldn't agree more.'

*

'Looks like everyone is celebrating,' said Mel.

'And we should too. We're making a habit of this, Sergeant Garvey. I hope that's acceptable.'

'More than acceptable, DI Pearce,' and hooked her arms round his as they walked off.

Chapter 63

Naomi

It wasn't supposed to happen like that.

That bloody knife. If only I hadn't left it in the shed? So stupid.

Panic. That's what it was.

I never thought they'd search the shed. I was their witness. I was pointing the finger at the other three. If it hadn't been for the knife, I would never have been charged. I should have got rid of it. At least there were no fingerprints. On a freezing night like it had been in February, everyone was wearing gloves. You couldn't not.

I hadn't thought they'd examine Josh's phone and find that footage. It showed how naïve I am about all things criminal. I'd thought about fingerprints but hadn't thought about disposing of the knife and hadn't thought about the phone. How could I have been so bloody stupid?

There were a hundred places I could have thrown that knife but I had to bring it home and just leave it in the shed for the police to find.

I wasn't supposed to have been charged. It nearly messed up everything.

I took the knife for protection. I wasn't going to let those bastards have another go at me. I didn't mean to kill Josh, just hurt him. Just punish him for getting me involved with that lot, for letting them do what they did. He'd never have known it was me as it was so dark and they were all hitting him.

But it had worked out in the end.

They had each got what they deserved.

Josh was dead and the other three would be locked up for a very long time.

Yes, I could have reported the rape. What good would that have done?

Even if they had been convicted, which I doubt, the footage would have gone viral. You couldn't see their faces. They'd just have said it wasn't them.

Reasonable doubt. I know what that means now. Ben Sutton would have posted it everywhere. He had a copy on his burner and the police hadn't found it.

If I reported him, everyone would know what they'd done. I just couldn't risk it. The humiliation would have been total. It was more than I could cope with. Imagine starting university with that. Everyone knowing. I would never have been able to shake it off. I would always be the girl that was raped. And they would be the ones that got away with it.

This way they had all got what they deserved.

Poor Josh. Not so poor after all. He was weak. He got himself, and me, into that mess. He let them rape me. He filmed it. He stood by and did nothing because he was spineless.

I feel sorry for his mum and dad. I had always liked them and can't imagine what it's like to lose a child but they didn't know the side of him I knew. I'm sorry for their pain but not sorry for what I did.

And the other three. Price crying like a baby, sorry for himself. He hadn't been sorry when he raped me. I still can't get the stink of him out of my head. The stink of all of them.

Smelling them all when I was in the dock was the worst bit of it. Being close to them again. Their smells came back to me, took me back to that place, that time.

No more smells now. They could rot.

Justice had been done. Or was it revenge?